This Book is dedicated to:

Ronald Webb

Rest in Peace Grandad Tax

BEFORE DUSK

DANNY HUGHES

Copyright © 2016 by Danny Hughes

All rights reserved. No part of this publication may be reproduced, distributed, or transmitted without the express consent of the author.

Act One

Amidst the Fallen Leaves

Day Ten

"Rob?!" he heard them shout as, suddenly the entire world slid back into place. "Can you see them? I thought I saw something"
His eardrums felt as if they had burst as the sounds of people panicking flooded into his ears.

When he looked around, Robert saw the worried faces of the survivors he had been travelling with the past few days. Many of them were huddled together in the corners of the old farmhouse, while others peered out of the windows, regrettably awaiting the inevitable doom that loomed outside. Their weapons were drawn and shakily pointing outwards into the great darkness beyond.

Pete stood beside him and the window they were both instructed to watch. Robert turned to him, waiting for him to answer. Rob didn't know what to say. Instead he looked down at the pistol in his hand. He was clutching it so tightly that his knuckles had gone white. He did not know the make of the handgun he had found on the corpse of the airport security officer. All he knew at the time was that if he hadn't taken it, then he was as good as dead. It was John who had told him that the gun still had the safety lock on when he first met him. Thankfully before then, he hadn't needed to use it.

Robert had never fired a gun before. When he was eleven he had owned a BB gun his uncle had brought him back from somewhere abroad. Rob used to take it and go to the field behind his house, wildly firing off shots into the trees.

He laughed as he remembered that thought. He had no idea how similar those days would be to his life right now. Rob looked back through the Farmhouse window at the dark shadows he thought he saw moving among the trees. He brought the gun up to the window sill and waited. He knew that he had one bullet less in the weapon, but he was unsure how many was in there to begin with. He had planned to ask John more about the gun when he got the time. John seemed to have some idea about how to use them.

As Robert stared out into the dark abyss before him, he thought about that missing bullet. He knew that the memory would haunt him until his final day.

A few days ago the creatures had chased them out of the city into the woods. The city was lost and staying there would have meant death. Heading into the woods gave the group a fighting chance at least. It wasn't too far into the trees that Robert fired his first shot with a real handgun.

It was someone Pete had shown up with, Rob couldn't remember his name. It was a youngish man, no older than twenty-five at the most. He had been grabbed by one of them as they tried to make it. The creature proceeded to tear at his abdomen, clawing its way through his stomach. Rob saw the man's intestines rip right out of him and slide across the dead leaves on the ground. The man tried to cry out in agony but no words or screams came out. Another one of the creatures joined in and began slicing the flesh off his leg with little effort. Its thick dark claws tore through him like warm butter.

The man lay on the ground on his back. His head faced back towards Rob and his cold eyes stared into his own. Rob felt as if he saw into the man's very soul. He could see all of his pain and torment as his insides were savagely pulled out piece by piece.

It was then that Rob swore that the man said the words to him clear as day. The rest of the world around them went silent. Maybe the man just mimed them, or maybe he didn't even say them at all, but Rob knew what he had to do. He could see it in his eyes.

"Kill me" he begged him. A split-second passed in what felt like an eternity as Rob brought the gun up and squeezed the trigger. The handgun kicked back and Rob felt his shoulder jolt backward. The bullet glided with such perfect precision. It made contact just above the man's left eyebrow, punching straight though his skull and into his brain. His eyes went dead a second later and after that he stopped struggling. He surrendered and gave into his fate.

The creature's hadn't noticed at first as they continued to disembowel him, but once they found their way to the beat-less heart, they both stopped and looked up towards Rob. As they hissed and snarled, the two of them rose to their feet. Their bodies obscured in the shadows of the trees all around. Rob could see them. He could see them plain as day.

As Rob went to back away, he felt their eyes pierce through his skin. They crept slowly away from the man's body as hot air fumed out of their mouths. He knew that if he did not act now then it would not be just their eyes that pierced his skin. Rob tried to take another step but his legs did not want to move. It was almost as if he was stuck, slowly sinking into the ground like quicksand.

As they went to make their move, a flash of light shot past Rob's face. He felt the intense heat of it brush past his skin. He caught a quick glance of it before it hit the ground. It was a whiskey bottle, square in shape, with a flaming rag hanging out of it. The bottle smashed against the hard ground and ignited almost instantly, setting fire to the dry leaves and sending a pillar of flames upward through the trees.

The creatures recoiled at the light and were hidden behind the blaze. Rob heard them roar through the fire as he felt a pull on his arm. He was spun around and saw John standing beside him.

"Let's go!" he demanded, pulling Rob out of his daze and deeper into the woods.

Robert looked round one last time after a while and he could still see the fire burning bright through the shadows of the trees in the distance. He saw movement flicker in front of the flame. They were being followed. They were coming.

"There!" John shouted pointing towards a light that they were heading to. Rob's head was a haze and he could barely focus on what it was until they were right in front of it; an old Farmhouse.

It wasn't much further until they managed to reach the rest of the group, those of them that had survived the escape from the city, who were hiding inside. Robert had been surprised at the number of people missing.

That was four days ago. Food had run out almost completely. There was only a small amount left, and that was being rationed. It was safe enough to venture out of the cabin during the day. The creatures didn't come out much when the sun was out. It was the shadows they needed to watch out. Recently the sky had become overcast. Thick dark clouds covered the sky above the Farmhouse and that meant the creatures were still out there... waiting. Rob knew they were waiting for them to come outside. They were hiding in the darkness... somewhere.

Karen had left the Farmhouse the day before last. She had gone with her husband to look for some food or anything that might have been nearby. Everyone had the same idea; a farm must have had some sort of food on its land, crops or any surviving animals that they could eat, anything they could get their hands on.

Shortly after they had left, the clouds had begun to gather. The shadows of the trees grew and stretched out over the ground. The entire place began to fall into darkness, and that was when they heard it.

Nobody could see what had happened to Karen and her husband, but almost everyone gathered at the windows as soon as they heard the gunshot. The trees shook as if they were trying to escape the terrifying screams that filled the forest and the souls of the people, watching inside the Farmhouse, with dread. She first called out for her husband for help. "Christopher" he thought he heard her cry. "Christopher".

After it was clear that he had either tried to flee or had been killed himself, her screams turned to shrills before they became distorted as if her vocal cords had been severed.

Silence came after that. Everyone inside held their breath for a moment and waited, listening to what came after. Gorging and inhuman squeals of excitement could be heard from just inside the treeline. The survivors stared out into the darkness and waited for it to stop, but the sounds appeared to go on and on. Every crunch sent chills deep into their bodies.

When the noises did eventually stop, it still took a few moments for the people of the Farmhouse to exhale.

Since then the survivors had not left the main living room of the old house. It was large enough for them to stay in the different rooms inside, but since Karen and her husband's death, no one had dared to leave the room. Thankfully a working toilet was located under the stairs, next to the basement door, that people could use.

John and a few others had done a quick check of the upstairs when they first had got inside, but that was the last time anyone had ascended the stairs. Now Robert and the rest of his fellow survivors were all, either keeping watch or trying to get some rest, inside a room the size of a shipping container.

Rob had been asked to watch the eastern windows and take shifts with Pete, but Robert hadn't slept in what felt like forever, so he didn't mind sitting here all night, like he had done the past nights.

It had only been less than two weeks since it all began, but when he didn't sleep, the days felt as if they dragged on and on. Day time was the only time he felt tired, but then there was so much to do and prepare for. There was the constant risk that the sun could go at any minute... and then the creatures of the dark would come out again.

That was why they needed to keep the lanterns burning. The lights in the Farmhouse were still working, but they couldn't run the risk of them cutting out and the survivors being left in total darkness. Robert even a kept torch with him... nearly everyone did, just in case.

Hours passed as Pete and Robert stared out in the night. Every rustle and every twig snapping caused Rob's heart to jump up and wind up in his throat, desperately trying to claw its way out of his body and make its escape. Robert wished he could do the same and just escape from this place.

He wondered where he would go. Was the rest of the country, or even the world, like this? Or was it just here?

As he sat there thinking about it all, he realised that they had no plans. Were they all going to stay here in the Farmhouse? As long as they kept the lights burning bright, then surely they would be safe here. It was better than travelling out into the woods, trying to find somewhere else, and be stranded when night fell upon them.

Rob thought about these things long into the night and when he did finally snap out of it, he looked over and saw that Pete had fallen asleep in his chair.

By the time that the sun began to grow on the horizon and sunlight flooded through the trees, Robert's hand had grown completely numb. He released his tightened grip on the handgun and sighed in relief that the new day had brought along the sunshine. It meant that people could venture outside once again and hopefully find some food for the rest of them.

He glanced around at the other survivors who had made it through another night, for now they could breathe easy. These men and women had lived horrors that no person should ever have to see.

Robert knew that they would have to live many more before this was over.

Day Eleven

"There were whispers out there" Robert said to Pete as they stood on the front step outside the Farmhouse.

Even during the day, with the sun blazing down on them, Rob could still hear them hiding in the shadows watching. He could feel their eyes on him. They sat waiting in the darkness, waiting for him to slip up and then they would be on him. Rob didn't want to end up like Karen and her husband. He needed to stay vigilant at all times.

He couldn't understand what they were trying to say to him, or even what they were saying at all. The words were so quiet that even breathing would be enough to hide them, but Rob could hear them still.

"I can't hear anything" Pete replied, looking around nervously into the trees. "Are you sure?"

Rob was sure he could hear them. Maybe the creatures were only talking to him, maybe Pete was just making too much noise to hear or maybe he was just losing his mind. He had already seen too many things that would drive a man insane.

"It's probably just the wind" Pete told him reassuringly. He had tried to make Robert feel better, even giving him a soft pat on the back, but it didn't help. Rob could hear the faint otherworldly whispers in the air. It was too hard to make out, and every now and then the rustling of leaves would disguise it.

Rob thought it was best if he kept it to himself for now. He did not want to let people think he was insane and become a risk to the group.

Over the short time that they had known one another, the group had become his salvation. There was safety in numbers, he had learned. The time at the beginning he had spent on his own was the hardest. When the city first suffered the blackout and the creatures appeared out of the darkness, it was a slaughter. Rob had to hide and run just to avoid becoming another victim. After days of cowering and moving quietly across the city, through the hundreds of torn up corpses that littered the streets, Rob was found by John and his group.

Since then, he stuck by them and never wanted to leave their side. He did not want to be alone in this new world. The strange fate that had befallen the planet; Rob didn't want to ever be on his own.

He did not know many of them in the group, some of the ones he did know had died getting here, while others had simply gone missing in the woods. Rob thought it was better that he did not get to know them, just so he didn't need to feel it when, or if, they died. The ones he did know, he had spoken to them quite a lot. It helped him to talk to other people who were suffering through the same situation as he was, or at least listen to them talk.

Out of all the people he had got to know, Pete was the person he had the spoken to the most. He was a short dark haired man, wearing the remnants of a once expensive suit.

John had stuck them together when the group was hiding in the church last week, and since then, the two had spoken a lot. Pete had talked about his jobs, who he was, and the early days before John's group had found him.

He had previously worked in marketing for some video game company. He had been working late the night it happened. It wasn't until he went outside that he witnessed the true horror of it. He said he saw a woman cut perfectly in half from the top of a building. Her torso fell and landed at his feet, exploding in a cloud of gore right before his very eyes. He said it was the most horrific thing he had ever witnessed. It was then that he realised he couldn't go home. He had to abandon everything and get out, his words.

Sometimes when they were on watch, they had spent all night talking. Rob wasn't much of a talker. He used to be, a few weeks ago, but since this has all started Rob had found himself talking internally more, spending long periods of time thinking. That's not to say that Robert didn't speak, but Pete did most of the talking when they did. He would talk not just about what was currently happening to them, but other things, normal things, things that no longer mattered in this new world. Rob found it comforting to talk about these things. Some things were too upsetting to bring up. Conversations about people that they knew or had lost were too much for Robert. He would quickly change the subject if the conversation ever started to head that way.
Pete had told him that he had "Abandoned everything", but Rob didn't ask him what it was he had left behind. It was a sore subject Rob knew, and he didn't want to know the suffering of others. He was worried it would be too much for him to bear, and all his feelings of the people he lost would come flooding in and drown him.

"Hey, I think they're back" Pete said pointing out towards the treeline.

As Rob turned towards the direction Pete indicated, he saw John and a few others emerge from the trees. They had left when the sun was above the treetops and ventured out in search of food. John was carrying a flaming oil rag tied around the branch of a tree. The flame was barely visible in the sunlight, but it was better to carry it to avoid suffering the same fate as Karen if the sun did suddenly go down.

John was the unspoken leader of their group. When Robert first met him, he was already commanding the small team of survivors he had with him. He had helped Rob with his handgun, calling it a Gloak or a Glock or something, and gave everyone orders of what to pick up, what to leave, where to watch, and when to be quiet. No one had ever questioned him. Even new members of the group had just done whatever John had asked of them.

John knew about weapons and survival skills, he was authoritative and his tone gave Rob the impression that perhaps he was once in the military or a police officer. He had never asked John his profession or got to know him at all really. Rob had just picked up this from the way John acted and looked.

He was a large man, both tall and broad, with short hair and a thick dark beard. He carried a makeshift belt of petrol bombs, or Molotovs as he called them, across his waist, and some sort of sub-machine gun at his side. He looked as if he was living in this new world long before it had even begun. Rob could imagine that John was just sitting around waiting for all this to happen.

One of the other people, returning with John, was a woman Rob knew as Maria. He did not know her at all but had often heard her name spoken. John seemed to like her. She was useful. The group had seen her fend off three of the creatures with a flare and a handgun. Since then John had always called upon her when he and a few others had gone out to look for supplies.

Robert noticed that she was carrying three or four dead rabbits. She had all of their legs gripped in her left hand. Their bodies hung upside down, dangling lifelessly. Rob envied them. The nightmare was over for them... if they had even known what was going on at all in the first place.

Pete's face lit up when he saw the rabbits. "Thank god for that!" he said excitedly.

Their find meant that the survivors had some more food for the next few days. Everyone in the group had started to get hungry. There were twelve of them in total, and it meant that they needed quite a bit to feed them all. The rabbits should be enough to go around for tonight and possibly tomorrow, but after that, they would need to think about the plan long term.

While some believed the classic story that the army was coming and would rescue them, others had the same idea as Rob; they knew that this was the world now. There was no going back to the way things used to be. No late night TV, no more eighteen holes early one Saturday morning. Robert knew that they needed to think of a plan. He knew that John felt this way. He was suited to this situation and Rob wanted to show that he was too.

As John approached, his Molotovs clanging together as he walked, he asked Robert and Pete if there had been anything to report. Pete shook his head and replied that it was quiet since they had been gone.

John looked up at the sky and into the sun, raising his arm over part of his face to shield himself from it. "Yeah... looks like it is going to be one of those days" he told them, before looking back at Pete and Rob and smiling.

Rob was not convinced by the smile. It looked false to him, as if John had learned how to smile from a picture in a book. Perhaps he was just trying to keep morale up.

Robert decided it was time to speak to John properly. "Excuse me, John" he said nervously as John turned around to look at him. "Can I have a word?"

John nodded and turned to Maria and the others. "Go inside and get those prepped for dinner later. We've got a few hungry campers who are going to be delighted by today's catch, you know" he told them. There was that smile again Rob saw.

Pete went to walk inside, but John stopped him. "Sorry, would you mind just sticking around out here a little longer? Keep an eye on the place?" he asked him.

Pete nodded and leaned against the door frame as, the survivor Rob had come to know as Matt opened the door and let Maria and the others inside. Rob could hear some talking coming from inside when they opened the door. It seemed some people were glad that they made it back in one piece, or maybe they were just excited at the sight of the rabbits, knowing that they would be eating well tonight.

John gestured Rob from the front step and towards the front garden. He walked and John followed him. When he stopped and turned around to face John, Rob realised that it was the furthest he had been from the front step since first arriving at the Farmhouse a few days ago. He thought he would be nervous, but somehow knowing that John was calm made him feel at ease.

"What can I do for you?" John asked him straight away. Rob had been excepting some kind of small talk beforehand. It seemed that John had other things that he wanted to get on with.

"I..." Rob went to say but the words stuck in his throat. He swallowed them and tried again. "I wanted to ask what the plan was" he told him. John gave him a look as if he didn't know exactly what he was referring to.

"Are we going to stay here? Or move on?" Robert asked.

"Do you have somewhere to be?" John replied.

Rob was taken aback by his response. Was he joking? Of course Rob didn't have anywhere to be.

"No, no" Rob replied. "I just would like to know. If we are staying here then maybe we should think about fortifying it. Taking wood from some of the inside doors and blocking off the ground floor windows". The idea came to Rob out of the blue. He was as surprised as John was by his plan. It appeared that under pressure, Rob was able to come up with a good idea. "If not then maybe a group of us could look around nearby and see if we can find anywhere better".

John nodded agreeing. "Well it is not really up to me, you know" he said, which Rob thought was a little strange given that, even though no one had directly said he was in charge, it was clear that he was. "But, in my opinion" John continued. "I think that we could defend this place. As long as we keep the lights burning then we are safe here. If we set up a few Tiki torches around the perimeter then we could stay here, so long as there is a good enough source of food and water".

"So you think that should be our next step?" Robert asked him. "To go and look for a source?"

"I think so" John replied. "I think there is a stream a mile or so that way. I want to go and check it out one day soon and see, if the weather holds up. David is going to stay here and watch over the others while we are gone. Maybe you should come with me". John smiled at him. It made Rob feel uneasy.

"Me?" Rob accidentally let slip from his trail of thought and out of his mouth.

"Why not?" John said patting him harder on the arm and knocking Rob a little off balance. "We'll talk about it more tomorrow. We have enough water to last us a couple more days. In the meantime, I'll get some of them inside to break a few doors and look for something we could use to attach them to the windows. It could be quite useful".

And with that he was off, heading back to the house. Rob stood there in the front garden watching John as he swaggered off towards the Farmhouse, then up the stairs, nodding at Pete, before stepping inside. The noise of everyone inside slowly died as the door closed behind him. Pete gave a slight wave towards Rob and looked around, checking any signs of anything.

As Robert stood there staring at the Farmhouse, he thought about John's suggestion. Heading out of the farm would be dangerous. He hadn't left since he first arrived. Was he ready to head back out into the wild again? Those things were still out there. He hadn't seen them since the man he shot, and he hadn't properly heard them since Karen's death. He knew that they were still out there though.

Just then the wind blew again. It brushed through his hair and past his ears. At first it was the faint whistling of the gentle breeze, but after a moment he could hear it. The whispers on the wind were back. They spoke in a soft unnerving tone through the shadows behind him. He could then feel their eyes back on him. He had forgotten it for a time, but the feeling of dread was back and now more than ever.

Of all the whispers, he could only make out one word. A simple word that means nothing on its own normally, but when used in such context, in that type of situation, it sent chills down his spine and into his very core.

"... Join".

Day Thirteen – Part 1

The next day was grey. Clouds had gathered in the sky and, throughout it, occasional rain would fall. It was the first time Robert had noticed it raining in months. He couldn't even remember the last time it was wet outside. He knew that it was before all this started to happen.
People in the group had attempted to put bottles out to collect the rainwater, under John's instructions, but strange noises coming from the woods had kept them from actually doing so.

One of the other people on watch, at the other side of the Farmhouse, thought he saw something moving through the forest. When he told the others and they checked it out, the woods were quiet. Most people thought he was just dehydrated or seeing things. Rob decided it was best not to get involved.

The constant threat that they were out there and waiting for them in the dark was enough to make anyone feel uneasy. If they didn't have John telling people what to do, Rob was sure that they would start to turn on one another.

All through the entire day, Rob was dreading John coming over to talk to him about heading out to find the steam. Every time John passed by him, Robert turned to the window and acted as if he was keeping watch.

By the end of the day, he had considered going upstairs just to avoid him altogether.

John had told people to break down a few of the interior doors to barricade the windows. It appeared that he liked Rob's idea to help make the Farmhouse safe, even a place that they could live for a while.
The thought stayed with him for the rest of the day. He thought about them moving people into some of the rooms upstairs, maybe even giving people a bit of a break from one another and a little privacy. He felt as if the toilet under the stairs was the only location he could really be alone with his thoughts, but whenever Rob went to go and see if at least he could try to use the toilet, someone would always knock on the door and ask how long he would be.
He thought about if they took the entire farm and secured it, maybe with a high fence and torches placed all around, what it would be like. There could have been more buildings on this land; a barn or a stable, somewhere where the group could move into. It would at least be the first step in getting the survivors back to normality.
It was still early days. Only a few doors were broken down during the course of the day.

In the evening they enjoyed the cooked rabbits from the day before and they seemed to fill everyone up. Pete offered to cover Rob's shift keeping watch so that he could get some sleep as he "looked tired", but Robert kindly refused.

The night flew past. Before Rob even knew it, it was morning and the sun had come out. As soon as he saw that first ray of sunlight beam through the trees, Rob felt a hand on his shoulder. He turned around and John was standing over him.

"Morning" he said proudly, as his voice boomed through the Farmhouse. Rob didn't realise that anyone else was up other than the man keeping watch in the kitchen at the other side of the house. Pete had once again fallen asleep, so it was good that Rob had decided to stay awake all night.

Before He could answer, John let go of his shoulder and asked "Are you coming with us today?"

It didn't feel like a question, more of a statement, or an order. Robert didn't want to feel like he was not contributing to the group, even though he had been wide awake, watching out of the same window, for the last few nights in a row. But the feeling he was getting from John, right at that moment in time, was that if he didn't come along today, then it wouldn't be long before Rob was out there on his own and fending for himself.

"Sure thing" Rob replied. It was another time when he spoke before he had actually thought.

John gave him one of his smiles. "Good man. I like seeing people pulling their weight around here, you know" he said, before heading off to tell the other people of the group what to do.

By the time the sun was starting to appear over the tops of the trees, John and the other people coming along were all prepped and ready to go. Maria was coming and another man Rob knew a little of. He was sure his name was Mike. Only John and Maria had any real weapons, John with his sub-machine gun, and Maria carried a handgun similar to Rob's. Mike needed to be pretty close to one of the creatures to actually use his weapon; a fire axe. Rob was thankful that he had managed to get hold of a pistol when did.

He was a black man who was wearing blue overalls. If Rob had to guess

Mike's profession before all of this, then he would have said that he looked like a mechanic. The fire axe led Robert to think that he might have even been a firefighter.

Before they left Pete came over to Robert and told him to watch himself out there. It was the first time they had been apart since getting separated in the woods early on and it seemed that Pete wanted his new friend to come back alive.

Rob laughed nervously. "I'll be fine" he replied not overly believing the words himself.

"Watch the place while we are gone, yeah?" John came over and told Pete. "Most people will be busy attaching the wood to the windows, but just keep an eye on the food and make sure no one steals any".

Pete looked over towards where they kept the food. "You think someone would try and steal some?" he asked.

John shrugged before turning to face the rest of the group nearby. "Okay, we won't be gone too long. Just going to check and see some more of the area nearby. If you could get those planks up on the windows, then we could really start fortifying this place for the long haul".

"Are we not going back to the city?" a woman in the group asked. She gave Rob the impression that she was hoping they would, to look for someone she had lost. The way she said it made him think that she thought the woods and the Farmhouse would be temporary. Somewhere they could stay for a few nights before going back to the city.

"I... I don't really know" John replied. "The city was quite dangerous. It might be best if we just hold up here for a while".

She did not seem very impressed with John's reply.

"We'll be back before you know it. If we manage to get any more food then we will, but we should have enough left over for tonight".

After a few nods of heads, John and his crew turned around and headed out the Farmhouse door. Robert took a deep breath and took that first step back outside, knowing that he would soon be far away from the comfort and safety of the Farmhouse walls and roof.

Outside the ground was still damp from the day before. Most of the dead leaves had been drenched and crumbled away in a small dirt creek filled with rainwater. The sun was still out, but the day itself was not particularly warm. The cold air rushed through the trees and slapped Rob right across the face. He listened for a moment but there were no whispers this time. He wasn't sure if it was just because he was with John, and the others; people who seemed to be able to handle themselves out here, or because the wind was silent, but Robert didn't feel the eyes watching him from the dark corners of the forest as he had done a couple of days before. This made him feel a lot better being outside.

They walked for a few miles through the woods. John was leading the pack with a flaming torch held in front of him.

Every now and again Rob would look up at the sun and feel the sunlight warm his face, before it disappeared behind a tree for a brief moment, only to reappear a second later. Robert was grateful for it. Once when he did this, he felt a strange sensation come over him and stopped to look around. Mike was staring at him strangely. Rob felt a little embarrassed but thought he would start a conversation to lighten the mood.

"Nice day, huh" he said.

Mike nodded. "Yeah... it sure is" he replied as he continued on behind Maria and John.

Robert didn't know whether to say anything more. By the time he thought of something mundane to say, Mike had already walked too far ahead. Rob decided to keep quiet and catch up.

A little while later, John lifted his arm up with his fist clenched tight. This caused Maria and Mike to stop moving. Rob took one more step before realising and stopped as well.

John stood there listening. Rob thought that maybe he could hear the whispers in the wind and so he tried to listen as well. They were not there. All he could hear was the gentle breeze rustling through the leaves hanging off the trees.

"No... Wait" he thought to himself. He could hear something else. It was the sound of rushing water. Nothing too loud or big, but softly in the distance somewhere, the sound of water flowing through a stream could be heard.

"We're near" John told them. He stood for another moment listening before facing a direction leading off deeper into the forest.

"That way" he said pointing.

The four of them trekked a bit further and the sound of the water began to grow louder the closer they got. It wasn't long before Robert began to tell that the stream was just through the trees up ahead.

John cleared through the woods first and arrived at the bank by the water. He stood beside it checking around for signs of anything. Maria knelt down beside him and started to go through her backpack, looking for something to collect the water in.

"This would be good... if it wasn't so muddy here" John said as Rob stepped out of the treeline and saw the stream in full.

The water was clear. He could see that it was a few feet deep and beneath the water the floor was littered with small stones and pebbles. The water looked cold, far too cold to get in and wash at this time of year.

Robert suddenly began thinking of the last time he had a shower. It must have been the morning of the first day. He always took a shower every morning without fail, but since he hadn't been able to, he hadn't felt clean in days. He hadn't even been able to brush his teeth either. His teeth felt furry and a stale taste lingered in his mouth.

"Mike!" John's voice boomed through the clearing. "Check out a bit further downstream. See if there is anywhere that might be easier to gather water from, you know. The banks here are nothing but sludge". Mike nodded, turned around and began walking along the side of the stream.

Rob looked at the banks. John was right. They were thick grey clay-like mud that made it difficult to get into the water. It was too far to reach with a bottle, and so they would need to actually step onto the bank. It was clear that if they did, they would most likely lose a shoe.

"Robert" John said suddenly, causing Rob's foot to slip out in front of him and onto the bank. His foot pushed its way through the grey mud, covering the back of his leg in wet dirt.

"Shit!" he said to himself before pulling his leg free and getting to his feet. "Yeah?" he asked.

John wiped his face with the back of his hand. "Go and do the same but head upstream, would you please?" he commanded.

Rob replied agreeing and began following the water to where it was coming from.

The stream curved around and back into the trees and it wasn't long before John and Maria disappeared, and suddenly Rob was on his own again. The thought didn't actually hit him until a little while upriver. The sound of the running water kept Rob's mind occupied for a time, but when he stopped, he felt that strange feeling again; eye's watching him from all directions. All around him he could feel the presence of them, watching and waiting.

It was the first time he had ever been on his own in the woods since this whole thing began. He had never felt more alone than he did right then. Somehow he felt more alone than he had done during the beginning. The city backdrop gave the felling that people could be nearby. Out here in the forest... there was no one.

He looked around in all directions and saw only trees. Different colours and shades of brown bark and dead leaves littered as far as he could see. His heart began to beat harder in his chest. He could feel it pounding against his rib cage. His breathing became more frantic and heavy. He brought his hand before his face and saw that it was shaking.

After a few moments, Rob decided it was time to calm down. He clenched his hand into a fist and took a deep breath, leaving it for a few seconds before exhaling. Robert did this three or four times and he began to relax a bit. His heart returned to its normal rate and he felt the watchful eyes slowly disperse all around him. He was alone again.

Rob took the handgun out of his belt, flicked off the safety catch and held it at the ready. He was not sure how far down John wanted him to check and so he decided upon himself that he was just going to go as far as the next time the stream curved around the trees, which was just up ahead, and then he was going to go back.

Right then Rob noticed something strange in the water. It was a thick pinkish glue-like substance floating through it. It was quite diluted here, but it appeared to be flowing through the water from somewhere upriver.

Rob began to follow it. He kept checking the trees every time he heard any noise other than the sound of rushing water, but there was always nothing there.

As Rob approached the corner, the red substance in the water was thicker here. It was floating along the top of the water, indicating that the source of it was not far off. The colour had changed as well. It had been a gradual change that Rob hadn't even noticed. It was clear to him now what it was. The liquid had turned a dark shade of red with every passing step. By the time he had got to the point where the steam turned off to the right, Rob knew that it was blood. Something was bleeding into the water.

He suddenly felt that feeling in his chest again. A lump of anxiety began to grow in his throat and his eyes watered. He brought his hand up to wipe his eye and he was shaking again.

"Get a hold of yourself" he said quietly.

He took a deep breath and thought for a moment. Should he go around the corner and find out what was in the water? Or should he just go back to John and the others. Whatever was bleeding into the water meant that it was unsafe to drink. John would want to know what it was. It would be easier to just check, rather than coming back with them and wasting time.

Rob gripped his gun tight and held it in front of him as he swung around the large tree on the corner, obscuring the view from the other side. When he could see around it, he saw that a tree had fallen long ago over the stream and to the other side. It was overgrown and made it impossible to see any further along the water. The blood was running beneath this tree. A thick flow of it was pouring from the other side and running downstream.

As Rob approached the fallen tree, he kept his gun pointed out straight in front of him. If anything was going to jump out from the other side of it, his plan was to shoot it, after that he had no idea what to do next. Another step and Rob heard crunch. It sounded like teeth bearing into soft meat. It was the sound of something being devoured.
The noise stopped Rob dead in his tracks. He waited for a couple of seconds, listening to the horrific sounds as they continued.

And then suddenly they stopped. The area went silent and only the sound of the flowing water could be heard. Rob stood there waiting. He stared at the fallen tree, waiting for whatever hid behind it.
A rustle of leaves came next, closely followed by the crunching of grass. The tree shook slightly as the source of the noise leapt up onto it. Rob saw a four legged creature stand before him. Its body covered in thick grey fur and its bright yellow eyes stared into his. He saw that blood had stained the fur around the beast's mouth and hot air rose out of its nostrils.

It was a wolf. A magnificent creature, even Robert could appreciate it in this situation. It was a natural survivor and a dangerous predator.

The animal must have heard Rob approach, or smelt him in the air. Either way he had disturbed its feasting upon a fresh kill.

A terrifying growl began to erupt from the beast. It was slow at first, but after a few seconds it was loud and fierce. Its eyes were locked into Rob's and the two of them stared at one another. Its growling continued on and on. Rob had no idea what to do. Did he shoot it? If he killed it then it would be a nice meal for the group back at the Farmhouse, but if he missed then he was as good as dead. Rob didn't have a clue what to do.

Just then the wind began to blow once more. The wolf stopped growling and started to look around either side of Robert. It jumped off of the tree and onto the wet grass below. The wolf turned to face Rob again. It barked and as it did Rob noticed that it lost the fierce look in its face. Its eyes no longer had murder in them. In its place Rob could see a sense of fear in the beast's eyes.

The wolf began to slowly back away from the tree. As Rob took a step forward, the wolf turned and ran off into the forest, disappearing through a large bush and then it was gone.

It took a few moments for Rob to get his head together. He thought for a time that he was as good as dead.

He decided to take this opportunity to look around the fallen tree and see the wolf's kill. As he peered over the fallen tree he saw that on the other side of it there was the body of a woman. It was a woman in her mid-thirties, wearing a blue dress.

Rob recognised her, but he could not say from where exactly. He did remember a woman who had been around with John and his group when Rob first met them. She was one of the people unaccounted for when the survivors made their escape into the woods and became separated.

Everyone had presumed she had died along with the other missing ones and nobody else had given it a second thought.

Rob was sure it must have been her. He was terrible with faces and names. Although he not remember her wearing the blue dress, and he was sure that he would remember something like that. Maybe she had it in her pack and she got changed for some reason. Perhaps it was to change out of her wet clothes, as her others got wet from the day before.

Or maybe it was a completely different woman altogether and she just did the same thing as they did and tried to escape from the city by heading into the woods.

There was a large section of the woman's chest cut out and missing, just around her breast. He was not sure if it was the wolf that had done this, or if it had been one of the creatures. A part of the woman's waist was what the wolf was eating, so it made Rob presume that the wolf had merely stumbled upon this kill.

Rob stood there for a while staring at the poor woman who's life had recently ended. He wondered who she might have been before all of this and what her life could have been if this hadn't happened. Did she have any children? Were they safe? Did she have a husband? Chances are they had all most likely ended up like her and suffered similar fates.

Just then the wind blew, and this time Robert heard the whispers again. They seemed to be coming from all around him. Inaudible words that echoed through the trees. The air grew colder, much colder than it had ever been.

And that was when Rob noticed it. He was standing in a shadow. When he looked around he saw the shadow reach up the side of the trees. It stretched and moved further out across the ground, further and further into the forest until all the patches of sunlight had gone.

Rob spun around and looked up at the sun. He watched as dark grey clouds began to completely cover it. They must have gathered over the course of the day out of view when they hadn't noticed, but now they were here and they had blocked out the sun.
The world around Robert began to fall into grey and before he knew it, everywhere was covered in a dark shadow.

The wind began to blow stronger. It rushed past Rob, blowing his jacket open. He could feel the eyes on him once more and then there was rustling in the bushes all around him. The whispers started getting louder and louder, and then they suddenly changed to inhuman noises coming from every direction. Screams and cries of terror and the torture of what was approaching.

They were coming.

Day Thirteen – Part 2

Robert stood motionless in the shadow of the clouds, waiting to exhale. He did not dare to breathe at all. When he finally did release, he felt his whole body begin to tremble. It started with his chest, as his heart beat frantically against it, then his arms and legs began to shake, and suddenly Rob felt weak. All he could do, at that point in time, was listen.

The dead leaves, which had once held onto their trees for dear life, had begun to break off and were now being taken away in the wind. They crackled like camp fires as they brushed past other trees.

As time slowly passed the stream appeared to quiet down. After a few moments, Robert could no longer hear the flowing water at all.

The whispers too had fallen silent, but Rob knew what that meant. They were coming. The sun had gone. The grey clouds looked as if they had taken over the entire sky. In a matter of moments, the whole world around him had fallen into darkness.

He knew that it was still the middle of the day, no later than one in the afternoon, but now it felt as if he was in the middle of the night.

"I shouldn't be out here" his brain kept repeating over and over. He should be in the Farmhouse with Pete and the others.

John, Maria and Mike were still out here with him. If he could get back to them then maybe he had a chance of returning to the Farmhouse alive.

Just then a noise spawned out of the trees. It started as a snarl but eventually turned into an inhuman wail of pain and suffering. It was a cry of agony and terror. It shot its way through Rob's skin, crawling beneath it like insects, before attempting to shut down his heart, brain and eyes. He became lightheaded and felt almost faint. His heart twitched, sending shooting pains all through his chest. And finally his eyes began to water. Rob almost felt as if he was about to cry.

The noise came again, this time far louder. It was joined by another, and then another. The noises came from all around him. Rob desperately looked around in hopes of seeing which direction they were coming from, so that he could run the opposite way, but there was nothing.

Robert turned and began to run, following the stream back towards the others. When Rob looked at water, he thought he could see that it had stopped flowing, almost as if it had nowhere to escape and so it was lying still in hopes that the creatures would pass by it unnoticed.
After a few feet, Rob's vision became blurred so much that he could not see where exactly he was going. His foot slipped on the wet mud banks of the stream. He stumbled to the ground and felt the grass smash into his face with splash of rainwater. His gun fell out of his hand on the way down and Rob heard it hit the muddy banks before he crashed to the ground. For a second, he thought that he would just stay on the ground and try to wait it out, but then another cry came from behind him somewhere in the distance.

Rob pushed himself back onto his feet and wiped the rainwater and everything else from his eyes. He looked around desperately for his pistol, but his first glance found nothing. The shadow of the clouds had made it difficult to see, but Rob thought that he should be able to find it regardless. His eyes scanned over the grass and the mud banks of the stream, but there was nothing.

"No, no, no" his mind repeated.

He had nothing else to defend himself with. He needed that weapon. Suddenly Rob remembered something. He did have something else on him. He reached into his coat pocket and pulled out his flashlight. He flicked the switch and a beam of yellow light poured out, illuminating a small area.

Robert lifted his arm and put his hand into the light. For a moment he felt better. He felt his heart begin to beat slower. He inhaled, waited for two seconds, and then exhaled. This made him calm down.

He aimed the light at the ground and began to search the ground. He checked the grass around his feet first, but there was nothing. Then brought the light over to the mud bank; nothing.

A noise behind him caused Rob to swing around and point the light into the trees. He moved the light all around the area he believed the noise had come from, but there wasn't anything there, so after a moment he went back to checking for his gun.

It wasn't until he moved the light over the surface of the water that he saw the pistol lying a few inches beneath it.

"Oh shit" he said aloud, instantly regretting it in fear that any noise he made would attract the creatures to where he was.

Rob knelt down and reached into the water. It was freezing. The cold stabbed at his fingertips as he grabbed hold of the pistol grip and pulled it out.

Thankfully the dark clouds had covered the diluted blood in the water, still flowing from the corpse of the woman in the blue dress upstream.

Robert brought the gun closer to his face. "Did it still work?" he thought to himself as he quickly looked it over. A piece of plant-life had become caught in the trigger. He pulled it out and tossed it to the ground.

Rob didn't know much about guns. He did know that if you got them wet, or submerged them in water, then there was a strong chance that they would not work or get jammed.

"How long can they stay under water?" he wondered. He had only fallen over a short while ago. Surely the gun couldn't have been too damaged during that time.

Rob thought that he should ask John to check when they got back... if they got back. For all he knew, the rest of the party he came out into the woods with could already be dead.

All of a sudden the wind began to blow. It whistled through the trees and froze the cold water on Rob's hand. He tried to brush it away, but the pain grew and grew. He fought against it and tightened his grip on the handgun.

Right then Rob heard it. It wasn't the whispers that were on the wind this time. What Rob could hear was a shrill cry of unspeakable horror that froze him almost as much as the wind did on his wet hand.

The cry felt as if it was clawing its way into his mind, sending him crazy. It stabbed at his brain as it passed by. Although he realised that it wasn't passing by. The wind blew and blew, causing leaves to rip away from the trees. The leaves had been holding on for their dear lives, but now they flew off into the distance.

The wails came again. This time they sounded like there were hundreds of them out there. The noise made Rob think that the forest itself was crying out for him. It hungered for blood and that was when he knew that he was trapped.

He ran as fast as he could following the stream down towards the clearing. He didn't remember it lasting this long coming up, but now it felt as it was taking forever for him to get back.

He knew that the others would not be waiting for him. They would have run back to the Farmhouse. Maria and John would have headed back the moment they saw the clouds begin to cover the sun. Maybe they had all known. Maybe Robert had been too stupid to check the sky when he was heading upstream. Mike could easily have come back at the first sign and they all headed back together.

He imagined that John would have said that Robert was expendable. He would have said that he was just another mouth to feed and someone else to look after. It was better if they didn't have dead weight holding the group of survivors back.

The noises followed him for a time, but eventually he managed to break away from them the further he ran. As he got closer to the clearing, the sound of thunder replaced them. It erupted out across the sky as a bolt of lightning shot out across the clouds. They were much darker now. They had become storm clouds. The sound should have stopped Rob dead in his tracks, but the will to get back to safety was too great. He was determined that today was not the day he died.

The rain began to fall. It started slowly, little droplets here and there at first, but after a while it began to pour down thick and fast. The dying trees above could not withstand the brute force of the rain and they provided no cover whatsoever. Robert began to get soaked.

His flashlight began to flicker. The bright yellow light became less and less with each passing flicker and before long it was gone entirely.

"No! Ah come on!" Rob said as he smacked the side of it with the end of his gun, but there was no luck. In frustration, Rob threw it into the steam beside him. He didn't even hear a splash, but he was too frightened to look back.

When he got to the clearing, his predictions were accurate. No one was there waiting for him.

"Fuck!" he shouted out at no one in particular. He knew that they were not going to be there, but the smallest chance had given him hope. The little voice in the back of his head had told him that they still might have been there.

Suddenly the unholy noises started again. For a split second they were distant, but the rustling in the trees grew closer and so too did the screams and wails. The creatures were closing in on him. They called out for his blood. Rob's heart began to thump as if it was going to pound its way out of his chest.

"What's that?" Rob said as his eye caught the colour of red on the grass in the middle of the clearing.

It was a red tube, no bigger than a foot in length, with a plastic top. It was a flare. John must have left it for him.

Rob almost cracked a smile, but that was soon taken away as a crunch and a howling roar broke through the sound of the storm behind him. He spun around with his arm held out, gripping the pistol tight. He felt as if the gun automatically spun him around to face the noise. It was fearless. Robert, on the other hand, was not. The rainwater was running down his face and the dark storm had made it difficult to see. He could not even see if there was anything in the shadows of the trees where he was facing.

Another rustling of trees and wailing calls came from various directions all around him. Rob desperately tried to find the source of any one of the noises. All he could see was silhouettes moving among the trees in the corner of his eyes. Every time he looked round at one, it was gone. He frantically looked all around him, but there was nothing.

He was just about to turn around and go to the flare when he heard another noise coming from beside him. He turned around so quickly that he felt a pain shoot through his neck, but he was quick enough to see it this time. A lone dark figure loomed out of the bushes between some trees.

Without hesitating, and unknowing if it would still work, Rob gripped the trigger of the gun and pulled it. The roar of the handgun blasted out over the sound of the storm and the screams. Its sheer force threw his wrist and hand backwards towards him, almost sending the gun flying out of his hand.

In that moment he saw the clearing light up. He saw hundreds of them in the trees; shadows of the creatures stalking him from out of the darkness. But in that light, Rob saw that it was not one of them that had stumbled out of the bushes to attack him. The light from the handgun's discharge had shown a man in blue overalls standing before him. The rain on his dark skin glistened in the light of the gun's flame. It was Mike.

Rob saw his eyes the moment before the bullet ripped through his chest, exiting out the other side and digging its way into the tree behind.

His eyes were still showing a type of relief. Robert guessed that it was due to finding someone else out here in the woods. Mike had probably thought the exact same thing that Rob had; that he was alone out here and was about to be ripped apart by the creatures of the dark, but instead he had been in the wrong place at the wrong time.

Mike's eyes changed to sorrow shortly after the bullet made impact. The struggle that had been fighting, to get this far, to get back to the safety of others or the Farmhouse, had suddenly gone. Rob could see it in his eyes; it had all been for nothing.

He dropped to the floor and crashed into the wet grass a short distance from Rob's feet.

"No! No! No!" Rob shouted, bringing the smoking gun down to his side. "What have I....?"

Mike's face was turned towards Rob's and he saw his cold expression upon it. He wanted to go over to him, but he didn't know what to do.

"I... I killed him" Robert said to himself. A lump grew in his throat and he felt as if he could cry.

It was not the same as the man from the other day, when they had first entered the forest. That man had wanted to die, whereas Mike had only ever wanted to live.

Rob didn't have time to think as all of a sudden a cry came out of the trees from where Mike had come from. He looked up to see the creatures slowly making their way out of the darkness. Their dark features hidden still, making them difficult to see, but Rob could see their inhuman forms as they made their way towards him. He could see their mouths opening slowly the closer to the treeline they came. Each one giving off a faint hissing noise as they approached. The hissing could be heard all around him. There must have been hundreds, all around him, coming from every angle.

For a second, Rob went to lift up his handgun and pull the trigger once more, but the noises from all around him proved that he was terribly outnumbered. Even if he was able to stop one, he could not stop them all. He had a better chance of surviving if he made it to the flare. Without hesitating he turned and made a dash for the flare. The creatures screamed out at him as he picked it up. The shadows picked up speed now and moved out of the trees. Their movements were jittery and distorted, their dark figures twitched and jerked as they moved.

Rob lit the flare and a bright red light shot out all around him. It burned bright in his eyes and caused the creatures to recoil backwards. The light from the flare made it hard to see how many there were, but they seemed to be all around him. They twitched as he moved the flare around.

The closest one roared out something Rob had never heard from them before and it caused some of the other ones to hiss.

Rob lifted the flare up high and began to walk back towards the direction of the Farmhouse. Some of creatures went to follow him, but they soon stopped and watched him, their eyes piercing through the flare's light and cut straight through Rob's very soul.

They stood there watching him slowly back away. Rob knew that if the flare was to go out, then he would be dead.

"Hel....p... me..." a voice called out from beyond the creatures.

Rob looked and could just see Mike reaching out towards him. It was difficult to see with the storm, the flare and the darkness, but Rob knew exactly what it was. He felt his heart sink into his stomach as Mike's pitiful plea brought the gaze of the creatures over to him.

"No" Rob said, not nearly loud enough to be heard over the hissing and the raging storm. He wanted to go over to him, so much so that he even took one step forward, but the fear was too great. Thoughts of logic were also running through Rob's mind. He had been severely wounded. They did not have the supplies to help back at the Farmhouse. John might know what to do, but what if he had been killed trying to make his way back there? Would the flare last long enough for him to make it over to him, pick him up, and help him back to the Farmhouse? Could he even lift him?

Rob did not know the answers. He stood there as he felt his body being pulled backwards, as if a magnet at the Farmhouse was drawing him back there.

The creatures turned away from Rob and began to surround Mike as he lay on the floor, bleeding into the grass and reaching out for Rob to help him.

"Pl.... please..." he pleaded.

Robert wanted to say "I'm sorry" before he turned and ran off into the forest, but the words never came out. He turned away and let the flare guide him back in the direction he believed would take him back to the Farmhouse.

The clearing disappearing behind him through the dark trees, and before Rob had made it more than thirty feet away, Mike's screams could be heard as the sound of the creatures tearing him apart ran out. They cried out with squeals of excitement as they were fulfilling their blood lust.

Mike's screams died down the further Rob went into the forest, and he knew that another dark stain had been left permanently on his soul.

Day Thirteen – Part 3

Rob ran and he ran and he ran, until his lungs were ablaze and felt as if they were burning him from the inside out. As he forced his way through the damp bushes, that smacked him as he passed, he thought that his whole body was going to spontaneously burst into flames. His thighs ached and his hands burned like frostbite that sent shooting pains all the way to the tops of his fingers. Rob felt as if, in a matter of moments, he was going to just fall apart. But he was determined to push on.

The flare was still continuing to burn in his hand as he made his way through the trees.

He knew that the Farmhouse wasn't too far now. Since the stream clearing, he had been running as fast as he could in, what he believed, was the right direction. The foliage was thick in this part of the woods. It was making it hard to see where he was going exactly. The flare shone brightly against the leaves as he passed, but that too made it difficult to see what exactly was coming up ahead of him.

Rob was being led by his instinct. He had always had a good sense of direction, and he was sure that the Farmhouse was not much further now.

As he ran he tried to listen to hear if anything was coming after him, but all he could hear was the beating drum that was his heart. He could feel his blood pumping past his temples with each step that he took.
Another hanging branch slapped him across the face, almost knocking him backwards onto the ground. He lost his footing for a second, but managed to stop himself tumbling over by pushing off the tree.
Rob could feel that his face was bleeding now. The branch had cut him across his left cheek and he felt the warm trickle of blood running down his face. He brushed it away, but made no real effort to clear it off. He knew that all he had done was smudge his own blood over the bottom half of the left side of his face and into his stubble. Rob didn't care. He was dirty, wet, and now had blood stains on his face, but he had far more pressing matters at hand.
He needed to get back. If he could make it back to the Farmhouse then he would be safe. Out here in the forest, he was as good as dead.

Thoughts of Mike tried to make their way into his mind. He pictured his face calling out for help as the creatures tore into his flesh. The moment he realised that Rob wasn't coming to help him.
"What could I have done?" Robert asked himself. There was nothing he could have done for him. Going back would have got him killed as well. He couldn't think about this now. He had to push this to the darkest corner of his mind.

Right then he noticed that the flare was starting to burn out. It began almost spitting out the flame, desperately trying to keep itself alive.
"No! Damn you!" Rob groaned and shook the flare violently, trying everything he could. He could see the light of the trees all around him slowly fade and turn back into darkness.

The flare hissed as it began to die. It was now only illuminating a small section around Rob.

"Fuck!" he cursed. "Fuck you!"

Rob was angry. He had made it so far and it was horrifying to know that he had got so close.

Suddenly a screech echoed all around him. It ricocheted off of the trunks of the trees and Robert could not pinpoint from which direction it came. He went to say something... anything, but nothing came out. It would have not have helped if he had done anyway.

The only light Rob had was dying in his hand, and the creatures of the night were closing in on him. They had finished devouring Mike, or tearing him apart, or whatever it was that these things did with their victims.

The flare fired one last spark out before becoming nothing more than a tube in his hand. The shadows surrounded him as Rob dropped it onto the floor.

It was then that he realised he had no idea which direction to head into. There was nothing but black abysses staring back at him in all directions. More sounds came from behind him, this time he knew, and Rob spun around checking if he could see what it was that was coming after him, but he could see nothing. At least he knew one direction he shouldn't go in.

The wind began to pick up. It whistled through the woods, sending dead leaves all around. The branches on the trees bent, and some even broke off.

Through their movement, Rob caught sight of something; a light. It was faint, but it was there, off in the distance.

"The Farmhouse" Rob knew and, without a second thought, he ran through the forest towards it.

He was feeling breathless, but it wasn't going to stop him. Rob kept running and running until he saw the old building his fellow survivors were living in. A torch burned on the fence post at the beginning of the path.

He could see the Farmhouse clear as day now. It had to have been less than a hundred feet in front of him. He went to call out, but something else managed to call out before him; a horrific howl called out to him from the darkness behind. It was not the sound like that of the wolf Rob had seen earlier by the stream, this howling came from the deepest part of hell.

As Rob made it past the torch, he felt safe. He was back. He ran up the path and could already see faces in the windows staring out at him as he got closer to the door.

"Open up! It's me! It's Robert!" he shouted as he banged the side of his fist on the door. "Open the door!"

He could hear rustling and hushed whispers from inside; the sound of people moving into position.

Rob's thoughts were suddenly on Karen and her husband. The two people the group had listened to die from inside the Farmhouse. Rob hoped that he would not suffer the same fate.

Another creature noise caused Rob to turn around. He could see the treeline beyond the Farmhouse's front garden fence. The hanging torchlight flickered nervously as if it knew what was coming.

"Open the fucking door!" Rob shouted as he banged his fist frantically on the door.

The Farmhouse door clicked and slowly opened. Rob saw barrels of handguns facing towards him as John stood at the front. His face was a mixture of relief, disbelief and anger. Rob knew of John's rule that they should never open the door when it's dark outside. When the sun goes down, they needed to barricade themselves inside and wait for the sun.

John reached out a large hand and grabbed Rob by his shirt. "Get in here!" he commanded as he pulled him inside. Another horrendous creature noise called out of the shadows before it disappeared behind the closing door.

The door slammed shut behind him and he heard the sounds of the door locking, and furniture being moved in front of it.

Rob felt the warmth inside the house. He saw a log fire burning at the far end of the living room, where everyone was still currently staying in.

All of the survivors were standing around and staring at Rob as he stood in the middle of the room.

Pete was there. He stepped out from behind the crowd and came over to him.

"Are you alright?" he asked.

Rob went to answer when he suddenly realised that some of his face was still covered in blood. He brought his hand up to wipe it away.

"Yeah... I'm okay" he replied. He wasn't. He felt as if his legs were going to break beneath him and he was going to crumble into a pile on the floor. Rob wanted to save face.

"David!" John's voice boomed out. "Get back to watching the window. You two, the same! I need you guys watching to see if anyone else comes out of the woods".

As the man John had called 'David' and the other two went off to their windows, Rob heard a voice ask "What happened?"

He turned around to see Maria standing there beside John by the front door.

Rob was still trying to catch his breath. He felt like he had been running for days on end.

"Here" someone handed him some water. Rob unscrewed the lid and gulped down nearly half the bottle.

"Thank you" he said, handing them back the bottle. He then turned back to Maria and John. "I..." Rob wasn't sure what to say, so he just decided to go from the beginning. "I went upstream to see if there was a better place to get water, like you asked" he said looking at John.

The man had a blank expression on his face that was making Rob felt uneasy. Maybe it was just the eyes of everyone in the room on him, but Rob was feeling anxious.

"I went about a quarter mile upstream..." Rob continued. "And then the clouds... they came out of nowhere".

"Yeah" Maria told him. "They just started to gather all of a sudden. It was crazy".

"The sun disappeared behind the clouds" Rob said. "Those things, they came out of the trees. They chased me... I ran back to the clearing where I thought you guys might have still been".

"Did you find a better place to get water from?" John asked out of the blue, almost as if he didn't care about hearing the rest of Rob's story.

"Wha... What?" Rob asked. He had been taken back by John's random question.

"Did you find a better place for us to get water from upstream?" he asked again, slower this time, making Rob feel on edge.

"Um..." Rob suddenly had a flash of the red haired woman in the blue dress. Her insides slowly seeping out into the water, her thick dark red blood flowing into the water and changing the colour of it. He remembered seeing the tight red strangulation marks around her throat.

"No..." Rob told him. "There was a body in the water... a woman. The water was running red with her blood in it".

A few of the other survivors were disgusted by the remark. A couple began to whisper to one another. Rob heard one of them say "Well I ain't drinking that".

"Could we have gone further upstream for it?" John asked. His sudden questions were making Rob's brain shoot all over the place. He had no idea what he was going to ask next. Rob's head was a haze and he was struggling to keep up.

"I... I don't know. Maybe" he replied.

"The fucking water's contaminated. Who is to say there isn't another corpse rotting in it a few miles upriver?" someone shouted out, Rob didn't see who.

"We can boil the water" John replied. "Clean it and making it drinkable". The person who had called out to John a moment ago began arguing with him. "You can't boil blood out of water!"

"Matt!" John called out. "I don't want to hear this shit".

"What happened to Mike?" Maria shouted out over the top of John and Matt.

Rob exhaled as the room fell silent. All the eyes were back on him. Rob didn't know what to say. Should he tell them the truth? Would they understand that he shot him accidentally? What possible motive did he have for intentionally harming him?

Rob looked around the room. He saw the eyes of people staring back at him. The whites of their eyeballs were as cold as arctic snow. They would never believe him, nor would they understand. They would call him a killer. He would become a danger to the group. There was no telling what John might have done.

Rob moistened his lips as he quickly thought about what to say. He turned to Maria. "The creatures got him" he replied, which was not entirely a lie.

The other survivors looked away as they all knew what it meant to be 'got' by the creatures.

"They killed him?" Maria asked.

"Yeah..." Rob replied.

Maria looked saddened. She, John and Mike had formed a little clique at the head of the group. They had gone scavenging together and John respected them. He had always asked them their advice on things. It was clear that he would be missed.

"Did you see it happen?" she asked him.

"Yes" Rob answered. "I grabbed the flare and tried to help, but they took him off into the trees and I lost them".

Rob suddenly realised that his lies came naturally to him. He had not even thought about what he was going to say, but the words came out.

He knew he should have just stopped with 'yes', but he wanted to feel a bigger man than he actually was for what he had done to Mike.

Maria turned away from him. She quickly walked off into the kitchen. Rob watched her go. After that the rest of the people began to return to their places around the living room. John went back to his usual position by the front door where a small window was fitted next to the door that allowed him to see out.
Robert went over to where the rest of his stuff was. The old chair cushion he had been using to sleep on, and a few other items he had picked up along the way.
Pete watched him walk over. "You okay man?" he asked as Rob sat down on the floor beside the windowsill.
"I'm okay. I am just a bit exhausted" he replied.
"Here" Pete handed him over a breakfast bar.
Rob reached out and took it. "Thanks" he said. He was starting to feel hungry.
"You did everything you could" Pete said as he patted Rob on the back.
A sickly feeling come up in Rob's stomach, and suddenly he wasn't hungry at all. He forced himself to eat. He knew his body still needed it.

The two of them sat there quietly as the dark day turned to an even darker night. The survivors in the Farmhouse went about their duties before they settled down for the night.
Pete had fallen asleep quickly once again. His snoring grew louder as the night went on. Matt had been asked to watch the window on their side of the house. John had not asked anything of Robert since he had got back. He probably thought that he needed to get some rest. Rob thought so to.

He lay down on his cushion on top of the carpeted section of the living room floor and closed his eyes. He had been thinking about Mike since it had happened. He could get it out of his head. He could stop thinking about what he said to the others, about how he had lied to them and not told them of the accident.

"That's all it was" Robert said to himself. "It was an accident... an accident, nothing more".

Day Thirteen – Part 4

The dream was almost too real. Robert stood back out in the forest once again. This time the world around him was immensely dark. He could not even see the trees around him. It was almost as if the darkness itself loomed all around. Only a lighter patch marked the clearing in the trees. The flare in his hand had gone out long ago. When he looked down to see it, the tube itself was blood red. It began dripping through his fingers before forming a pool around his feet. Before he knew it, he was standing ankle deep in bloody water.

He looked at the palm of his left hand as the flare had become nothing more than a bloodstain. It was still running. The thick droplets ran down the side of his hand and joined one another at the tip of the fingers, before dripping off and splashing into the water.

Rob suddenly felt a weight appear out of nowhere in his right hand. When he brought it up to see what it was, he realised that he was holding his handgun. Grey smoke fumed out of the barrel as it floated upward to join the black sky above him. He watched it until it disappeared into the dark void above his head.

The sky itself was black and soulless. Not a single star could be seen. The wind began to blow as the clearing in front of him grew larger. A lighter, almost grey patch of the darkness opened up, but Rob could not see ahead of it.

As he tried to run for it, his legs dragged at the ground beneath him. He felt as if he was being pulled by some strange unknown force backwards... back towards the darkness. And it was then that he began to hear the voices.

"Help me...", "Help me" they cried.

Rob had heard them before. He knew them well.

The voices continued on and on. They came from all around him.

"Help me... help me!" they cried, but Rob could not see where they were coming from.

"...M... Mike?" Rob called out. He thought he saw Mike's face appear in the darkness ahead, but when he looked closer, there was nothing there. The wind and voices stopped. An eerie silence had fallen all around him. Rob turned and tried desperately to see if anything was approaching him, but nothing came.

Right then Rob noticed that the clearing had gone too. Now the black walls around him felt as if they were closing in.

Rob took a few steps towards the clearing in the shadows ahead. He walked and walked in the silence but felt as if he was not getting anywhere. It was meaningless to try.

The crack of a twig broke the silence and almost made Rob jump out of his skin. He spun around and saw the Wolf standing over the corpse of the woman in the blue dress, as it had done by the stream, only this time she was still alive. Rob could see her beating heart through her opened wound. Her ribcage was pulled outward exposing her insides. She lay there helpless as her chest rose up and down.

The Wolf turned and continued feeding from the woman. It pulled at her

skin with its teeth and began to chew on flesh chunks it pulled off.
Rob watched in horror as her throat began to tighten. He could see deep red marks form on her neck, right before his very eyes.

Suddenly a voice called out to him. "Kill.... me!" it begged. The sudden cry shocked Rob to his bones as he spun around and saw the creatures tearing into the man Rob had shot when they had first entered the woods. His mouth was moving but the words were not coming from him. "Kill... me" they echoed all around him.

Rob looked back for the Wolf, but it and the woman had both disappeared. When he turned back, he saw that expression on the man's face. It was the same one that had haunted him for days. The man was pleading for death once again.

"Kill.... Me..." the words cried out and the man extended his arm and reached out.

Rob pulled up his gun... the same way he had done it before and went to pull the trigger.

Just then the creatures stopped and looked up at him. Rob could see them clearly now. They released their hold on the man and stared at Robert, the man's blood dripped from their chins.

Rob was staring at two exact copies of himself. Their faces were distorted at times, but they were his. They were covered by blood and hidden by shadows, but Rob could see it clear as day.

The two creatures stepped out of the darkness and walked closer towards him.

"Join" they said as they stepped closer and closer towards him. The man they had been devouring and tearing apart faded into the black.

"Join" they said again, but this time the words came from all around him.

When Rob looked around, he began to see creature versions of himself step out of the shadows and walk towards him. Rob was powerless to move. He stood there motionless, watching as they slowly staggered towards him.

When they finally reached him, the closest one reached out and touched him, resting his hand on his chest. Rob felt a cold stabbing pain there and clenched his eyes shut for a few seconds, desperately trying to wake up. "No... Wake up!" he said to himself, but it didn't work. When he opened his eyes they were still there, only this time his face had gone. Instead they had their original creature forms. They had surrounded him. He could see their dark black skin and grey claws, their bone white teeth and their piercing eyes.

They began tearing into Rob's skin, ripping chunks of flesh from his bones. His blood poured out all over them, but the creature's black hides were too prominent and the dark red blood disappeared in their dark aura.

Rob felt pain racing all over his body. He wanted to call out for help, but he knew that no one would come. He could not do anything to stop them. He was helpless. All he could do was stand there and let them do it, acceptance.

"Join". The word echoed all around him as the creatures began tearing out Rob's organs and feasting on them.

Rob's vision became blurred and soon the black sky above him had turned blood red. He looked up towards it as the creatures themselves began to merge together and consume one another. He too was fading into the darkness. As he lifted his hand to try and reach out towards the sky, the arm was gone. Nothing came out of the black surrounding his body. He could feel the arm lifting into the air, but nothing was there.

One of the creature's arms oozed out of the black void and placed its hand over his face, pulling him downward. The hand ripped the skin from his face as it pulled him under. Rob didn't fight it.

He closed his eyes and let the darkness take him. He felt his body being torn apart and each section of him devoured.

And that one word sounded over and over in Robert's head. It repeated as he seemed to fade away into dust as the black abyss was all he could see now.

"Acceptance".

Day Fourteen

When Robert woke, the darkness faded away and the dream went with it. Rob felt as if his body had reattached itself as he was pulled awake by the blinding light he felt hitting his eyelids.

As he opened his eyes, he saw a silhouette beside where he was sleeping. It was difficult to see at first, but as Rob sat up, he saw that it was John squatting down beside him. He was still feeling groggy and out of place after his disturbing dream, but something in John's face made Rob feel different and a whole new fear crept over him. This feeling he had seemed so much more real than the one in his dream.

At first Rob was confused and thought that he might have still been sleeping, but a moment later, after his eyes had adjusted to the new day sun glowing through the windows all around the Farmhouse, he saw it. John had Robert's gun in his hand. He immediately knew it was his as he saw John's still nestled safely in the holster attached to his belt.

Rob's stomach felt as if it dropped out of him. He felt as if he was going to void his bowels, but he tried desperately not to show the worry on his face.

"He knows..." he thought to himself as he met John's gaze. "He's going to kill me".

John gave him an insincere smile that somehow made Rob feel even worse than he already did. He tried to look away but his eyes kept being drawn back to John's. He glanced over to where he left his gun the night before. He had left it beside his cushion facing the window, just in case any of the creatures came for them.

But now the gun was gone. It was definitely his one in the broad man's hands.

His eyes went back to John's as he spoke. "Morning" John said calmly making Rob feel uneasy.

Rob quickly looked away again, trying desperately to look around nonchalantly, as if he was just seeing what was happening in the house that morning. "Hey" Robert replied, bringing a hand up, pretending to wipe his eyes. "What's up?"

Right then Rob realised that they were alone in the Farmhouse's living room. Every morning there had been people busily getting on with tasks and duties to help out around the place, but today was different. No one was around. There was a faint hammering sound coming from somewhere outside in the distance, but Rob wasn't sure if that was the sound of work being done, or just something banging against the side of the house in the wind.

"Where's..." Rob went to say, but John interrupted him abruptly saying "Everyone's gone". John's smile slowly disappeared from his face.
"Gone?" Rob thought. "Where have they gone? Have they left me?"
John must have seen the confusion on Robert's face because right then he said "I sent a lot of them out on salvage missions. Just around the farm itself, you know. Trying to work out exactly how much land we have to work with here".

Rob sat there confused for a bit longer. He wasn't sure if John's answer had satisfied him. What of the older people of the group? Surely it was too dangerous for them to leave.

"Even the oldies?" Rob asked. He had no idea how else to word it.

John frowned. His thick black bushy eyebrows went into a V-shape on his forehead before returning to their normal positions.

"The 'oldies'..." he said quoting Rob. "They are checking out the upstairs. Maria already did a sweep of the upstairs earlier today. It's silly of us to all be in the same room". John turned to face the window. "It's pretty clear they can't get in here if we have a light going... figure that this place is pretty safe and secure. We may as well spread out here... take the top floor and let people get a bit of breathing room, you know".

"Was that a question?" Rob thought to himself.

Rob's eyes went to his own pistol clutched in John's hand, resting against his knee. John must have seen this too as he lifted his arm, bringing the gun up closer to his face.

"I saw your handgun on the floor. It looked dirty. You need to keep this thing clean, you know" John told him.

"Oh..." Rob replied. "Yeah, I slipped on the bank of the stream... coming back to the clearing yesterday. It fell out of my hand and landed in the water".

"Oh yeah?" John muttered.

"Yeah... I actually wanted to speak to you about it" Rob told him. "I wasn't sure if it would still work, as I did hear that they jam up if they get wet".

John looked the gun over. "Well you need to keep them clean, but you are supposed to use solvent or special gun oil... not water".

John continued talking about the best way to clean a handgun for a while. Rob sat there pretending to listen and take it all in, but John was using unknown words that Rob had no idea where on the gun it would be found.

"What the hell is a guide rod?" he thought to himself as John went on and on.

Rob was not sure if he was showing off about his knowledge of the inner workings of weapons, or if he was just being thorough, either way Rob could see that John was enjoying himself talking about it. It appeared that guns were a favoured subject matter of his.

Eventually John's presentation came to an end.

"Right... Okay, I'll be sure not to get it wet then" Rob said, trying desperately to show that he had acknowledged the drawn out conversation.

"Right..." John replied with a slight hint that he too believed that Robert didn't have a clue as to what he was talking about. "Anyway..." he continued. "You should take care of these things, you know. You don't want it jamming up on you in a bad situation".

An awkward silence crept upon them. "So" Rob said, desperately thinking of something else to say. "Do you think it would still be alright to fire?" he asked.

John lowered his brow again, and that was when he dropped the bombshell. "Well... you should know. You have fired it recently".

"Shit!" Rob thought to himself as he felt a lump bulge up in his throat that came from the deepest pit of his stomach, the same place he had been suppressing his guilt over Mike, and suddenly his thoughts were of the feeling of the trigger being pulled, the kick of the weapon, and the look on Mike's face as the bullet ripped through his chest.

"Oh... right" Rob managed to say. He swallowed hard but the lump would not go. "Yeah... I fired it at those things on the way back here. I forgot about that. The flash thankfully scared some of them off".

John didn't say anything. He stared straight through Rob. It felt as if his eyes were watching for some kind of hint from Robert's body language that he was lying.

Rob tried to keep his cool. "I didn't know if... because that one was in the top part of the gun..."

"The chamber..." John informed him brusquely.

This threw Rob off his trail of thought. "Emm... yeah, right" he said, struggling to get his brain back on track. "The one in the chamber fired... but I didn't know if... Emm... if any of the other bullets would be damaged or jammed, or whatever".

"No..." John said softly. A moment of silence passed before he continued. "It should still be working fine. Maybe just dismantle it and dry it out to be sure, you know".

John climbed to his feet, the Molotovs on his belt clanged gently as he did. He was still holding the pistol firmly in his hand.

"So did you manage to kill any of them?... you know... with the bullet you fired?" John asked. The tone in his voice made Rob feel even more uneasy than he already did.

"N... no" Rob stuttered clumsily. "I only scared one of them off... after the flare had died down".

"No, I didn't think so" John replied. "I haven't seen any of them die by conventional means". John went to walk off. "Well it was nice talking to you Robbo".

"Was it?" Rob wondered. He felt as if he had just been interrogated. John gently tossed the pistol on to the cushion beside where Rob was sitting. "If you need any help with drying it out, then give me a shout, you know" John said to him.

He mouthed a fake smile at him once again, and Rob quickly tried to reply in kind. He grinned, showing nearly all of his front teeth at John. It was clearly false, but then what did John know about smiling?

The man nodded before heading towards the kitchen doorway. "Oh" he said, turning around. "We might need your help with setting up a few things outside. Your friend Pete is out there. When you are feeling up to it... be sure to come and give us a hand, you know" and without waiting for a reply, he disappeared to the other side of the house.

Rob let out a sigh of relief and slumped back into his seat. He hadn't realised it, but his heart had been beating profusely during that whole conversation. He took a few deep breaths to try and calm himself.

It was not a good way to start the day. He had already spent all night dreaming of what he had done. But when he stopped to think about it, he really couldn't remember any of his dreams. He remembered that he died, that seemed to be a reoccurring theme of his dreams. Somehow though, the small memories he had of it made it seem as if this one was much more significant.

Fragmented still shots burst into his head of the man he had shot in the woods, and then of Mike.

After that all he could remember was that it was his own face staring back at him.

Robert got to his feet and looked around. He could do with some fresh air.

As he looked around, the Farmhouse was eerily quiet. The hammer sound had disappeared now. He glanced down at his handgun and sighed once more. He thought that he was done for. John had discovered he had fired a shot, but Rob's story was believable enough. There was no way that they could find out he was lying, just so long as he kept his cool.

Rob started to think that maybe this wasn't the best place for him. The Farmhouse could be a safe haven for these survivors, but would it be safe enough for him?

Day Twenty

The next week flew by with great speed. Every one of the survivors had been pulling their weight and helping to secure the Farmhouse and the surrounding area. John had made sure that no one was slacking off. If they weren't helping to build the fence, putting together Tiki torches, or moving furniture, then they were keeping an eye on the treeline for movement, or clouds that would cover overhead.

The days were hot, which was strange for this time of year. The sun shone brightly and there was not a single cloud that Rob could remember seeing. In the evenings, John had called everyone to get inside the Farmhouse before the sun had even reached the horizon.

At night, they had sat guarding and watching the woods for anything, but nearly every night had been quiet. They did hear the creatures one night. Rob remembered it was almost midnight and they heard them snarl and roar from among the trees. Everyone had been on alert then and no one was able to get any sleep after that. Rob remembers that he had sat there watching the same spot for hours, waiting for those things to show their faces from out of the darkness, but they never came.

Another night, Robert had heard the whispering again as the wind blew. A lot of the group had fallen asleep at this point, including Pete, whose turn it was supposed to be at this point in the night, but ever since his dream Rob had not been able to sleep more than a few hours, so Rob didn't mind taking over for Pete, whenever he had dozed off.

The whispering had come when the night was at its darkest. The full moon had disappeared behind thick dark clouds and the only light outside was coming from one of the Tiki torches. Rob couldn't make out what the whispers had said this time, but he knew they were calling for him. He felt it deep inside of him. Almost as if they were calling to his very soul.

After that the nights had been quiet. Rob stayed up for most of the night, watching and waiting, but nothing ever came. During the days he had mainly helped with the fence.

While searching the area, the survivors had discovered three other structures on the land. One of which was at the back of the land. It was some kind of Storehouse, with multiple rooms and large enough to house a good few people inside it. They had found that one of the rooms was filled with canned goods. The survivors had thought that they had hit the jackpot, until they discovered that a lot of the cans in the back were actually just old paint cans. The canned food itself was still good to eat. Maria had been in charge of taking an inventory of the remaining food. It seemed that they had enough to last a month. Twenty-two people were quite a few mouths to feed. They could easily get through all of the food that they had in a day, if John had not begun rationing it. None of the group had seemed to mind. John had explained the importance of survival and it was not as if they were starving.

Next to the Storehouse was a Tool Shed. There had been some useful equipment in here to help people build the fence and make repairs on the Farm and Storehouse. John had put Pete in charge of cataloguing the tools and making sure that a lot of them were returned to the tool shed at night, so that everyone knew where they were if they needed them. Rob was not sure if John had a little obsessive compulsive disorder, or if the fact he was in charge was slowly getting to his head. Rob had always suspected he had been a police officer, and his recent power trip had made this seem more likely. He had recently taken to ordering people to do things, instead of asking them as he had done before. Nobody seemed to care that much, as his orders were what most people were thinking of doing anyway. He had just given them a better way of implementing them.

The other building had been an old barn to the west of the Farmhouse. It had been renovated in the last year or so, and that the second floor was being used as an office of some kind. They had found a desk and pieces of paper here. There was nothing interesting about the paperwork, but it had given them an insight into the previous owner. The Farmhouse had been deserted when the survivors had arrived nearly two weeks ago. They had assumed that the original owners had left or been killed by the creatures, but the paperwork had hinted that a family had lived here previously. The dates of the documents stated that they had gone on a family holiday quite recently. It had made Rob wonder if this was happening all over the world, or was it this little island that was plagued by the darkness.

Rob had hoped that the family would never return to this horror. He wanted the place that the Farmer and his children had gone to, to be a safe haven and completely isolated from all of this. He had wished he could have got out as well, before this all started, and spent the rest of his days relaxing on a beach somewhere.

In the bottom section of the barn, the group had found hundreds of pieces of wood behind an old tractor. There were beams, planks and boards piled up all around the ladder to the office. This was when John had the idea of the perimeter fence. The Farmhouse already had a bit of a fence around it, but that stretched out across the entity of the Farm itself. Lots of sections of this fence were missing to allow tractors to tend to the fields, so the rest of the area was easily accessible. John had ordered people to start building a fence that connected from the fence already running around the Farmhouse. This new fence ran up to the barn, connecting it to the back wall of the barn, then it went across to the Storehouse, behind it and around the tool shed, before finally running down and connecting back to the Farmhouse's already existing fence. This had created a safe zone in the middle of the Farmhouse, the Storehouse and the barn. The fence was only waist high, which meant that people could easily climb over it if they needed to, but it was not easy enough for someone to step over.

The tractor had been moved outside the barn and the group discovered it had been full of oil. They used this to make a few Molotovs and soak the Tiki torches John had ordered the group to build and plant all around the inside of the fence. There were a few issues with this Rob knew. For one they would eventually run out of oil. They must have only had a quarter of the tractors tank left, and secondly a few people had to go around and light the torches as the sun started to go down. Many nights only a few of them had been lit, mainly in the areas that people were ordered to keep watch on. The rest were too out of the way to light before the night came. Many people had forgotten. Rob could only recall one night when John had ordered the whole lot of them lit. Matt and Rob had been elected to run around the Farm and light them all. It had taken well over an hour and by then, the sun had nearly gone from view entirely.

Many of the older survivors; the weak or useless of the group, had helped to clear out the middle section between the buildings of the overgrown plant life and debris that had just been left here. They had made a large bonfire in this middle section, which people had taken to calling the "Courtyard". John occasionally sent people out to gather firewood from the forest, or they would use old scrap wood that was not good enough to help build the fence. A few evenings they had lit the bonfire and stood around it. The light was bright and made them feel safe to be outside at night. Of course as it got darker, they soon moved inside.

By day eighteen, people had started to feel safe here. Some people had moved out of the Farmhouse and gone to various different locations around the Farm. Some of the rooms in the Storehouse had been fixed up and people moved a couple of the beds out of the Farmhouse, across the Courtyard and into the Storehouse, while other people moved into the rooms in the upstairs of the Farmhouse. This gave people a lot more space and almost a touch of normality to their lives. Many people had been used to living as a community and these new living arrangements had helped people feel as if things were slowly turning back to the way things once were.

Rob had no illusions. He knew that a lot of these people would not even speak to one another had the world not turned to shit. Every one of them had lost loved ones, their homes, and their old lives. The world was different now, no matter how much you didn't want to hear it. Rob knew that many of these people just wanted to survive. They wanted to live their lives without fear of when the sun went down and the creatures of the night would prey on them.

Robert had moved to the front bedroom of the Farmhouse. It was the smallest of all five bedrooms in the Farmhouse. Rob did not mind. He did not have many things. He had brought up the cushion from downstairs, as the bed in this room had been moved to the Storehouse and now someone else was enjoying it. So the room itself was pretty bare. Again he did not care that much. Some of the other rooms in both the Farmhouse and Storehouse were being shared, but Rob seemed to prefer being on his own and left to his own company.

Pete was in the room next to his, along with Matt. The three of them had been ordered to take shifts and keep watch at night. So recently at night Rob had gone into their room and sat with them to keep watch.

John had moved into the office area of the barn. He accepted the self-appointed role as the leader of the group and taken it upon himself to move into a location that was away from everybody else, apart from his own little group who had set up an area each at the bottom of the barn. Rob had not been to the place John had taken as his own accommodation, but on day twenty Maria came to Rob while he was helping a few others with a section of the fence that had blown down in the wind, and said that John wanted to speak to him.

This had made Rob feel incredibly uneasy. Other than the normal orders that John barked to everyone, he had not spoken to Rob directly since the morning after Mike had died.

When Rob got there, the bottom of the barn was where Maria, David and another guy Rob had not spoken to slept. They had made the corners of the barn their own and in the back was where the group kept all their remaining food.

He needed to take a ladder up to the floor where John lived. When he reached the top, he saw that John had made a hammock for himself to sleep in. The desk was still in the same place they had found it, but now John had dismantled various firearms and the different parts were all laid out across it. On a shelf in one corner, John had stood all his Molotovs upright, with the oily rag hanging from them. The whole place stank of petrol. Rob had quite enjoyed the smell in the past, but the room was thick with the smell.

John was busy looking at what appeared to be an old map. He turned to Rob as soon as he heard him get to the top of the ladder.

"Ah yes. How are you doing Robert?" he asked.

Rob could tell that the man did not actually care how he was doing. The way he had asked it felt almost patronising. John was taking his role as the leader of the group very seriously.

"Yeah... I'm okay" Rob replied, unsure of what to say to the man.

"I need your help with something" he said, ignoring Rob's answer.

"Do I have a choice?" John wondered.

"As you might know, I've sent David with a few others to check a small town that should be just a few miles east of here". Rob did not know this.

"I've got another couple of people just following that stream from the other week. I want to see if it goes to lake of some kind. Maybe we can get some more water from that. Maybe we could have a few people do some water runs, you know. Make it a regular thing".

Rob was wondering where this was going. Did he want him to do these water runs? Did he want him to go and meet up with them? Rob had not been out into the woods since that night with Mike. Thankfully John had not asked him to go out there again.

Robert realised that John was staring at him. He must have been waiting for Rob to respond. "Oh... right" was about all that he could manage to say. His mind was racing with what the hell John wanted to speak to him about.

"Come and take a look at this" he said, urging Rob over.

Rob went to the desk and looked at the map. It was a crumpled piece of paper that had been flattened out. The corners were bending upward and one whole section of the map was missing, apparently it had been torn out. The map showed a layout of the Farm. The fields took over most of the page, with a section on the right showing the Farmhouse and the other buildings here.

John pointed to another small structure on the map just slightly north of the barn. "Here... do you see that?"

Rob got a little closer to the map. "Is it another building?" he asked.

"I believe so... it isn't very big. It is not big enough to house any one... not that we have enough wood to build the perimeter fence all that way, but it might be worth checking out".

"Ah... here it is" Rob thought to himself. "Here it comes".

"With my best people out already..." John started saying, which didn't give Rob the greatest confidence considering that he did not think of him as one of his 'best people'. "I would appreciate it if you could just go and check this out for me, you know. The day is still young and there is not a cloud in the sky. David and the others should be back before nightfall, but I wanted someone to go and check this out, you know".

"Why can't you go?" Rob suddenly blurted out. As soon as the words left Rob's mouth, he knew he had messed up.

John's eyebrows formed their famous V-shape, but he must have seen the fear in Rob's eyes as they widened over the last few seconds that John brushed off the comment.

"I would love to... but I have to keep watch here. This is a good thing we have going here. I need to make sure that we can keep this up until..." John paused.

"Until what?" Rob thought, but did not dare say. John gave Rob a strange feeling in the pit of his stomach. It was the feeling that he could snap him like a twig if he wanted to, which he did most likely want to, but was somehow resisting the urge to do. So Rob kept quiet. But what was John thinking? Until they got rescued? Surely John, of all people, did not believe that they were going to be rescued.

John turned back to the map. "If you need anything then just let me know. You can ask someone else to go with you if you want. But if you could get this done before the evening, then that would be great, you know".

Rob took this as a hint to leave. He made his leave and went back down the ladder.

Once Rob got back to the fence, the rest of them had finished. Maria had offered to help in his absence. With the fence back up he thought it was best to go and check out the structure in the north. He would have asked Pete to come with him, but he couldn't remember if Pete had actually been beyond the treeline the whole time they had been here. He didn't want to force a job onto him, or put him on the spot the way that John would have. Earlier today Rob had walked in on Pete crying over something in his room. Rob apologised and left. He knew that Pete must have been sad over the people that he had left behind. Pete would often hint at them, but Rob would never push the conversation further.

With that in mind, he decided to ask Matt instead. Rob had become quite friendly with him, and Matt had always tried to be as helpful as possible around the Farm. He had been outside the Farm a few times now and Rob knew that he was no stranger to the dangers they might face out here.

The two of them headed out of the Farm's fenced area a little while later. Matt told him that due to the position of the sun, it was most likely around two o'clock in the afternoon. Rob looked up at the sky and saw that the sun had passed the highest point in the sky, but other than that, he could not have worked out the time.

The woods were well lit and only occasional areas were covered in shadow. At first Rob felt nervous. His thoughts were back on Mike once again. It had been the last time he had ventured out this far from the Farm in nearly a week. But as this part of the woods was still on the Farm's land, it did not feel as bad as the forest that surrounded it.
It took them around twenty minutes to reach the structure. Matt saw it first and called out to Rob who had stopped to take a leak behind a tree. When he was finished, he quickly caught up with Matt and saw what he was pointing at. It was an old shack in the middle of the woods. It looked as if it had been unused for years and that the previous owners had not bothered to fix it up. The shack's roof had been half destroyed and collapsed inside and the door was almost rusted off.
Matt opened it and they both saw that hundreds of spiders had made their webs across the ceiling.

"I'll... I'll wait out here" Rob told Matt.

"What? Are you scared of spiders?" Matt asked him mockingly.

"No. It just looks like this is a waste of time. I can already tell that there is nothing we can use". Matt laughed and went inside.

Rob took a walk around the shack. He could hear Matt inside scurrying about and moving things. A crashing sound erupted a moment later. It sounded as if a box or something had fallen over.

"You okay in there?" Rob asked.

"Yeah... yeah. I thought I saw a rat" Matt replied, laughing.

Once Rob made it back to the front of the shack again he took a look inside. He saw it was dank and dark, with the only light coming from the hole in the ceiling, but that was still blocked a bit by the overhanging trees.

He saw that there were a few piles of old boxes. They appeared to be wet and the contents inside damaged.

"Anything?" Rob asked.

"Nah... I don't think so. I think you were right".

Rob laughed and turned back to face the woods. When he did, something caught his eye. It fluttered in the soft breeze, before slowly landing in a bush just near the base of one of the larger trees here. It was a piece of newspaper. Rob went over to it and pulled it from the tree. One of the pages ripped and the breeze caught it, carrying it off into the woods.

The rest of the paper was relatively fine other than being a little damp. It was only two pages that had got themselves stuck together somehow in the fold. Rob thought he would take a look.

It was dated from three days before this all happened. "Twenty three days ago" Rob thought to himself as he reflected for a moment. He wondered if he would have done anything differently if he was back at this date. He would have most likely prepared himself better and made sure he said his goodbyes.

The newspapers front page was covering the story of a serial killer the media had called the Bridgefield Butcher. Robert had been familiar with the story and had seen some news coverage about it before the creatures appeared. The police had found several corpses with their heads decapitated. They were never found. The article stated that the police were doing all they could to capture him. Rob thought that this Bridgefield Butcher would most likely fit in well with the monsters that stalked in the shadows. He was sure that people like that would have probably been right at home in this new world of theirs.

Another story in the newspaper told of a wealthy CEO who hanged himself after being caught cheating. Rob stopped reading it. He remembered that that this was the reason he did not bother reading the newspaper. He did not even watch the news. He always found both to be nothing but stories of a depressing nature that did nothing more than make him feel bad for the world that they had lived in. Upon reflection, Rob would have given anything to have been able to go back to it.

As he was just about to toss the paper away, his eye caught something. There was an article about a husband and wife who been accused of murdering their young child. It was another depressing story, but the picture next to the article was what had captivated him. There in black and white was a picture of Karen and her husband. Her hair was different in the photograph, but Rob was adamant it was her. Her husband looked exactly the same as he had done the night that they had gone out into the forest, before being torn apart and taken away by the creatures. The story said that they had been charged with killing their son, but a lack of evidence had acquitted them of the crime and they were released. The newspaper had gone to calling them 'Monsters' and 'Murderers', stating that this was a clear injustice of the legal system. The photo was of them being escorted from the courthouse to the back of a police car, as angry onlookers and journalists shouted abuse and took photographs.

Just then the wind began to get colder. Hairs started to stand up on Rob's arm as Matt emerged from the shack. "There is nothing here" he told him as he brushed off some cobwebs from his jacket. "We should be getting back. I think it's starting to take a turn for the worst". Matt looked over to Rob, still holding the newspaper. "Hey, what have you got there?" he asked.

Rob automatically let go of the paper and the wind carried off through the trees. He could hear a faint rustling sound as it brushed past old dead leaves, before disappearing out sight and sound.

"No, it was nothing" Rob told him lying. He was not sure what good it would have done to have told Matt the truth about Karen and her husband who had died a week and half earlier. "Let's get back then".

On the way back, Rob's thoughts were on Karen. He thought about how they had been sharing a small house with murderers, but then again he remembered that they had been acquitted of the crime, and that the media had a way of painting a bad face onto everything.

He suddenly remembered how he too was now a murdered. The man in the woods when they first had entered the forest was a mercy kill, Rob knew. He had pleaded for him to end his suffering. Mike on the other hand had been different. He knew it was just an accident, but the way he kept it from the others and had lied about it, especially now that so much time had passed, had made him no better than Karen or the Bridgefield Butcher for that matter.

When they got back to the fence, Robert saw that David and his scouting group had returned. John was speaking to them in the middle of the Courtyard near the bonfire. A few other survivors had gathered around to hear what they had found in the nearby town.

As Rob approached, John took a glance over to him, smiled that fake smile of his, before turning back to David.

"It seems untouched" he heard David say as Rob shuffled in between two people to get a better view. "It's deserted... we didn't find anyone".

"Okay good" John told them.

"Good?" Rob thought to himself.

"We did find something strange" David continued. "All the streetlights have been smashed. It looks as if that place is pitch black at night.

"Okay" John replied. "We will begin salvaging what we can from there and bring it back here. We'll need to make sure that we are out of there before nightfall. I'll begin preparations and arrange for a team to go and start bringing stuff back tomorrow". John turned towards Rob. "What did you manage to find?"

Rob shook his head. "Nothing. The place is half destroyed and no use to anyone".

"Okay good" he replied.

"There it was again... good?" Rob wondered. Was he even listening?

"I want volunteers to go on the first salvage run tomorrow. Any takers?"
As soon as the question left his lips, the survivors went quiet. David raised his hand along with a couple of others from the group who had just arrived back from there, but no one else did.

"Robert?" John turned back to him. "What about you?"

Day Twenty One – Part 1

Rob sat there on the edge of the forest for a while as the others caught up. He stared out of the trees and down the hill he could see the small town David and the others had scouted yesterday.

It had been weeks since Robert had been this far from the Farmhouse. Even the stream had not been as far as this. It was strange to see a normal civilised place such as this. There were cars and shops, benches and street plants, all of which looked as if they were frozen in time, like a photograph. If it wasn't for the fact that the wind was blowing, causing rubbish to float around, then Rob would have thought that this was in fact a large billboard. He could hardly believe his eyes.

Rob had never seen or heard of this place before. He had lived in the city for most of his life, but he never knew of such a small quiet town twenty or thirty miles out. The whole thing felt surreal, but he brushed it away, thinking that it was most likely due to the fact that he had spent so long in the confines of the fenced Farm.

The entire town was deserted, as David had said. It was a ghost town. There was no indication that there was anyone alive in there, but they didn't want to take any chances. Rob carried his handgun and the rest of the team all carried various bludgeoning weapons and firearms. Normally the rustling of the wind blowing through the dead leaves created a background noise, but here, on the edge of the forest overlooking this ghost town, there was only silence.

Glancing around Rob saw the broken street lights littered all around the streets. Broken pieces of glass lay in heaps beneath them. "What could have done that?" Rob wondered. Anyone who smashed them was only causing problems for themselves, and he knew that the creatures would not go near them if they were actually up and running, at least that is what he believed.
The more he thought about the monsters in the darkness, the more questions he asked himself about them. Nobody really knew anything about them or where they had come from. They had emerged out of the darkness one night and consumed all that they had come upon.

On the journey to the town, Rob had kept to himself. John had come along for the first salvage mission. It seemed he was eager to get back into the thick of it, rather than hiding behind the fence and Tiki torches of the Farm. Rob thought that it was strange that he had sent him to check out the shack the day before, stating that he had to keep watch over the other survivors, but now suddenly he doesn't need to watch over them, especially on a much more long winded and dangerous mission as this. Rob did not seem to understand the man's way of thinking at all. He had asked Maria to keep a watch on the Farm while they were gone.
David and Matt had also joined them, as well as a couple of other people from David's group yesterday who now knew a little bit of the lay of the land. Rob did not know them, nor had he ever spoken to them, so he had decided to just keep himself to himself on the road up here.

When the trees began to thin out, they knew that they were getting close. Rob offered to go ahead and check it out, to which John had agreed. John smiled at him, but this time it was not one of his fake smiles that looked as if he learned how to smile from a book, but instead it was a slight grin that gave the impression to Rob that John liked his suggestion.

By the time the others caught up to him, Robert had a good look over the town.

"What have we got?" John asked as he and the others came out of the trees and took a knee beside him.

Rob cleared his throat. "We... um... its dead here. It's a ghost town". John stared out over the area. Rob thought it was best to continue.

"Everything looks untouched as David said. It honestly looks as if everyone just upped and left one day... which is pretty different to what happened in the city".

Rob remembered that the streets were utter carnage. There was blood and bodies all around, as great fires burned buildings and darkness swept over them all.

Or was it? Rob couldn't remember now. It had been a few weeks since then, so perhaps it hadn't been as bad as that.

"What about the buildings themselves?" John asked. "David? Care to shed some light"

David rubbed his nostril, the way that he always did, and told them that there were three main buildings he thought they should check out. He said that he had found an electronics store, a small police station, and a supermarket. John told them that they should go in teams of two and check out each one. John decided that it was best if each of them went with one of the people who had already come here yesterday, and so John and one of the unknowns would go to the police station. Matt had mentioned that he knew a little bit about electrical engineering, so John had asked him and the other unknown to go to the store, and that left David and Rob to check out the supermarket.

"Okay, if anything happens, we'll meet here on the edge of town. Keep an eye on the sun and make you stay out of darkened areas" John had told them.

No one knew if the creatures hid inside dark buildings during the daylight hours. No one had seen where they had come from or where they retreated to when the lights came on. It was safe to assume that they lay in wait in the shadows, watching for when the sun went down.

They moved down the hill and arranged a time to meet back. Anything they could carry, they would bring here and leave it, just in case anything was to happen, that way they could always come back and grab it if need be. This didn't fill Rob with the greatest confidence.

Clouds had begun to gather, but they did not give Rob any cause for concern. The sun should still be able to shine through them.

David was a strange man. He had always stayed close to John, but he was always out of the loop. John seemed to like to have only two other people with him, and the rest of them were the ones he ruled over. After Mike died, John seemed to have promoted David to being one of his 'lieutenants', as Rob called them. They were in charge of following John's orders back at the Farm. This involved mainly passing orders down and advising people what they were going to do next. David seemed to fit into the role nicely. Whenever he gave someone an order that had come from John, he had always given them an arrogant remark, making them feel as if they had no choice in the matter. Maybe people felt as if John would kick them out of the group and exile them from the Farm if they did not do what they were told and pull their weight.

David looked as if he went down the gym a lot in the old world. He was not massive, but he looked as if he had kept himself fit. It was a fad that almost everyone was into before this had happened. Rob had been meaning to get himself down the gym as he had started getting a bit heavier as he got older.

Rob laughed to himself as he thought about that. Maybe this was one good thing that came out of all of this. He had run more in the last few weeks than he had ever done in his whole life, and he was eating far less now that the group was rationing food. He had spent all of last week helping to build the fence, and now he did feel a little lighter because of it.

Rob wasn't sure what David was before all of this happened. He could imagine him in a nightclub with his top button done up, heading into one of the toilet cubicles to do a line of cocaine with three other guys. The fact he kept rubbing his nostril gave Rob this idea. It could have just been an itch for all he knew, but he often found himself assuming the worst in people.

"It's this way" David said, pointing to a street around the next corner. As Rob followed, he felt a crunch beneath his feet that broke the awkward silence between David and him. This whole time "It's this way" had been the only thing either of them had said to one another. Rob looked down at his shoe and saw that he had trodden on broken glass and plastic from one of the street lights. He glanced up and saw that the entire bulb had been smashed along with the outer plastic covering that protected it.

He wondered if the monsters had done it to make it easier to swarm the town on the first day, or if the power outage had affected this place as well, and the street lights were smashed to stop survivors from using them should the power ever get turned back on.

Other than them the town was perfectly intact. There were no smashed windows, no crashed cars, or fires, no blood trails, or bodies. The entire town was just empty.

When they arrived at the supermarket, the doors were locked. David tried pulling them and kicking them but they did not budge. The sound the doors made when David kicked them caused Rob to check around and made him uneasy. The creatures only came out in the dark, but Rob wondered what else might have been hiding in this ghost town.

Rob walked over and peered into the window. It was dark inside and difficult to see, but it looked as if it might have been full.

"Let's check round back" David suggested as he began moving quickly round the side of the building. Rob thought it would be best to follow. They moved across the car park to the rear entrance, but that too was locked tight.

"Fuck sake" David complained, kicking the door violently.

But then Robert saw it. "There" he said pointing, almost excited at the prospect of getting inside. He had had enough of being outside by this point.

David glanced up to where Rob had directed him. A vent cover, large enough to fit a full grown man, had been removed, exposing the dark shaft within. "One of us could probably fit in there". As soon as Rob had said it he realised that he would be the one going into the vent. David was bigger than he was and he was not sure if he could actually hold up his weight as he climbed into the vent. "Shit" he thought to himself.

David held out his hands flat and Rob climbed up and into the vent, as he did he cut his hand on a piece of metal sticking out of the side. He resisted swearing or letting David know that he had injured himself and pulled himself inside.

The silence was broken the moment Rob was in. The wind followed faintly behind him, rushed past and echoed off into the dark distance. He heard David call up to him, but he could not make it out. The outside world was now distant and muffled behind four thick walls of steel. Rob just decided to shout something back, making an assumption to what he had said. "Yeah I'm in... I'm okay" he called back and the words too echoed off.

He continued onward and crawled through the vent shaft towards a grating a little bit further forward. He realised then that he had been leaving bloody hand prints all over the route behind him. He would need to find something to bandage it up, but at least he was in the right place to look for some sort of medical supplies. "Maybe this place has a pharmacy" Rob thought to himself as his fingers slipped through the grate.

Just then he stopped. He thought he had heard something. "A footstep?" he thought as he waited for a moment and listened to see if he could hear anything else.

A minute passed of silence, other than the noise from the wind behind him. He went to put his hand back on the grating and then he saw it. It was movement from below. It was quick and in the corner of his eye, but he was sure that he had seen it. Whatever it was made no sound and was gone before Rob got a decent look at it. "Shit" Rob said under his breath as his hand hovered over the grating. He felt a droplet of blood drip from the wound on his hand and fall through the grating to the ground below. The droplet made no sound at all upon impact, but that didn't stop Rob from thinking that perhaps whatever was down there could have heard it.

He waited a few more minutes. He knew that David must have been getting impatient, but he wanted to make sure that whatever he had seen had gone.

After a bit he grabbed hold of the grating and went to move it. It came away easily and he moved it to the side as quietly as he could.

He poked his head out of the vent and saw that below him was a dark corridor at the back of the supermarket. There was a manager's office, male and female toilet doors, one door that must have entered the actual store, and another at the far end which David must have been waiting behind. The door to the supermarket was blocked by a vending machine that had toppled over. It was the first sign of any chaos since the broken street lights, if chaos was the appropriate word.

The rest of the hallway was empty. Rob worked out that with the store doors blocked and the door leading outside locked, the Manager's office and the toilets were the only place whatever he saw could have gone to.

He waited one more minute before climbing down. Whatever he had seen had now gone. Before getting David, he drew his gun and pushed the Manager's Office door open with the end of it. The door was locked. "That's three down" Rob thought to himself, referring to the doors. "Only the toilets left".

He took a step forward towards the Female toilet and rested his palm on the door. It too was locked. Rob let out a sigh of relief, until he released that he was now sure whoever, or whatever, he had seen was behind the fifth door.

Rob took a deep breath and went towards the Male toilet door. He tried to swallow the lump in his throat but it would not go. He raised his hand up and went towards the door. Suddenly a bang brought him back and made him jump out of his skin. He swung around and saw David's face looking at him through the window of the rear entrance. "Come on man! Let me in, then you can go for a piss" he said waving Rob over to the door.

Rob breathed a little easier and went over to it. When he got there, he looked out the window behind David. The clouds were still light, but they should probably get a move on. He pushed the emergency exit bar and the door unlocked, opening. Rob has half expecting an emergency alarm to ring out, but thankfully the only sound he heard was David pulling the door open and stepping inside.

"Good work" he said giving Rob an almost sarcastic pat on his back before going on ahead. "You took your time". Rob closed the door behind him and followed.

Further down the corridor they came to the entrance to the main store. Rob did not know what to expect. The supermarket had looked pretty full up from the outside, but it had been dark and it could have easily been misleading.

"Give me a hand with this" David said with one hand already on the vending machine.

Rob knelt down and used both hands to push it upward as David pulled it back into place. It was heavy but thankfully the machine had been empty at the time it fell.

Once it was back upright, Rob went to open the door until he suddenly remembered something.

"There was someone here..." he blurted out.

"What?!" David said surprised. "Why didn't you tell me earlier?!" he asked drawing his pistol from his belt strap.

"I checked the other doors. It was only this one left" Rob told him, pointing to the male toilet door.

"Well what are you waiting for?" David replied.

Rob didn't know what to say. His question had caught him off guard. He did not realise that he wanted him to go in there alone. Just as Rob was about to answer, David shook his head and went over to the door. He kicked it and the door swung open, before storming inside with his pistol drawn at the ready. He disappeared as the toilet door closed behind him.

It was then that Rob heard it. A whisper. It was faint and on the wind now flowing through the open vent above him. It raced around the corridor, sending a chill all over Robert's skin. At first he thought it was only the sound of the wind whistling through the ventilation shaft, but then he heard a word. It was that word again, the one he had heard on the front grass of the Farmhouse two weeks ago. He remembered it. It haunted his dreams and made him think of horrifying things.

"Join" it said... "Join".

Another noise drew Rob's attention round towards the store entrance and as he turned, he saw the face of a woman staring back at him. It caused Rob to flinch backwards. Her face was white and her eyes were cold. They had thick black circles all around them and her skin looked as if it was ready to peel off over her blue dress and pile all around her on the floor beneath her feet.

He stared into her eyes for what felt like an eternity. Her eyes grew darker and darker as the seconds passed. Rob's skin began to crawl and he felt as if he could not move.

The door beside him opened and David reappeared, causing Rob's head to turn away from the woman's glance.

"It's empty" he said, tucking his gun back into his belt next to the combat knife he always carried.

Rob turned back to the store entrance, but the woman had gone.

"You okay man?" David asked.

Rob did not know how to answer. He did not want to tell David that he saw someone, as he was sure not to believe him, after sending him on a wild goose chase a moment ago. The woman could not have been the person Rob had seen in the hallway, as she would not have been able to get to the store given that the vending machine was blocking the way. There had to have been someone else here. Or maybe there was no one here at all. "Perhaps I am losing my mind" Rob thought as David looked at him with a confused look on his face, waiting for Rob's answer.

Rob shook his head slightly and replied. "Yeah, I'm fine".

David smiled at him. "You must have been seeing shit man" he told him.

"What?" Rob replied thinking how could he have known what Rob had seen.

"The toilet was empty... not even any toilet paper hanging up" David said, causing Rob to understand what he meant. "There is something strange that went down here".

Rob wondered what he meant by the term strange, if he was in fact comparing it to all they had witnessed over the last few weeks.

David turned the lock on the store doors and pushed opened both of the doors. They swung open and into the walls beside them, making a loud crashing sound that echoed through the aisles of the supermarket.
Rob looked at David and saw that a smile was beginning to creep onto his face. He turned and stuck his head around the door, and then he saw what David was smiling at.
The supermarket was untouched. The fruit and vegetable sections had started to go mouldy, as well as some of the bread, but Rob had expected this place to have been ransacked during the first few days.
The shelves were stacked with cans and packaged goods as far as the eye could see. There were trolleys sitting and waiting for them to stack as much as they could into them. Behind it all was a large unlit neon sign in one of the far corners. The word 'Pharmacy' was what the letters spelled.

An even bigger grin began to grow on David's face. "Jackpot!"

Day Twenty One – Part 2

The clouds had begun to gather in the sky by the time they had got back to the meeting point. Rob could see John, Matt and the other two unknowns already waiting for them. Matt and the other's faces seemed to light up at the sight of David and Rob pushing large amounts of canned food and other goods in shopping carts down the street towards them. John was too busy sorting something else out behind what appeared to be a large lawnmower. As they got closer, Rob could see that it was one of those portable generators he had seen on buildings sites.

"What's all this?" he asked as they got a little closer. It was only then that John looked up and acknowledged them. He stood up and as he did, he brought what he was doing on the floor.

"We've been waiting for a while, you know" he said as he threw a large shotgun over his shoulder.

Rob was taken a back a bit by the sheer size of the weapon. He completely forgot what he was about to say. Thankfully David chimed in.

"Jesus man, where the fuck did you get that thing?" he asked with a hint in his voice that made Rob think he was jealous of the weapon and hoped John had managed to find him one.

"We picked this up and a few other things from the station" John replied, bringing the gun down to his other hand and almost caressing it. It was clear to Rob that John was incredibly pleased with his find.

"Anything for the rest of us?" David asked, confirming Rob's suspicions. John laughed at his question, but did not try and answer it. Instead he asked him what he and Robert had found.

"All sorts of good stuff man. We tried to get as much as we could" David told him, pushing one of the carts towards them. Matt took a step forward and stopped the cart, glancing wide-eyed into it.

"Wow" Matt said amazed. And he was right to. It was the most food any of them had seen since this whole thing had started. The survivors at the Farm had been living off of the few cans they had brought with them into the forest and the ones they managed to find in the Storehouse, but they had started to run a little thin. Rob had noticed that the rations John and the others had started to give them had been a little bit smaller than the day before. The food was well needed.

"Look at all this stuff" one of the unknown survivors said as he reached in and grabbed hold of a can of hot dogs.

Rob and David had just grabbed whatever they could and filled up two full shopping carts each. There were twenty-two of them back at the Farm and they knew that one cart each would have been eaten in a matter of days. At least now they would last that little bit longer.

David had been more interested in the pharmacy section. Rob noticed him looking over a lot of the pain medication and nicotine patches. He grabbed quite a few different things from all over the shop and stuffed them into a couple of shopping bags that were now hanging off of his carts.

When Rob had approached him, needing to find a bandage for his cut hand, he saw that David had busted open the door to the backroom and was piling in as much as he could.

Rob asked him about it and David replied that the group would need the medication and other items if they were going to survive. That made sense to Rob. Medicine and bandages were almost as important as food in this type of situation.

But when Rob looked over the bags, he saw a lot of things that he had no idea what they were or what they did. Drugs that he had never heard of; Seroquel, Klonopin, Chlorpromazine and loads of other stuff Rob could not pronounce. He was going to ask David if the group really needed any of this stuff, but then he did seem like he knew what he was looking for. This had blown Rob's theories of what David was before out of the water. Maybe he had been some kind of pharmacist or medical student. The way he spoke and acted didn't give Rob the impression that he was well educated, but he supposed he should not judge a book by its cover.

As David had been busy gathering more medicine and drugs, Rob noticed he had packed some pregnancy tests and condoms, and not just the normal kind, David had seemed to grab whatever he could from the shelves.

"Was he hoping to get lucky with one of the other survivors back at the Farm?" Rob wondered. He had been spending a lot of time with Maria at the bottom of the barn, so perhaps there was something going on there. It had only been a few weeks since everything went down, surely people had not already resorted to sleeping with one another, but then again, what with the urges that human beings have, it would not have been surprising.

It would have been better to use protection than to bring a child into all of this, Rob knew. The thought of the world never returning to what it once was, was terrifying enough for Robert, let along having to bring up a baby in all this horror.

It was too early to think about all of this Rob had known. For all he knew, the military could have been taking care of the creatures and securing the cities, setting up safe zones and protecting people. It could have explained why all the people in this town had just left it, without any signs of a fight.

Matt had brought Rob back to the moment at hand. "Check out what we've got" he said as he tapped the top of the generator with one of the cans he was holding.

"The hell is it?" David asked.

A puzzled look appeared on Matt's face. "It's... it's a generator" he said, almost questioning the words as if it was not clear enough to see.

"We are going to hook it up to these" John said, holding up a bag of LED lights. There must have been hundreds of them in the bags behind him. "We'll string them up all along the fence around the entire perimeter of the Farm... then we'll run the generator at night and that should keep those bastards out".

This was a good idea Rob knew. At night, if the bonfire was not going, then they were forced to lock the doors of whichever building they were staying in. At night the Courtyard was just as dangerous as the forest itself. Even with the bonfire burning, anyone outside would have to stick close to it, as there were too many dark areas all around, so it was better to just remain indoors.

"We can stick it in the tool shed and keep it out of the rain" Matt suggested.

John seemed to like that idea, giving him a slight reassuring nod.

"What else did you find?" Rob decided to ask the four of them.

John drew his eyes to a duffle bag at his feet. He must have been loading the shotgun here when they first arrived as there were a few shells lying beside it. "We got a few bits and bobs from the police station, you know, but nothing that interesting. Only a couple of handguns and some magazines".

"Magazines?" Rob thought, but he remembered not long after that he meant the thing that holds the bullets in.

"What about you two? Is there more food to grab?" John asked.

"Loads more" David said interrupting.

"Okay, we'll need to do a few runs here in the coming days, you know. Anything else to report?"

David looked over towards Robert. "Yeah" he said slowly and from his tone, Rob knew what was coming. "Our friend here thinks he saw someone".

Everyone's eyes went to Rob. "Oh... I... err" Rob stuttered.

"Did you see someone?" John asked.

"Well, yeah... I thought I did. But it must have been nothing" Rob said, half lying and the other half knowing what he had seen. They would not have believed him about the woman in the store. Rob had seen her clear as day. She had not been a hallucination or a dream or anything. She had been standing in front of him on the other side of the doors as real as Matt, John and the others were now. Rob had even kept an eye out for her when they were searching the supermarket. He had approached each aisle with great caution, but no one else had been there.

"Maybe I am losing my mind" Rob thought to himself as everyone seemed to lose interest and carry on with their discussion.

"There are a few other places I would have liked to check out, but I don't know how much longer this weathers going to hold" John told them staring up at the sky. His gaze then turned to the shopping carts. "We ain't going to be able to bring all this stuff back through the woods in one go. Not with the generator and the lights, you know".

"We could always go and get some others to come and help" Matt suggested.

"No, it would take too long" John replied. "We'll have to stash one in the woods and come back for it later".

As they loaded what they could and arranged who would take what, they began moving the carts and other goods through the forest back towards the Farm. They left one of the shopping carts in the bushes at the edge of the forest. They had put an enormous branch over the top of it and covered it in dead leaves in hopes that anyone passing by would not take it. It was a risk, but they already had too many things to carry as it was. The clouds had seemed to remain where they were in the sky for the journey back. The sun was still shining brightly through the trees.

It felt as if the journey back took hours. Rob and the others were exhausted. The shopping carts had been a bad choice. They were incredibly difficult to move over the dirt. Rob was sure that it would have been easier to take all of the cans out and carry them individually. Every now and again they had to stop to get the cart unstuck from holes or tree roots that it had become stuck on.

"Man, fuck this!" David shouted at one point and was kicked one of the carts over in anger, knocking its contents over the ground.

John had given him a stern look that shut David up instantly and somehow telling him to pick it all up. That had taken a good chunk of their time up.

It was mid-afternoon by the time they had got within a few hundred yards of the Farm. They could see that the bonfire in the Courtyard was lit and smoke was blowing off in the direction of their approach. Rob felt a sigh of relief as they got closer, knowing that he could sit and rest for a while.

John whispered something to one of the unknowns who ran on ahead with the duffle bag of stuff John had found in the Police station, leaving Matt to push one of the carts on his own. Thankfully the ground on the Farm's land was much smoother and, at this point, one person could handle this easily.

A few other survivors came out to meet them as they returned. The looks on their faces as they saw all the stuff they had brought back made Rob feel like he was really doing his bit for the good of the group.

Maria came out of the crowd and headed over to them, taking one of the bags David was carrying, giving Rob the inkling that his theory about them two might have been right. Another few unknowns came out and helped bring the carts and the generator into the Courtyard. Rob caught his breath and rested against the fence. He could see that the survivors had finished making the repairs they needed to the Storehouse while they were gone.

Pete was there and came over to Rob. "Hey, how are you doing?" he asked.

Rob nodded his head, still taking the time to get himself together.

"Did you manage to find anything useful?"

"Food mainly. Oh and a generator of some sorts. John wants to get up a load of lights all around to keep the Courtyard lit at night" Robert told him.

"Ah cool" Pete replied glancing over towards the pile of stuff they had brought back with them from town.

A moment later the unknown, John had sent ahead came, rushing back with two large backpacks someone might have if they were travelling around the world. He ran over to John and handed them to him. John gave him a nod and turned to Rob.

"Robert... Matt. I need you two to go back and get the other cart" he commanded in his usual authoritative voice.

"What?" Rob replied. He was beat. The thought of having to push another cart through the forest was agony.

"You can't expect us to do that again can you?" Matt told him, who was clearly just as annoyed at the idea of having to push another cart as Rob was.

"No... No" John said laughing. "Take these". He tossed the backpacks at their feet. "Just go back and load the stuff up into these. As much as you can carry. We can't risk losing it, you know... and I would like to have as much food as possible so we can catalogue it".

Rob and Matt exchanged a look to one another.

John must have sensed their frustration. "Look" he said stepping over to them and sounding as if they were good friends. "We still have a good three hours of daylight. It will take too long to send someone who does not know where we stashed it to find... if they found it at all. It should take you less than an hour there, a little bit to put all the stuff in the bags, and then an hour to come back. You will be back in plenty of time. Just in case, take these". John handed them each a flare. "You'll be back before it gets dark" John assured them.

Rob didn't like it, but John's words had sort of made sense to them. They would have enough time to get there and back, before dusk, before the forest got dark.

"Fine" Rob told him, leaning over and grabbing hold of one of the backpacks.

Matt and Rob headed back through the forest towards the town on the same path they had taken on the journey back. It had started to get a little gloomier in the sky, but not enough to warrant any concern. They trekked quietly for a third of the way before any words were exchanged. "This is bullshit!" Matt said kicking the dirt beneath his feet as he walked, almost like a child. "Why couldn't he have sent David or someone to do this?"

"It's okay. We'll be back soon enough" Rob replied. "At least we don't have to bother hanging up all those Christmas lights".

"Yeah that is true... but still".

Matt kicked the dirt once again and suddenly Rob heard a crunching sound. He looked round to see Matt cry out in pain as he crumbled onto the floor. He hit the ground with a thud and dirt rose up all around him. "Ah shit! My ankle" he cried, clutching at his leg.

Rob ran over to him, dropping the backpack onto the ground. "What the hell happened?"

"The fucking branch broke and my foot slipped. Agghh it hurts so badly". Rob knelt down and took a look at it. "It doesn't look too bad" he said. "I think it's broken... I think my ankles broken" Matt told him.

Rob couldn't help but laugh a little. "I think you might have just sprained it".

Matt appeared to be displeased with Robert's laughing. "Ah fuck you. It feels like I've broken it".

Rob helped Matt to his feet. "Can you walk?" he asked.

Matt took a step and Rob saw the painful expression on his face. "Agh... yeah. Yeah, I think so".

"You ain't going be able to carry any stuff back with you are you? We still have about two thirds of the journey to go... and then back. Are you sure you can do it?"

Matt looked around and then to him. Rob could already tell what he was going to say. "I don't think so. I think we need to go back".

Rob toyed with the idea for a moment. He could help Matt back to the Farm and get some rest. John would understand since Matt was clearly in pain. But then again this was John they were talking about here. Any normal person would understand, but Rob was not sure about the man in charge. He would be pretty annoyed if they came back empty handed. He wouldn't be surprised if he sent Rob out again with someone else. If they made it back to the Farm now then they might still have enough time to get back before dark. If not then they always had the flares John had given them.

The more he thought about it, the more he did not like the idea.

"You go back" Rob told Matt.

This seemed to surprise him. It surprised Rob himself. "What?" Matt asked.

"If you can make it, then go back. I'll go and grab some of the stuff and bring it back. It shouldn't take too long". Rob was not hundred percent with the idea of being stuck on his own in the forest so close to night, but he didn't like the idea of going back to the others without the food.

"Are you sure?" Matt asked him, grabbing a part of the branch that broke a moment ago and supporting himself with it.

"Can you make it back to the Farm?" Rob wondered. He did not want to leave Matt alone in the woods with a busted ankle.

"Yeah. It wasn't too far. I can follow the trail back".

They parted ways a short while later. Matt used his new branch walking stick to help him back to the Farm, and Rob took both backpacks in search of the cart they had left behind.

When Rob looked back around, Matt had gone. He had disappeared off into the forest behind old tree trunks and bushes of dead leaves. He was truly on his own now. This is what it would be like if Rob was to just leave the group completely and never go back. He could take the food from the cart and just go in search of other survivors. There must have been something else than the Farm out there. If they were just hiding in the woods then their chances of being found were slim.

Rob thought about leaving as he hiked his way back to the town, but he did not think he would survive long on his own. He had escaped the creatures of the dark in the forest before, but it had cost him a piece of his soul. Shooting Mike had left stains inside of him. He felt different now, like he was not the same man who had gone into the woods.

When he arrived at the edge of town he found the cart straight away. The wind hand blown one of the branches off of it and another at the front had just toppled over, exposing the cart to the town below.

"It was a good job we didn't wait until tomorrow" Rob thought.

"Someone could have easily seen this".

He began loading the packaged goods and the remaining cans into the backpacks. He thought he might be able to carry one bag on his back and another in his hands, doing the work of two people. At the very least he could have stashed the other backpack easily and it would have remained well hidden as opposed to the shopping cart.

By the time Rob had finished, he was starting to get tired. It had been a long day of walking through the woods and exploring the town. Rob thought of nothing but getting back to the Farm and sleeping. It was not his turn to keep watch tonight. Most likely Pete would have done this, if he could stay awake past midnight.

He picked up one of the bags and threw it over his shoulders. It was heavy but not so much that he couldn't bare taking it all the way back to the Farm. The backpacks were so large that he had managed to fit enough of the food into one, so the one he carried in his hands was light enough.
He glanced back at the shopping cart and remembered how much of a pain it had been to push it all the way back. He was glad that he didn't need to do it this time.

The sun was starting to go down and more clouds had begun to gather. It was starting to get a little bit dark but Rob knew that he still had a couple of hours to get back and inside.
He turned and took one last look at the town. He was not sure if he would have been ordered to go on any more salvage runs here tomorrow. Especially now that he was bringing all this extra food back single handed. He was sure that John would give him a break.

But something he saw made him drop the bag he was holding. At first he had not noticed anything out of the ordinary about it. Under normal circumstances it was something so simple, but given the situation, it could have meant a number of things. He had definitely not seen it before. No one had. John would have made them investigate it.

He took the other bag off of his shoulders and placed it beside the other one on the floor, before moving closer to the tree up ahead to get a better look.

It was just across the road and down the first street from him. It appeared to be a small apartment block, with rows of six windows across five floors.

And there, on the top floor and the second window in, was a light.

Day Twenty One – Part 3

The rusty iron gate of the apartment building creaked as Rob pulled it slowly open. The sound seemed to echo down the dark passageway towards the inner door. Travelling across town had spawned fear inside of him. He knew it was stupid to go and check out something like this alone. He had left the supplies back in the bushes at the edge of the forest, and run down the street towards the apartment. The whole time Rob's mind wondered what could be causing the light. It was not sunny out, so that removed any chance of it being the reflection of the sun. He had stared at it for some time before heading into town, making sure that it was not a reflection of anything else, glare on the windows, or if the building was on fire. No, it was definitely a light of some kind. Either the building still had power and someone was using it, or it was someone's own personal light source of some kind that they were using against the creatures in the shadows.

There was a chance that it could have just been nothing. An old flashlight that was still on and the batteries had not died yet, or even something reflective inside. Either way, Robert felt strangely compelled to find out what. If it was someone, then they might have been alone and in danger. The light could have been a signal they were trying to use to let others know that they were in there. There could have even been an entire new group of people living in the apartment building. They could have been better defended and have the place more secure than Rob's group did back at the farm.

Rob wondered what it would be like to live with another group. It had only been a few weeks, but he had not seen anyone else other than the people who were either living at the farm, or who had died getting there. The rest of the people he had seen, since this whole thing started, were disembowelled corpses and severed limbs. The thoughts still lingered in Robert's brain, but they were fading with each passing moment. Now some of them only seemed like strange dreams he had long ago, remembering only segmented still shots of it, like a horrific graphic novel.

The inner door was locked. Rob looked around for another way in, but there seemed to be nothing that was obvious. He had considered taking a walk around the entire building, similar to what he had done back at the supermarket, but the day only had a few hours of light left. "There is still time" Rob kept saying to himself over and over. All he needed to do was a quick check of the light, speak to anyone if there was in fact anyone, and then get back to the Farm. If all worked out then he would be back there before the sun even set.

The sky was turning grey at this point, but thankfully the sun must have still been shining brightly elsewhere. Hopefully that should keep the monsters at bay for a few more hours.

Rob wondered what the survivors would do in the winter, when the sun rose later in the day and set earlier in the evening. In this part of the country, Rob felt that some of the days in the winter, the sun didn't even come out at all. He needed to make sure he was somewhere safe and secure before then. That was why the possibility of finding other survivors or another group excited Rob. John had made him feel uneasy. The way he was running things back at the Farm had made Rob doubt the safety of it. John had been keeping them safe up to this point, but Rob knew that he could throw them out at any point he liked.

If Rob found another group, living maybe in this very apartment building, then he wondered if he would in fact tell them about the Farm, or if he would even go back there at all. John would probably send a search party out, most likely with the secret agenda to find and collect the supplies Rob was supposed to bring back, but they would not look too hard for him. If he did not go back, they would have assumed that the creatures had got him. Something could have distracted him and he couldn't get back through the woods before the night came.

A sudden feeling of dread shot all through Rob's body and with it, a horrible thought echoed through his brain. "What if that was what was happening?" he wondered. What if he was just getting distracted... and he wouldn't be able to make it back before dark?
Right then Rob knew that he should go back. He shouldn't have come here alone. If Matt was still with him, then he could have watched his back, or better still; convince him not to come at all.

Rob turned and went to walk back down the passageway towards the iron gate, when something glimmered on the floor and caught his eye. When he looked down, he saw a brass key sticking out from beneath the outside door mat. He leaned over and picked it up. An insect of some kind scurried off from under it as he lifted it off the floor. The bug retreated under the mat and disappeared.
The key was surprisingly heavy for something of such little size. He turned

it over and saw the word "Entrance" written on it. When Rob looked back up, the key hole on the locked inner door of the apartment building seemed to call him. It almost felt as if the lock was stretching open ever so slightly. Without a second thought, he plunged it into the lock. The key slotted in perfectly like a puzzle piece, and as it did, Rob automatically turned it, hearing a satisfying clicking sound as he did. One of the doors came away from the other gently.

"Well... there is no harm in just sticking my head in I guess" Rob thought. He rose a hand up, placed his palm firmly on the window of the door and pushed. The door swung open silently. It gently glided across the floor until it made contact with the doorstop and stopped dead as it did. Rob stuck his head inside and waited a moment, listening.

The apartment entrance was silent. A set of stairs lead upwards in one corner, while an elevator, that did not look like it was functioning, was in the other corner. The door was open to it, and none of the lights inside were on.

The non-functioning elevator dissolved the idea that the building still had power. That made Rob feel uneasy. He had hoped that there was in fact another group of survivors living in here, a group as big as the one back at the Farm. He could have stayed with them and not had to be answerable to John and his little crew anymore. All the suspicious eyes would have disappeared and maybe he could have felt a little at ease for once, within reason given their overall situation.

Rob realised that he had wanted to find another group so badly. Maybe that was what had driven him to follow the light, unlock the door, and step inside. In fact, when Robert realised this, he was already at the bottom of the staircase looking up. He had walked through the door and passed the letterboxes. One of his feet was lying flat on the bottom step. He did not even know what he was doing. It was almost like he was in a trance, or being lead like a puppet.

When he looked up, he saw that the top of the stairs was dark. Rob knew that he would need to climb to the top floor to find the light source. From what he could see, the staircase did go all the way to the top, but it didn't show any signs of getting brighter the further up it went.

A lump grew in Rob's throat and he swallowed hard, debating whether or not to go up. He had already come this far, but every moment he stood there debating, he was wasting precious daylight hours. It would be dusk before long, and he needed to be back at the Farm before that happened.

"No, I should get back" Rob said to himself and turned away from the stairs, but as he did, he heard something. It was ever so quiet and he was not even sure if he had in fact heard it. He stopped and listened, in case he was hearing things, but there it was again. It was the sound of movement coming from above him. Someone was definitely up there. Rob went to grab the handgun in his belt, but then thoughts of Mike began to creep back into his head. It had been a similar situation that had made him take out his weapon and shoot accidentally him.
He let go of the gun handle right then. He was not going to make the same mistake if someone else came out in front of him.

The noise moved. It sounded almost like faint footsteps that wandered off out of earshot.

Rob went to call out "Hello?" or "Is anyone there?" but then he wondered if he should. He did not know whether to just go up there and see, but then again, if they were living up there on their own, then they could have easily been more on edge than Rob was. He could have ended up being the person with a bullet in his stomach.

He took a deep breath and looked up towards the top of the staircase. "Hello?!" he shouted out. The word blasted upwards, echoing down hallways as it did. It seemed to magnify the sound by ten, booming out across each floor as it reached the top.

Once it had fallen back to silence, there was the sound of movement again. It was only one person, Rob could tell. The sound moved across the floor and stopped as it was loud enough to be in the stairwell.

"Who's there?" a faint male voice called back to him.

Rob was shocked. He had found someone. He was right, someone had been living in this apartment building.

Robert didn't know what to say. "Emm..." he started with. He had no real reason to believe anything Rob said, and nor did Rob have any reason to believe anything this person said. For all he knew it could have been a trick that the creatures were using; trying to lure people out away from the light and from groups, and using human-like voices to draw us nearer. He had heard their whispers on the wind; words that sounded like "Join" and that other J-word Rob had heard they say, but he could not make out what it was.

Rob swallowed again and spoke. "I am not here to hurt you" he said, almost feeling stupid as heard his own words echo back at him. "I am from a group... not too far from here".

"Are you alone?" the voice called out to him.

Rob was not sure how to answer. It seemed like a bit of a strange question, but at the same time Rob could understand that the man could have just been playing it safe.

"Yes" Rob called back.

"Are you armed? Do you have a weapon?" he shouted down.

Rob looked down at his gun. He could have lied, but he wanted to make sure this man knew that he would defend himself in case anything did happen.

"Yes" Rob replied firmly. "I have a gun". He had decided that honesty was the best policy. He did not want to lie to the man he had only just met. Or had he? He could not see this person. He could only hear his voice.

"Come to the railing... please" Rob asked. "Are you human?" He felt stupid again, but then again it was a good idea if Rob too was thorough with his questions.

The man laughed a little. "Yeah... yeah I'm human".

"Are YOU armed?" Rob asked, and the man replied "I do not have a gun, but I have a weapon". That made Rob feel a little bit better. He had the advantage if anything bad was to happen. The man had not come to the railing however. This made Rob feel uncomfortable.

"Come to the railing" Rob asked again.

"I can't..." replied the voice. "I am injured. My leg... I think it is broken. I can't move".

"Oh..." Rob said. He had not expected that. "Hang on" he suddenly thought. "I heard you moving up there" Rob shouted up.

"No... I was throwing a piece of tied up curtain. I need to get my flashlight from the windowsill. It's going to be dark soon".

"Oh shit, yeah" replied Rob. "Okay... I will come up". He put one foot on the first step.

"Okay. Don't make any sudden movements" shouted down the voice.

He was just being caution Rob knew. If he was in a similar situation, then he would have done the same.

As he climbed the steps, the apartment building fell silent. The only sounds that could be heard were that of Rob's feet treading on the creaky steps. He went past the first floor landing and up another flight of stairs. Then past the second, then the third. When he came to the fourth, he could see that the next floor was the top. The man had not said another word the entirety of Rob's journey up, although neither had Rob for that matter.

"Are you still there" Rob called up as he crossed the fourth floor landing and made it to the bottom of the last flight of stairs. No one replied.

Rob stopped still on the first step and waited. He felt as if he was standing there for an hour, when it reality only a few minutes had passed, all of which were silent. The man did not say anything.
Rob didn't know whether to go back down and leave, which was what his brain was trying to tell him to do, or to just get up there and see. He was now almost at the top. It would have been a shame to just leave without seeing, especially if it had turned out to be a genuine reason, such as the man had passed out due to his injuries.

"Hello?!" Rob shouted out as he climbed a few more steps, just enough to look out over the landing. The word bounced off the walls and disappeared down the hallway. The man did not reply.

When he looked across the floor, he could see the darkened hallway ahead of him. All the doors were shut except for one about halfway down. It was open and light was gleaming off the door. That must have been where it was coming from.

The man's silence had caused Rob to draw his pistol. It was worrisome in case he did accidentally shoot this person, but he also knew that it was wise. He had no idea what this man was capable of.

Rob got to the top of the stairs and walked to the entrance of the hallway. It was quiet. The window at the far end of the corridor could be seen from where he was. The sun was still peeking through cracks in the grey sky. That made him feel a little better. There was still time.

He headed down the hallway, his gun held at his side, and arrived at the open door. "Hello?" he asked again. There was no point in hiding. The man knew Rob was in the building. He had probably heard him climb the stairs, if he was still in fact conscious.

He stuck his head around the corner slowly. The light made everything in the room seem bright. It looked comforting inside. The glow of the lamp, set on a table by the window, gave the room a warmth.

Rob entered the room. The apartment was small and unfurnished. The kitchen was set right beside the living room and were both visible as soon as he had entered. A door was to his right and another one on the far wall of the living room. He saw that there were old chocolate bar wrappers and apple cores rotting in a pile in the corner of the room. The sink was filled with dirty water, and a glass of water was resting beside it. A torn sleeping bag was lying on the floor. The man had been living here for some time. He was unsure if he had seen him, David, John and the others when they entered the town earlier to gather supplies. He could have been watching them from the window the whole time.

The man was nowhere to be seen. This was now becoming dangerously unsettling. Rob crept through the apartment as quietly as he could and headed for the lamp. When he got there, he put his hand on the side of it and felt that it was hot, as if it had been on for quite a while. Rob had previously thought that perhaps he was hearing things. Maybe the man's voice had not been real at all, but the lamp and the warmth he felt on his hand, made him feel that the person he had heard was real.

"You are like them ain't you" a voice said, breaking through the silence and shattering it. Rob felt his heart pound against his chest, as the blood pumped faster through his veins. He spun around and saw a hooded man standing at the open door on the other side of the room. He was dressed in shabby clothes, stained with brown and green. He wore a large pair of black boots, caked in mud, and his hands were hidden beneath his hooded grey jacket.

"Wha..." Rob went to say, when the man spoke again.

"The darkness... it stalks you" he said.

"The darkness?" Rob thought confused. "You... you mean the creatures?" he asked.

The man lifted his head and Rob could see his eyes. They were white, glowing out from a darkened face beneath the shadow of the hood.

"You can't escape from the darkness" the man said.

"No... But you can stay near a light and you'll be safe" replied Rob.

"Safe? There is no such thing. Not now... not in the new world". Suddenly the man's hands lowered from the sleeves of his jacket and Rob saw he was carrying a knife.

"Whoa!" Rob called out. "Take it easy guy". He felt his trigger finger twitch and his hand tightened around the handle of his gun.

"The darkness will come for you too... and then, you will know"

"Know what?" Rob asked.

Just then the man leaped into action. He ran across the room and crashed into Rob before he even had a chance to lift his gun. The two of them hit the floor, Rob beneath the man. The hood had come off and Rob saw the man had a thick matted beard.

He struggled to realise what was going on for a moment, until the man sat up and held the knife up.

"NO!" shouted Rob, grabbing hold of his wrist and trying to get the knife off of him.

The man punched Rob in the face with his other fist, splitting the scab Rob had on his face and cutting his lip. Another punch felt like Rob had been hit by a train. The man's fist had hit him with enough force that he felt like he was about to go through the floor. Rob let go of the man's wrist, not intentionally. The force of the punch had disorientated him and caused his hands to loosen their grip.

Another punch knocked Rob's head against the floorboards and now his head was in agony. His eyes were hazy and his vision now blurred. He saw the white in the man's eyes once again and then he realised it was his own. His own face was reflected off of the knife that was now held above him. The man's face was now behind it as the knife plummeted towards Rob's chest.

A second later, an explosion rang out in the room. The whole place got brighter for a heartbeat and Rob saw the man's face turn to pain. He fell backwards off of Rob and collapsed on the floor beside him. In his wake, Rob saw his own hand there, pointing the pistol upwards, smoke still rising from the barrel. The empty shell casing resting on his chest, right at the point the knife would have entered his body.

After that the world seemed to grow dark. He felt his right hand drop to the floor under the weight of the gun, as his left did the same, only this time it was into a pool of the man's blood.

Rob's eyes grew heavy and closed.

Day Twenty Two

When he awoke again, he saw the man who had tried to kill him staring back at him. His cold dead eyes staring into his. They did not seem as pure white as they had done before. The blood had poured out across the floor and Rob seemed to have been lying in it for some time.
His head hurt. There was a pounding unlike anything else he had felt before. Rob felt as if he had just awoken from a dreamless sleep. When he looked around, he realised he pretty much had. The room was darker than it had been before, much darker. The lamp's light was now more intense and it burned a yellow glow that stretched out across the walls and ceiling. The window was pitch black. When Rob saw it, his heart sank.
"Shit!" he said as tried to climb to his feet. He put his hand down to support himself, but this only rested in the pool of blood. The blood was now sticky instead of wet. His clothes were soaked with it and they felt sticky as well. The man had been lying there, bleeding over him for what must have been hours. It had still been quite a while before it was going to get dark, but now it looked as if it was in the middle of the night.

When he finally got to his feet, he felt his head wobble as if it was going to fall completely off his shoulders. He rested his hand on the table with the lamp and got his bearings. When he looked out of the window, he could see the dark streets below. Clouds had gathered in the sky and there was not a single star in it. The moon was nowhere to be seen. He had come to think of the moon as the only saviour when the sun set, but he was not even sure if the creatures did still attack in the moonlight.

The streets were dead. There was nothing out there. Rob hadn't seen the world up high at night for a while. He looked out over the town and could see the edge of the treeline at the top of the road. Everything was black. He remembered that all of the streetlights in town had been smashed. This meant that, even if the power in town was still operational, the streetlights were no help.

He knew it was dangerous down there. There was no way he would be able to make it back to the Farm tonight. The other survivors would have to think he was dead until the morning. A quick thought popped up in Rob's mind. What if he didn't bother going back at all?

"Could I really do that?" he wondered. He could have just taken the supplies and went off on his own, in search of more survivors or somewhere else to live.

But then his thoughts were of the man he had just killed. He turned around and looked down at the body.

"This is what I would turn into" he said to himself.

He saw his gun on the floor and reached over to pick it up. As he did, he looked over at the man's face once again. "I've killed him" Rob thought, but he did not feel anything. He seemed more concerned with the fact it was night time and he was stuck in this apartment building in the middle of god knows where.

He had killed three people since this had all began. The first man he had shot because he begged him to do it. The creature of the night was clawing him and spilling his insides onto the forest floor. That had been a mercy killing.

The second had been Mike. He had come out of the shadows when the clouds had gathered over the sun and caused it to go dark. The creatures were coming and Rob had mistakenly shot Mike in a panic. That had been an accidental death.

And now Rob had murdered this man. The strange crazed man who had been living in the apartment building alone. He had lured Rob up the stairs and then attacked him with a knife. There was nothing he could have done. It was either kill or be killed.

He looked down at the man's body. "It was self-defence" Rob said out loud, almost justifying taking the man's life.

It had been twenty-something days since Rob's world had fallen apart, and already he had killed more people than he could have ever imagined himself doing in his whole life.

"One was too many" he thought to himself.

Suddenly a tap came at the window. It made Rob almost jump out of his skin. He spun around towards it, with the gun held out in front of him, but there was nothing there. Only the dark night could be seen. He went over to it and peered out again. The streets were just as silent and still as they had been before. Even the trees were not blowing in the wind.

He stood there, watching out of the window at the darkness, for some time. He guessed that it was most likely about one or two in the morning. He would only need to wait another four or five hours for the sun to come up. After that he could leave. But until then, he was trapped here. The lamp had been the only source of light, which meant that the rest of

the apartment must have been dark, which also meant that it was not safe to leave this room without it. He did have a flare on him still that John had given him in the backpacks he handed over. But after the last time he had used one, in the woods after shooting Mike, he knew that they did not last as long as he would have liked them too.
But what was the alternative? Was he to sit in this small unfurnished apartment with the corpse of the man he had just killed?

Another tap broke his trail of thought. It was louder than the one before. Then suddenly another echoed out, only this time it was inside the building. Rob gripped his gun tighter and moved over to the door, sticking his head out of the room and into the hallway. It was dark. It was so dark that he couldn't even see the staircase at the end of the hall.
He waited there for a moment listening, waiting for another tap. He stared down the hall, waiting for whatever had made it to make themselves known, but nothing ever came. He stood there for a few moments more before turning back into the room.
He walked over the body and over to the kitchen. The glass of dirty grey water did not look at all inviting. The water in the sink looked even worse. "Was he drinking it?" Rob wondered.
He opened up the fridge beside it and peered inside. It was empty other than a single chocolate bar. It had peanuts in it, but Rob didn't care. He ripped it open and wolfed it down, almost not touching the sides. As soon as it had come, it was gone again. The only thing he had eaten that day was some bread that had not yet gone mouldy at the supermarket. He thought he would have something big when he got back to the Farm later that night, but now he wished he had gorged himself when he had the chance.

He had hours to kill, and nothing to do. He wished Pete was here right now. He would have entertained him with some story that went on and on while Rob watched the world from the window. That was how he had spent most nights since living at the Farm. Even when they had their own separate rooms, him, Matt and Pete had still worked together to keep watch in shifts when it was their turn.

Now Rob was on his own. He was alone in this ghost town, at night, with only a corpse to keep him company.

Another tap drew his attention to the window once more. "The fuck is that?" he thought as he went over to it. When he looked out onto the streets below, he saw movement. Something shot past the road and behind the building in front. Another flicker of movement caught his eye. This one moved across the other side of the road. Then another one at the top of the street. There was movement all around down there.

He couldn't see exactly what it was, but things kept moving in the shadows down below. He knew it could only really be one thing.

Suddenly he realised that all the movement was coming towards the apartment building. Whatever it was were getting faster the closer they got and Rob began to see that the entire town was full of them. A dreaded feeling came over him, not unlike the one he had felt out in the woods when he was running back on his own. His heart began to beat faster, almost irregularly, as the shadows moved towards the iron gated entrance of the perimeter border. He saw the gate swing upon with such force that it was almost taken off the hinges. The rusty creak screamed out into the night, and that was when Rob heard them. The creatures were coming.

Rob leaned into the window to try and get a better look down below, but he could only see darkness. A sound echoed from behind. A smash and a roar, no, many roars could be heard. They had got into the ground floor of the apartment building. Rob could hear them clawing and snarling their way through the hallway and towards the stairs.

"Oh god" were the only words Rob could muster as he turned and went for the door. He took two steps and he felt his legs go from under him. He had completely forgotten about the body of the man he had killed. He tripped on him and toppled over, landing flat onto the sticky blood soaked wooden floor below.

He pushed himself up a moment later and could hear the creatures were climbing the stairs. There must have been hundreds of them. The sounds of bodies shuffling together and clawing at the walls and metal railings as they climbed, grew louder and louder with each passing second.
Rob needed to shut the door. He had to seal himself in this apartment until morning. That is what this man had obviously done. He needed to do the same.

He got to his feet and ran for the door. In a matter for seconds, the noises were so loud that they didn't even have time to create an echo before they had reached Rob's ears.

He got to the door and grabbed hold of it, kicking the doorstop into the hallway and slammed it shut. As he did, he saw the shadows burst round the corner. Their squeals almost sounded as if they were delighted by the presence of Rob.

The door shut and Rob turned the lock. The door began to shake as the creatures pounded and clawed at it from the other side. He took a step back and watched in horror as he knew that hundreds of murderous monsters awaited him on the other side of that door. The apartment

door and the small metal lock, were all that was stopping him from having his throat torn out, or having his skin peeled off of his bones.
He took a few more steps back and tried to calm himself down. He felt as if he was having a panic attack. When he took another step back, he felt his foot hit against the body of the man. He looked down and saw that when he had fallen over him earlier, he had moved him. His face was now staring up at Rob's, but it wasn't the face of the man he had killed anymore, it was Rob's own face staring back at him. His cold dead white eyes pierced holes through him.

The lamp flickered for a second, but Rob wasn't sure if he had blinked. It flicked again. "No..." Rob thought. "Not now".
It turned off completely. When it did, Rob was surrounded by the creatures. They were all around him. They stood beside him staring at him. They snarled and hissed as their eyes stared into his. He could not see where one of them ended and the other began. He could just see a sea of shadows all around him. They loomed up over him and he saw claws emerge from the shadows. The claws looked almost chrome as the space between them grew smaller. Rob felt hands around his throat and the tips of claws poke at his flesh.
"I'm going to die" Rob thought.
Now all he could see was their faces. Their horrible faces of the abyss.

The lamp flicked back on and it was all gone. Rob felt the hold around his throat loosen and he could breathe again. He looked around the apartment and it was quiet once again. The creatures were no longer banging or clawing at the door.
He looked down at the body of the man and his face had returned to normal. It was still the unknown man he had met and killed earlier.

Hours had passed before Rob had even realised it. He had sat by the window staring at the front door for what seemed like a lifetime. He had no idea how long it had actually been. It was only when the sun had shone through the window and hit him in the face that he realised the night was over.

He climbed to his feet and looked out of the window. The sun had been up for a little while. It must have been about eight or nine in the morning by now. He hadn't slept a minute all night. He was tired and ached, but most of all he was looking forward to getting back to the Farm. All the thoughts about just taking the bags and leaving on his own had disappeared. Now all he thought about was the bed he had made for himself back in his own room at the Farmhouse.

As Rob went to leave, he took one last look into the room. The man's body lay perfectly still on the floor in a solidified pool of his own blood. Rob realised that it had started to smell, but he had not noticed before. The lamp in the room flickered once more as he left, but then continued to shine on.

He opened the door and saw the horrific gouges on the outside of the apartment door. They were around ten centimetres deep and some of them stretched across the door for about a foot or more. The scratches were all along the wall leading downward towards the staircase. Rob followed them across the hallway and down the stairs.

Outside the air was cool. The wind was blowing and sent a shiver across his whole body. The sun was out and the day was looking promising. He made his way across the street and over to the edge of the forest, where he found the bags waiting for him.

He knew he would have to do a lot of explaining. John would want to know what had happened. He wanted every detail. Did he tell them about the man he killed? It was then that he suddenly noticed his clothes were completely covered in the man's blood. He had nothing else to change into. He had considered stealing the man's clothes, but then again he thought that might have been a bit much, especially after murdering him. The man's clothes were also most likely covered in blood as well. Rob knew he would not be able to get back without them asking about his clothes. So he knew he would need to tell them something.
The man had attacked him and he had defended himself, surely they would understand and believe that. It was only a problem if they started to think about Mike. They might start to wonder if Rob had killed him also.

Rob shook off the thought as he grabbed the bags of supplies from the bushes. He threw one over his shoulder and the other he carried as best he could, mostly dragging it across the ground.

It was almost midday when Rob made it back to camp. The Farmhouse had appeared up ahead and Rob could see movement. It had been Maria who had seen him first. Rob could not hear her but he could tell what she had said. "I don't believe it".
Rob couldn't believe it either. It was nice to see the Farm once again. For a while, back in that apartment room, Rob had thought that he would never see it again.

Maria had obviously told someone Rob couldn't see to get John. The big man stepped out from the side of the house as Rob approached the perimeter fence. David, Matt, Pete and a few others came out of various locations. Pete and a couple of people had come out of the front door of the Farmhouse to greet him, while Matt and David had come from behind John.

Everyone had seemed happy that Robert had returned after being missing for the night. It was only as he opened the front gate that people's expressions changed. Rob knew that they had seen the blood on him. John's face turned from a satisfying smirk to an authoritative concerned look. Everyone else's face looked worried. Matt came hobbling over.

"Ah you okay? Are you bleeding?" he asked.

"I'm fine" Rob replied. "It is not my blood".

Rob knew that his comment would raise further questions. More of the Farm residents had gathered out the front of the house now. Nearly all twenty-two people were there, staring at him as he walked up the path. Matt stood beside him.

As he got to the Farmhouse steps, Pete grabbed the other bag. "I thought you were dead" he told him. Rob couldn't help but laugh.

He took the bag off of him and Rob pulled the other off of his back, turning to John. "I got the supplies we left" he told him, almost cockily. John did not seem amused.

"Whose blood is that?" John asked firmly.

Rob took a deep breath and started to talk. He told them about his and Matt's journey back to town, Matt's fall, he told them about taking the supplies out of the shopping trolley and putting them in the bags, he said about the light, and he told them about the man. Some of the survivors turned away when Rob told them that he had to kill him, that it was either him or Rob. John seemed to understand. He didn't ask any further questions about it, he just let Rob talk.

Rob told them about the night he had spent in the apartment, about the creatures clawing at the door. The light flicking out and them inside the room. Rob could see the horror on their faces. He was scaring them. The thought that they could be inside the very same room as you, and the moment you turn off that light, they are there, emerging from the shadows to kill you. The very idea terrified them.

Rob told them everything. John and the others took it better than he could ever have hoped for. He even believed that John might have respected him a little more for what he had done.
And when it was all done, everyone went back to their work. Rob took a look around the Courtyard and saw everyone working hard.
Suddenly a single thought appeared in Rob's head. He knew that at that moment he had only one thing on his mind.

"I've got to get some sleep".

Day Twenty Five

The next few days were a blur to Rob. As the rest of the survivors had spent their days repairing parts of the wall and hooking up the new lighting Matt had found in town, Rob had spent his days sitting in his room, lying on his makeshift bed, and thinking long and hard about anything and everything. It was clear that people believed Rob had been through a lot the last few weeks; Mike's death, being attacked, killing in self-defence and being left out in the unknown after sunset. All the other survivors avoided him. Nobody knocked at his door, not even Pete. Rob was not sure if John had told people to leave him alone or if people didn't want to disturb him. So he was left entirely on his own for days.

He had eaten nearly all of his own rations he kept in his room. Tins of Spam and other soggy meat that came in a can, as well as all of the breakfast bars he had stashed in his bag.

Occasionally he would get up and look out of the window. Here he could see the others setting up the LED lights. It seemed they were putting them around the entire perimeter of the Farm, all along the tops of the fence. It seemed like a good idea to Rob, and something that could actually work.

Every now and again, someone would glance up towards Rob's window and see him staring down and watching them, so they would quickly look away as if to pretend not to have seen him.

One afternoon Rob saw John walking around the front of the Farmhouse with Maria. It was clear that they must have been checking up on how the maintenance was going. John carried his newly found shotgun everywhere he went. Every time that Rob had seen him from the second floor window, John had his weapon gripped tightly to his stomach, with his right hand always gripping the handle.

By the third day, Robert decided that he had spent far too much time alone. Thoughts of Mike and the man in town were the only things that he thought about. The looks in their eyes were what seemed to appear in flashes in his head.

One time in particular, Rob had fallen asleep around seven in the morning, due to being awake thinking all night, and had only been asleep for an hour before Mike's bloody contorted face appeared out of the darkness to him. His skin was almost completely peeled off and the dream had jolted Rob awake.

It was then that he decided to leave his room. He got up and went over to the door. As he reached for the knob, he could hear voices coming from the other side that caused him to pause for a moment. He was having mixed feelings about leaving. On the one hand he wanted to interact with other people, but at the same time he did not want them to ask how he was or ask him anything about the night he had spent in town.

As he listened, he recognised one of the voices. It was Pete. He appeared to be chatting to another man in the hallway, but he could not hear what they were saying. He opened the door and went out. The conversation filled the room but was suddenly cut short as Pete and another survivor,

Rob did not know the name of, stopped talking to look over in amazement towards Rob's room.

"Hey!" Pete said, almost as if he had been caught doing something he shouldn't have been. He came running over to Rob, leaving the other man to himself. "How are you doing? Are you okay?"

Rob didn't mind Pete asking. He knew that he would have to get this over with in order to carry on as normal.

"Yeah, I'm okay" he replied. His voice was crackly from sitting in silence for a couple of days. He swallowed hard.

"Ah, that is good to hear" Pete told him, as Rob caught sight of the other man heading down the stairs and disappearing to the floor below. "We were getting a bit worried about you. We could hear you moving in there and some people saw you from the window, so we knew you were alive, but we thought it was best to leave you in peace until you wanted to come and talk to us".

Rob laughed, it was the first time in a while anything had amused him. He was not even sure what Pete had said was funny at all. "Sorry" Rob told him. "I thought that was the case".

"Yeah..." Pete replied, steering the conversation elsewhere. "Anyway, the lights are almost up. Have you seen them?"

"Yes" said Rob. "I saw you guys hooking them up from the window. Do you have them all the way around?"

"Yeah. They circle around the entire Farm" Pete told him. "Matt has hooked them up to the generator they have set up in the Tool shed. John has someone guard it most of the time".

The idea was not surprising. If the lighting system worked, then it might have meant that the survivors were not limited to having to stay inside the buildings at night. Rob had seen that John still ordered people to light the Tiki Torches at night, but he was not sure if that would be the case after they got the lights working.

Rob followed Pete down the stairs of the Farm, passing by David who gave Rob a strange wink as they got near to one another. The gesture made Rob feel strange and he turned away to look at the living room of the Farmhouse.

When they had first arrived, all twenty-odd survivors had lived here and the kitchen adjacent to it. Now the living room was deserted. Nearly all of the furniture had been taken and either put in someone's room who had wanted it, or had been broken down to help make repairs and patch up the surrounding fence.

When they got outside, they saw that the bonfire was burning. It was mid-afternoon, but already the group had lit the bonfire in preparation for the evening. It was clear that they were ready to test the lights and needed the bonfire as a kind of backup plan in case they didn't work. Quite a few people were huddled around it, as the day had begun to grow cold.

While in Rob's room, he had noticed that it was beginning to turn colder in the evenings and at night. He knew that it would be winter in a few weeks, and that the nights would be growing longer. It would have been good for the group to get those lights up as soon as possible, maybe work out any kinks that needed to be sorted before they needed them.

Pete lead Rob over towards the tool shed where he found Matt kneeling before the generator. The noise of them approaching must have alerted him to their presence, as he looked round. Rob saw by his face that he was caught off guard. He had not expected to see Rob walking around.

He climbed to his feet and smiled.

"Hey man" he said.

Rob waited for a second for him to ask if he was okay, but thankfully he never did.

"Hey" Rob replied with a smile.

"How is this going?" ask Pete. "Do you think we'll be up and running tonight?"

"That's the plan" replied Matt. "All the lights are up, I am just trying to get these all connected. We have so many different power leads that need to be put together. I think I almost have it".

Rob looked around. He could see a lot of people going about their business and carrying on their duties, but he could not see John. He looked over to the Barn, but the place looked empty.

"Where's John?" Rob asked.

"He... err..." Matt knelt back down and carried on his work, almost as if he would get into trouble if he did not have the lights up and running. "He went into town to get some more supplies. Seems there was a lot more food there than we originally thought. He left Dave in charge".

Pete turned to Rob. "John said we would have a bit of a feast tonight if we get the lights working. He said it would be good for morale".

"Right..." was about all Rob could muster. What he was really thinking was how 'nice' it was of him to horde all the food and choose when people could eat. Especially arranging a feast only if the lights got working.

It was getting late when John, Maria and a few others returned from town. Rob had found out that John had arranged a few trips into town over the last few days. He had even allowed people to go without him out on scouting runs, some of which resulted in quite a lot of useful supplies.

The old Storehouse was brimming with stuff, as well as now being fully converted into a place for people to live. In the time between speaking to Matt and waiting for John to return, Rob had taken a walk around the Storehouse and seen what the living conditions were like.

The building had around ten rooms inside of it, one of which was being used to hold various goods such as clothing, that a few of the older survivors were washing with water they obtained from the stream further up from where Rob had found the body of the woman a few weeks ago, and the room also contained useful house hold equipment and other such items that were useful.

As always the food was held at the bottom of the barn, where David and Maria slept, with John watching over from above, and the tools were kept in with the generator.

A few of the rooms in the Storehouse actually looked better than some in the Farmhouse. A lot of the rooms in the Farmhouse had been scavenged when they had first arrived there and so they had already moved a lot of the furniture and other bits about, mainly to board up the windows.

As Rob looked into one of the rooms, he saw a young woman sobbing. There was another person inside who closed the door and blocked Rob's view. He was unsure if there was some kind of domestic thing going on, or if the weight of it all had taken affect. It was hard living in a world where nearly everyone and everything you had ever loved was gone.

Soon after the door had closed, Rob could hear a voice shout out from the Courtyard outside. It was John's voice. It was clear that he was calling everyone over, so Rob decided it was probably best not to get on his bad side, so he went and joined them.

Outside Rob found most of the Farm survivors crowded round near the bonfire with John standing before them. Rob walked over and slipped unnoticed into the back of the mob as John started to talk.

"I think that is about everyone" he said to no one in particular. "I'd like to thank you all for coming, you know".

Rob looked around at the group. It was not like anyone else had anything better to do. Everyone here did exactly what was asked for them, so it was not like they actually had a choice in the matter.

"It has been a tough few days" John continued. His voice still sounded authoritative while trying his hardest to be compassionate. "We have lost many people along the way, and while we have been living here, you know. All of us have been working tirelessly to help build the fence around this place, collect wood, gather food and supplies, take inventory, and wash our clothes. I mean I really appreciate not smelling". He said the last part jokingly, which made a few onlookers laugh. "Every one of you has brought something to this group, even the sick or being older than the rest, you have still offered your support in making this place what it is... and so I thank you, you know".

Rob wondered if he truly meant that. He could have probably done all of this himself, but it had taken far less time with this many people. There was also a safety in numbers that Rob had realised all too late a few days ago.

"I know it has been tough" John went on. "But we are making this place better, every day. As you know, we have been setting up a series of lights all around the area. Matt there believes that he has just about got it working, and so I would like you to witness them going on. With these up and running, I think that this place will be even safer. We will no longer need to hide inside when the sun goes down, you know. We will be able to walk outside at night without the fear of being taken away by those..." John turned away for a moment. Rob saw something strange in the corner of John's eye. It lasted only for an instant before John turned back to the crowd. "Anyway Matt... Would you mind?"

The crowd looked over towards Matt at the Tool Shed. He nodded and flicked a switch on the generator. It began to rumble and shake. He took a step back as sparks shots out of the top of it. Rob saw a few concerned faces among the survivors, but then the generator shook harder and suddenly the lights came on. It looked as if there were hundreds of them. They lit up all around the Farm, as well as through the few trees inside the Courtyard. The strings of lights connecting one side of the fence, through a tree near Rob, and across to the other side of the Courtyard lit up. Rob had to turn his head as the sudden intense light was far too b for his eyes. He brought a hand up and rubbed his face, wiping away some dirt from the corner of his eyes.

When he lowered his he hand, it looked as if a hundred stars were burning brightly all around them. The Courtyard was lit up like a Christmas tree. People cheered and clapped, overshadowing the rumbling sound of the generator.

Rob did not realise how dark it was starting to get until the lights came on. He glanced over towards the fence where he found it difficult to see anything on the other side of it. A nearby Tiki torch looked unlit in comparison to the white lights shining above it.

From what little Robert knew about the creatures that stalked them from the darkness and when the sun went down, the amount of light the LEDs were creating, should be enough to ward them off.

"Well met" John said proudly, as if he had actually just created the light himself similar to how God had done. He looked impressed himself, as if he was not expecting the generator to work or the lights to come on. "We will need to conserve this, you know" he said, cutting through the clapping and cheering like a knife. This caused a few of them to stop and listen concernedly. He couldn't let them have this brief moment. He needed to tell them that this was not a luxury. "We will turn them off around one in the morning. No point in having them running all night. We will need fuel for the generator, but David found a good source of that back in town. So tomorrow we will start gathering it. If it gets dark during the day, then we will have it up and running then. No point sitting around indoors when we could be out here. We'll keep the bonfire going at night, and I want the Tiki torches lit every night, regardless of the lights. It is always best to have a plan B in case something happens, you know. Anyway we'll leave these on for tonight. I have arranged for some extra rations to go out to everyone, thanks to the efforts of supply runs into town. Just come over to the barn and Maria will sort them out for you. Enjoy".

John headed off towards the barn as the crowd of survivors began to disperse. Rob saw Pete approach him.

"Some 'feast' Huh?" Rob said as he approached.

"Well... it is more than we have had since we got here. So I guess it is a feast of sorts" Pete replied, brushing off Rob's comment.

Matt came over and joined them. "Well I'm starving. I am not going to look a gift horse in the mouth".

"Come on... let's go and get some before..." Pete's words were suddenly cut short as David called out their names.

"Robert... Pete!" he shouted beside the bonfire, holding a long piece of wood with a burning oily rag around the end of it. "Come here".

Rob looked over towards Pete, but he was too focused on David and had already begun to walk over to him. Rob then turned to Matt.

"I'll speak to you in a bit, okay" he said and Matt nodded, before turning away and heading over to the small group of people gathered outside the barn.

He could see Maria handing out canned and packaged goods, as John climbed the ladder to the top of the barn in the background.

"Hey! Robbo!" David shouted and drew Rob's gaze over towards him. Pete was already standing over near the burning bonfire, nothing but a silhouette of him. "Hurry up man".

When Rob got there, David handed him the burning piece of wood. Rob took it, feeling the intense heat against his face.

"John wants you two lighting torches behind the Storehouse" David told them, lighting up another oil soaked rag, wrapped around a piece of wood, and handed it over to Pete.

"Sure" Rob told him. He wasn't hungry anyway.

Pete was quiet until they got around the back of the Storehouse. It was darker here than the rest of the Courtyard. The LED lights were shining brightly, but they were only over the fence and a small section of the back of the Storehouse. There were no lights overhead, which made the area significantly darker, especially now that it had begun to turn to dusk. Rob could tell it was making Pete nervous. He had not once stepped outside of the boundaries of the Farm.

"You okay?" Rob asked him, lighting the closest torch.

Pete jolted out of his trsin of thought. "What? Oh... yeah, yeah. I'm fine" he replied.

"You want me to just do it?" Rob asked.

"No, no, no" Pete responded almost instantaneously. "I'm fine".

They lit the six torches, three each, before meeting at the last one right on the Farm, right beside the fence.

"Do you want to talk about it?" Rob asked, trying to get a bit of conversation out of him. Pete had been acting strange since he had come back here. He knew that something was on the man's mind. He had not got close to any of the other survivors. He would never have bothered finding out if something was wrong with any of them if they were acting different, but Pete had become the closest thing to a friend in all of this. He was not sure that under, different circumstances, he would have been friends with him, but since they had been together, the two of them had got attached. Pete had done most of the talking, but whenever he mentioned anything of his past life, before all of this had gone down, Rob had changed the subject. He knew that he should get it off of his chest. Pete looked over to him. "I don't know... I am just thinking a lot about them". Rob knew who he meant, even if he had not mentioned it before; the people they had left behind. "I know we have this whole new life now... but I just miss them. I used to talk to them every day... we would all meet up and chat. It was the best. But..." his voice began to tremble. "But I just left them. I just ran and left them back in the house". Pete looked as if he was about to cry. A single tear grew in the corner of his eye and slowly dripped down his cheek. "I just loved them so..."

Suddenly the wind whistled through the trees all around them. The burning flames, on the end of the wood they were both holding, began to flicker nervously. The lights above them shook.

A strange feeling crept over them. Rob knew it all too well. He also knew that Pete was feeling it as well. The look on his face said it all. The tear on the side of his cheek looked as if it had frozen, almost too scared to move, as they both were feeling.

The wind blew harder and harder and the leaves that still clutched to the trees, started to shake. Rob began to feel lightheaded and as he brought a hand up to his head, he heard the whispers once again.

At first they were inaudible and Rob could not make them out. He looked over to Pete to see if he could hear it too, but Pete gave no indication that he could.

The whistling sound of the wind weaved through the trees and flew behind them. Rob could hear the words now as if the person saying it was whispering it into his own ear.

"Kill" the darkness said.

Rob's heart began to beat fearfully. It felt like a squash ball being beaten around a court, bouncing off his lungs and stomach.

Rob went to speak, but the words didn't come out, instead the word echoed all around him once again, softly at first, but growing louder and louder each time. "Kill... kill... KILL!" until the word felt as if someone was shouting it into Rob's brain.

It was them. They were here. They had come to kill them Rob knew. The call must have been some kind of threat, to strike the very fear Rob was feeling inside of him. Even though the new lighting system was up and running, and the torches burned all around them, Rob felt vulnerable.

"Did you hear that?" Rob managed to ask.

Pete turned to him. "That... that noise?" he replied. "The screams".

"Screams?" Rob echoed. He had not heard any screaming. He had heard only the threatening call of the monsters in the shadows. The words they had called had been clear as day.

The whole world around them began to grow cold, colder than a winter night.

"What do..." just as Rob went to speak, Pete interrupted him.

"There" he softly said as he lifted his hand, pointing towards the trees. Rob saw it too. It was the slightest of movements, but both of them had seen it. Rob saw the figure standing there amongst the trees. It was long and thin. The shadows obscured it, but then Rob realised that its body was almost completely shrouded in darkness, as if it was a shadow itself. Its long claws extended downwards, as its other hand scraped along the side of the tree. Its head turned towards them both and bright white eyes pierced through them. It was brighter than any of the light sources they had on this side of the fence.

The two of them were stunned, staring straight at the creature. They watched as it slowly opened its mouth, revealing a darkened pit that was blacker than anything he had ever seen before. It hissed gently at them, sounding almost like a snake, before turning and disappearing into the darkness.

Pete and Rob stood completely still for a few moments as the wind began to calm. The Tiki torches flickered once more before returning to normal, and the trees stopped shaking. A second or two later Rob felt the hairs on his arms and the back of his neck fall as his skin grew warmer. His heart began to return to normal.

Pete, almost trapped previously in a daze, snapped out of it and turned to Rob. His face was still locked in a stunned look of fear and bewilderment.

"Did... did you fucking see that?!" he asked, his voice cracking halfway through.

"I..." Rob went to speak, but then he realised he had no idea what in fact to say.

"It's been so long since I have seen one" Pete went on. "I knew they were out there, but I hadn't seen them since we got here. I had forgotten how stunted they looked".

"Stunted?" Rob asked. He knew them as being nearly a foot larger than him, which made them nearly two feet taller than Pete.

"Yeah... the fact that they end at the shoulders freaks me the hell out" Pete replied.

"What the fuck are you talking about?" Rob blurted out, no longer having an inner monologue with himself.

"What do you mean?" Pete asked.

"They weren't..."

Just then a voice shouted out around the corner. "Hey! What is taking so long? You guys are going to miss out on the food" Matt shouted, sticking his head around the side of the Storehouse.

"Oh yeah, right" Pete said, lighting the remaining torch and turning around. "That was close. We are lucky to be alive. We would have been dead if it had not been for these". He held up the burning wood in his hand. "... and those lights. Must remember to thank Matt. We should probably let John know it does in fact keep those bastard things out. Maybe now we will all sleep a lot better at night". Pete sounded like he had returned to his normal bubbly self. The sight of the creature and living to tell the tale had obviously made him forget his past troubles. In a few moments he had disappeared behind the side of the Storehouse.

Rob stood there at the back of the building in the dimly lit area of the Farm for a moment. He turned and looked at the treeline, but there was nothing there, at least, there was nothing he could see. They were most likely still watching him from the shadowy abyss. He could feel their eyes on him all the time now.

He turned back to the Storehouse, seeing the light from the bonfire and the LEDs above the Courtyard creeping around the side.

"End at the shoulders?" Rob repeated out loud, echoing Pete's words to only himself. "Stunted?"

A horrible feeling began to befall Robert in that instant. A dark thought crept its way through the innermost reaches of his brain. It was a question, one that he knew he did not want to know the answer of. In a matter of seconds it took over his mind and he found himself asking it out loud. The words faded off into the shadows around him.

"What... what did he see?"

Act Two

Within the Darkness

Day Thirty – Part One

The world the survivors had created for themselves at the Farm had begun to turn strange. At first the lights had brought hope to the group. Many of them had sat outside at night and enjoyed evenings together in the Courtyard, watching the bonfire burn, or looking up at the stars in the clearing above the Farm, but a couple of days later, the mood of the group changed entirely.

At first Rob heard it as a rumour, when he couldn't help but overhear two other survivors talking on the landing of the Farmhouse, but it wasn't too much time afterwards that he could see how John was acting and that confirmed it. Apparently someone had been stealing food from the supply at the bottom of the Barn. Originally they had left it open and people could go in and out as they pleased, but there would always be someone in there, either keeping guard or taking inventory, who would stop anyone from just walking out with anything.

But now they kept the Barn doors locked and John had someone standing guard in front of the door at all times, day and night. The bright lights above the entrance would keep them safe during the evenings, but John still insisted that someone must stand there all night until dawn. Thankfully Rob had not been chosen for this duty, as he was sure that John suspected everyone but a close circle of followers, which included

David, Maria and three others Rob did not know very well at all.

It wasn't until around the twenty-eighth day that John told the group. He called them all together, outside the front of the Barn, and said that they must shorten the rations given, in order to make sure they lasted. This raised a few eyebrows and not to mention a few concerned voices. Eventually he told them that food supplies had started to go missing and that he suspected that someone had been stealing them.

Rob saw a wave of worry creep over the faces of the Farm survivors. A few of them exchanged looks of fear, knowing full well that John was not the sort of man who would stand for something like this. They knew that they would all suffer for the actions of one individual.

Robert watched as John gave his speech about survival, and he also watched the group for signs of anyone who might be acting strangely upon hearing the news. Rob knew that John was doing the same. Every now and again he would pause to scan their faces, looking for guilt, before continuing.

"I am afraid that due to the amount taken, we will need to cut back on the rations and so we will not have as much as we did, until we begin to utilise the farmland".

John had mentioned this before. He had said that they should look into growing crops and harvesting food, but they all knew that winter was on its way, and once that hit, they would not be able to grow anything. It was the wrong time of year to be thinking of this.

"We have taken all we can from the nearby town, but a group as large as ours does require a lot of food to feed, you know" John said, still clutching his shotgun tight, as if he was preparing for the group of fifteen or so strong to try and overthrow him as leader, and chuck him out beyond the fence for the creatures of the night to feast upon.

By the time John had finished, everyone left the discussion disappointed. The last speech John had made had given them hope that their community would live on through this crisis. That their lives would return to normal, or as close as it could, given the circumstances. It was what everyone wanted. Everyone that was but John. Now the group would need to start rationing. Rob knew that this was not going to go well. Over the last few days, people had enjoyed and got used to having a lot of food available to them. They had eaten breakfast, lunch and dinner, as well as any snacks they had wanted if they went up to the Barn and asked whoever was working that day. This time when lunch rolled around, they went hungry. There was no call for food, as there had been on previous days. At dinner they had about half the portion they had the day before. People were unhappy, but nobody said anything. Everyone was a little on edge about being the one accused of stealing.

Earlier that day John had David, Maria, and the others who were not guarding the Barn, question a few people and ask if they knew anything about it, or where someone might have been hiding such quantities of food or other supplies that had been stolen that the rest of the group might not have been aware of yet. It was clear that John was using them to police the community.

At one point before dinner, Rob decided to go back to his room to change his top, and found Maria in the middle of it, kneeling on the floor and looking underneath the bedside table. Rob was taken back by her sudden appearance in his room. Nobody really went into his room. Whenever he was on watch duty with Pete or Matt, he would often go into their room and watch from the window. It was easier if Pete had fallen asleep.

"What are you doing in here?" Rob asked her. Maria spun around as she got to her feet. Her face told Rob that she was a little embarrassed being caught in the act. It was already clear that the big man had ordered her to come here and look through Rob's things. That did not stop him feeling annoyed by her presence.

"What are you doing in here?!" Rob asked again, only this time allowing the anger to show in his voice.

Maria cleared her throat. "I'm looking for something" she replied.

Rob knew exactly what she was looking for. "The food isn't here. So you can get out" Rob told her firmly.

Maria smirked and held up her arm, Rob saw that she was holding a wrapper from one of his breakfast bars. "Then what is this?"

Her attempt to accuse him of stealing the food was laughable. Rob himself couldn't help but laugh. "You cannot be serious" he told her. He saw in her eyes that it was a desperate attempt and her arm lowered. "Everyone has a little food in their rooms. I have had those stored up since we arrived here".

Maria's face changed and now she looked as if she was scared. "Look... I..." her voice was trembling. "John wanted me to check out a few rooms and report back to him. He said to do the top floor of the Farmhouse while David did the Storehouse. I... I didn't mean anything by it. We are all on edge at the moment".

Rob almost felt a bit sorry for her. It was clear that Maria had attached herself to John in a desperate attempt for protection and to remain higher up in the food chain of the group, but now that John was acting the way he was, she had to carry out his bidding. She was already too far gone to stop now.

"I don't know who took the food" Rob told her, tossing his gun onto the bed.

Maria left without saying anything more. She would have had to go back and tell John she found nothing in Rob's room. Maybe then he would stop staring at him with accusations in his eyes.

Rob knew that whoever had stolen it, if in fact it hadn't just been miscounted or whatever, then they better hope they do not get discovered. He knew that John would not give out a light punishment to the culprit. It was best for everyone if they just forgot about it and moved on with their lives. They were not starving. It was not like they had not found a mass of food in the supermarket back at the town. It seemed that John was taking his leader status a little too seriously.

Over the last month, Rob had witnessed John's change. When he first met him, he seemed like a reasonable and resourceful guy. He had jumped on the apocalypse like he had a guide sitting at home that he had read every night leading up to it. He taught them how to make Molotovs, how to bandage up wounds properly, and how to load firearms. It was clear that he had some kind of background in military or law enforcement, Rob could tell that from the way he spoke to people, the little things he would say, and the stuff he knew about. At first Rob had mistaken him for a police officer, but there was just as much evidence to support the fact that maybe he was a video game and military fanatic, sitting at home and looking at guns online, all the while preparing for the Zombie apocalypse.

John had never claimed that he was the leader of their group. He used to say a few options on what they should do and give the reasons why they should or shouldn't do it, ultimately leaving it up to the rest of the group to make a decision. Of course this always led to people doing whatever it was that he wanted to do, but he gave them the illusion of choice. He would always do that fake smile whenever he suggested a plan that he secretly knew was the best option.

It was his suggestion that they get out of the city and make for the woods nearby. He said that they might be able to find the caves on the other side and live out in one of them, catching their own food and waiting for all this to blow over. Even then Rob knew that this was never going to just blow over and everything would return to how it was.

They lost their way on the track and found the Farm a day later. After that, John thought it would be best if they stayed there. The idea of sleeping in a cave did not appeal to everyone, so nobody suggested otherwise. When they got to the Farm, John started to give out a few more 'suggestions'. However nicely he asked someone, these were orders. Overtime the facades of these suggestions slipped away. It wasn't until they started to make a life for themselves here, that John assumed control over the group and people referred to him as 'in charge'.

Now his fake smile had all but faded. He ruled over the survivors of the Farm with an iron fist. People had begun to feel that they would suffer the consequences if they did not do what they were told. Defiance was not something Robert had witnessed since John had self-appointed himself their leader. At times he had wanted to see what would happen if someone was to say "No" to him. Would they have been killed? Or exiled out into the wilderness? Whatever John was before the darkness came, he was a different man now.

After dinner Matt came over to Rob with an annoyed look on his face.

Rob contemplated asking what was wrong, but before he could open his mouth, Matt spoke.

"This is fucking bullshit" he said sitting down in the kitchen of the Farmhouse where Rob was eating his dinner with Pete. Matt's ankle had healed up nicely and his walk was back to how it had been before he twisted it.

"What do you mean?" Pete asked finishing what remained of half a can of tuna and a stale cracker.

"I am still hungry. I am starting to get a pain in my stomach" replied Matt.

Pete laughed a little. "Don't be so dramatic. I am sure you won't starve". Matt brushed off the comment and gave him a look that told Pete he was not in the mood. It seemed that the hunger replaced his patience. "Nah... It's rubbish. You are eating half a can of tuna you had to split between you two" he said, fixing his gaze on Rob.

Robert shrugged. "Well getting pissed about it isn't going to help" he told him.

Matt sighed and opened up a bottle of water, taking a swig of it before wiping away the remaining water from his mouth. "Makes me wish I had stolen that food. Did you know that prick David came to see me this morning? He pretty much accused me of taking it. I was this close to punching him".

Rob wondered what would happen if someone was to hit one of John's main crew. David had been on a bit of a power trip since John tightened the rations. He like to throw his weight around. Rob never really trusted the man. He was always hanging out with one of the girls in the Storehouse. A few people had gossiped that maybe they were sleeping together, but most people thankfully stayed out of each other's business, which was how Rob had managed to avoid nearly fifty percent of the group over the last month and keep himself to himself.

Pete broke in and cut through Rob's train of thought. "Yeah he asked me if I knew anyone who is acting suspiciously... and he asked me about you".

Matt looked surprised. "About me?" he replied. "What did he say?"
"Emmm..." Pete thought for a moment, looking down at what remained of his tuna cracker. "He was just asking where you kept your stuff".
Rob decided to interrupt. "He has probably gone through your stuff" he said, almost anticipating Matt's reaction of anger. "I went up to my room earlier and Maria was going through it".

"You caught her?" Pete asked, a huge smile breaking onto his face. "That's classic".

"John asked her to go through a few rooms upstairs" Rob continued.
"That son of a bitch!" Matt said, standing up and swinging his arms, almost knocking over the flask Pete used to drink his green tea. "They can't just go through our stuff like this".

"I am sure he has good reason" Pete replied. "I mean someone IS stealing food from us. One person is ruining it for the rest of us".

"Fuck off you pussy" Matt told him, as he knocked the chair back onto the floor and turn to storm out of the room.

There in the doorway, John stood. Maria was standing beside him but she was almost completely overshadowed by the sheer size of the man. His shoulders almost touched the moulding. His face looked unimpressed and suddenly a wave of worry fell over the three other men. Rob looked over to Pete, whose face had turned bright red with embarrassment. Matt took a step backward as John entered the room, Maria in tow.

"How are we doing here fellas?" he asked, moving across the room to one of the side windows.

Rob stayed silent and Matt looked away. Pete was the only one who answered the man's question. "Um... yeah. Everything is fine" he said. From his tone, Rob thought he was going to add the word 'sir' onto the end of his sentence.

You could feel the tension in the room. Rob wondered how much of their conversation the man had heard.

Maria stood in the corner of the room, leaning against one of the walls and watching over them. She didn't say a word. It was her gaze that was making them feel uneasy first of all, but when John did speak again, it changed back to the big man carrying the shotgun.

"I think we might have a few issues among us, you know" he said resting the weapon on his shoulder, raising it up into the air. The tip almost touching the ceiling. He took a few steps over towards the table, as he did, the Molotov cocktails he had dangling from him clanged together. The air in the room filled with gasoline.

"I think we should just try and clear the air here boys".

Matt turned towards the door. "I have to get back" he said as he went to leave.

Rob saw in the corner of his eye John's gun fall down and the barrel into the firm grip of his other hand. "Take a seat with us Matthew..."

An awkward silence flowed through the air. Pete looked over to Rob, but his gaze, like John's, was fixated on Matt and what he would do next.

Matt turned around. "Are you asking me... or telling me?" Matt questioned.

Rob had a horrific vision in his head of John pulling the trigger and blasting pieces of Matt all over the kitchen of the Farmhouse. He looked over and saw that John did not have the gun pointed at him.

"I am just asking you for a chat" John said and that smile made another appearance. It had been a while Rob had seen it. The serious nature of someone stealing food had caused it to be replaced with a stern look of distrust.

Matt went over and picked up the chair from the floor, moved it over towards the table and sat on it. He was trying his best to show him he was not afraid of him, but at the same time, John was a big man and carried an even bigger gun. Matt on the other hand was rather skinny and didn't look like he would be much good in a brawl.

"What do you want?" he asked and suddenly John's fake smile disappeared.

"I know this food stealing business has got us rustling a few cages, you know" John started off by saying. "I don't want this to cause any issues around the camp, but the fact remains that there is a thief amongst us. Someone has been going into the Barn and stealing our food right from under my nose". It was clear that the end part was what angered John most about the whole situation. "I have asked a couple of people I know, and trust to take, a look around the Farm, ask a few questions, and see if they can't bring this person to justice".

"What kind of justice?" Matt asked abruptly.

John smiled again. This time, however, Rob saw something in it that made him think that this one was real.

"The kind that sees the guilty punished. The kind that stops this thing from happening again, you know" John told them.

The thought of it seemed to stop Matt in his tracks from the follow up question he had planned in his head. It was clear to Rob that he had not anticipated John's honesty.

Rob was still concerned by John's answer and decided to question it himself. "Are you going to kill them?" he asked bluntly.

This question caught John by surprise. "Ha!" he laughed aloud. "I don't know if it will come to that. But we need to restore order here. We can't have people coming and taking whatever they want, now can we". He stood up and walked over to the other side of the kitchen, bottles clanging together with each step. "In the old days, if you stole from someone else, and you got caught, then you were put on trial. If found guilty then you went to prison. It is as simple as that, you know".

"So are you going to lock them up?" Rob asked.

"I have an idea of what will happen when I find the person responsible". Rob decided it was best if he didn't say anything more.

John rubbed his thick black beard and walked over to the doorway. "Look" he said, turning back to the table where Pete, Rob and Matt sat. "I am not accusing you of anything. As far as I am concerned, it could be anyone. There is only a few people I trust with this, so I wanted them to try and find out anything they could. Maria here says that you three are not suspects. Listening to what you were saying a moment ago, I believe that to be the case as well, you know".

Pete turned away with embarrassment. Rob felt that his face had started to turn red as well.

"In the meantime, I have a couple of jobs for you. Matthew?" Matt reluctantly turned towards John. "The generator has started to smoke. Might just need a little oil, but I don't want that thing going off on us at the wrong moment in the middle of the night. These people want us to keep the lights on, so I suggest you take a look at it".

Matt didn't say a word. He climbed up from his seat and left the room, not so much as exchanging a glance at John as he passed him in the doorway. John let him go.

"Pete" John carried on with his orders. "I have a job for Rob". He laughed to himself at the words rhyming. "I have a task I need Rob's help with, so you will be on watch yourself tonight".

"Yeah, sure thing" Pete replied almost instantly. Rob had noticed that Pete had become a bit of a lackey as of late. He had not questioned anything John had ordered or implemented, and sometimes even gone so far as defended the boss's actions whenever Matt had mentioned anything when the three of them were on watch together. This had led to a bit of hostility between the two of them.

"You can go if you like" John said to Pete in a way that told him that now was the time for him to leave.

Pete did not take more than a few seconds to quickly grab the remains of his dinner and scurry out of the room, leaving John and Rob alone. Maria still stood in the corner, leaning against the wall, but for all she said and did, she may as well not have been there.

John came over to the table and sat down opposite him. Rob began to feel his intense stare on him that always made him feel uncomfortable. It was worse now as he wondered what he could have wanted him to do.

"Now..." John begun, almost hushed as if he did not want even Maria to listen. "I feel like you are one of a handful of people I can trust, you know".

This came to Rob as a bit of a surprise. He had not expected John to say anything like that. He was stunned and unable to respond.

"I..." John cut himself off. "Maria, go and make sure the torches are lit tonight would you. We need them lit every night, without fail. I don't want people slacking off in case something happens with the lights". Maria replied with a simple "Yes" and left the room, leaving the two men truly alone. It almost felt as if he was embarrassed and didn't want anyone else to hear what he had to say.

"I need someone to watch the Barn tonight. Just standing out the front of it keeping an eye on everything. The lights up top will protect you fine. We even have the bonfire going again tonight, so it will be warm enough. I am giving Maria a night off, and I need David and a couple of the others to do something for me, so I need someone I can trust. I saw how you have not said no to anything I or anyone else have asked of you. I know you did everything you could to save Mike..."

The name hit a sore spot in Rob's chest and it felt as if the word had pierced through his heart.

"Last week you went to that town and you got yourself trapped there. You did what you needed to in order to survive... and you brought back food for the rest of us. You have been a team player since I met you, and so I want you to do this job for me. Can you do that tonight?"

John stared at him with almost compassion in his eyes. It was a strange sight for Rob. He did not know if he preferred John like this or how he was before.

A few moments passed and Rob knew that he needed to answer. All he could say was "Sure", and he wondered what else he could have possibly said.

"Good" replied John. "Come on over to the Barn at dusk... when the sun is setting. If you need anything then we can..."

Just then the Farmhouse door was flung open, crashing against the wall and knocking a hanging picture onto the floor. David burst into the living room, his gun in his hand. Both Rob and John shot up to their feet. Rob reached down for his gun but realised he had left it up on his bed earlier. John held his shotgun with both hands.

"What the hell..." John went to say but David called out to him.

"John... we've... we've got... there's people here John" he said, struggling to get the words out.

The word 'people' caused John's eyes to go huge. "What people?"

"Other people John" David replied, turning back towards the door, staring off through it towards the front gate.

"Other survivors".

Day Thirty – Part Two

"Please... my wife, she is sick" the man pleaded as he held the woman beside him tightly.

He had light brown hair, was wearing a ripped grey shirt and a pair of jeans, with a hole exposing a section of his leg. The woman did not seem as if she knew what exactly was going on. She kept her head down with her hair covering her face. She was pale and wore a long maroon sports t-shirt that appeared not to belong to her. Her hair was matted and Rob thought he could see a leaf or two amidst the dark straw colouring.

John stood at the bottom of the steps of the Farmhouse entrance with Maria and David either side. Although John did not have his shotgun pointed at them, he gave everyone the impression that he would do it and pull the trigger in a heartbeat. The other two minions stood with their weapons drawn as well, Maria with her handgun and David holding the knife he always carried on his belt.

Rob watched from the doorway as John leaned over to the David and whispered something into his ear. It was too far away for the strangers to have heard, but Robert heard it as if he had said it to him. "Make sure no one else comes out here" he told him and, without question, David turned and ran off around the side of the house.

The man went to take a step forward, maybe to try and enter, maybe just to get the big man's attention, either way he had succeeded and John turned, moving the barrel of the gun closer to their direction. "Easy now" John told him. It was a combination of dominance while at the same time trying to be friendly and non-threatening.

"Please" the man said again. "We have been out here for days. It is getting dark soon. Those things..." he took another glance at his wife before turning back to face John. "Those things are out there".

John stood there silently, watching them as if he was waiting for them to suddenly pull out weapons and begin shooting. Rob anticipated some kind of gunfight breaking out and wished he had not left his weapon upstairs.

From where he was standing, he could not see if the woman was genuine or not. The light from the nearby Tiki torch had hit her which cast a shadow across her face.

The man went to speak again, but John cut him off. "Where have you come from?" he asked.

The man looked as if he did not understand the question. "Wha...?" he muttered.

"Where did you come from?" John repeated. "You ain't been living out in the woods in the dark for all this time. You don't even have a flashlight on you, you know".

He was right. Rob looked over at what the man was carrying. In one arm he clutched the shoulder of his wife, while in the other he was holding a shopping bag that looked as if it didn't carry anything more than a couple of bottles of water.

"A building... on the edge of the city; a shop. We have been living there for a few weeks now. It had food and since it was just the two of us, we were living there" the man replied.

"So why did you leave?" John asked. It appeared as if he was thoroughly questioning them before he did anything. "Sounds like you had it pretty sweet there, you know".

One of John's other goons showed up at the doorway and pushed passed Rob. He carried another handgun. He walked out onto the porch and stood against the post, watching the newcomers. It seemed this made the man uneasy.

"I..." he went to say, but the woman almost collapsed, but he managed to support her. "The power went out. The building must have had some kind of backup after the city went dark... we couldn't get it back on and they were coming. The city is crawling with them. The whole place is covered in shadows. We couldn't stay there. So we thought we might find a car out on the road".

The man's answer did not seem to satisfy John. "So how did you end up out here?" he asked. Rob could hear the accusations in his tone.

"We ran into another group. They seemed friendly enough. The second night they tried to kill us. They got our friend. My wife and I made it into the woods, but she was injured. I think it is infected. Please... you have to help us".

The man's voice had started to get louder. John looked around to see who was nearby, before turning back to the man and holding up one of his hands as if to quiet him down. He took a step closer.

"Okay... okay. I understand. Look..." John took another look back, this time however, he looked directly at Rob. Their eyes met for a moment and he instantly knew what was coming next.

"Look..." John repeated. "We have a bit of a food shortage here. We'd love to take you in, but we haven't got enough to feed ourselves, let alone anyone else".

"What?!" the man said shocked. "We just need somewhere out of the..."

"I want to help you... I do. So we'll give you something for your wife. Maybe even a torch if we can spare it. Maria" he turned to her. "Run inside and grab one of them first aid kits I made up. There should be one in the kitchen".

Maria ran inside. John turned back to the man, whose face looked as if he was in utter disbelief at what was happening. "At the end of the day..." John paused for a moment. He stood there gripping his shotgun tighter and tighter with each passing second. It felt like a life time of silence before John spoke again. "We don't know you from Adam, you know. We need to protect our own. Your story doesn't add up. I suggest you take this". John tossed the flashlight he had on him at the man's feet. The man looked down at it and went to speak, but John interrupted him. "Take that, and the first aid-kit... and go".

Maria returned. Rob moved out of the doorway to allow her to pass. She was carrying a small bag containing a few supplies for treating a wound that John had made up himself a week or so ago and placed around for people to use if need be. Maria passed it to John who did not take it. Instead he gestured towards the man and woman and Maria took the hint. She walked over to them and passed it to the man who grabbed it with the hand still holding the handles of the shopping bag.

"You... you can't do this" the man said. "You can't just throw us back out there. We won't survive!" The man's voice was starting to get louder once again.

His wife started to look up and Rob caught a glimpse of her face for a brief instance, before it fell back down.

Robert started to get a feeling a guilt inside of him, as if the man was telling the truth. He began to feel sick in his stomach.

"You motherfuckers!" the man almost shouted. John's face turned to anger and he looked around, as if expecting to see the whole of the Farm survivors standing around him and watching. Thankfully for him, no one else other than Rob and John's lackeys were there.

John took a few steps forward and moved the barrel of his gun to face the man. "I suggest you take your leave" he said, cold and stern.

Rob went to step out of the doorway. "Hey, wait a..." he tried to speak but the unnamed goon on the porch turned around and pushed Rob back inside. "Get off of me!" Rob said as pushed the man's hands away. "Shut your mouth. This doesn't concern you!" the lackey told him.

"Please" Rob heard the man plea, but it appeared to have no effect on the leader of the Farm.

"Pick that light up... and get out of here. You don't want this to get ugly" John told him.

Rob went to leave again, but Maria and the man walking back inside got in his way. From over their shoulders he saw John still standing there in the middle of the front garden. The man had moved himself and his wife backwards past the fence.

"You're killing us!" he shouted.

"I told you to keep your god damn voice down!" John shouted back.

Rob heard a few people enter the Farmhouse as if they were coming over to see what the commotion was.

"There is a town..." John told the man, trying his best to sound calming. "It is a few hours that way. You'll be able to find shelter there. You can make it before it gets dark".

Rob looked up at the sky. John knew what time it was in the day, he did not truly believe that, did he?

"Please... we'll die out there" the man pleaded with John, but from the tone in his voice, it already sounded as if he knew that the man with the shotgun was not going to let them inside. He turned back to the treeline. "We need your help".

The two strangers disappeared behind the trees and almost fade off into the background. The evening sky had started to appear and the world began to grow dark.

A small crowd had gathered inside the living room of the house to see what was going on. Rob saw John standing in the front garden, staring off at the trees where the strangers disappeared to. He did this for a few moments, illuminated in the orange glow of the nearby torch, before turning around and walking back inside. It was completely silent other than the sound of the bottles on John's chest clanging together. As he entered the living room, Maria closed the door behind him.

The crowd of around six, including Rob, stood there patiently waiting for John to speak. Rob felt almost sick to his stomach at the thought that he did nothing to stop him from turning them away.

John rubbed his beard and then his mouth with his hand. "They were sick... diseased. We don't know enough about what is going on. For all we know, it could be a virus. An epidemic".

"What?" Rob said out loud, but thankfully John ignored it and continued talking.

"We are in a crisis here people, you know. We do not have enough food to feed the rest of us, let alone letting in people who could very well contaminate us. We still do not know what we are dealing with". John's voice had now turned as if he was giving a speech before a nation. "We have hid away from the outside world for nearly a month, living out here and protecting our own from the horrors of the world. I will not allow anything that poses a risk to our people. We need to protect one another. We cannot risk anymore of our lives".

Rob looked around the room at the faces of the other survivors. From what he could see, they seemed to be hanging on to his every word. "I gave those people aid... and I gave them a light to help them find a place of their own" he said as if attempting to convince the people, but Rob knew they were already on his side. "I suggest we keep a better watch tonight. Report any unusual sightings right away".

John walked off and after a couple of seconds, everyone went back to their business. Rob was left standing there alone in the middle of the living room. He felt strange. He did not believe anything that John had said about the people, other than giving them a few things to help. As far as Rob was concerned, they had enough food to feed just two more people. "Surely not that much food could have been stolen?" Rob wondered to himself. He knew that John was just hoarding and rationing it until the thief was found.

Did John truly believe what he had said about the disease? Could this whole thing be some kind of virus outbreak? Or had he just said that to justify not taking in those people?

Rob went over to the window by the front door and looked out. In the early days, only a few weeks ago, he and Pete and sat by this window and kept watch. He looked out at the trees as the sun was starting to set in the distance. The warm glow of sunlight shone across the sky. It always felt brighter at this time of day, as if it was the calm before the storm, when the light disappeared from their world and they were forced to face the darkness that awaited them. Rob knew that time had come. He knew that the flashlight John had given the man would not protect them both from the creatures that stalked the shadows.

He could not explain how he felt inside. Rob already had a lot of blood on his hands. Since this whole thing began, he had now killed three people, but this was different. John had signed the stranger's death warrant, and Rob did nothing to stop it. What could he have done? John's word was gospel around here. He was the Lord of this Keep.

A thought began to form in Rob's brain as he stared out at the trees in the fading sunlight. He thought about the creatures and began to imagine what it would be like if the entire Farm was to fall into darkness. If they came for them and the lights were out. Would John be able to protect them then? The power he had over their little group of survivors and all the weapons he carried would not be enough if the lights went out and the monsters came. In that moment, he would be no more powerful than anyone else.

To the creatures in the dark, we are all the same.

Day Thirty – Part Three

The night grew colder with each passing hour. At first, Rob didn't seem to mind so much as he stood out the front of the Barn doors as the burning bonfire kept him relatively warm, but as many of the survivors had gone to bed, there was nobody to tend to the dying flames. The fire flicked nervously, trying as hard as it could to hold onto what little life remained before it finally died out a short while after midnight.

If it was not for the string of LED lights shining brightly above Rob's head and around the Courtyard, the whole place would have been in total darkness. The few Tiki torches that had not gone out, their flames danced and swayed in the cold breeze that blew its way through the trees and disappeared off into the darkness.

Rob got a sudden chill the next time the wind whistled by. He brought both of his hands up to his shoulders and began to rub them to get warm. He was less than halfway through his shift and he knew that it was hours until morning. John had said that at sunrise, David would take over.

Rob wasn't sure if it was because of what John had said to him earlier at the kitchen table, that caused him to agree to standing out all night in the freezing cold, guarding the entrance to the place the man was sleeping inside, or if it was because he did not want to get on the wrong side of him.

All different thoughts crept into his head. He thought about how he could get the bonfire lit without having to leave his post. The fuel was kept at the entrance to the Storehouse at the other side of the Courtyard.
He thought about why John had really given him this job. Was it that he truly did in fact trust Rob? Or was it because he just needed someone to give David a night off?
He thought about how good it would be, come morning, when he could return to his small little room in the upstairs of the Farmhouse. His makeshift bed was calling him. He was already beginning to feel tired, but he was used to staying awake most of the night. Especially when he and Pete were keeping watch at the front of the house, and Pete would often fall asleep.

Rob had changed over the last few days. He was feeling himself getting into a routine. He no longer stayed awake most nights, lying in bed and thinking about the horrific events that had befallen them. Instead he found himself drifting off nearly every night, and when he did, he didn't dream the way he had done when he had first come to the Farm.
Rob's appetite was back as well. He wasn't sure if it was because of the abundance of food they had found at the town that had brought it back. Maybe scrounging for scraps had made him used to not eating much, whereas now, at least, before the rationing, he had got used to eating more and now his body was beginning to crave it.
John's plan to ration the food had made everyone agitated. No one was particularly happy with it, and since it had come into effect, everyone seemed to be getting hungry. Rob was hungry too. He could feel his stomach gurgle and clench every now and then. To help counter this,

Robert kept taking sips of his water every fifteen minutes or so, although he knew that this would eventually lead to him needing to urinate and leaving his post.

As he took another sip of his water, Rob realised something. He had not thought about Mike or the strange man from town, for a while. Nor did he think much of the man he had killed when they first went into the woods. The feelings of guilt for their murders had left him. He had thought that maybe he finally believed that they were not his fault, or at least, not done with bad intentions. The mercy killing, the accident, and the one in self-defence.

Rob thought about them for a moment and didn't feel anything. He tried to think about Mike's eyes, the look on his face when Rob pulled the trigger, but nothing came. He could not remember. It was only a few weeks ago, but Rob now felt as if his mind was letting go of the guilt.

When he thought about guilt on the other hand he felt guilty about another thing entirely. His thoughts were on the man and woman who had shown up earlier at the Farm and John had sent them away. Rob still thought about how he stood there and did nothing. He had tried to say something, but that goon of John's had stopped him. Rob didn't put up much of a fight. Thinking back he should have punched the man and called out to John that it was not right. He was sure that the man would not have been knocked out of the way, so he would have probably hit Rob right back and it would have resulted in a much worse situation. John could have brought them in. He was sure they had enough food for two more people. If he truly believed the infectious disease thing, then he could have quarantined them.

But then again, what if he was right? Rob believed that this nagging thought was what stopped him from actually doing anything earlier. What if they were trouble? The man who attacked Robert in town was a clear example of how dangerous strangers could be. For all he knew, the woman might have been playing sick. They could have got inside the Farm and done anything. They could have killed someone, someone that they knew. For all Rob knew, they might have been sneaking into the Farm at night and been the ones stealing the food.

Just then Rob caught a glimpse of something in the corner of his eye to his left and he spun around to see what it was. His thoughts were of the man and woman, and god knows who else, hiding in among the trees and stalking them, ready to attack and try to take their food or try and hurt them.

When Rob looked over towards the forest on the left side of the Farm, all he saw was darkness. The bright LED lights made it difficult to see anything. He scanned along the dark abyss and the thoughts soon left him.

"If they were out there... watching us... in the dark, then the creatures would have got them" Rob said to himself, and he was right.

The monsters hunted everyone and everything in the shadows. If you were out there after dark, and without a light, then you were done for.

A rustle of dead leaves turned Rob's attention to a section of trees near the corner of the fence, just a little way from the Storehouse. It was some kind of movement.

"Hello?" Rob asked desperately, to no one in particular and praying for no one to answer back.

There was no response. He stood there, watching the dark shadows for a moment, before taking a few steps closer.

The lights above guided him all the way to the Farm's perimeter fence, where another set of LED lights shone above them. He was at least six meters away from the Barn door, the place he was supposed to be guarding, but he was sure he heard something.

Other than that wolf Rob had seen early on, and the rabbits John had hunted, there had been no other animals sighted around the Farm or anywhere in the forest at all for weeks. Now that he thought about it, Rob was not even sure if he had dreamt that wolf, it's huge wide eyes and snarling teeth staring at him, until it sensed the approaching darkness and fled.

The fact that no more rabbits or even a squirrel had been seen in ages gave everyone the impression that the creatures had taken to killing animals. No carcasses had been found, but every single hunting trip people went on, before the survivors had found the town, had turned up nothing.

This was why Rob was so curious about the sound of movement he heard, coming from the trees just beyond the fence.

Rob heard the noise again and peered over the mismatch of wooden slats and the remains of an old door, and watched quietly for a moment. He was half expecting one of the creatures to step out from behind one of the trees and screech that awful sound at him, but nothing came.

As Rob stared he noticed something. It was not too far away and was quite possibly the source of the rustling sound he could hear. He saw a flicker of light shoot out from the shadows. It was faint, as if being obstructed by leaves, but it was there. It stood out in the black all around it; a bright long yellow glow. It was no bigger than the light that a flashlight gave off.

"A flashlight?" Rob thought to himself.

There would be nobody else out there, that he knew of, who would have a light like that, other than the one John had given to the man and woman.

He watched the light for a short while and noticed that it did not move. Were his suspicions correct? Was someone out there watching them? Or was it the man and woman, who simply did not take John's threat seriously, or who were just so desperate that they were willing to get on his bad side, just so they could have a chance at surviving the night.

Rob suddenly remembered something. The shack that he and Matt investigated a while back were in that direction. They could have possibly been taking shelter inside of it, but then again, it could have been someone else.

He waited for a moment, contemplating what he should do. John had specifically asked him to stand guard outside the door. If he was to come out and see that he was not there, even him being as far as the fence, then he would be in serious trouble. He knew he should go and tell them. That was the obvious thing to do, but he was worried about what John would do, especially if he found out that it was the man and woman he had sent away.

"Would he kill them?" Rob wondered, turning back to look at the Barn where he knew the big man slept inside.

Out of nowhere a pitiful cry came from the direction of the light. Rob's head turned so fast towards it, that it felt as if he had pulled something in his neck. The cry went again. It was a woman's voice. Rob could not hear the words exactly, but he could hear someone calling.

"They could be in trouble" Rob thought, and he realised that he had a chance here to redeem himself for not doing anything when John turned them away.

He thought for a second about how he could smuggle them inside. Everyone was asleep so they could stay in his room. John would not like it, but he thought it was better than leaving them out in the dark to die, while this group of survivors slept comfortably and happily in their beds, all safe and sound.

The cry came again. It would have been far too quiet for anyone else to hear it, but there, on the edge of the Farm and leaning over the fence, Rob heard it.

"Please" the woman's voice said. It was hard to hear it exactly, but Rob knew the word that time.

"Shit..." Rob said aloud, as he grabbed the nearby torch and pulled it free from the ground.

He put one hand on the top of the fence and hopped over it gracefully. His feet crushed the grass on the other side. Here, the grass had not been trampled by the survivors and so it was left to grow without interruption. It climbed up the back of the wooden planks.

It was instantly colder on this side of the fence. Rob felt a chill rip through his entire body. Maybe it was the wind, or maybe he was thinking too much about what would happen if John found out he had left his post.

He would only go to the shack and back. It was a relatively straight forward path. Through the trees and into the forest. The distant light should help guide him. As for getting back, he imagined that the Farm was quite possibly the brightest place for miles, maybe even the entire country, if this nightmare was as bad as everyone thought it was. He should be able to get back easily enough. Hopefully he could be quick enough so that no one would know that he was gone.

His biggest worry was if the thief was someone in the camp and they went in while Rob wasn't there. He imagined that would be the thing to tip John over the edge. He had no idea what he would do if that was the case.

"No everyone is sleeping" Rob told himself.

He knew he could get there and back within twenty minutes or so. It would be far too coincidental if the thief was to strike during that time. If the woman was injured or needed assistance, then he would have to go back and get someone. Matt or Pete was his first thoughts, however, Pete had become a bit of a follower of John's of late, so he was sure that Pete would confess everything to the big man at the first chance he got. Matt was the better choice. He would have probably been awake at this time, keeping watch of the front as Pete slept. He could easily get him to help.

As Rob moved forward, the bright lights of the Farm's Courtyard faded behind the thick black shadows of the trees. The torch was providing adequate lighting for the time being. It showed no signs of going out any time soon. Rob also carried the flare John had given him when heading back into town a while back. He had not used it, but kept it close at hand just in case.

As he drew nearer to the source of the light, fear began to take a hold of him. He grabbed his gun and took it out, flicking off the safety catch, as John had shown him before.

He thought about what the man had said; that there was another group who had tried to attack them. What if this was them? Or what if the man and woman were here to cause the Farm survivors trouble?

If Rob was outnumbered, then there would be no hope for him. His gun only had around seven or eight shots inside of it. Rob had lost count. He knew that if he fired a warning shot, then that should hopefully scare off the attackers, he hoped. At the very least, it would alert the people back at the Farm. It would be then that he was glad if John was on his side. But would he? Rob had betrayed his trust and did not do as he was ordered.

Rob's hand was trembling as the Shack appeared out of the darkness ahead. He could hear the gun tapping against his belt with each step he took. He moved his arm and brought it up, pointing it towards the light that was just up ahead.

He slowed right down now, taking one foot off the ground slowly, before placing it further forward a moment later, trying his best to minimise the noise as much as possible.

As Rob approached, the light was resting on a section of brickwork that was sticking out. It was a flashlight Rob could see. He could not tell if it was the same one that John had given the stranger, as he had not got a good enough look at it when he did. But if it was not the man and woman, then who left it?

The door to the Shack was open. The hinges were rusted, Rob remembered, and so the door was left ajar. The light from his torch shone inside, and when Rob took a deep breath and stuck his head inside, it was cold, dank and empty. No one had been living in here.

"Please!" the voice called out again, this time from behind him. The voice was louder than before, almost as if the woman was standing right nearby.

Rob spun around, knocking the flashlight off the wall and onto the floor. The light flicked as it hit the ground and pointed off towards the Farm. With his gun pointed outward with one hand, he held the torch up higher with the other, hoping to make the area brighter, but it did not help, he could still see nothing. No one was there. The source of the shout, the woman, was nowhere to be found. All Rob found, when he turned around, was the darkness staring back at him. The small clearing around the Shack was empty, as far as he could see in this light. He took a few steps away and looked around, trying to check every crevice and every shadow, but nothing was there.

Rob began to feel a little light headed. He thought that perhaps it was the adrenaline pumping through his body, or the fear of what would happen to him if John found out he had left, but right at that moment his head started to feel strange. He took a few deep breaths and closed his eyes. He could hear a ringing in his ears. He knew that it was not a noise out in the forest, but something his mind or his ears were doing.
He felt the warmth of the torch light heating his face, and faintly, through his closed eyelids, he could see the fire burning.

After a few seconds the ringing suddenly stopped. When he slowly opened his eyes, he was confused to find himself no longer standing in the clearing of the woods near the Shack, surrounded by trees. Instead he standing in a dark alley on a drizzly rainy evening. The sounds of the city could be heard in the distance. They were sounds Rob had become familiar with throughout his life, but he had not heard them for weeks now. It was the sound of cars and buses driving past the alley. They splashed nearby puddles as they passed and some even honked their horns to show their frustration at other drivers. Rob could not see them but he heard it. From where he was, he should have been able to see the lights from the cars, but all he saw was a dark endless pit at the end of the alley.

He tried to move, but he felt as if he was stuck to the floor. He did not feel as if he was even there, as if he was having an outer body experience and seeing through the eyes of someone else. He looked down, expecting to see his own body below him, but when he did, all he saw was the wet cement floor below.

He could not feel his arms or his legs. A phantom pain trickled through his nervous system, tricking his brain into thinking that his body was still there.

The plea came again. "Please! No!" she cried and Rob turned around to see a young woman appear out of the darkness behind him. She was dressed in dark colours and her face was obscured like someone in a dream.

"Am I dreaming?" Robert wondered to himself as the woman came charging towards him.

He saw that her clothes were torn around the sleeves. They hung from threads and dangled by her side as she ran. It was not a fast run. She struggled as if her feet did not work properly. She stumbled and leaned into a nearby wall and desperately pulled herself forward towards Rob. "Help" she called out. Not to Rob. Her gaze was fixed in the direction of the road behind him. She stared through him as if he wasn't there. Maybe he was not there at all.

As she got closer, Rob got a better look at her face. It was blurred and unrecognisable. She didn't look as if she had suffered any surgery or horrific mutilation. She appeared almost like a hallucination.

Out of the dark behind her, another person appeared. This time it was a man. He was walking slowly, but still moving faster than she was. Rob watched as he walked down the alley towards the girl, who at this point had collapsed from exhaustion.

The man was hooded and carried a small knife in his hand. The glimmer of steel stood out in the dark surroundings.

"Where are you running off to?" the man asked her.

The voice sent a chill through Rob's body, at least, what little feeling in his body remained. It was not the words that haunted him, instead it was the voice. Rob knew the man's voice. He had heard it before.

The man reached out a hand and grabbed her. The woman went to scream but he brought the knife to her throat and she stopped. She sobbed and breathed heavily as the figure loomed over her. He grabbed her by the collar and pushed her down onto the ground.

"I am going to enjoy this" he said as Rob saw the man release his grip on her and fumble with his belt buckle.

Rob tried to cry out and tell him to stop. "Get off of her!" he shouted. "Leave her alone!" But the words never came.

Rob had previously had dreams similar to this. Dreams where he had tried to call out to someone but his voice did not work. No matter how much he forced it, no matter how much his throat felt as if it was ripping apart, he could not speak.

The same was happening here. Rob tried again to shout but it was no use.

Suddenly in the blink of an eye, Rob could see it from the woman's perspective. The huge man, who almost looked beast-like at this angle, stood over her. His hoodie fluttering in the wind as rain dripped down all around them.

The hoodie was open at the front, and Rob could see a set of blue overalls, undone and open now, his belt hanging loose like a dead snake tied around his waist. The smell of motor oil was thick and strong. It drowned out the usual smell of an alley in the city.

It was here that Rob got a good look at the man. He saw a face staring back at him, frozen in that moment. It was a face he knew well, one he had almost forgotten about, but the whites of the man's eyes made it all come back. It was Mike. The man who was about to rape this poor woman was the very man Rob had shot by the stream a week earlier. The last look Rob had seen on the man's face was of pain and suffering. He had died an agonizing death at the hands of the creatures as a direct result of Rob's actions. Now his face was filled with hate. He looked pleased with himself and the glaze in his eyes made Rob think that he felt powerful in what he was doing.

That moment froze in time for a while before everything went dark again. The screams and cries of the woman rang out and echoed in the darkness. The buzzing came back a few seconds later, and after that, Rob felt the heat from the torch burning once again by his face.

When he opened his eyes, he was back in the clearing. His pistol held out in front of him, and the torch upright in his other hand. The alley was gone, and so too was Mike. The buzzing faded shortly after, and the whole world began to slip back into reality.

Rob stood there for a moment, alone, in the clearing just staring off into the trees, confused by what he had just witnessed. It had felt like a dream at first, but Mike's presence had made it feel as if it was, on some level, real. Almost as if it was some kind of memory.

Day Thirty – Part Four

On his way back to the Farm, Rob's mind was racing with everything he had seen in his vision. For all he knew, it could have been a strange hallucination, or even some kind of post-traumatic stress disorder as a result of witnessing all those deaths. Maybe his situation was finally catching up with him. It could have been a number of things, but Rob somehow knew that what he had seen was real. It was the past. It was Mike's evil past. He had raped that woman, and god knows how many more.

Rob felt like a weight had been lifted from his shoulders. If that was the type of person he was, then there was no telling when he might have tried to do that to one of the women back at the Farm. He had done them a favour, without them even knowing it. The survivors would have thought of Mike as a nice, normal guy. Someone who helped John hunt in the early days, but Rob knew the truth. Would they have believed him if he told them the truth? How could Rob have possibly known?

Rob no longer felt what little guilt remained for killing Mike. When he saw the man's eyes a moment ago, he felt the feelings come flooding back. He remembered the look in Mike's face when they both knew that the bullet Rob had fired at him, had ripped through his chest and he was going to die. Now Rob didn't feel anything about it. In fact, he was feeling the smallest bit of pride. It was peculiar. He did not imagine that he would feel like this for murdering a man in cold blood, but now that he knew exactly what the man was, everything had changed.

The Farm seemed further away than it had done before. He could see the small glimmer of light in the distance, through the trees up ahead, but the lights looked small and insignificant at this distance.
Rob looked back and the Shack disappeared behind into the darkness. He had left the flashlight there. The light had gone out at this point. Either the battery was low or it had somehow switched itself off when it fell, but the light was no longer on. Behind now was a dark empty void of nothingness.

A fallen tree blocked Rob's way up ahead, so he had to walk around it. It was strange. He didn't remember passing this on the way out.
The distance lights of the Farm kept hiding behind trees and branches, making it difficult to find his way back. Rob began to feel nervous, as if he was going to lose his way and get stranded on his own once again. The flame of the torch made him feel calmer. It looked as if it still had a good few hours left on it. The only probably was that it was so bright, that it sometimes made it difficult to see exactly which way to go. He had a general idea of how to get back, but things he kept seeing made him doubt himself.

There was something in the trees nearby that he had not seen on the way to the Shack. From this distance, it looked like it was just a huge black oval, stretched down from one of the branches. It was quite large. Rob was sure he would have seen it earlier as he was adamant he had passed this way.

The object was in his way. He would need to get closer to it and pass it in order to reach the Farm. Just behind it, the string of LED lights illuminated a small section of the woods between two thick trees. At first he thought that it was probably just part of the tree, but it wasn't until he was halfway there that the oval began to take shape. It curved in near the middle and then he realised that the bottom section of it was not one shape, but instead two. They hung down like small pillars, but did not touch the ground.

He held the torch higher and moved in closer, now only ten feet away, Rob began to see parts of it more clearly. The hanging pillars were not anything of the sort at all, they were legs. A crack at his feet drew his attention downwards, but it was only a stick, when he looked up, he saw the mangled carcass of a person strung up in the tree. He was hanging on by his arms, similar to how Jesus was on the cross. His arms were stretched out with vines wrapped around them. It looked almost as if the tree branch itself had been tired around his arms and was pulling them tighter apart.

The head of the person hung down, facing towards the ground. The light from the torch shone and revealed light brown hair. His grey shirt was ripped to ribbons and hung off his skin like Christmas decorations, scattered sporadically all around his body. At his stomach, his abdomen had been sliced open. The wound looked jagged and his intestines along with other bodily organs Rob did not recognise, were hanging out. His jeans were covered entirely in blood, giving them a deep purple colouring. Trickles of it ran down his legs and were dripping onto the floor from his ankles. His feet were gone completely. At the ground, there was no trace of them whatsoever. All that remained were tears that exposed the bone and muscle where his ankles met his feet.

It was truly a horrific sight. Rob had taken a step back and found himself bringing his hand up to cover his mouth. His hand was still gripping his handgun tight, so all he ended up doing was placing the top of the gun to his open mouth.

Another scan of the body revealed that sections of the man's scalp had been torn open. The skin hung like strips of processed meat in between his hair.

Rob took another step back and felt something hit against his foot. He thought that it could have been a root or possibly a rock, that would have been the most obvious thing he had hit, but as soon as he touched it, he felt the cold hand of another touch him. He turned frantically and almost leapt backwards toward the hanging body. When the torch moved round, it uncovered the remains of a woman, lying down in the grass and mud. Her hand was extended outward, as if reaching out for the man in the tree. It was this that Rob had made contact with. Her cold hand had touched his leg, just above his sock at the exposed warm flesh. The fingers had burned into Rob's skin when they made contact.

The woman's back was torn apart. Sections of her spine could be seen and the entire left side of her body was ripped open, as if someone had been clawing at her while she lay on the floor.

Her head was face down in the mud. Thankfully Rob did not need to see her eyes to know that she was dead, or who she was for that matter. The long maroon sports shirt, showing the remains of a number seven on the back of it, proved that these were the two people John had sent away earlier today. It seemed they had not got too far into the woods before they were attacked. The sun had already begun to set when they had left, but they could have been killed at any point afterwards. No one had heard any screams. It was possible that they had been hiding near, or even in, the Shack, given that the flashlight there had to have been the one that John gave them.

Rob knelt down at the woman. Her straw hair was now almost completely bright red, stained with her own blood. It looked as if she had been attacked first, although he couldn't say for sure. From the direction she was facing, it seemed they might have been coming back to the Farm, maybe to try and beg to be let in.
The man had probably tried to help her, only to be strapped to the tree and mutilated.
"Why would they leave the light?" Rob wondered to himself.
They had no chance of making it from the Shack to the Farm in the dark. If it was down to stupidity, then this was their own doing, but Rob was not sure that they would have survived this long if they were stupid. Maybe they had spent too long in one place, living off the resources there and dying a few days after leaving. He imagined it was common for people to become lazy and slow, maybe even a little stupid, the more safe they thought they were. He could already see it happening with the survivors back at the Farm. They were beginning to feel too safe, what with the lighting system and their fearless leader making all their decisions for them. Rob hoped that they would not suffer a similar fate.

When he got to his feet, Robert could feel a slight breeze from the wind. It started off as a tickle on his arm hair, but shortly after the wind began to pick up. The trees above him began to shake as the wind grew fiercer with each passing second. The torch flame, now almost horizontal, moved as if it was trying to detach itself from the wood and make a run for it.
Rob turned around and saw the corpse of the man rocking back and

forth. His head flung as if it was attached by the smallest part of skin, before eventually being forced backwards. The head hung abnormally far back, over his shoulder blades and revealed that his throat had been cut. Blood slowly poured from the wound as the head flew back, almost ripping off completely. As it did, Rob caught a look at the man's contorted face, frozen in his last moments of agonising pain before his death.

Rob took a step away from the body of the woman, and then another towards the Farm. He needed to get back. As he went to move, he began to hear it. At first it could have easily been mistaken for the rustling of leaves, but as each moment passed, Rob could hear the whispering from the shadows speaking once more.
As always, the words were unknown to him. It sounded like many voices whispering words from a distant or ancient language. The words he heard did not make any sense at all. They weaved in and out of the trees and sounded as if they came from all around him, echoing off of nothing and hanging there in the darkness.

Then one word forced its way out from amongst the others. It was a name.
"Joanna..." the whispers said.
At first Rob thought it was maybe the name of the woman who was lying dead no more than a few feet away from him, but he felt something different inside of him. It felt as if someone was holding onto his heart and squeezing it tight. His chest felt as if it was going to explode. He struggled for air and his vision became dizzy. He blinked, but it seemed to last for an eternity. The blackness covered his eyes and it was ages before it disappeared. At first he thought he was going to pass out. He struggled for air and his head went light. His mouth was dry and he felt his brain

rolling over and over inside of his head. The name had pierced a hole and he felt as if liquid oozed and begun to pour out, filling up his head.

After a short while he began to feel normal again. The sensation he had felt when the whispers had started appeared to leave him. As Rob felt himself calming down, the whispers still continued on in their inaudible tone.

He thought he saw a flicker of something nearby, a flash of blue maybe? But when he turned, all that was with him was the mutilated bodies of the strangers.

The name came again. It swooped across the ground and twirled all around him.

"Joanna" the whispers said again.

Rob turned, almost as if to follow it, and when he did he saw a figure quickly move behind a tree.

"Who's there?!" Rob called out, but no one answered.

He stood there, watching the spot he had seen the person, for a time, but nothing happened. The wind began to die down after a few moments and the whispers faded off into the distance, being overshadowed by the sound of the dead leaves, some of which rained down all around, as the wind turned back to normal.

Confused, Rob decided it was best to get back to the Farm. It was far too dangerous to be out in the forest on his own, not to mention strange. The last half hour, or however long he had been gone for, had left his brain in a scrambled mess. It felt as if it was trying to push its way out of his skull. His mind was racing, but that didn't matter now, Rob needed to get back before anyone noticed he was gone.

He did not look back at the bodies, instead he just made his way through the trees towards the distant lights up ahead, towards the Farm.

The lights drew closer and the silhouettes of the Barn and Storehouse begin to come into view. With his mind racing, Rob didn't even notice the overhanging branch and whacked his head against it. "Shit!" he said as he rubbed it with the back of his hand.

Suddenly, almost out of nowhere, a gunshot blasted out from across the way. The suddenness of it spooked Rob and he ducked down as if he was somehow under fire. The shot sounded as if it came from the other side of the Farm. The noise was still lingering in the air, quietly ringing and fading slowly, as the sounds of commotion could be heard at the Farm. Rob realised that he needed to get back to his post, especially before John left. Rob not being there would be the first thing the man noticed when he stepped outside of the Barn.

He picked up the pace and ran through the remains of the forest, out of the treeline and stopped halfway to the fence, when he saw a crowd had gathered over by the corner of the Farmhouse. A few other people were coming out of the back of the building, as well as some were still crossing over the Courtyard towards it.

Rob could not see John there yet. The bonfire had all but died now making it easier to see straight across to the place where the crowd was standing. From what he could see, it looked as if they were all facing towards the man who had stopped Rob from interfering with the strangers earlier today. Smoke was still rising from the barrel of his gun and amidst the noise of people chattering, wondering what was going on, he could hear the man calling over the top of them.

"There was someone out there" he cried.

Even at this distance, Rob could see the fear grow among the survivors. Their faces showed worried looks as they began glancing off in all different directions to try and locate the 'someone' the man was referring to.

Rob walked over to the fence and went to climb it, when suddenly the door of the Barn swung open. John appeared, clutching his shotgun and dressed as if he had been sleeping in his full gear, including the Molotovs. His hair was a bit of a mess, Rob noticed.
"What's going on?!" he shouted across the Courtyard to the crowd, but no one answered him.
With David and Maria, both armed with handguns, as well as David carrying his knife in his other hand, they stepped out of the Barn's entrance and walked a few paces forward.
John shot a glance over to Rob, now standing on the wrong side of the fence, and gave him a quizzical look, as if to say "What the hell are you doing there?"
Rob thought about saying "I was taking cover" thinking that this would please the military minded man, but he was not sure that would be a good enough excuse for leaving his post.
Rob went to speak, but the words stumbled in his throat. He just about managed to get the word "someone" out, before coughing and saying "I thought I saw someone as well over here". It was not overly different from what he was actually doing over there, but he hoped his excuse would suffice.
John did not seem fazed by whatever Rob had said. Instead he turned his head to the commotion and kept walking.
Rob hopped over the fence, catching his foot on the top and he almost tumbed over it, if he hadn't stabbed the torch into the ground to support

himself.

When his feet were firmly on the ground on the other side of the fence, he saw John questioning the goon who had fired the shot. Everyone was standing around, overlooking the interrogation silently, eagerly listen to what the man had seen, or thought he had seen.
Many of them looked as if they had been in their beds or sleeping sacks. A couple had realised that they were not in any immediate danger and had gone back to their bedrooms.
He could see Pete in amongst the crowd. He was standing near the front and hanging on every word that the man said about the 'figure' he had seen standing near the fence.
"For god's sake, you can't just fire off a shot unless you are in danger. You will create a panic" John told him, trying to defuse the situation. "The lights keep them out... it's late" he said trying to calm the other survivors nearby. "You might have just been mistaken, you know".
"No way man" the goon told him. "I saw it... it was huge and it was animal like".
John could see that a few people were starting to get scared at the man's comments. "Come on now. Let's go back to the Barn and you can tell me everything".

The goon firing his gun had distracted everyone from Robert. He breathed a sigh of relief in knowing that he had not been discovered sneaking off into the woods and abandoning his post in the middle of the night.
He watched as John let go of the shotgun with his left hand, his right still gripping the trigger, and reached out for him. "Come on" he said softly.

It was right at that moment it happened. At first Rob thought that he was suffering the same thing he did a moment ago when the whispers came and his eyes went dark, but then he realised it was much worse.
In half a second, the entire Farm fell into darkness as the lighting system shut down. At first no one knew what was going on. They had become so used to it. They merely thought of it as it was; a simple electrical error. In the old world they would have just reset the breakers or flicked a switch, maybe even needing to call someone to come and fix it, but the truth of the matter, in this new world that the Farm survivors were living in, the darkness meant that an unspeakable horror was coming for them.

The Tiki torches still burned here and there, but many of them had gone out. At this late in the night, no one was up to relight them. All of the lights inside the Farmhouse and the Storehouse were still on. It appeared that it had been the generator in the Tool Shed that had blown a fuse or something, shutting down the rows and rows of lights the survivors used for protection against what awaited them in the dark.

A couple of seconds passed and suddenly panic erupted amongst the group.
"Shit!" and "Oh my god!", as well as "No, no" were some of the phrases uttered by the crowd as the realisation of their situation had kicked in. The majority were more than ten meters away from the nearest light source. The torches near them had been blown out earlier that night. Thankfully the torch Rob had just recently returned to the ground was still near to him.

It all happened way too fast for anyone to realise. The wind picked up throughout. It started off as a gentle breeze, that someone might have thought was normal, but after a few seconds it grew more and more ferocious. The whispers didn't come, instead of the hushed words, hidden between the trees, screeches and roars boomed out of the shadows of the forest. The inhuman squeals of excitement raged on all around them.

There was no saying how long they had been there. No one was sure if the creatures spawned out of the darkness to attack, or if they had been watching the Farm from the treeline, out of sight, and waiting for the perfect moment to strike. Either way, they descended onto them quickly. The first one leapt out of the top of a nearby tree and grabbed onto the goon. Everyone turned and was frozen in a moment of terror as the man was ripped from his position and pulled back into the abyss. His scream rang out before changing to a plea for his life, which ended abruptly. This caused mass panic to burst out of the crowd. They all began running off in different directions. Some of them headed back to the Farmhouse, while others ran for the other two buildings nearby, all the while some of them being picked off and grabbed by the monsters.

They clawed at them, one man Rob saw, got slashed across his face, three sharp jagged cuts appeared on his face in a flash. It sliced him downward from top to bottom diagonally, popping his eyeball as it did. A pure white substance oozed out of it and mixed in with his blood. Another survivor; a woman, was grabbed from behind and the creature dug its claws into her front, ripping open her chest cavity and her insides toppled out like puzzle pieces.

Screams poured out from all around the Farm. Rob could not see where most of them were coming from as it looked like there were people and carnage absolutely everywhere. The long thin creatures moving between and striking whoever they could.

Blood spewed out all around. Even in the darkness, the unmistakable sprays and splatters of blood appeared to shoot up all around.

Out of the darkness, a bright red glow of light emerged. It shot up in a flicker of smoke and John appeared, holding a flare in his other hand.
"Get inside!" he shouted, as if no one had already had that idea.
Another flash appeared beside the Barn that drew Rob's attention to his right. This time it was a flash of flame and a small explosion occurred. The Molotov ignited and one of the creatures became more visible at this angle to Robert. It's thick black skin recoiling from the fire before scurrying off behind the Barn.
Maria stood at the other side of the fire in a position that indicated she had been the one who threw it. She retreated backwards through the Barn entrance.

A loud gunshot blasted out, and when he turned, Rob saw John firing a shot or two off into the dark.
"We need to get the lights back on!" John shouted out.
Rob, without thinking, acting almost instinctively, grabbed the torch and ripped it from the ground.
A snarl came from behind him and he spun around, swinging the flaming torch towards the noise, where he caught sight of one of the monster's faces. It went to roar but ended up pulling itself back from the fire and ran off, disappearing over the fence.

Most of the screaming had stopped in a matter of moments. As Rob made his way across the Courtyard and towards the Tool Shed, the same direction he could see John's flare glow moving towards, he realise that the screaming had all but died down. There were still a few here and there, as well as the sounds of people panicking inside the various buildings of the Farm. The noises had now been replaced by the feeding frenzy of the beasts tearing into the flesh of their victims, ripping them apart, or dragging them off into the woods to do it elsewhere.

Rob could hear a few cries for help. They were pitiful and soon replaced by a gurgling sound as blood began to fill up their mouths as they died.

When he reached the Tool Shed, he found John already kneeling beside it.

"We've got to get this fucking thing back on!" he said, more to himself than anyone.

"What can I do?" Rob asked him, and when he looked around, he realised that there was no one else out in the Courtyard.

Everyone had been so unprepared and reliant on the LED lights, that they had not bothered taking any kind of light out with them.

"Just... just keep them back" John said, having to put his flare on the ground so he could use both of his hands.

Rob looked around again and saw that Rob was the only person John had here to watch his back. David was nowhere to be found, and Maria was hiding safely inside the Barn.

The sounds of the creatures were still screaming out from all around, but Rob could not see them. He saw quick flashes of movement in front of the few torches that remained, but there was nothing coming for the two of them. It seemed that the flare and the torch was enough to keep them at bay.

"Why won't you start, god damn it!" John said angrily as he pretty much punched the side of the generator.

The machine looked dead. The magnitude of lights hooked up to seemed as if they had somehow overloaded the machine.

A different noise came out of the darkness behind Rob. He turned and saw that there were faces in the windows of the Farmhouse. He saw Pete staring out towards them. Rob breathed a sigh of relief, happy that the man had managed to make it to safety.

Matt appeared at the backdoor of the Farmhouse. It looked as if he was about to run across the Courtyard, empty handed, and save the day. Another survivor was trying to pull him back inside. He was fighting against him.

Matt shouted something that did not make a whole lot of sense to Robert, but John appeared to know exactly what he meant. Rob looked down at him as he grabbed one of the jumper cables and hooked it up to the generator. An explosion of bright yellow sparks shot out and suddenly the generator was up and running.

The lights came on in a heartbeat, which given the speed of how fast Robert's heart was beating, was incredibly fast.

They shone all around the Farm and lit the entire place up. Screeches of agony from the creatures burst forth from all around. They could not be seen, but they could be heard. Noises of them fleeing back into the forest surrounding the Farm, and distant roars filled Rob with terror. He knew what they were saying; they would be back. He knew that this would never be over.

Rob looked down to John, still kneeling down on the ground by the generator. The machine rumbled and shook as it powered their main protection against the monsters.

John shook his head before hanging it down. He seemed exhausted. It was an almost human moment that the man was displaying.

Another noise caught Rob's attention and he turned to see a few people had braved coming out of the back of the Farmhouse to see if they were alright. Rob went to give them a reassuring wave to inform them that they were, when suddenly he noticed something.

From where he was standing, he had a perfect view of nearly the entire area inside the Courtyard. The bonfire pile was blocking a section of it, but that only hid a small part of the blood bath that had befallen the survivors 'sanctuary'.

In that moment, as he looked around at the puddles of blood and the piles of body parts, Robert wished that they could have turned off the lights. He wished that the creatures would leave them alone long enough so that they did not have to witness the gore he could see laying scattered and splattered all around the Farm.

"Turn it off" he said to himself under his breath. "Just... turn it off".

Day Thirty One – Part 1

The next day was cold. A chill breezed through the air beneath grey clouds that had gathered overhead. It was a gloomy day that suited the mood of the Farm perfectly. Blood still lingered in the air.

In the aftermath of last night's attack, there were only fourteen of them left. Pete, Matt, Maria, David and John had managed to survive the attack, as well as eight others Rob had not bothered to learn the names of.

Some of them had spent the morning gathering the bodies, or in some cases the body parts, of the dead and taken them to the section of grass just the other side of the western fence. There they had dug shallow graves to bury them in. There were around four or five bodies altogether. Some of them still had missing appendages that just could not be located, no matter how much they looked. One was just a section of arm that did not seem to belong to any of them. The rest of the bodies were gone. The creatures had grabbed them and taken them off into the woods. John had not arranged a search, and no one had asked to look for them. Everyone knew what had happened. From the Courtyard, they could not see the bodies hanging in the trees like the two strangers Rob had seen the night before. There was no trace of them.

Nothing remained of the goon who had fired the shot that brought everyone out into the Courtyard. Rob thought that if it had not been for him, then very few people would have been killed when the lights went out.

Everyone had agreed to give the few bodies that remained a proper burial, so Rob and a few others had been busy digging graves all morning. It was not a particularly bad job. John had told them that some people needed to do it and Rob had volunteered. Other jobs included going around and searching for any leftover body parts, with some discoveries leaving permanent scars on people's minds, while some of the other survivors were trying to wash the blood off of the side of some of the buildings. Others had volunteered to help make repairs to the fence that was damaged during the attack.

John was keeping everyone busy. It was a good thing as it stopped people from wallowing over the dead, whom many of the other survivors of the Farm had become friends with, or who had been together since the beginning.

Rob heard a couple of people crying every now and again. One man's partner had been taken from him during the night. Rob had not spoken to these two people since they had been living together on the Farm, but he had always seen the two of them together. The man sobbed as he hammered nails into the fence. His partner had been one of the survivors who were taken in the darkness, and so nothing of her remained. For all he knew she could have been alive, but the man appeared to know the poor woman's fate as much as Rob did. No one was going to convince him otherwise. Rob imagined that it was worse for him, not having a body to lay to rest must have been the hardest thing of all.

A woman, charged with washing blood off of the Storehouse's door, was crying almost hysterically, as she soaked the blood stained sponge into the pink water and scrubbed it against the wall. Rob did not know who she was either, but he had seen her with a man at times, never paying either of them much mind however. It appeared that he had done the right thing by not getting to know them, or even half of the people he was living at the Farm with. The only people he really knew were Matt and Pete, as well as John, a little. David and Maria he knew by name really, nothing more. The rest of them were strangers to him. If he got to know them, and they died, it would have been hard for him as well. Watching the woman cry over her loss, made him feel glad he did not know them. It seemed cold hearted, but in this world, someone they loved could have been taken away from them at any minute. Last night proved just that.

Matt and Rob grabbed the body of a young man by his ankles and wrists and lifted him up into the air. At this point a snapping noise could be heard and blood slowly ran out of a wound on the man's back, similar to a low running tap.

As they placed him, as best they could, into the grave, Rob took a long good look at the man. He did not know him, but that was nothing new. He hadn't seen the man around the Farm before, although it was difficult to see him clearly as large sections of skin on his face was now missing, revealing the soft bright red muscle beneath.

"Who was he?" Rob asked, merely out of curiosity over the fact he was unsure if he was even part of their group.

"That was Daryl. He was about twenty-four, I think" Matt replied. "We did a supply run to the town a few days ago. He was a nice guy".

Rob picked up the nearby shovel off of the ground and scooped up some dirt. He stared at the disfigured remains of 'Daryl' for a few moments before pouring the dirt over him. The soil fell into his eye sockets and filled up his mouth, still stuck in the position of his last scream as his life left him. Rob had wanted to bury his face first. He needed to get rid of that look that was plastered on the corpse as he stared up at the sky. Before Matt had picked up his shovel and helped, Rob had already covered the entire head of the dead body with dirt.

It was a few hours past midday when they were on the last corpse. It was the top half of a woman that they had not managed to find the legs for. One of them Rob suspected they had buried with a completely different body, but he was not prepared to dig it up and check. She wore a maroon coloured hoodie that was now stained a deep red.
By this time most of the blood had been washed up and any chunks of flesh and gore that remained had been removed. Some of the remaining survivors were trying to get the bonfire going. It appeared that the kindling they were using had somehow got damp during the night, and now it was difficult to light. Everyone else had gone inside to avoid the cold.
The chill that surrounded the Farm that day had got worse as the hours went by. Rob's fingers were beginning to feel numb and he started to see him own breath appear as a mist before his face.

Just as they had finished digging the hole for the poor girl, Rob heard a familiar noise; the clanking of bottles, the tell-tale sign that John and his Molotov's were nearby. At first he had thought that it was just off somewhere in the Courtyard, but as the etched got louder, he realised that John was coming towards them.

Rob stabbed his shovel into the ground beside the grave and turned around. At this point Matt too had his back towards the direction that John was approaching from. When Rob looked over, he saw that the big man was storming towards them, anger crawling across his face, with two of his goons in tow.

Questions raced through Rob's mind until he suddenly realised that John had finally come to enquire as to where Rob had been last night. He had abandoned his post and wandered off into the woods in the dead of night, instead of guarding the bottom of the Barn.

At that point in time Rob felt dread befall him. He thought he had got away with it, but John seeing him last night on the other side of the fence must have been playing on the man's mind. He had clearly been too busy dealing with the chaotic aftermath of last night's attack, but now it seemed that he had the time.

A single droplet of sweat formed on Rob's forehead. It was warm and felt as if it burned through his skin like acid as it ran down the side of his face.

"Matt!" John boomed out towards them, his eyes almost burning with the same heat as the nearby Tiki torch.

Matt, squatting down towards the grave to pull out a root that was in their way, turned his head around. He had not been John's favourite person as of late. The two men had clashed a number of times over the last few days, and none as awkward as yesterday morning in the Farmhouse's kitchen.

John stormed closer, seemingly picking up speed and spreading the distance between him and his goons. Rob noticed that his shotgun was strapped behind him with a makeshift sling made out of a couple of old belts.

At this point Matt realised that something was wrong, got to his feet and turned around to face whatever wrath was coming his way. Before he could even say a word, John pushed him with both hands and with such force that he fell backwards into the side of the grave, tripping down the step they had dug and crashed on the dirt beside it.

"What the fuck!" he managed to shout as he fell.

It was clear as day that John was not here to speak to Rob about abandoning his post. He was here for something else.

Rob felt his hand reach for his shovel, but he realised that one of John's henchmen was already holding it. He had pulled it from the ground and held it down at his side.

"You fucked up the lighting system!" John told him, as Matt picked himself up. "You got a lot of people killed!"

"What the hell man?!" Matt shouted back, attracting a few people who were still working in the Courtyard.

Thankfully there were only a couple left. Most of the survivors had gone inside to escape the cold.

John raised a finger towards him. "You said you had fixed the generator, that it would power the lights". John's hand turned into a fist. "But it stopped fucking working when we needed it".

"This is not my fault" Matt threw back as he stepped forward towards them.

"Hey" Rob interrupted, thinking he could try and defuse the situation. "Come on man. The generator is an old piece of shit. It is not his fault if..." Suddenly John gave him a burning look. Rob felt the stare cut straight through him. He held it for a few moments before turning back to Matt. "We needed those lights to keep the people safe. Without them we are as good as dead!"

"It is not my fault they went out!" Matt barked back at him. "I did what I could".

"These people are DEAD Matt!" John slammed back. Rob could hear the anger in his voice. "You told me it would keep them running as long as we have the fuel" he said.

Matt turned to Rob, puzzled, before turning back to the big man. "I said it SHOULD keep running. The whole thing is held together with extension cables and duct tape. I gave you no guarantees".

That must have angered John. He threw a punch at him, making contact with the side of his face and hitting Matt with such force that he fell to the ground. As Matt landed, he fell into the corpse of the woman with his hand landing in the soft blood soaked dirt and sinking into the ground.

Rob felt a hand reach for him as one of John's men must have anticipated Rob lending a hand here and doing something stupid.

"Get the fuck off of me" Rob said as he pulled his arm away. The man lifted up the shovel, as if to smash Rob over the head with it, when John's enormous hand grabbed a hold of it by the handle.

"Enough" he said and the other man let go. The shovel dropped to the floor. John turned to Matt. "You let the lighting system go down. Whether you meant to or not doesn't matter. Your negligence has caused the deaths of these people".

Matt didn't reply. He was on his hands and knees now beside the torso, still probably a little stunned by John's blow.

"Take a long look at her" John continued. "That woman's blood is on your hands now, you know". One of the goons sniggered slightly at the irony that Matt's hand was in fact covered in the blood and mud from where he had put it down to try and brace himself when he fell.

Rob went over to Matt and started to help him up. He knew it was not a smart move to do it in front of John. He did not want him to think he was picking Matt's side over the self-appointed leader, but he knew that John's accusations were insane. It was not Matt's fault that the lighting system had failed. Rob was sure that he had done the best he could with it, given the tools and the time he had to build it.

Rob didn't' look towards John as he helped Matt get to his feet. He knew he would be giving him a cold stare.

"You best fucking pray that system is working right this time" John told him. "We can't afford another fuck up like that, you know". John turned around. "Let's go. There is still stuff to do".

He walked off towards the Barn, his two men following close behind.

At this point Matt was now on his feet and rubbing the dirt off of his face. His cheek was now a bright red colour.

"Are you okay?" Rob asked him.

"The man's fucking lost it" Matt replied, staring at the blood and mud mixed together on his hand. After a few moments he watched as John disappeared behind the Barn's doors, with one of his men following him inside, while the other stood guard out the front of it.

"We can't stay here... not with him".

"What?" Rob asked stupidly. He knew that John was getting worse, but he was keeping them all alive.

"That man is a fucking psycho!" Matt blurted out. "It is bad enough the world has gone to shit... we have those inhuman creatures out there. We don't need another monster in here as well!"

"A monster?" Rob thought to himself. He had not really looked at it that way, but recently John had become somewhat of a tyrant around the Farm.

"We need to get the hell out of here" Matt told him. "Me and you. We need to leave the Farm".

"What about Pete?" Rob asked.

"Fuck Pete!" he replied. "He follows that fucking piece of shit. He is just another one of John's lackeys".

"Jesus" Rob said. "Look... go and get yourself washed up, alright? We will talk about this a little later".

Matt was too angry. He was not paying attention to Rob and was staring off towards the Barn. His wet hand now dripping onto the corpse beneath him.

"Hey!" Rob said loudly, finally getting Matt's attention. "It is too cold out here. Go and get yourself inside. Wash your hand. I will finish up here". Rob gestured towards the grave.

Matt paused for a moment. He did nothing but watch Rob as he went over and picked up the shovel from the ground where the goon had dropped it.

"Yeah..." he finally said. "Yeah I'll... I'll be..."

It appeared Matt was having difficulty finishing his own sentence. His mind was racing with what had just happened, as well as thoughts of escaping from the Farm. Rob decided to force him along.

"I'll see you in a minute" he told him. "We will talk about it then".

And with that Matt turned around and headed off towards the Farm without saying another word. Rob watched him go. His mind too was racing.

"Leave the Farm?" Rob wondered.

Rob wasn't sure about all of this. Matt was angry and Rob could understand why, but leaving the Farm? Where would they go? They had already picked clean the nearby town as best they could. They could have found some other morsels of food there, but how long could they really hope to survive out in the wilderness on their own. They would need light if they were to avoid being ripped apart by what waited for them in the darkness.

Rob's thoughts were on the strange man he had killed in self-defence in the town.

"How many more of them were hiding there?" He wondered.

Rather than attempting to lift the torso of the woman on his own, he decided it was best to drag her into the grave. After a moment Rob realised it was the better of the two option as only one organ fell out of the gaping hole in her stomach. Rob didn't have much knowledge of human anatomy, but the organ itself was not something he knew the name of, nor had ever seen before.

When the woman was in the hole, Rob slid the mushy deep red hunk of meat with his foot. It rolled over the side and splatted down beside her. A month or so ago the sight might have made Rob gag, but now he was used to it.

As he began shovelling the dirt over the top of the woman, his mind started thinking things from the other point of view. John had created some tension around here of late, but his attack on Matt could well have easily have just been out of anger or frustration for letting down the people he had vowed to protect. They saw him as a leader. No one else was willing to do the things that needed to get done. John had. Was that all so bad?

He had just simply done what was best for the Farm and the other survivors. He had kept them fed, kept them warm, and kept them relatively safe. The deaths from last night's attack had left people with a sour taste in their mouths. They thought that they were secure here. They had become lazy and had begun getting their lives back together. In reality they were far from safe. Last night had proved just how easy it was for the creatures to come and get them. They had shown up within seconds of the generator cutting out. The one who had caused all the fuss had been taken in a matter of moments after the lights went down, so it meant that they were never too far away.

Just then Rob felt their eyes on him. They were watching him through the trees. He looked up and tried to find their breath vaporing through the thick foliage, but there was nothing. For all Rob knew they did not breathe.

He started thinking about what Pete had said about them having no head. A memory flashed in his head of the dark teeth of the beasts as they tore into the flesh of the survivors last night. He had heard them feeding on their suffering as he stood guard beside the generator whilst John desperately tried to get it back up and running.

He realised shortly afterwards that his mind was all over the place. He needed to think on what Matt had said. He didn't think that they should try and make it out there on their own. He honestly did not think they would survive for very long. How far could they really get? Would John really just let them go? Maybe he would Matt... but would he want to run the risk of them running into other survivors and telling them what they knew of the Farm? Rob knew how John was with strangers. The poor man and woman who had shown up here yesterday had proved that. They had tried to make it on their own and ended up mutilated in the woods only a few hours later. He did not want to endure that fate.

All of a sudden Rob felt his stomach growl. He was hungry. He had been working for nearly six hours and he still had not had breakfast. No one had been hungry this morning. It seemed that losing people you knew and had lived with in a limited space for a month had made people lose their appetites.

That was another thing that put Rob off of Matt's idea; what were they going to do about food? There was no way John would let them go with their packs full of food, if he let them go at all. Would they steal from the Barn? The thought made Rob's hunger fade. He felt sick at the idea of what would happen if they were caught stealing, or even after they had stolen the food and were on the run. John would hunt them down. He and his men would search the forest until they found them. They would have been accused of stealing the other food from a few days ago.

Rob was convinced that trying to leave the Farm was all in all a terrible idea.

He grabbed another load of dirt on the end of the shovel and went to pour it into the grave when he noticed that the woman's maroon hoodie was no longer covering her. Instead a section of the mud was revealing a navy blue colour between them. Rob had seen this colour before.

He pushed some of the earth away with the end of the shovel and it was clear that the woman was now wearing a blue dress. Something was different. It was not the same woman as before. Her skin tone was lighter than the woman who had been cut in half. This woman seemed younger.

Rob moved the shovel up to the soil covering her face. As it moved away, he could see that the face was completely different too. The sight of her started to make Robert's heart beat faster. It thudded in his chest more violently with each passing second. As more earth moved he saw that face again. The woman... he knew her. Her eyes opened. They were pure white, but Rob could see them staring straight at him. He turned his head away.

Just then the wind began to blow. The cold air stabbed at Rob's skin and froze him to the bone. His eyes began to water and then blink three or four times. When he turned back and looked down, the blue was gone. All that remained was the half buried remains of the woman in maroon. Her eyes were closed, one was filled with mud.

Rob's head began to throb. These visions were getting more frequent. He had seen a lot of things over the last few days, so much so that his head was killing him. He realised that not only had he not eaten all day, he had not drank anything either. He thought that it would be best to finish up and get inside, out of the cold, and get himself something to eat.
Darker clouds were gathering above, and Rob had spent as much time as he had wanted to with the dead.

Day Thirty One – Part 2

It was late afternoon when Pete came over to Rob with a tin of plums and offered him it. The living room was cold. All of the Farm's citizens were inside. Some were in the Storehouse or upstairs, but the kitchen and living room were the busiest he had ever seen them. Even with this many people inside, the temperature of the rooms was still cold. The wooden foundation of the Farmhouse had begun to show signs of aging. Cracks had appeared all around and these were letting in drafts of cold air. At this time they had not got the heating working and so a lot of people inside were still wearing their coats and hats, whilst others had quilts thrown over them. Whenever any of them so much as breathed, Rob could see a small cloud of air vapour appear.

It was clear that winter was now here. People had spoken of its coming for a while now, but it had finally caught up to them. It had seemed like only a few weeks ago that the sun had been out. They knew that this was just the beginning. It was going to get a lot colder.

Rob, already having finished a lukewarm can of tomato soup and some stale bread about a half hour later, refused Pete's offer politely. He had been sitting in the Farm's living room in the corner alone, staring out of the window at the flames from the torches in the front as they flickered in the wind. Rob had been sitting there alone with his thoughts until Pete had approached him. He had been thinking about the dire situation that they were in. Tension between Matt and John had caused some concern around the Farm. He had heard some hushed voices mention it, but nothing he could make out. Only a few people had seen what exactly happened earlier today beyond the fence. He was sure that there were rumours going around, but Rob didn't want to get involved. By sticking up for Matt he already felt far too involved than he should have been.

"So, what's going on?" Pete asked him after Rob's refusal.
"What do you mean?" Rob replied. He knew exactly what Pete was referring too, but he had hoped that he was mistaken.
"You know... the thing with Rob and Matt"
Rob felt his stomach tighten and he stopped himself from sighing with frustration. He knew that it was only a matter of time before people came around and asked him. He had wondered if one of the other people he did not know would attempt to speak to him. Would they have started off with some awkward small talk or would they have jumped right in with the big question? Either way he didn't mind as much because it was Pete.
"Yeah... emm" the words caught in Rob's throat. He was not sure how to put it. "He... John blames Matt for the generator going off".
Pete stared at him for a moment with a puzzled look on his face. "Oh right. Is that why he hit him?" Pete asked.
"Yeah" Rob said turning back towards the window.
After a few moments of silence Pete spoke again. "I didn't think that generator would have run all those lights".

From that statement Rob knew that Pete had already sided with John. He had wondered for a brief moment who he might have picked, but as of late he had agreed with nearly everything the big man had said.
"It can run them fine" Rob said annoyed. He could tell from Pete's facial expressions that he was picking up on his annoyance. "There was something dodgy about the generator itself".

"Oh right" Pete replied and began to turn away. "Do you think someone should go up and see Matt?"

By someone, Rob knew that he meant him. Pete would not have gone to see if Matt was okay as it might have made him look as if he was in Matt's corner; a place no one wanted to be in this very delicate situation.

Rob didn't turn away from the window. He gave the slightest of nods that Pete thankfully acknowledged and walked away. He knew he was right. Someone needed to go upstairs and make sure Matt wasn't doing anything stupid. His nod had spawned from that thought. Pete must had assumed that the nod meant that Rob would be the one to go and do it. He knew no one else would do it, so he guessed that it was up to him.

Matt had been quiet since he came inside from his run in with John earlier. When he last saw him, Matt had disappeared inside to clean his hand and get his head together. It seemed that no one had heard or seen him since ascending the stairs a few hours ago. Not even Pete had spoken to him, and it was even more awkward for him as the two of them shared one of the larger bedrooms in this building together.

There was another bathroom up here with a sink that he had probably used, after which he had probably gone into his room to sulk like some adolescent teen, which was understandable. He must have felt like the only person who could see John for the man he was becoming.

"Or has already become" Rob thought when he reached the top of the stairs.

A glow had caught his attention from the window beside the staircase. The view showed most of the Courtyard behind the Farmhouse. From here he could see the side of the Barn, the Tool Shed, and a bit of the Storehouse, which was obstructed by a large overgrown tree. The glow had come from the bright flames emitting from the bonfire. It was clear that someone had got the thing lit. Hopefully that might produce some more heat to help get them through the night.

He could see the large light grey clouds forming over the top of the farmland. They looked as if they would burst at any moment. Snow was the last thing the survivors needed right now. It was getting hard to forage in the woods as it was. Rob hoped that the food they had got from the Town might have taken them through the winter, especially with John rationing it.

Just then he saw a flicker of movement by the Storehouse. A figure was running across the Courtyard in the direction of the Barn. The trees and the flames concealed him for a time, but just before he disappeared inside the Barn, he saw that the person was David. He was carrying something close to his chest. He vanished behind the wooden door a moment later and the Courtyard faded back into stillness. If it was not for the flickering of flames then he would have thought that the window was a painting.

Just before Rob's hand made contact with Matt and Pete's bedroom door, Rob suddenly realised he did not know what to say. He knew that if it was the other way around, then having someone asking if he was okay would have really pissed him off. So he stood there for a moment, his hand still frozen in a pre-knocking fashion. He thought it would be best if he asked him something else, that way he could gauge the situation and how Matt was doing. It was a similar tactic to what Pete had done earlier to Rob, but this was different. Rob was not here to snoop for information and gossip.

Matt had a large supply of batteries in his pack, Rob knew. He had collected them and stored them in his backpack since the town. This was just in case they found or needed to use something that didn't have a battery. In a world where flashlights were a means of keeping yourself alive, it was always best to carry around a few spare batteries.

He knocked on the door. After a short while Rob heard movement coming from within. The door clicked open and Matt's face appeared between the door and the frame. Rob was glad to see that he had not tried to make a break for it, or worst still, tried to kill himself. He could see the mark on it from where John had hit him. It looked sore.

"How's it going?" Rob asked almost slapping himself in the face with the palm of his own hand. The greeting had come automatically to him. He was not going to ask how he doing or if he was okay. He was here to get some batteries for his flashlight and work out how the man was doing. Just before Matt could answer, Rob cut him off. "I just wanted to see if you had any double A batteries. My light is dimming and I don't really want to be caught out there with my pants down, right?"

Was that a joke? Was it a question he expected Matt to answer? Rob wasn't quite sure. Thankfully Matt replied to Robert's original question. "Yeah... sure thing" he said as he pulled the door open. Rob looked at his hand and saw that he had in fact washed it, which was good to see. He had also changed his clothes from the ones he had got dirty earlier. That was something Rob had not actually done yet.

He went inside and the door closed behind him. It was warmer in here than it had been anywhere else in the Farm.

The room itself was a bit of a mess, but it had often been that way. This was slightly different however. Normally Matt's bed was always made in the mornings, but the cover looked as if he might have been sleeping in it.

"Did I wake you?" Rob asked.

Matt went over to the corner of the room where a pile of clothes covered a few boxes and bags. "No... I mean yes" Matt replied. "I didn't sleep at all last night. No one did. I was just trying to catch up on some". He started going through the items, pulling clothes off of the pile and throwing them onto the bed. "I couldn't sleep at first. I kept thinking about earlier". Rob noticed his tone had changed. He sounded as if he might have been upset. "I have been doing some thinking".

"Right..." Rob said inquisitively.

Matt stopped what he was doing and turned around. "What if it was my fault? The generator... last night's attack. What if I had done something wrong and it blew a fuse? I could easily have messed up the wiring by mistake. What if it was my fault those people died?"

Rob felt a stab cut through him. It was sad to see Matt taking the blame for what had happened.

"Come on Matt" Rob said surprisingly sympathetic. "Don't beat yourself up over this. You couldn't have known that was going to happen. For all you knew it could have just been a pretty shitty generator". That made Matt laugh. "Don't listen to John. He was just angry and looking for someone to blame. He wants to protect everyone here... or he wants to keep this place going. The type of guy he is... he doesn't know how to deal with something going wrong like that. He has to find someone to be responsible for it".

Rob was surprised where all that had come from. As Matt nodded and turned back to the pile he was searching through, Rob actually felt as if he had cheered him up a bit and that the matter was kind of settled. It seemed that his ideas of running out on the Farm had faded away, along with his anger. He thought about saying a bit more, but he didn't want to ruin it and end up saying something that might have annoyed him further. He thought it was best to just stop there. Matt seemed okay. He just needed some time.

"This will all sort itself out in a couple of days and then everything should be back to normal" Rob thought as he turned towards the bedroom door. He could hear a slight commotion going on downstairs.

"Oh... where the hell has that got to?" Matt asked, himself more than Rob, as he pull down one of the boxes and put it shoddily onto the bed. The box slid off and crashed onto the floor before Rob even had a chance to react and catch it. Matt didn't seem to notice or even be bothered by it.

The sound of a commotion travelled up the stairs. It sounded as if a whole herd of people were running up them.

"What is...?" Rob went to say when Matt drew his attention.

"My pack... it's gone!" The noise moved across the landing outside the bedroom and grew louder and louder with each passing second. Matt still had not noticed. "Where the fuck has that gone? I always leave it right here".

In that moment the door burst open. Rob brought his hands up to somehow defend himself, but the display looked almost comical. Both he

and Matt stared on, stunned, as Maria, two of John's goons, and another two people from downstairs swarmed into the room. They were armed.
"What the hell is...?" Matt went to say when one the men smashed him across the face with a wooden pole that made a horrific crunching noise that Rob was not sure was Matt's skull or the pole itself breaking.
Rob himself was shoved aside in the chaos and fell backwards onto the bed as another one of the men kicked Matt in the side of the ribs. He tried to speak and shout out, but he was cut short by further kicks.
Maria stood at the door holding it open. "Come on" she told them. "Let's get him outside".
Rob barely had a moment to realise what was going on as the men began dragging Matt out of the bedroom by his feet and arms. It was not unlike how he and Matt had held the corpses of the people who had died the night before when they had chucked them into their graves earlier.
"Get off of him!" Rob called out as he climbed to his feet, but by that time they had disappeared out of the room.
When he got to the doorway, he saw the men taking Matt down the stairs. He was struggling a little, but most of the fight had been hit out of him. Maria lead the party, which at this stage had caught the attention of the entire Farmhouse. An older couple were peering out of their bedroom door to see what all the commotion was about. Rob ran past them and followed the party down the stairs.

Maria held the backdoor of the Farmhouse open as the men took Matt outside. Rob managed to catch up with them at the door leading outside, but a crowd of onlookers blocked his way. He pushed his way through them and as he did he could feel the cold air hitting him in face. It was bitter.

Outside he saw John standing before the bonfire. Beside him he could see David and all around them a few of the other survivors had emerged from their quarters. A few were coming across the Courtyard from the Storehouse, clearly attracted by the noise, and the rest were shoving their way out of the Farmhouse to form a troop before the big man as his men brought Matt before him.

The sky had begun to turn dark now. Dusk was approaching and the snowy clouds above removed any warm orange glow from the sky. John's two goons and the two men who had got involved had dropped Matt at John's feet and stepped back, creating a barrier between them and the other survivors. Rob tried to make his way forward. One of the goons turned around and pushed Rob in the chest, causing him to fall a little backwards. Before he could even say anything, John began to speak. He started by asking David for something. David, still clutching whatever it was he had tightly to his chest, released his grasp on it and handed it over to him. At this point Matt had managed to get his bearings and sat up slightly on the grass. Rob could see that the back of it was now covered in wet mud and a little bit of his own blood.

Very few people in the crowd had any idea what was going on. Rob saw many bewildered faces amongst them and he knew that his face just as confused by the entire ordeal. None of them said a word. Rob expected to hear a few questions murmured between them, but there was nothing.

John stood there staring at the beaten man on the ground in front of him as the fire burned behind like hell had opened up all around. After a while he spoke.

"This yours?" he asked, not so much a question as more of a statement. John knew that whatever he had belonged to Matt. He threw it onto the ground. It was Matt's pack. As it hit the floor the unfastened flap at the top opened and the contents of the bag flew out across the ground.

A couple of gasps could be heard, closely followed by the murmuring that Rob had expected earlier, but he could not see what it was that had come out. The larger of John's two henchmen blocked his way. Rob risked getting another shove, or worse, and he moved in closer, peering over the man's shoulder.

There, laying scattered on the floor between John's feet and the half beaten man on the grass, was an assortment of cans, tins and packets of different foods.

"The stolen food?!" someone in the crowed cried out and a few more gasps could be heard, as if the whole lot of them now completely understood what was going on.

"I've never seen that! That wasn't in my pack!" Matt struggled to defend himself, still clearly quite injured from the attack a few moments ago. He brought his arm up and wiped the blood from his mouth with his sleeve. John just stood there, staring at him silently. His eyes burned as much as the bonfire did behind him.

"So this isn't your bag then?" David asked cockily, knowing full well it was.

"It was just full of junk" Matt told them, but it made no difference. Rob could see from the faces of everyone around that no one believed him.

"Stop this!" Rob called out, shoving his way past the man in front of him, who immediately turned and grabbed Rob and tried to hold him back.

"Get the fuck off of me!"

John looked over towards him for a brief moment before turning back to the pleading man on the floor. As he turned back, another one of John's men ran over to Rob and grabbed him as well. The two men pushed

Robert onto the ground. He felt the cold wet dirt hit him in the face. The ground had been thoroughly trampled and so the Courtyard was a lot wetter than the rest of the surrounding grassland.

"I didn't take anything" Matt said, sounding pathetic. Everyone could tell he was a broken man.

If anyone else wanted to stop whatever was going to happen, then no one else dared intervene. Rob had been the only one to try and put a stop to this madness, and he was now held down on the floor with, what he could only assume, was one of the men standing on him to hold him in place. As for the rest of them; the survivors of the Farm, they were standing gawking at everything as it transpired. Some of them were nodding with approval, ready to spectate whatever was to follow.
Rob tried to shout out, but as he opened his mouth, mud and water began to pour into it.

Matt pulled himself up slightly, now kneeling before John. "You have to believe me... I didn't take the food".

John, with his cold stern face, stared at him. After Matt had finished pleading, the whole Courtyard fell silent for a few moments. All that could be heard was the sound of the wind gently blowing. John began to speak.

"We have all suffered, you know" he started by saying to his followers. "We bore witness to our world fall apart. Our lives changed that day the darkness came. Our friends and families were taken away from us all". He lowered his shotgun to his side, gripping it by the barrel of the gun and letting the handle almost touch the ground. "We have had to struggle every single day to survive since the day the world died. We all have had to fight to hold on to our humanity. We started a new life here in this place... a place we managed to secure, defend and use to try and get what lives we have back to normal. But it has not been easy. We have lost friends and family here as well. Last night was the most we lost since the day that this all began. I blamed this man for that. He had helped set up the lights you see above us now... and I blamed him for what happened last night. But the truth of it... the deaths are on me".

Rob was taken aback by that. He was shocked to see John taking responsibility for what happened.

"I should have made sure they were working properly. I should have checked that they did not go out in a time when we needed them most. I can see that now, you know". He called out as loud as he could so that everyone could hear him. "I do not blame this man for that".

The crowd was completely silent, hanging on every word that their faithful leader was speaking in his moment of wisdom.

"But this..." his voice changed. The tone in his voice turned harsher as his hand gestured towards the open bag on the ground. "This we cannot have".

Rob could almost hear the sound of everyone's hearts skip a beat as John fell silent.

"Please..." cried Matt, now tears beginning to stream down his face. "I don't know how that..."

Suddenly John swung his shotgun across like a baseball bat. It crashed into the side of Matt's face, sending a spray of spit and blood across in the opposite direction like a scene from a boxing movie. The whole thing happened so fast that it caught everyone by surprise. Matt hit the ground hard. He was still conscious, but barely.

Rob struggled and managed to throw one of the men on top of him off. He tumbled backwards and tripped over his feet into the mob behind. He grabbed hold of the collar of the shirt of the other man, now trying desperately to keep Rob down on the ground.

As a fist, from somewhere, made contact with Rob's face, he caught a glimpse of John standing in front of the fire with his gun now being held in both hands. He had a tight grip on the handle and his finger was resting on the trigger. He could hear the strange buzzing sound once again that felt as if it was spewing out of his skull and filling his head up with liquid. His eyes began to water and when he blinked, he saw that the bonfire was now a small mudbrick building with a wooden roof. The fire burned more intensely than it had done a few moments ago. The ground around them was now nothing but sand, and Matt had been replaced by a young Arab man, now pleading for his life.

John stood in exactly the same pose as he had been in front of the bonfire. His weapon had now changed to some kind of automatic rifle, and he now wore military fatigues. The sound of a helicopter raced over, but when Rob looked up into the air, he could not see anything but the strange dark colourless void that surrounded them.

Another blow to the face and Rob was back in the Courtyard. The helicopter sound faded along with the buzzing. Rob blinked a few times and the world faded back to normality. John still stood before Matt, who was now bleeding profusely from a wound that had opened up on his cheek.

"You have stolen food from us" John's voice boomed out like a preacher shouting out the word of god. "More food than any one person should have in these harsh times. Such selfishness when we are all struggling to continue. A thief amongst us is like a cancer eating away at our survival. What gives one person the right to steal from the group? Stealing food from us is as bad as putting a gun to someone's head and pulling the trigger. By taking what little we have, you are sentencing us to death".

"I didn't..." Matt fought to say but the other words never came.

By this point John had convinced most of the other survivors that Matt was guilty and deserved whatever punishment was coming to him. A few of them were almost at the point of cheering whatever John said. Rob saw Pete there in the crowd. His expression told Rob that he too was following John and welcomed whatever was to follow.

"We need to make an example of this man... you all need to witness what happens when you try and destroy all we have built here".

"No!" Rob cried out as he managed to get free of the two men holding him back. He charged forward across the open space in the Courtyard. John did not take the slightest bit of notice of Rob's approach. As Matt reached a hand upwards towards John and prepared to mouth something along the lines of "Please" or "Don't", John pulled the trigger. The shotgun exploded in an eruption of bright intense heat and a colossal blast of noise that rang out, for what seemed like, hundreds of miles around.

Rob was almost stopped dead as the pellets from the shotgun shell shot through the small space between the end of the barrel and Matt's head, making contact with his face almost instantaneously and exploding his entire cranium into a mist of pink and red vapour as segments of his skull and flesh, muscle and hair, flew out all around in different directions. Everyone was stunned by the display of execution and the people on the right, their legs were almost covered in Matt's blood. His body fell lifelessly back onto the ground and all that remained of his face was the bottom half of his lower jaw. An artery spat out stream after stream of deep red blood as his leg twitched on the ground, digging into the mud by John's feet.

Rob stood there in shock gawking at Matt's body for a few seconds before he felt the burning rage form in the pit of his stomach. He felt the anger force its way up his torso and into his lungs, almost igniting them. His teeth ground together as he turned his gaze upon John, who had now turned to face Rob. The end of his barrel was still red hot with a small trail of smoke coming out of the end of it and rising up into the air. Rob, without thinking, charged towards the big man. It was a stupid thing to do as it was completely based on impulse and adrenaline. There was no rational thoughts running through Rob's mind at the time. He had no idea what he was going to do when he reached him, but he was sure he had a pretty good idea of the outcome.

When he got there, John had already had the time to prepare and with one quick motion, he swung the end of the gun into Rob's already beaten face and knocked him out onto the ground. In the short instant before everything went dark, Rob felt the burning sensation in his stomach fade away, as if the fires inside of him had been put out with icy cold water. The heat had been replaced by the scorching metal of the shotgun's barrel as it made contact with his face. This passed within seconds as he felt the cold wet dirt hit him as he fell to the floor. In his last few moments before blacking out, he saw that Matt's leg had finally stopped twitching. He could see the silhouette of their tyrannical leader as the fires burned all around him.

After that everything seemed to fade into darkness.

Day Thirty Two – Part 1

Out of the dark depths came a bright light. It shone through the trees and all behind him was nothing but a powerful white. It was all that could be seen. When he looked up, Rob could not see the treetops. They were still hidden behind the darkness. From where he stood, it felt to him that the trees merely faded away to nothing the higher they went.

When he turned back to the light, Rob could see that the intense white was pulsing frantically, almost violently. He could feel it pulling him towards it. He reached out and felt the tips of his fingers go numb as some of the furthest away trees were swallowed by the light. In the middle of it, Rob thought he could see faces. They were faces from his past; his friends, his family, and his co-workers. They were all there. He could see memories of his former life. He saw ones from when he was a child and others from long before the darkness came. They were frantic and fragmented, flicking on and off and distorting the longer they went on for. They were colourless somehow. Rob felt as if he could have stood there forever just staring at it.

Soon the images turned evil. The faces became tormented with looks of anger or anguish upon them. They were not his memories. He realised that he did not know the people at all. He recognised a few faces here and there, but they were from the group of survivors at the Farm. They seemed as if they were individual memories.

He saw the flames burning once again with John standing before them in some war torn country. He saw a woman hit a man with her car and drive away. There was a man holding his hand over the face of a loved one in a hospital bed. He saw Mike before he raped that woman in the alley. One man was handing out packets of powder to a teenager. Another woman was opening her arm up with a razor. A man was stalking another from the shadows before creeping up on him and driving a blade into his throat. Again the images were all disjointed and broken. As if Rob was staring at a moving jigsaw that seemed impossible to put together. The woman in the blue dress appeared before finally a severed head of a different woman in ice could be seen. The images began to flash too quickly that Rob could not even begin to keep track of them. Some of them were horrific but soon disappeared just as quickly.

He began to step away from it. It started as a few slow paces backwards, but as soon as the white light started moving closer through the trees, Rob knew that he needed to run. He turned and saw the darkness before him. The trees stretched out for what seemed like an eternity up ahead. There was no sign of anything in that direction, but that didn't stop him. Rob could feel himself being drawn towards the white. It felt as if it was pulling him apart piece by piece. He started to run. He ran as fast as he could but it did not seem to help. The white light was chasing him. He tried to look over his shoulder, but it was no good. All he could see was the trees he had just passed, fade away behind him.

As he ran, Rob saw that the trees in front of him were reappearing in exactly the same place that they had been before he passed them. He was running but he did not seem to be getting anywhere. He felt the white light yawning at his heels. He thought about turning around and facing it. He knew that if he did, he would not be able to escape. It would close around him and swallow him whole.

Flashes of white light shot out from beside him as he ran. At first Rob didn't pay attention to them. He was too focused on trying desperately to get away from whatever it was that was chasing him.

After three or four more, he finally took notice. They flashed like lightening within the trees beside him. They were images again. The flashes depicted events that had transpired since all this had started over a month ago. He saw the creatures emerging out of the shadows as the city's lights went out. He saw his party moving through the woods before the face of the man Rob had killed mercifully appeared. He mimed the words "Kill me", as he had done the night Rob had shot him. Blood was still trickling down the side of his face as the creatures tore into him. Another flash on the other side of the forest and Rob saw Karen and her husband being torn apart. The creatures disembowelled them and he saw Karen's face turn to agony as she called out in a muted scream. After that Mike's face appeared. Rob saw himself with him beside the stream. The two of them looked flushed and out of breath. The Rob in the image lifted up his gun slowly and pulled the trigger. The bullet flew through the air and hit Mike square in the chest. Another flash showed Mike's facial expression as he fell to the ground, his eyes growing cold.

As Rob continued on through the nightmare that was this never ending forest, the flashes came more frequently. He saw the faces of the other survivors on the Farm. Pete, Matt, Maria and the others. Suddenly another burst of light appeared and he saw the face of the homeless man in town. He had the same insane expression that was on his face when he had tried to attack him.

Finally images of Matt's death flashed up. John hitting him across the face with his gun, Matt pleading for his life, and the crowd doing nothing to stop it. This was before it showed quick flashes of Rob trying desperately to fight his way through them, being knocked to the ground, and finally the execution of Matt by John's hand.

Just then a voice called out. "Robert" it said. It was faint but he could tell that it was a woman. Rob knew that voice. The white flashes of light almost recoiled from the noise. They tried to force their way around Rob as they had done before, but the voice came again and the light withdrew.

"Robert" she cried out, only this time it was slightly louder. It was ahead of him, somewhere in the darkness beyond. The woman called to him and drew him in a particular direction. Rob felt his feet head towards it and the voice grew even louder than before. "Please… this way" she called out to him. "Join…"

Now he could tell he was heading the right way. The trees began to change and the white light that was chasing him seemed to fall behind. He ran with everything that he could, all without feeling at all tired, towards the noise.

As the white faded, the world all around him began to grow darker. The trees themselves began to disappear up ahead and soon he was just running towards a black emptiness that stretched on and on. He ran like this for a while before the voice came at him again, this time it was so loud that he felt the woman's warm breath brush up against his ear. "Join us".

"Robert!" she said and suddenly he woke up.

Rob jolted up and saw that he was back in his bedroom at the top of the Farmhouse. He gasped for air as his food slipped off of the bed and knocked over something that had previously been stacked against it. "Wha?" he said confused as his hand touched the painted wooden wall beside him. Rob was checking to make sure the world around him was real. The dream had been so vivid that he had felt as if he was standing somewhere in the darkened woods, running from the strange white light that was chasing him.

Suddenly an intense sharp pain came rushing back to him as everything slid into focus. He brought a hand up to his head and felt a lump, along with a couple of improvised stitches that had been sown over a small wound on his forehead. As soon as he touched he, his mind flashed with images of what had happened before. He saw Matt pleading for his life, John standing over him with his gun as the bonfire burned away. He remembered the cold and wet mud hitting him in the face. When he looked at his collar, he saw that he still had dried blood and dirt stained on it.

"We didn't think you were ever going to wake up. John certainly did hit you for six" a voice called out to him. It was a woman's voice but different from the one in his dream. When he looked up towards the source of it, he saw Maria standing in the doorway. "What were you dreaming about?" she asked him, taking a casual step forward.

"What did I dream of?" Rob thought to himself, almost saying the sentence aloud. Instead he managed just a simple "I..." before losing himself in his thoughts. "What did I dream?" he asked himself, trying desperately to remember. It seemed as if the memory of his dream was fading away with each passing second. He remembered the woods and the darkness... and running. Or was he? He could not remember.

"I don't know" he finally said as the look on her face was making him feel unsettled.

"How are you feeling?" she asked him.

Rob rubbed his eyes. "I feel like shit" he told her. All of a sudden he remembered the blast from John's gun as Matt's head exploded. "What happened to..." his name became stuck in his throat. Maria thankfully knew what he was going to say.

"To Matt?" she replied. Rob gave her a nod. "John umm... John had him taken into the woods".

The words pieced through him. "The woods?" he repeated. Rob imagined the crows pecking at his corpse. "My god..."

Maria decided to change the subject. "Listen... John knows that you were acting out of anger over what happened to Matt". She was trying her best to sound sincere, but it seemed like she was just listing the facts. "We all knew that you were friends with him. Nobody holds it against you or thinks that you were in anyway involved. John wants you to know this. He feels pretty terrible about what happened to you".

"But not Matt?" Rob asked. Maria didn't answer.

"He wants you to know that you are still a valued member of this community, and he hopes that this unpleasantness hasn't changed you in anyway". She sounded like an office middle manager talking to a colleague.

"Why isn't John telling me this?" Rob asked. He was sick of this bullshit. "Where is he?"

"John is out with a hunting party. They are hoping to catch something big for dinner tonight".

Rob thought about the fact that they had not seen any animals in the woods for weeks now. What was the chances that something would now have suddenly turned up?

"Listen" Maria said, her tone dropping and she almost sounded normal. "I know what happened to Matt sucks. It wasn't a very pleasant thing for anyone to witness... and I know he was your friend. Just take it easy okay? Just lay low for a while and help out where you can. I am sure this will all blow over".

Rob didn't reply. He turned towards the window and stared out of it, not looking at anything in particular.

Maria left it a few moments before speaking again. "I've got to go and catalogue the food... now that we have the stuff back that Matt stole..."
Rob cut her off. "Matt didn't steal anything". He could tell that she knew she had made a mistake, but it was already far too late.

"Right... well I will be going" she said as she turned around and went to leave without saying goodbye.

As the door closed slowly, Rob thought of the people living at the Farm. None of them had made any attempt to try and stop John from doing what he did. All of them stood idly by and watched as John obliterated all traces of Matt's face. No one other than Rob dared to stand up and make a stand against him.

The more Rob thought on it, the more he could feel his blood boiling. The pain in his head was growing and he felt his hands clenching tightly. He tried to breathe and relax, but he couldn't shake away the thoughts running around in his mind. How did John know he was the thief? Rob knew that Matt's bag had only been used to store bits and bobs he had found while out exploring the town. He carried a variety of different battery types in there he knew, but he didn't think he would have put the stolen food in there. There were a hundred better, and far less incriminating places he could have stored it. Outside would have been Rob's suggestion. Somewhere where if it was discovered, then it would not be able to be traced back to him. It would have been stupid to have left the stolen food where he slept, inside his own pack. He may as well have spray painted his name on the Barn's doors, informing them that it was him who had done it.

There was definitely something wrong here. The backpack could not have been Matt's. Which was a possibility since a couple of bags around here did look rather similar to one another, given that most people had taken them from the sports equipment store in town. That was one possible solution. Unfortunately Matt's bag was missing at the time the one with the food in had showed up.

Another solution could have been that someone had framed him. They had taken the batteries and electrical stuff out of his bag, stashed them elsewhere and then replaced them with the food. John was already angry at Matt and blamed him for what happened the night before last. Rob did not believe for an instant what John had said yesterday about it. He knew that the big man still held a grudge against Matt for the lighting system going down. His talk of himself being accountable was nothing but bullshit. Rob could see it on his face. It was all a facade to get the mob on his side.

Identifying Matt as the culprit would have been just enough to send John over the edge. There was no way the person who had done this could have known that John would have killed him. But he would have known that John was close to the breaking point. It was the perfect plan, as it left the true perpetrator off the hook and life at the Farm would have continued as normal. John might have lifted the strict rationing regime.

Rob felt he owed it to Matt to find out what had happened and who was behind it. He knew that he had not taken the food. Someone else must have done this, whether intentional or not, and there was only one person he needed to talk to about this.

David had been the one who had shown up with Matt's backpack. Had he taken it from Matt's room? Or did he find it elsewhere? Had he found it on his own, or had someone handed it over to him? There were too many unanswered questions. Rob knew that it was not going to bring Matt back from the dead, but at least he could find some closure in knowing who had really stolen the food from the Barn. David did have access and Rob did not trust him. He was another one of John's lackeys who followed him blindly. He would need to go and have a chat with him. Without John here in the Farm, it was the perfect time to do so.

Rob could not have anticipated the events that would unfold as the day went on. No one could have seen what was waiting for them on the horizon.

Day Thirty Two – Part 2

Outside the world was bitterly could. The heat that the bonfire gave off was not doing anything. Frost was beginning to form on the grass in the Courtyard. As Rob moved, he could hear the crunch beneath his feet as the thick grey clouds hung overhead all across the sky.

Few people were outside. Only the ones that were committed to the tasks they had been given dared to brave the cold, and even then they wrapped themselves up in hats, socks, scarfs and multiple layers of clothing.

In hindsight, Rob had not had the idea to dress like this. All he wore was his jacket over the top of a T-shirt and jeans. Inside the Farmhouse it had been surprisingly warm. Rob must have taken it for granted and not realised that it was most likely due to the amount of bodies that were huddled together inside. He thought about going back and putting on a few other layers, but decided it would be better if he just made his journey across the Courtyard as quickly as possible.

As he headed towards the Storehouse; the place David spent most of his time of late, Rob tried to stick as close to the bonfire as possible. He could feel a slight warmth coming off of the flames that gently touched the side of his face, but it was soon replaced with the harsh stab of cold as it burned against his skin.

He passed by the spot where John had ended Matt's life. The last time Rob had been here, John had smashed him in the face with his shotgun and it had sent him onto the floor beside Matt's corpse. He remembered each moment from that part of yesterday as he walked past a large section of flattened grass. It could have been the very section where Matt lay before John pulled the trigger.

Rob could feel the burning sensation building up inside him again as he thought of it. He remembered Matt's pleas for mercy that fell upon John's deaf ears. He was going to kill him, Rob knew. John had already made his mind up long before Matt was even dragged out of the Farmhouse kicking and screaming.

"Hey Rob" a voice called out behind him. He turned around to see Peter exiting the Farmhouse. "What are you doing?" he asked.

Rob felt conflicting emotions boil up inside of him. On the one hand Peter was the closest person to a friend he had in this place, especially now that Matt was gone, but on the other, he could remember seeing Peter's face in the horde of watchers who did nothing to stop John from murdering.

"What..." Rob said, abruptly stopping as he realised he had nothing else to say.

Peter was caught off guard and stuttered a bit before finally speaking up. "Are you okay man?"

"What is you want Peter?" Rob asked him coldly.

Peter stared at him for a moment before saying "Never mind", turning around and heading back towards the Farmhouse.

Rob watched him for a few moments before calling out to him to get him to stop. Peter did. He turned back around and came over to him once more.

"Look, I'm sorry" Rob said apologetically. "It's been a rough couple of days... and all that shit that happened last night..."

Peter cut him off there. "That is what I wanted to talk to you about. I know Matt was your friend..."

"He was your friend too!" Rob told him.

Peter looked at the floor. "Yeah... well, after everything that happened yesterday. It might be best if you just kept out of the way for a little while, you know, for your own sake". The words angered Rob. He could feel his fist clenching and thoughts of smacking Peter across his face began to flash in his mind. Peter must have seen it. "All I am saying is that maybe we need a few days for this to blow over". Rob stared at him, not saying a word. After an awkward few seconds, Peter spoke once again. "I don't want you to go and do something stupid and get yourself in trouble, is all. We should just try and get through the next few days as quickly and as quietly as possible".

Rob turned and walked off towards the Storehouse as he was originally doing before Peter stopped him. He could feel Peter's gaze upon him and then a short while later he heard him ascend the steps outside the Farmhouse's backdoor and go back inside.

Peter had fallen in line with the rest of John's men. They were all under his reign now. He had used the execution of Matt as an example to the others to show them who was in charge and what would happen if anyone tried to mess with him. Everyone was now under his command. Rob felt like Matt was the only one who could see through the man, and now he was dead, leaving Rob questioning as to whose side to take.

Would he dare try and oppose John and risk everything? Or did he blindly follow him as the rest of them did, like a shepherd with his flock?

Rob didn't know the answers, but he was beginning to not care. He knew that Peter would go running off and tell the big man as soon as he got back from his hunting trip.

"Tell him what?" Rob wondered to himself. All he was doing was finding David to ask him about Matt's bag. At least that was what his brain kept telling himself, but he knew that something was on the horizon. There was a storm fast approaching at the Farm. It was all just a moment away from striking.

By this point Rob was near the Tool Shed. He could hear the engine running on the generator. Even though it was the middle of the day, the string of LED lights that circled around above the Courtyard were still on. He wasn't sure if they had been left on since the night before last when the Farm was attacked, or if they had been turned off for a few hours here and there. He seemed to remember them being on all throughout the day as he and Matt had dug shallow graves for the victims of the creatures, as well as during Matt's 'trial' and execution.

Beside the Tool Shed were the piles of fuel canisters the group had collected from the nearby town. They were being transported to the entrance area of the Storehouse to escape the cold. Two men, one of whom had been one of the goons who had held back Rob yesterday, were passing the canisters to the other as they took it inside.

As Rob got closer to the door, the goon looked at him. He met Rob's gaze and they stared at one another for a moment. Rob could see that the man was still harbouring resentment against him. He could see that the goon had a sore looking mark on his face and a bit of a black eye forming. Rob remembered that he had elbowed the man in the face during the struggle yesterday. The guy scowled at Rob for a while before turning back and picking up the next canister. Rob could feel a smile almost form on his face, but he decided to hold it back. He continued on past the pile of fuel cans and went through the doors.

The Storehouse was a dark and dingy building on the inside. It was the first time Rob had set foot inside of there since they had converted it into a series of different rooms. When they had first discovered it, the building had piles and piles of wood scattered all throughout, as well as a few bales of hay. The group had used the wooden boards to build themselves improvised walls, separating the Storehouse into multiple rooms to give people a little extra breathing space. It wasn't until they had started salvaging from the town that the survivors had furnished these small living quarters. Someone even had the idea to get hinges from the hardware store and make doors, giving people a little bit of privacy. They reinforced the makeshift walls and added carpets and other household goods. Some people had given their own rooms little touches to try and make their own space personal.

It was different to the way that people were living in the Farmhouse. The furniture and homely decorations were already in place. No one had really bothered trying to make their rooms something of their own. Rob's room, for example, was bland compared to a couple of the living quarters in the Storehouse. All he had in there was a bed, a chest of drawers that he didn't even use, as most of his stuff was piled up into the corner beside the bed, and a wardrobe that Rob didn't even think he had opened. The room had been bare when he had first moved into it. It was clear that the previous owners did not even use it.

It wasn't too far until he reached the door to the room where David had spent most of his time. It was the room located at the furthest back corner of the building. In fact the room was at the furthest part of this side of the entire farm. It was the perfect secluded location. David had lived in the bottom of the Barn in the past, in one of the makeshift living areas beneath John's, with crates of supplies creating a divide between his and Maria's lodgings.

As of late he had been shacking up with some girl who lived in the room Rob was now outside the front of. She had been quiet from what Rob could remember of her. She had never voiced her opinion during any group meetings or gatherings. She had mainly just faded into the background. Half of the group probably didn't even know her name. Rob didn't, but that was not usual.

Before knocking on the door, Rob leaned forward and pressed his ear against it, trying to listen for anything inside. There was nothing. Suddenly the outside door burst open and cold instantly filled the hallway. The noise startled Rob as he pulled himself away from the door and turned to look down the hallway he had just traversed, as another survivor entered the Storehouse. He looked up, rubbing his hands together.

"It's freaking freezing out there" he said, giving a half-hearted smile. Rob could feel his face reddening with embarrassment at getting caught trying to listen through the door of a young woman's room. He could feel a lump forming in his throat as he tried to speak, but the words never came.

The man must have realised who Rob was, as his facial expression dropped. He blew hot air into his hands, as he continued to rub them together, before turning and going into one of the rooms, shutting the door behind him. By this time the outside door had closed and the hallway fell back into darkness, but the cold air still lingered.

Rob turned back to the door and without thinking, he knocked on it. A few moments passed, but nothing happened. No one came to the door and there was no noise inside the room. A short while later, he knocked for a second time. Once again there was no answer.

Rob's first instinct was to turn the handle and walk inside, however, he had no idea what he would find in there. He could catch the woman undressing or her and David in the middle of something. He already had a bad reputation now around the farm, the last thing he wanted was to be known as the resident peeping Tom.

If there was no one in there, then what was he going to do? Was he going to snoop about and look through all of the girl's possessions? And he wasn't even sure what it was he was looking for. He needed to talk to David. If he wasn't here, and she wasn't here, then Rob wasn't going to get any answers. Besides, he remembered how it felt when he came home to find Maria going through his own room. He did not want to be in that situation.

Rob thought it was best to leave it. As he turned away from the door, his ears picked up a slight murmur coming from inside the room. He stopped. He waited a moment, standing there, perfectly still, in the cold hallway just listening for the sound again. A moment later he heard it. There was defiantly someone in there.

"Hello?" he said, as he knocked gently on the door.

There was no response. Rob grabbed hold of the handle and turned it. The door clicked open, as he pushed it, the door was wedged slightly between the floorboards. It was clear that the door had not been properly cut to size when it was first put up.

There was no light being fed into the room from the hallway as he entered, instead the only light source came from something in the back. An odd smell immediately flooded out of the room. It was heavy and hung in the air, filling Rob's nostrils and almost burning them.
As he pushed the door as far as it would go, Rob stepped through and entered inside. It was only around ten feet by ten feet and windowless, but the room did have a lot of stuff inside of it. There was a bed behind the door, with a pile of large quilts scrunched up on top it, which Rob barely glanced at as his eyes were being drawn towards the desk on the far side against the back wall. It was here that the light was coming from. A small lamp gave off a warm orange glow that illuminated the equipment laying on the desk. There was a large glass bowl that had a strange brown chemical floating inside of it. It was so thick that the light could not penetrate it. A tube ran from this and into a large tin can of sorts. This can was suspended over the top of an ashtray filled with burnt paper and wood. The ash pile was still smouldering as if it had been used recently.

Rob took a few steps towards it. He reached out and could feel the heat coming off of the can. He decided to leave it. He continued to look and found a bottle of bleach and a bottle of some other household chemical sat atop the desk. Beside them he found burned kitchen utensils, such as spoons and spatulas, some of which had been bent, while others were burned black. There were a few other bottles of liquid, needles and prescription drugs that Rob recognised. They were branded with the logo of the supermarket in Town he and David had searched. He had a sudden moment of realisation as to what all this was.

"A drug lab?" he said aloud.

Suddenly the murmuring sound appeared, only this time it was louder and came from the direction of the bed. He spun around to see the quilt move. He reached for his gun, but stopped himself remembering where he was.

A foot slid out from the bed beneath the quilt. It was a woman's foot.

"Hello?" Rob asked. "Are you okay?"

The woman moved and so too did the blanket. As it did it revealed her gaunt pale face. Vomit stained the pillow beside her, and a crust of dried blood lined the ring of her nostril. She took long deep breaths and as she exhaled, Rob could hear a faint wheezing noise. He could see her eyeballs flickering frantically beneath her eyelids. He went to take a step towards her, but hesitated.

"Are you okay?" he repeated.

Her arm slid out from underneath the blanket and Rob could see injection marks surrounding the joint in her arm where her bicep met her forearm. There were scars surrounding this area, some of which looked as if they had been there for years. It was clear that she was whacked out on whatever drug her and David had been cooking in here.

"What you doing Robby?" a voice beside him called out. He turned and saw David standing half sticking out behind the door. He could see his gun tucked into his belt, but in his hand was the blade he carried around with him. "You shouldn't come barging into other people's rooms" he said, taking a step inside, before quickly checking the hallway behind him for anyone else.

As he entered the woman's bedroom, he let go of the backpack he carried, which fell to the ground. He proceeded to grab the door by the handle, lifting it up slightly off the ground, and then gently pushed it closed. That was the way they had dealt with stopping the door from being wedge on the floorboards.

Rob wasn't sure what to do. He glanced back at the woman on the bed, who had now rolled over, face first into the sick stain on her pillow. Just as he was about to say something, David interrupted.
"Some things never change. Things we might have thought lost from the old world…"
He began showing off with his knife skills, flicking the blade around in his hands and between his fingers. "Can still be brought over into this new one". He gave a gesture towards the desk with the homemade lab equipment on it.
"You are talking about drugs?" Rob asked confused.
David sniggered. "Robby… I am talking about everything. The old world is gone. It has faded away into a deep dark hole. We are all that is left of it. Our pleasures that were lost when the world went dark… or that might have been regarded as 'wrong' in the old ways… those days are gone. They are dead along with everything else. We can do whatever we want. We can create this life in whatever image we desire. Jennifer…" he said as he moved his hand towards the bed and the woman in it. "She used to do all kinds of sinful things in order to get what she wanted. But now, all she needs to do is ask. We are not short of the shit we need to make it".
"What are you some kind of dealer?" Rob asked him bluntly.
David's expression dropped. "Think of me as a chemist. We don't need the rules we followed before. With so few of us left, we can do whatever we like with what little time we have left.
"Is that what you used to do before… before all this? Sell drugs?"

"It doesn't matter what we were before Robby". He flicked his knife around once more, most likely to try and intimidate. "All that matters is who we are now. Take Maria for example…"

"What about her?" Rob asked.

David walked over to the woman kneeled down and put his hand on her head, before standing back up and facing Rob. "I recognised her the moment we met her in the city. Her face was in the paper a few weeks before all this happened. She was wanted in connection with that rich business tycoon guy, the one who ran that big building downtown, you know the one?"

Rob shook his head.

He sighed. "Anyway… the guy hanged himself as his mistress was blackmailing him. Turns out he was having a bit on the side and this woman was threatening to tell his wife if he didn't pay up the goods. The guy clearly couldn't hack it and was found hanging from the railing of his balcony. Maria's face was all over the paper. 'Industrialist's Mistress released due to lack of evidence', if I remember correctly. Everyone seemed to have forgotten, but I knew. I knew as soon as I saw her on that first day".

"Why are you telling me this?" Rob asked him.

"I… I am saying, she wasn't a good person… but here, she is free to do whatever she wants. People look to her for protection. She is free to do whatever she wants, and she is not constricted because of laws she might have broken before all of this went down".

Rob took a few steps towards the door. David stepped in between. "Look… at the end of the day, she wanted this. I know how to cook. She doesn't need you or anyone else judging her for what she chooses to do in whatever time she has left. None of us know when we might be grabbed and ripped apart by those things. What harm is there in spending that doing something fun?"

Rob took a glance at the woman on the bed. Her back had a few sores on it. "She looks like she is having a lot of fun" he said sarcastically. "Look... I don't care what you are up to here" Rob confessed. "I am not going to rat you out to John if that is what you are worried about. I came here looking for you".

David seemed surprised by this. "For me?" he repeated. "Why are you looking for me?"

"Where did you find Matt's bag?" Rob asked boldly. He stared at him for a moment before saying "I know you took it out of his room. He didn't steal the food".

David went to speak but stopped to lick his lips. "What?" he said, trying to smile to hide his guilt.

His eyes flicked down towards the backpack on the floor. It was so quick that Rob almost missed it. He looked down towards the backpack and it was right then that Rob knew.

"You took it" he stated. "You have been the one stealing the food". He could feel the fire burning once again in the pit of his stomach. "You got Matt killed".

David could clearly feel Rob's anger. He pointed the tip of the blade towards Rob. "Look... I don't know what you are on about". "I just cooking a little something to take the edge off. People like Jenn..." he said gesturing the knife towards the woman on the bed again. "I am just trying to make their little lives a bit more manageable".

"What is in the bag then?" Rob asked, reaching out towards it.

The knife darted forward towards his hand. "Get out of here!" he demanded. "Who the hell do you think you are?!" He grabbed him by his coat collar, the blade drawing closer to Rob's face. Rob went to hit him but as soon as he felt the cold steel pressed against his cheek, he lowered his hand. "Get the fuck out!" he shouted, spinning the two of them around before letting go and pushing him towards the door.

Rob stumbled backwards and fell into the door. He was surprised that he didn't go through it. It must have been put together better than he had thought.

David stood in the middle of the room staring at him. With his blade in one hand, Rob saw him reach down for his gun with the other. Rob knew that this was now escalating out of control. In a panic, Rob didn't even think about reaching for his own gun, instead he leant down and grabbed hold of the bag.

"No!" David shouted as he pushed forward and barged into him, spilling the contents of the bag on the floor.

To Rob's expectation, tins and packets of food spilled onto the floor.

"You mother fucker!" Rob heard himself say as he drove his fist into David's stomach.

He felt the man wrench forward, but as he did, his arm flayed around, swinging the knife as best as he could. It slashed Rob right across his other hand as he desperately tried to grab the knife off of him. The cold metal almost burned to the touch. Straight away he could feel his own blood trickling through his fingers as he grabbed hold of David's hand. "Let go of me" he hissed.

For an instant, Rob thought he was going to bite a chunk out of him. As the two of them struggled, Rob suddenly brought up his foot and pushed David away with it. He staggered back, knocking into the table and some of the chemical jars fell over, spilling the contents inside. Rob used this opportunity to pull open the door as quickly as he could, using the method he had seen David do only a few moments before. He grabbed hold of the handle, lifted the door upwards and pulled it open. By this point David had managed to get to his feet and was now going for his gun again.

"Was he going to shoot me?" Rob wondered in his head. He was not going to stick around to find out. He squeezed through the gap in the door and shot out of the room as quickly as he possibly could. He heard David shout something as he did, but by that time Rob was already halfway down the hallway.

The goon, who had given Rob a filthy look earlier, was now loading the petrol canisters inside. He had one of them propping open the door, as he moved back towards the pile outside of it.

Rob looked back and saw David forcing his way out of the gap of Jennifer's door when Rob made it to Storehouse's entrance. He sprinted outside, pushing past the goon, who mouthed some profanity at him as he went by, but Rob was not able to hear it over the sound of his own heartbeat.

He had no idea where he was going to go or what he was going to do. His initial idea was to just get outside in the hope that the public would stop David from doing something stupid. The man's identity as a drug dealer/maker had been revealed, not to mention the fact that he and Jennifer were currently cooking and taking their homemade drugs in the back of the Storehouse. Rob also had proof that the man was the one behind the missing food, and wrongful execution of Matt. David had a lot to lose by Rob getting his words out.

As he got within five feet of the bonfire, he whirled around and saw David stepping out from the building. His gun was now resting back in his belt, but his blade was still in his other hand. The goon at the doorway looked at him and then turned back to Rob. It was clear that he could see that something was up.

"ROB!" a voice boomed out over the trees and echoed all around. The word bounced off of the buildings and caused the very ground beneath him to shake.

At first Rob thought that the word had come from David, but the man was busy turning towards the source of the noise at the edge of the Courtyard. Rob began to feel an unspeakable amount of dread building up inside of him. His heart was beating differently now. Before it seemed as if it was being fuelled by his adrenalin to escape from David, but now it felt as if his heart was trying to rip its way out of his chest and flee before whatever was coming for him got there.

Rob slowly turned his gaze, from David, over towards the direction of the noise. As he did, the wind blew into his eyes, causing the water that was already there to glaze over his vision. He blinked a few times before bringing one of his hands up to wipe it. When it was gone, he saw John standing over near the fence. Beside him he could see two other men from his entourage. The two people, who had been working on the fence, had moved the panel over to allow them access into the Courtyard and were now replacing it behind John, who began walking forward across the grass.

Rob didn't understand what was going on. Everything was happening too fast. He looked over his shoulder and saw a few other survivors coming out of the Farmhouse and watching. Peter was there in the crowd. The cold air blew again and glazed his vision once more, but this time when it was done, Rob could see that John was carrying something behind him. No, he was dragging something behind him.

Rob turned and took a step or two forward before stopping dead at the site of it. He saw that John was holding a leg by the ankle and was dragging the body of man towards them. He heard a few gasps from the onlookers as they could see who it was the big man was dragging. Rob did not know what was happening. The flames of the bonfire were obstructing his view of the body, right up until John was only twenty feet away. The look on his face was the same it had been when he had murdered Matt in cold blood. The same look of madness in his eyes, that burned with the same intensity that he had in Rob's vision of him, shooting someone dead in a war-torn desert town, were present as John stopped and pulled the body around so that it was in front of him.

At first Rob didn't know what to do. He stared only at John until the man pointed with his eyes down towards the corpse. The wind began to pick up slightly. It whistled through the bare branches as it had done many times before. He felt his breathing rapidly increasing as his heart beat violently inside of him. His eyes began to look downwards towards what John was looking at. There was a noise on the wind. It was the same familiar sound he had heard before. It was the same word he had heard before, all the way back in the beginning. The wind moved through his ear canal and lodged itself into his brain as he gazed upon the body of the man. He was rotted, but it was clear that this body had once had dark skin. A blue dirt stained overall covered his torso.

He could feel the word pierce him inside his head.

In the middle of the man's stomach was a hole that looked as if something had ripped through him. The whole area around it was stained with blood.

He could hear the word as clear as day. It came again and again and again.

"Join… Join… Join…" it said over and over.

The body was Mike's.

Day Thirty Two – Part 3

The silence stretched on without end. The wind had died down and the whispers had faded away along with it. All that could be heard now were the soft murmurs of the gathering crowd as they looked on and waited for the chaos that was fast approaching. This moment could have easily have been described as the calm before; the time when the eye of storm was about to reveal itself and bring nothing but destruction.

Rob could see it brewing all around him. John stood before him silently watching Rob's every movement. Every time he moved his eyes to glance down at the body on the ground, he could feel John's own eyes following. Behind the big man, his cronies stood watching and waiting as the other survivors did. None of them dared to say a word until their fearless leader spoke first. David stood behind Rob, previously gunning for him and ready to end Rob's life, he was now standing patiently. It all felt as if no one knew what to do.

A quick glance into the crowd and Rob could see Peter standing there, looking over the shoulders of the man in front of him. His confused face was the exact same as everyone else's. Everyone was clearly trying to process what was going on. They had all of the pieces, they were all just trying desperately to put them all together and figure out what was going to come next.

Mike's body was perfectly intact. It looked as if he had been dead for a while. His skin was decaying and bits of it had been ripped off, which was clearly from John dragging his corpse all this way. That was the strangest thing about it. Rob remembered seeing him being torn apart by those creatures. The darkness had surrounded him and devoured his flesh as he screamed out in terror. The memories of that day had come back to him as his eyes turned back to the body at John's feet.

So why was Mike undamaged? He remembered that he had actually fled before Mike was consumed by the monsters. From what he could remember, as soon as he had fallen backwards into them, Rob had turned and ran for his own safety. The smoking gun still burning in his hand. He remembered Mike's eyes when he had pulled the trigger, far too late to stop it from ripping into his flesh. When Rob looked over the body on the cold frosty grass, he could see that bullet hole in the middle of his chest. It had ripped through his overalls and dried blood had accumulated around the open wound.

A millipede crawled out of the bullet hole and scurried off under the body, almost as if it too knew what was coming.

Rob's eyes glanced upwards and met John's. Just before either of them spoke, Rob remembered the vision he had of Mike, the woman in the alley on the rainy night. He knew who Mike really was and what he had done. He had done that before, Rob knew. It had not been the first. He did not feel remorse for Mike's death anymore. The strange vision had shown him the true nature of the man he had killed. The new world was a better place for it.

But that was not going to hold up here. John wanted answers. He knew a bullet hole when he saw one, Rob was sure of it. He knew Rob's story of how the creatures had got him and ripped him apart. A story that, at the time, Rob believed to be true. He had just left out the part before. But now this corpse had disproved Rob's tale. The gaping hole in his chest, the morning after when John had been inspecting Robert's gun, and now the story he had told was nothing but lies. John knew everything. He had put two and two together and got the whole picture laid out perfectly in his own mind. The man was not stupid. It was obvious that he wanted Rob to admit it, or at least try and defend himself. It had been the same with Matt only the night before. John was a ticking timebomb, ready to explode. Rob could see the fire building up inside of him and ready to come out, dealing out the same kind of punishment that had befallen Matt.

Would it be two John kills in as many days? The thought made Rob feel cornered and alone. He quickly looked around at the other survivors and he could see that some of them were also putting it together. Their eyebrows lowered in accusation as their gaze turned from Mike's body to Rob. He felt as if the entire Farm was now staring at him and waiting for him to speak. It was time to give them what they wanted.

Rob didn't know exactly how to word it. He could feel the right words to say dissolving in his mind and disappearing off into the abyss. Everything else just seemed like nonsense. They all needed an explanation, John most of all. His face had not changed from the moment he had first locked eyes on Rob from across the other side of the Courtyard.
Rob needed to pick his words carefully. Was he going to be honest and tell them everything? There was no way that they would believe the

vision of Mike's true self. That part would need to be left out of his story. But what should he say? That he shot the man accidently in a panic, and that he ran? Would they even believe him? He had already been caught out in a lie.

"I..." Rob finally started. Any sounds that were around the Farm quickly dispersed as everyone listened intensely. "Wha... what..." he said desperately trying to think of what to say.
John spoke up. "You said Mike was killed by those things". His words lingered in the air like a foul smell. Rob could feel his heart heating rapidly once again. "You said that you fired randomly at those things". Rob could tell that he was getting angry the more he spoke. "You blamed it on THOSE THINGS!" John almost shouted the last two words as he took a step forward. Rob wanted to take a few backwards, but he thought it was best if he stood his ground. He wanted to do anything he could to prove his innocence.
"What happened?" Maria's voice called out from behind John.

Rob just stared for a time. His mind was racing but nothing concrete was forming. He didn't know what to do.
"I... I killed him" he suddenly blurted out. It was more of a surprise to himself than to anyone else. He had no idea where the words had even come from. Everything that was running through his head did not feature those words once. The brutal honesty had come completely out of nowhere.
His eyes tried to look away, but they couldn't help themselves but met John's once again. The big man's own eyes were huge with a thick dark pupil dominating.
"Was he happy that I had admitted it?" Rob wondered to himself.

His thoughts were full of all the terrible things that were waiting for him. Matt had denied stealing the food, but that had only granted him a shotgun blast at point blank ranged to the face. What was going to happen to Rob for confessing?

He suddenly realised that he had left it far too long and now the crowd had begun to look at one another in utter disbelief. Rob needed to say something. He needed to make them see that it was not how they thought.

"It was an accident…" he said almost pitifully, like a helpless child caught red handed by their parents. He knew that alone would not be enough. "The sun had gone…" Rob continued, louder this time, making sure that everyone in the Courtyard could hear him. He could see John was studying his every word. He needed to make sure that they knew the truth. Only then did he stand a chance of getting out of this with his life, and even that was as slim a chance as any.

Rob licked his lips and went on. "And they were coming; the creatures… the darkness". Everyone was hanging on his every word. They all wanted to hear the truth. "I was lost and alone in the woods. I couldn't find John, Mike or Maria out there. Everyone had gone. Those sounds…" Rob could faintly hear them now. Were they in his head or were the creatures watching in the dark of the nearby trees? "They were coming for me. I managed to find the flare that John had left. I fired it up and stood there in that dark clearing for what seemed like forever. I could hear them coming from all around me. They were closing in from everywhere. I thought I was going to be ripped apart, like Karen and her husband. I took out my gun and held it out towards the direction of the noise. Suddenly a loud one came from behind me. I…" the words caught in Rob's throat. "I just turned and fired. I didn't even think. I thought that Mike had gone back to the Farm with everyone else. It was far too late when I realised it was him". Rob looked around at the crowd. Some of them had turned their stare away from him. It was clear that they understood. "It was an accident. I didn't mean to shoot him".

"Why did you not tell us?" Maria asked.

Rob felt a flood of shame wash over him. "I panicked. I didn't know what to do. I thought that you wouldn't believe me. I thought they had grabbed him and ripped him apart. When I ran..."

"You ran?" John cut in. Rob felt his stomach sink. It had been the wrong thing to say. "You left him?"

"No... I..." Rob tried to say, defending himself, but John kept on.

"You shot him and left him to die at the hands of those things... even though you had a working flare?"

"I wouldn't have been able to get back to the Farm" Rob told him. "I had to..."

John's nostrils flared and his eyes grew large as he lunged forward towards Rob. He hit him in exactly the same place he had hit him the night before, only this time it was with his fists and not the butt of his shotgun. It still felt just as hard. The force of the punch had knocked Rob backwards onto the ground. His eyes went blurry and everything was a haze. His face was pounding. He tried to look up but all he could see was John's silhouetted hulk looming over him, creating a sense of déjà vu from last night.

"MURDERER!" John's word boomed out deafening Rob's ear drums.

"It was an accident" he tried to say, but the words never came. All he managed was parts of each word.

"No!" another voice called out. "Leave him alone!"

Rob's eyes had started to clear and he looked over towards the voice. It was Peter. He had pushed his way through the crowd and was now charging towards John with his gun in his hand. It was not pointed towards him, but he gave the impression that he was ready to use it. A few of John's followers, Maria included, drew their guns and held them in Peter's direction as he approached the big man. John at this point had turned, clanging his Molotov bottles as he moved, and was now facing towards Peter.

"He said it was an accident! He didn't mean to kill Mike!" Peter shouted out at him. "Leave him the fuck alone!"

"He left him to die!" John shouted back at him, making sure it was loud enough so that everyone could hear. "He shot him and left him to be eaten by those things! It is not the first time he has killed! He shot that man in the woods the first night we ran from the city! He lied to us about Mike and now he is lying now!"

"No!" Peter responded. "He was scared... scared of what YOU would do to him. You have become something else John. You murdered Matt last night and now you are going to murder Rob?!"

Rob could see the rage building up inside of John. The fire was only going to be held back for so long. He tried to reach out and stop all this, but John had hit him so hard that he had nearly given him a concussion. It was strange. Only last night Rob had been the one trying to defend Matt, and now he was on the other side of it. The similarities did not fill Rob with hope that he would not befall the same fate as Matt.

"You're the fucking monster John. Leave him along!" Peter continued. John took one step towards Peter, who everyone could see was now beginning to tremble. He tried desperately to maintain his stand and hold his ground. Another step and Peter lifted up his gun. This time it was straight at John's face. Everyone else who had their weapons drawn lifted them up and pointed them at Peter. John gave a hand gesture that told them not to shoot.

Rob climbed to one knee. "No" he managed to say. "Don't do this".
John turned and kicked him in the fact, knocking Rob back down to the ground. "Shut the fuck up!" he said like a cobra spitting venom.
Peter moved in closer. "I said leave him a…"

And with that John turned and grabbed hold of the gun, pushing it to one side. The gun went off and a deafening blast of noise erupted from the scuffle. The bullet ripped into the dirt beside Mike's corpse, only a foot away from the wound that had caused all this in the first place.

John pulled Peter closer to him and smashed the top of his head into his. Peter's nose exploded in a burst of blood as his head flew back. John pushed him away and as he was falling back, proceeded to hit him with each of his fists. His rage was now in full swing as he pummelled Peter's ragdoll body continuously as he fell back onto the ground. Even when he was on the mud, John continued to hit him. Over and over and over again he punched Peter's unconscious body. Blood flew out of fresh wounds and bruises instantly formed beneath his skin. John gritted his teeth as he drove each punch into him.

It felt as if the savage beating went on for hours until a few of the crowd rushed over to pull John off of him. The first one to try and intervene had suffered a hit of his own and was now standing on the side-lines holding his stomach. It was clear that he had the wind knocked out of him.
John stood over Peter's beaten body breathing heavily. His hands were dripping with blood. After a few moments his gaze turned back to Rob, who at this point, had been helped up by two of the others.

As Rob looked over at Peter, he could see that the man was still breathing. He was alive. "Thank god" Rob thought to himself. He did not want the man to have died on account of him and his lies. Rob already felt awful over all of this. Peter had been differently lately. He had always sided with John and defended his actions. He had never spoken out of turn and had not said a bad word against the leader of the Farm for quite some time. Peter had not intervened once during Matt's trial and execution, so Rob had not expected him to get involved in this. He was well and truly surprised by him.

That being said, he had not wished for this to happen. A couple of the other survivors had rushed over to Peter and were currently trying to help him, bandaging his wounds and cleaning his cuts as he lay there motionless on the ground.

"Get him out of my sight" John told one of the helpers working on Peter. He then turned to Rob. "And you...". He didn't say a word. He just stood there for a moment breathing heavily. Eventually he took a really long deep breath and exhaled a moment later. This seemed to calm him down. It was clear that his rage had been unleashed upon Peter and so now he was thinking clearly. He grabbed a cable tie from his pocket and tossed it on the ground. "Tie him up" he told the two people holding Rob up. "We will figure out what to..."

Suddenly, almost as if by magic, Rob could see that an idea had popped into his head. John resisted smiling. Rob knew that this would not have been one of those fake smiles, but something far darker and far more real. He turned to Maria and one of his other henchmen. "Grab the tools and those sheets of metal behind the Storehouse. We are going to have to repair that Shack in the woods before we can lock him in there".

John turned back to Rob. "Let's get to work".

Day Thirty Five – Part 1

It only took the group the rest of the day to get the Shack up to standard. They had used the sheets of metal to fill in the holes in the roof and the section of destroyed wall. As for the stuff inside of it, they had worked tirelessly for around two hours, taking the stuff out and piling it up outside. John had watched over the entire reconstruction, occasionally barking orders or at times finding it easier to just do it himself. The entire time, Rob had been forced to sit on the ground beside a tree and wait. One guard was kept on him at all times, as the rest of the survivors, who had joined John, were busy working. They would change shifts every hour or so, and then that person would go in to help out in the Shack wherever they were needed.

John had not once looked at Rob, nor spoken to him. He had made sure that Rob and the guard watching him were in his peripheral vision, just in case Rob decided to make a run for it or attack the guard. Rob was not feeling so stupid. He knew that one slip up and John would shoot him dead without hesitating. At this point Rob was just thankful that he was not already dead, but he wondered if what awaited him next was worse. They were planning on leaving him locked up in the Shack. For how long, he could not say, but he knew that he would have to wait in the Shack, alone and in the dark, until John had decided on a suitable punishment. For theft of food, at least in this case, the accusations of theft of food, given that David had been in fact the one to steal it and had got away scot-free, John had executed Matt. Now that the big man had calmed down, Rob wondered what could have been worse than the death penalty. He was sure he was going to find out.

He had decided to keep the information about David to himself. There was no point in incriminating anyone else and having John kill them. David was a scumbag. He had cooked drugs in his past life and no doubt supplied them to anyone willing to buy. Rob had wondered how many lives had been damaged by what he had done. But did the man really deserve to die? Especially by the same gruesome end that Matt had met? Rob did not know. Besides he was not even sure that John would believe him. He would have most likely assumed it to be a tactic to try and get out of his own situation, but at least it would have left lingering suspicions.
Rob's conflicting thoughts had left him with the idea that he should remain silent as the survivors continued their work on his own personal prison.

By the time that the sun had started to set behind the great grey clouds, they had finished. They had made a barricade to place over the door once Rob was inside. They had done it so it was easily removed from the outside for when they wanted to get him out, but Rob knew that it would not be as easy from the inside.

As they got Rob to his feet and ushered him towards the Shack, Rob thought about asking "Are you just going to leave me alone in there? In the dark?" but he decided to stay silent. He figured that it was for the best.

Someone grabbed hold of the cable tie and cut it off of Rob's wrist, leaving behind a deep red mark. He glanced over and saw Maria, who looked away when she met his gaze. He could see that she was ashamed by what they were going to do to him, but at the same time, Rob saw that she believed John. In that moment he remembered what David had said about her. She had blackmailed a man which resulted in him taking his own life. Rob could have called her out and told everyone who she was as well. Her dark past could have caught up to her with one slip of the tongue. What would have happened? Would she have ended up sharing the cell along with Rob? Or would John have decided that past crimes no longer apply in their new world? John's hands were dirty as well. Rob had seen the murders he had committed. They were all guilty of something.

They shoved Rob inside and went to close the door. Just as it was about to close, Rob turned around and saw one of them toss something inside. He could see John standing there, staring back at him as the door was shut and the sounds of the barricade being set into place could be heard seconds later. The Shack fell into darkness. A small amount of the remaining daylight was seeping through the cracks between the original bricks and the new sheet metal. He knew that it would not last forever.

When he looked down, he saw a flashlight laying on the ground beneath his feet. Someone had kindly given him the smallest glimmer of hope before locking him inside the small building in the middle of the darkened forest. He had no idea what to expect. Other than the one night Rob had spent in the Town, he had slept every day in the Farmhouse. He had been surrounded by the other survivors, all of them armed with guns or some other form of weaponry. But now he was all on his own. He would have to ride out the night enclosed in his own tomb. He just hoped that the brickwork and barricaded door was enough to keep those creatures from getting to him.

The first night was the worst. As soon as the light had faded away and the Shack became submerged in total darkness, that was when they came. At first it had just been the wind, as it always was. It picked up after each passing second. He tried to look through one of the cracks, but there was nothing. All he could see was an endless black void. Rob thought it was best if he stayed away from there. He thought about sitting in one of the corners and waiting, but then again, if the wall wasn't enough to hold them back, then he didn't want to be sitting right on the other side of it. He decided to sit right in the middle of the empty shack. The hard broken and rotted wooden floor was uncomfortable, but there was nowhere to sit on and nothing to rest against. He turned the flashlight on and sat there, listening and waiting.

It wasn't long after that the whispers came. They spoke in the strange language of shadows. At first it was inaudible. It was nothing but hisses and murmurs, but moments later came the words that sent pains all through Rob's skull. "Surrender" they said in the whispery inhuman voices. "Join", "Kill", "Kill", "KILL".
After that the screeching started. The unnatural animal noises that sounded like squeals of excitement, or cries of agony echoed all throughout the Shack and the surrounding woodlands.
Rob could hear scrapes on the walls. The sound not unlike long fingernails dragging down a chalkboard. The scrapes came from all around. They

were trying to get in. The scratched and clawed at the walls and door for hours. All through the night they screamed and cried, desperately trying to get inside. Rob held his hands over his ears and tried everything that he could not to listen, but it was no good. It felt as if their noises were coming from inside his skull. He could feel his brain throbbing as the noises never stopped once.

Eventually the creatures' attempt to get inside became more and more threatening. They smashed at the walls and hissed. Some of them must have had their faces pressed up against the gaps as Rob could have sworn that he saw movement when one of them cried out. He could feel their dark eyes watching him from all around.

At one point he heard movement on the roof of the Shack. A thudding sound moved across above him, occasionally stopping to bang heavily on it. They were looking for a weakness, Rob knew. They wanted him. They wanted to do whatever it was these creatures did.

At first Rob had thought that it was to eat and consume their victims, but after what had happened to Mike's body. Rob wasn't sure. He knew what he had seen and what he had heard. He had seen what had happened to the people in the city on the night that all of this had begun. He knew what he had seen when he discovered the bodies of the two strangers from a few days ago. Their mangled carcasses strung up in the trees like obscene Christmas decorations.

So why had they left Mike's body perfectly intact? Were they playing with Rob? Did they do all of this so that they could get him alone out here in the woods?

Rob's train of thought continued like this for the rest of the night, as too did the creatures' relentless attempts to get inside the Shack. Rob was grateful that John and the rest of the survivors had done a good job with fortifying the small building, otherwise the small flashlight would have been all that he had to protect himself from them.

A few minutes before dawn the next day, the creatures stopped. Their scrapes and scratches, squeals and screams suddenly stopped, hours after they had begun. Rob had not managed to get a single bit of sleep. Every time there was a moment of quiet in the middle of the night, Rob had started to doze. Seconds later he had suddenly awoken as one of the other creatures had cried out, ripping Rob away from his slumber.

When white light began to feed into the Shack, Rob flicked off the flashlight. The wind stopped and so too did any trace of those things. The fear and adrenaline was feeding Rob and keeping him warm. Now that it had faded away, along with the darkness, he felt freezing. All that he had was the clothes he had been wearing the day before; his flimsy coat with a t-shirt beneath it. It was not the right kind of protection to wear in this kind of weather. The Shack was clearly providing no warmth whatsoever. He took this opportunity to rest in one of the corners and tried to drift off to sleep.

It was cold and uncomfortable, but after the last few days, he felt like he needed a good sleep. He felt dirty and damp from the frosted grass he had spent most of the previous day sat on. His skin felt flaky, as if the cold air was drying it out and he was just crumbling away. Trapped inside that freezing cold building was starting to feel like hell.

Eventually his body gave in and he fell asleep. He did not dream. The cold kept waking him up every hour or so, but he persevered and managed to fall back to his slumber shortly after.

When he finally did wake, later that day, he realised that no one had come to check on him the entire time he had been in there. No one had brought him any food either. He was starving. He could feel his stomach in knots as it began to feed upon itself.

The day seemed to pass in an instant. He had done nothing but sit there, trying to keep himself warm and thinking on everything that had happened. Even when the darkness came again, bringing with them the creatures of the night, they did not break Rob's thoughts. He was tired and cold and uncomfortable. He did not care about the monsters on the other side of the wall this night. He did not even bother to move back to the middle of the Shack. If they had not managed to get inside over the course of the previous night, then they were not going to get inside now.

After an hour or so of the creatures trying once again, it almost seemed as if they gave up and went away. The silence managed to bring Rob out of his thought process and back to reality. He sat there for a moment listening, but nothing came. There was no wind and no whispers. There was nothing. It had only been dark for a short while.

Suddenly he noticed that he hadn't even turned on the flashlight. He had been sitting there in the dark for a while now, and nothing had got inside. "They can't go through walls" Rob thought. This was quite the break through. No one knew anything about them and what they could or couldn't do. All that they knew was that if you had a light source, then you were okay, if you didn't, then you were not going to survive.

He went to turn it on, but then realised that there was no point. If the creatures couldn't get inside the Shack, then he had no reason to try and get rid of them. From the sounds of it, they must have got rid of themselves.

When the next day came, the bitter cold had got worse. Rob felt like he was at the point of starvation. He was tired and the entire Shack reeked of the faeces he had done during the night in one of the corners. It was when the white light from outside hit him in the face that he had a sudden horrific thought. "Was this what John had planned for him?" It seemed to make a lot of sense. They had decided to starve him or freeze him to death out here, away from everyone else. It was clear that John didn't want to exile him or anything of the sort, due to the fact that Rob could have been a danger to the rest of the group. He didn't want to kill him himself, so instead, he had decided to leave him to die, locked up in this small Shack.

It had been nearly two full days since Rob had been thrown inside and the door shut behind him. He was freezing and starved almost to death. He had eaten some strange plant that was growing on the inside of the Shack through one of the cracks. He was not sure if he was getting any sustenance or nourishment from it, but it helped to ease the crippling stomach cramps.

Rob worked it out to have been around four or five in the afternoon when they finally came for him. It had started as a distant whistle. Rob thought he was imagining it at first, but as it continued, it seemed to get louder. Then came a strange crunching sound that also became louder the closer it came to the Shack. When Rob realised that it was someone, he leapt to his feet and moved over to the door. He didn't stand directly behind it, but instead a few feet back to allow anyone wanting to come in not to feel threatened by him. In truth Rob did not feel very threatening at all.

The sounds of the barricade being moved could be heard and moments later the door opened. A blinding white light filled the room and Rob had to look away for an instant. When he turned back, he saw three figures standing in the doorway. Behind them was a thick white layer of snow covering the entire clearing and the tops of the trees above. It was clear that the great grey clouds had finally given in and unleashed their cargo upon them. It gave the forest an even stranger feel than it had already. One of the figures leaned into the Shack, grabbed hold of Rob by his coat, and pulled him outside. He was marched out of the doorway and passed the other two of John's goons. Rob glanced back around at the man who was shoving him forward into the snow. It was David. He smiled an insincere smile when their eyes met.

Rob turned back around as his foot made contact with the snow. The same crunching sound from earlier could be heard when Rob's foot was swallowed by the white. It must have been at least half a foot deep. He could feel a cold wet sensation surrounding his foot. He wanted to stop and go back inside, but David pushed him forward.

A few more steps and now both of his feet were submerged beneath the snow. He looked up and saw the grey clouds were still hanging overhead. It was clear that they were not done. Rob wondered if he would live long enough to see it snow again. The thought was suddenly dashed when he saw John move from behind a tree up ahead. He had just been fixing something to the tree. When he saw John's face, he instantly knew what was coming. He tried to turn back, but David pushed him forward. He was tired, hungry and didn't have the energy to resist David's shoving.

John untied the section of rope fastened to the tree and the noose fell down from the thick branch running straight above him.

John's words were cold and to the point. Rob had expected no less.

"It's time…"

Day Thirty Five – Part 2

The cold air was still. It lingered all around them like time had completely frozen. The trees all around were motionless. All that could be heard were the sounds of snow crunching beneath feet as a man marched forward towards his own death.

"Where is everyone?" Rob managed to muster the words to say as he looked around. All he could see was John and three of his men in the clearing around the Shack.
John didn't say a word. He looked away and grabbed hold of the rope by the noose.
"It's just us today" David's voice called out from behind. Rob looked round at him. He smiled again. "Everyone else is back at the Farm in the warm".
"Yeah, could we hurry this up?" one of the other men called out. "It's fucking freezing out here".
Rob took a deep breath before saying "So... this is it, huh? You have just decided to string me up?" The words caught John's attention. His eyes glanced over in Rob's direction. "No one else knows, do they? You are just going to kill me and make up whatever story you want".

John was checking the strength of the rope when he finally spoke. "You shot Mike and left him to die, Robert" he said in a cold voice that was nearly as cold as the harsh weather all around them.

Rob thought about telling him how much it was an accident, but somehow he didn't think that John was open to listening. He didn't have the energy to argue with him in a dispute that had already been decided. "Why have you left it this late? It's going to be dark soon" Rob questioned.

John gave a look over to the other men, looked at each of them for a few seconds, before turning back to Rob. "The creatures will claim your body Rob, you know". His trademark phrase managed to show itself which gave Rob the indication that John was calm and thinking clearly. "We will leave the door open and just say you got out. No one has to know what happened here".

Rob looked down and caught a glimpse of the big man's shotgun resting against the tree on the ground. The barrel sticking out of the dead white snow.

"You're a killer Robert… plain and simple" John continued. "You are too much of a danger to keep alive, you know. You are a threat to the entire group".

"What about David?!" Rob yelled as he pushed David's hand off of his shoulder. "A man you supposedly trust, cooking drugs and stealing food right from under your nose?" Rob was feeling desperate now. He was not sure how this was all going to play out.

John gave David a quizzical look before bringing it back to Rob.

"I don't know what the fuck he is on about" David told them as he took out his knife from his belt and held it to Rob's face. "This sack of shit is lying. I say we forget the lynching and bleed him".

Rob turned back to John, the cold steel of David's blade still pressed against his face. "And what about you? Your hands are not exactly clean. You left those two people to die. I found them in the woods that night. They had been ripped apart by those things. That is on you!"
John laughed. "I can't protect everyone. Those people were a threat to this community"

Rob cut him off. "A threat? A threat?! That is all you ever say! You are the only threat here! You murdered an innocent man in cold blood for something one of your men was doing!" He gave a gesture over in David's direction.

Rob felt the blade pull tight to his face. "Shut your mouth, you fucking liar!" David told him. "I didn't have anything to do with that!"

When Rob looked back at John, he saw the man's eyes squint, as if he was processing all of the information and some of what Rob was saying was actually making sense. He turned and gave David a look that made him with draw the knife from Rob's face. As the blade left his cheek, he felt the warm sensation of blood as it trickled down his face. It was the warmest part of his body.

Rob decided now was the time to reveal the truth about John himself. His vision of John dressed in military fatigues over the bodies of an Arab man pleading for his life as the fires of their houses burned all around him.

"And what about you!" he started off accusingly. "You murdered all those innocent people in that village". Rob looked and saw John's eyes widen in complete dismay.

"Wh... what?" John managed to say, tripping over his own words.

"The Arab's... you slaughtered them the same way you murdered Matt". John's face had changed dramatically over the course of the last few seconds. Rob could see that his mind was desperately trying to process how Rob could have possibly known that information. The truth of the matter was that Rob didn't even know. He had seen it all in a few visions. The same kind of vision he had seen with Mike, and the woman in the blue dress.

"How do you..." John started, but then suddenly remembered where he was. He had almost let himself slip and reveal that Rob's words were in fact the truth, but at the last second he managed to grab hold of himself and come to his senses. He turned to David. "Let's get him up" he said bluntly.

As David grabbed hold of Rob's arm and pushed him forward, Rob continued. "You are a fucking murderer John. Those people still haunt your every waking moment". A strange sensation began to wash over. At first he thought it was nothing but adrenaline, as his heart was beating so rapidly, but that soon passed the moment he heard his own words reach his ears.

"That is what is waiting for you in the darkness".

Rob suddenly realised what he had just said. "The darkness?" he thought to himself. "Where had that come from?" For a moment there, it had felt as if he had not been in control of the words that had come out of his mouth. It was almost as if some great power had control over him. It must have been that same strange power that gave Rob the energy to do what came next.

Without even thinking, Rob brought an elbow up to David's face. He heard the crunch of his nose break as he released his grip on Rob's shoulders and toppled backwards to the ground. The hit had taken him completely unaware. He crashed into the snow as blood trickled down his lips.

John must have still been trying to work out how Rob could have possibly know all that, as it took him a few seconds to register what was happening. This thankfully gave Rob the opening he needed. He did not know whether to hit Rob or reach down and grab hold of his gun, resting against the tree, so instead he did neither. He simply threw his head back in surprise, having been caught off guard. Rob ducked behind the nearby tree as the other two men marched forward towards him. John used this time to shout the words "Get him!" as he eventually made the decision to go for his gun.

By this time, Rob had managed to weave in and out of the trees, trying to put as much distance between himself and the clearing. He ran as fast as he could, trudging his way through the snow as best he could. He knew that the very act of hitting David and making a run for it was enough to make him look guilty in anyone who had doubt eye's, and it also gave John enough justification to shoot him dead, but out of the choice between trying to live and being hung from a tree to be feasted upon by the creatures of the darkness; Rob knew which option he would rather take.

He could hear the crunching of snow and the distant shouts of the men following him. He was not sure if John himself was following him, and if David had managed to get himself up off of the ground and join in the chase, as Rob did not look behind him once. His whole entire body ached from the last few days of restless sleeping, shivering from the cold, and sitting uncomfortably in that small Shack, but whatever energy that Rob mustered, was giving him enough drive to run.

He moved through the trees some more, trying desperately to think on his feet and make his tracks in the snow impossible to follow. He knew that the bright white snow made the forest floor more illuminated in the daylight than the deep green and brown coloured foliage that had previously covered the area.

"GET BACK HERE!" he heard John's voice boom out through the woods. The words echoed off of the trees and sounded as if it had come from every direction. It was distant however, giving Rob the impression that they were further away than he had thought.

A blast rang out a second later. That too sounded too far away to actually affect Rob, but he knew exactly what that sound was. He recognised the sound from when John had unloaded a shell into Matt's face a few days ago. The sounds of wood chippings flying in all directions could be heard from behind Rob. The blast had made contact with a number of trees, that no doubt Rob has passed moments earlier, and he imagined that large chunks of them were now laying scattered atop the snow.

"ROBERT!" John's voice cried out once more as the shotgun blast faded off. The shout was not unlike a battle cry that Rob imagined men in historical wars would do when they charged into the face of their enemy; bayonets pointed out in front.

If there had been any animals in this forest, then they would have fled as fast as Robert himself was running right now.

At this point, he had gone further north than he had ever done before, since arriving at the Farm. He had no idea what was in this direction. From what he could tell, the path ahead of him was nothing more than a continuation of the bleak forbidding forest that had entombed him and the other survivors for the last month.

His chest was tightening, as he finally began to feel the strain that he was putting his body through. Forcing his way through the snow had been incredibly difficult. His legs ached with a deep burning sensation running through his calves. His face still stung from the knife wound David had given him, and he had not realised it until he began to slow down, but Rob must have scrapped himself against the trunks of one of the trees, as he now had a tear in his coat, one that had managed to slice through the inside of his shirt and into his flesh. It did not hurt at this point, but he could feel the warm blood trickling down his forearm.

Rob went to exhale, but it felt as if he was breathing out steam generated from the fire burning deep within his lungs. As he tried, his chest tightened even more, making it almost impossible. He brought up a hand and rested his arm up against a nearby tree, taking a moment to try and catch his breath. It was clear that whatever was fuelling him, making him run as fast as he could, had now run out. His head felt heavy and his eyes were glazed over. He swung his head around to look behind, but as he did, he felt as if his brain crashed into the side of his skull. His eyes seemed to be responding slower than his head, as it felt like it took a few extra moments for him to be able to see what was back there.
It was silent. There was not a soul to be seen. The Shack was not even remotely visible. He had no idea how long he had been running and how far, but he was sure that he must have put a good distance between himself and the Shack, and even further from the Farm itself.

He had not realised it, until he took a moment to look up in the sky, as he discovered that the grey clouds had begun to grow darker, now that the sun had started to set.
"Shit" Rob wanted to say aloud, but the pain in his chest and the fear that John would hear it, stopped him from doing so.
It was clear that John and the others had given up the chase, knowing full well that it was going to be dark soon. After all, that was John's original

plan; to string him up and leave him for the creatures. Now Rob had made it all the easier for him. All he needed to do now was say that Robert had escaped from the Shack and disappeared into the woods. He had no flashlight, flare, or even anything to make a fire with. He was as good as dead when the night came. And he was right. Rob, for a few moments, stood there and thought about how well and truly screwed he really was.

"You fucker" a familiar voice spoke out beside him, bringing Rob struggling to his feet and sluggishly turn around, almost losing his footing and resting his arm against the tree once more.
He turned and expected to see John and all the others standing there, weapons drawn and ready to finish off what they had set out to do. Instead only David stood amongst the trees. Blood was slowly dripping from the end of his nose as one of his nostrils was completely covered in a coat of deep red gore. A line of it had previously run down his face and had got tangled up in his beard. Sections of it were now caked in a sunburst red.
In his hand he held his signature blade. The same one he had used to threaten Rob back in that young girl's room a few days ago, and the same one he had pressed against Rob's face only moments ago. Rob still could feel the slight sting from the cut on his cheek.

It was clear that David did not concern himself with the fast approaching darkness. Either he had some kind of death wish, or he believed that he had enough time to get back to the Farm before it was too late. It was clear that it was already far too late.

"Why did you..." Rob said lethargically, but David soon cut him off, not by speaking, but instead charging straight towards Rob with the blade tightly held down by his side, ready to drive it up into Rob's stomach.

Rob, managing to muster as much strength as he could, moved around to the other side of the tree, putting it between him and David. The knife came flying towards him from the left side, causing Rob to quickly duck and move around the right. David muttered something inaudible due to the fact that all Rob could hear was the sound of his own blood pumping through his temples.

He swiftly grabbed hold of David's knife wielding hand and pulled him towards the tree. He heard the man thud into it before pushing himself back up and moving around to come face to face with his enemy.

"You should have kept your fucking mouth shut" he said, now pointing the knife out at Rob. "This could have gone so much easier, but you had to be difficult. I should have cut your throat in that supermarket in Town".

Rob, panting like a dog as the burning sensation continued on in his lungs, tried to speak, but the words never came. He wanted to tell him to go back, that the night was coming and he would not survive, but he knew that it would not have mattered. David was hell-bent on killing him. He would not be leaving this section of the woods until Robert was good and dead.

Suddenly Rob saw a look in David's eyes. It was a cold dead stare with a flicker of excitement that told him that David was thinking; "It is time to end this". Almost as soon as the thought ran through Rob's head, David was now racing forward. Rob, never taking his eyes off of his blade, followed it and anticipated the attack. As soon as it was in range, Rob pushed David's hand away with all his might, leaving himself open for the man to tackle him to the ground. The two of them toppled into the snow, carving a large crater as their arms and legs flung around.

Rob's hand was tightly gripped around David's hand, keeping hold of it so that he knew at all times where that knife was. Meanwhile David's other hand had turned into a fist and was desperately trying to hit Rob as many times in the face as he could. He got a few in, but the sheer chaos of the situation caused him to hit the cold ground beside him more often than not.

With a firm push, Rob grabbed David and managed to roll over and was now on top of him. A slip of David's hand and it was free from Rob's grasp. He quickly utilised the moment and slashed the smooth sharp edge towards Rob wherever he could. The knife made contact with his other arm, creating an almost identical gash to the one he had got on his other arm from presumably a tree during his escape.

This time he felt the blade go in, as a shot of blood squirted out and spread itself across the snow beside them. The deep red on white contrast stood out almost instantly in the borders of his eyesight. He could not focus on it now. Rob was too busy staring at the knife as he grabbed hold of David's wrist once again. The weapon tore upwards and a small chunk of flesh came out of the cut in Rob's jacket, along with the knife itself. Rob clenched his teeth to try and absorb some of the pain, as his gaze turned back to David's.

"Get off of me!" Rob guessed that he shouted. The whole situation had caused so many different emotions to be flowing through Rob, that he was deafened to everything. He could not hear the sound of David's hand smashing against a rock, or the noise the knife made as it soared across the air and disappeared beneath the untouched snow a few feet away.

He did not hear the sound that took place moments later, when Rob drove his fist into David's face, causing his broken nose to start bleeding again. He suddenly realised that he was holding the same rock in his hand that he had just used to disarm his attacker. Rob had no recollection of grabbing it.

As David turned back towards him, Rob hit him again with the rock, this time smashing out a couple of teeth and causing a few more to fall back into his throat. Rob used this opportunity to let go of the rock and begun to wrap his hands around David's neck. He squeezed tightly as he saw the skin around his hands begin to turn red. David brought a hand up to Rob's face in an attempt to claw it, but it barely made contact with him. The rock strike had disorientated David and his head must have been spinning like a cartoon character being hit on the head with a mallet.

In the moments that passed afterwards, Rob felt his hands tighten and tighten around David's neck as he felt him struggle for breath, coughing up the fragments of his own teeth and blood, now running back through his nose and pouring down the back of his throat. His eyes locked onto Rob's in that instant. Rob could see nothing but horror in them as the man's life was slowing draining out of him.

Right then Rob had a second of déjà vu. A long forgotten memory flicked inside his brain, almost as if a light switch had just been turned on inside his head. He had no idea if it was his own memory or another vision, but suddenly he was hunched over the body of a woman. She had soft pink skin and a blue dress. Her long slender fingers tried desperately to fight off her attacker, but it was no use, the hands wrapped around her throat were too strong as they squeezed tightly, cutting off her air and strangling her. She was beautiful, Rob could see, even in her dying state.

As the vision continued on, Rob realised what he was doing and tried to let go of her. He had no control over his hands. It was almost as if they were glued there. He watched as the woman's eyes went dead and her face drooped downward.

Only then could Rob let go. When he did, he could see that it was David's throat that he had just released his grasp from. His body lay motionless on the ground. The tight strangulation marks were clearly visible around his neck, looking almost like purple rope had been tied around it.

Rob pulled himself to his feet and stood over the corpse, staring down at it. The man who had abused substances and made them, with the intent to sell, was dead. He had lived a life of feeding off other people's misery, like he had done that poor young woman back at the Storehouse on the Farm. He had stolen the food from the supply and in the process, he had got Matt killed. The Farm, and for that matter the new world, was a better place without him in it. But he knew that the others would not see it that way.

Rob quickly looked around for signs of John or the other two goons, but there was nothing. There was not a soul anywhere nearby. He leaned down and checked the dead man's pockets, but there was nothing. If he had a firearm on him then he must have lost it back at the Shack clearing. He had no lighter, no matches, no flashlight, or no light source whatsoever.

"His knife" Rob suddenly said to himself, turning over in the direction of where he had remembered it falling to. He stepped over David's body and kneed down.

The blade was buried under a few inches of snow. A perfect impression of the knife showed where it had fallen through the soft crust. He reached in and grabbed hold of it, before staggering back onto his feet.

With the knife in his hand, Rob took another long look around the area. All he could see was the trees growing darker and darker with each passing moment as the sun slowly began to set behind the gigantic snow clouds overhead. A trail of foot prints, left by Rob and David, could be seen leading off back in the direction from where they had come, but other than that and the clear crater where the two of them had fought, the rest of the snow was perfectly untouched.

An incredible sensation of being alone swept over Rob as he scanned the treelines looking for something... anything. There was nothing but the trees. There was no houses, no farms, or buildings of any kind. Nothing to use to make a fire, and nothing to help fight against the darkness that was slowly creeping up upon him. All that there was, right there in that moment, was the looming sense of dread that built up all around, but when Rob looked, there was nothing there at all.

All was quiet in the deep dark wood.

Day Thirty Five – Part 3

It started to snow a few moments later. The heavy grey clouds delivered their payload over the horrors of the land. The dead and decaying trees were once again coated in a layer of white. All the tracks Rob had made from the Shack to where he was now, were long gone. As he walked, aimlessly through the snow, as the darkness crept up all around him, he imagined David's body slowly vanishing beneath a quilt of snow, as his cold dead eyes stared upward before eventually disappearing.

It had been only a few minutes since Rob had ended the life of another survivor and had now staggered off in a random direction from where it had all gone down. He had no idea where he was going or what he was going to do. He was moving haphazardly between the trees, desperately looking for shelter or some sort of light. The forest was nothing but a bleak wasteland, and the further that he went, the more everywhere looked the same. The falling snow had hidden the path he had trod, so he was not even sure if he was heading in a new direction or simply walking around in circles.

It took him a few moments before he realised he should head back to the Shack near the Farm. John and the others would have retreated from it when they first caught sight of the sky turning dark. The flashlight Rob had in there would have been enough to keep him alive. If he could just figure out a way to seal the door, then he could spend yet another night in there and ride out the night. Of course come the morning, Rob knew that John would be out and looking for him. By then he would have most likely told the others, back at the Farm, that Rob had escaped, probably when John and David went to 'release him'. If he knew of David's death by then, then John could just tell them that Rob killed him, which was not far from the truth, but it would have been another nail in Robert's coffin. At this point, it was undoubtedly too late to return to the Farm and continue living as he had done over the last month. That time was over. If Rob could survive the night, then he would have to start fending for himself. He knew that the Town could be a good place to try and make it on his own.

Although the Farm survivors were sure that they had picked the Town clean, Rob believed that maybe he could find something there. Surely they had not searched every room, every corner, and every garage. There had to be something there. The crazed man in the apartment building; another one of Rob's victims, had managed to survive there on his own for quite some time.

It was not a good plan, but it was all he had. Of course, the entire thing was hopeless and even trying to come up with a plan was a waste of time. As Rob glanced around him, he could not tell which direction the Shack or the Farm, were even in. He was hopelessly stranded and lost, all alone in the calm moments just before the darkness came. And when it did, it would be the end.

He had had a good run. Rob had managed to survive just over a month in a world of horrific terror. Every one of those days had been a struggle. Did he really want to continue living in such a world? Would it not have just been easier to give up? He had tried to fight against it, but ever since the lights went out in the City, everything, even Rob himself, had changed.

He was a murderer now. He had killed four people. No matter what excuses he had given to justify their deaths, the blood of those men still stained his hands.

"I am no better than those things" he said to himself, bringing his hands up to his face and looking at them. It was then that Rob realised he was bleeding from his hand. He turned it over and looked to see that one of his nails had been ripped off. "It must have come off during the struggle" he knew. The cold air had thankfully numbed his hand and he could no longer feel the ends of his fingers. The exposed pink and blood stained flesh beneath looked as if it would have hurt a lot, if Rob had any sensation left.

Just then a noise crept out of the darkness behind him. It was a stage whisper, much louder than the ones he had heard before. The word sent an involuntary shiver down his spine. Although he was already freezing, this quivering shudder seemed to creep through his bones, as if his very marrow was trying to get out.

The word came again a few moments later, only this time it came from the opposite way. At first Rob had thought he had been hearing things. His head was pounding and it felt as if all of the cuts and scrapes he had suffered over the last few days, were all burning with intensity, but now he realised that word he could hear out of the shadows was in fact his very own name.

"Rob... ert... Robb... eeerrrrt" the voices went. There were more of them now. The same word snuck out of every fallen tree and dead branch, from beneath every snow covered rock and every snowflake falling from the sky. They had to have been at least fifty of them. All of them were calling for him. There were not saying the horrifying words and phrases Rob had heard throughout his time here, instead they were now calling out his very name. The creatures knew what they wanted; they wanted him. They wanted him so badly that they had somehow learned his name and were taunting him from behind the trees and in the darkest recesses of the forest, waiting for the time when the night would finally come, and along with it, Rob's own demise.

"Rob... errrrrt" the voices called out again.

This time, as soon as the words touched his ears, Rob turned in the only direction he thought had the slightest chance of being okay, and fled. He was aching badly and every single one of his muscles hurt. He pushed himself as hard as he could, but he knew he was not moving very fast. The snow appeared to have either increased in size, or somehow increased in weight, making it almost impossible to move through it. He did so at an incredibly slow pace, one that he knew that if he was being chased, then they would have caught up with him in a matter of moments.

He knew it was hopeless. He had a better chance of turning around and surrendering, but some strange emotion, lying dormant at the very core of Rob's heart and mind, urged him to keep going. It told him to keep pressing on, to keep trying. He wanted to survive. He didn't want to end up like Karen, her husband, the man and woman in the woods, the Farm survivors when the generator went down, and all the other people in the world. The sensation inside of him told him to stay alive, by any means necessary.

It had been the same emotion that had swept over him when he had fought with the crazed man in Town, when he ran after shooting Mike in the chest, and when he battled it out with David only a short while ago. It had always been sitting there inside of him, waiting for the right time to make itself known and give Rob that little extra boost to help him on his way.

That very thought gave him the feeling of hope. It told him that there must be a way out of this. That he would see tomorrow and the next day and the one after that. The hope was shattered as quickly as it had appeared.

The sky around him fell to darkness. The change was almost instantaneous. It was as if someone had just turned the lights off. Previously the forest had been a dark shade of grey, littered with a white coating of snow spreading itself across the ground, but within a few seconds, the world around went black.

Rob's legs seemed to give up in that same instant. They collapsed beneath him and he toppled to the ground. He placed his hand out to save himself, but it was swallowed up by the snow. The coldness seemed to burn at his skin as it fell through the crust.

It was only then that he realised that the whispers had stopped. He could not tell if they had faded or simply cut out the moment that the lights went out.

As he tried to pull himself up to his feet, his legs trembled at his own weight. He fell down onto his knees. A second passed and there was still nothing. There was no sound coming from anywhere, other than Rob's own exhausted heavy breathing. He raised his head up and looked around, casting an eye over the entire area, trying desperately to look for any signs of movement, but there was nothing. Moment after moment passed like this and nothing seemed to be happening. The small flicker of hope tried to ignite itself inside of Rob. It tried frantically to get itself ablaze, but never came.

Just as Rob attempted to pull himself up once again, multiple inhuman screeches erupted out from all around him. The noises came so suddenly and abruptly, that they made Rob's skin almost jump off of his body and try to make a run for it. He felt as if his own heart had suddenly stopped beating as it hung motionless inside of his chest in total terror.

He managed to move his eyes across the forest floor and towards the nearest cluster of trees. It was then that Rob saw figures standing amongst them. He looked from tree to tree and saw that they were all around. The dark humanoid silhouettes with strange hunches and long slick claws hanging down. Their forms were a darkness that was unlike anything imaginable. They were made up of such an eternal blackness, that they stood out against the pitch black background behind them. They somehow made the rest of the world seem brighter in comparison. They hissed and squealed as some of them moved in closer.

Rob looked over his shoulder and saw more of them closing in on him. They had surrounded him. "This is it" he thought.

The other ones began to step forward. The snow did not seem to hinder them one bit. They glided through it, not leaving footprints behind them, but instead deep cut paths in the snow could be seen, almost as if they somehow melted it with their touch, or the snow was somehow forced out of their way by some unknown supernatural power. Rob could see that the ground was now clearly visible in their wake. That was until more of the creatures moved in the way and formed a solid wall around him.

He felt his head go light and something strange happened inside of him. He could feel himself growing calm. It must have been a similar thing with people who accept their death moments before it happens.

Rob mustered the energy to climb to his feet. He staggered slightly, but managed to hold his footing, believing it to be best to face his inevitable departure face first.

One of them was a lot closer than the others. He stood ahead of the pack and stared into Rob's eyes with his own. His gaze burned through him almost in the exact same way that they themselves had burned through the snow.

Silence had crept over the forest now. There was no sound at all. All of them stood there motionlessly staring at Rob, who in turn, tried his hardest to stare back at them.

The creature at the front slowly lifted his arm out forward. It reached out for him, the dark claws looked as if they would cut through his flesh with the greatest of ease. Rob closed one eye and recoiled away slightly in anticipation of the pain that was soon to come. The claw drew closer to him and as it did, the other creatures surrounding him began to give out a faint hissing sound that grew louder and louder.

The creature's claw abruptly came into contact with him. Rob couldn't tell if it had grabbed hold of his ripped coat, or just placed its palm onto his chest. Either way he suddenly felt an agony pool out from the point of contact and something merciless began to infest his entire body. Rob felt his eyes roll back into his skull as his brain swelled up and pushed against the inside of his skull, growing in mass within a few milliseconds. He felt his heart stop beating and the pain sensation wash over him, leaving behind a strange numbing feeling that caused the joints in his body to twitch.

The sounds of the hissing faded away as Rob felt his mind and soul leave this plane of existence. He knew that he was still standing there in the middle of the cold dark forest, but his consciousness was ripped away and was now flying through the darkness. As he flew, images began to form all around him.

John back in the Middle-Eastern village once again. This time it was a different segment of that memory. He had just kicked in the door of a hut and was now wildly firing into the room. Blood shot out and spat against his face as Rob felt himself being pulled into his eyes. He saw the enjoyment the man got from the deaths he had bestowed upon others. As quickly as it had come, the image was gone. It had now been replaced with the woman David had been making the drugs for. Rob felt himself sucked in to her needle and pumped through her vein. The creatures were the drugs, only this time they were in liquid form. They carved at her from the inside and Rob could see her body slowly break away. Further down the river of blood that he was now riding down, Rob saw more of the Farm survivors. Maria stood beside the corpse of a hanged man, the rope was suspended by nothing. The creatures stood all around her. Another man was cruelly beating a woman. Another had a gun in his hand a stocking over his head. The images began to come hard and fast now. They flashed intensely and Rob began to see all of the darkness that were in the very souls of each and every one of the Farm survivors. Horrifying phantasmagorias began to form in every direction. He could not tell when one ended and another one began, nor who they were related to. The creatures were always nearby. They watched from the side lines in some form or another. He saw people stealing, committing adultery, murdering, beating, and causing misery to each other. At one point he even saw a group of severed heads resting on a side. The faces were all contorted and unfamiliar to him, but he knew what all of this meant. The façade of the survivors washed away in a sea of blood. Their own questionable past lives had now revealed themselves. The new world had given them a chance to hide the suffering they had caused others, but the creatures knew. They wanted them to suffer. They wanted them to be punished for their sins.

Right then, Rob saw what they wanted from him. The visions changed to an aerial view of the Farm. It was night. Rob couldn't tell if it was this exact night, or if it was from another time. The snow had stopped falling but was still present on the ground. The string of LED lights shone brightly as they hung all around the Courtyard. He could see other light sources coming from windows in the Farmhouse and at the top of the Barn. The world began to shift and Rob felt his consciousness floating down and around the area. He saw that the bonfire was not lit and that only a few people were present in the Courtyard. One man stood beside the entrance to the Barn, while another was standing next to the Tool Shed. He felt himself being drawn towards it. As he got closer, he could hear the generator running inside.

Rob's soul moved nearer to the closed door, before walking through it like a ghost. Inside he saw the generator. It rumbled away, sending power to the string of lights all around. The rumbling sound was louder now. He could see the replacement belt Matt had attached to it after the night the power went out. It seemed to be holding up alright and running without a hitch.

A moment later everything went dark again. Unlike it had done before when Rob was in the woods and the darkness fell upon him, everything this time seemed to turn to the same abnormal black that the creatures were made up of. The endless void of nothingness where not even light could penetrate it. It was all Rob could see.

He began to hear whispers inside of his head. They spoke of what they wanted. Their words began to soak into Rob's mind. The corruption bled into him before that one word lingered once again.

Rob felt an unrelenting force push his eyelids open. He was back in the night forest once again, except this time all of the creatures were gone. It was just him alone in the woods. He glanced around and saw that there was no trace of them. The melted sections of the snow were still present, but they gave no indication of where the creatures had gone to. His head was killing him, but it slowly got better the further time went on. When it had finally disappeared, he was left with a feeling of euphoric light-headedness. He felt as if he was still dreaming.

He turned around slowly and the world took a few moments to shift with him. As it did, it looked as if a haze of static covered over the area. As he looked at the pure white layer of snow on the ground, he could see small speckles of moving shapes flickering between white, grey and black. It was something similar to a badly tuned in television channel.

Ahead of him, Rob could see a faint glow of light shining brightly through the darkness. He was not entirely sure what the light was exactly, but a voice inside of his head told him that it was the way back to the Farm. He went to take a step forward, when he suddenly realised that the lingering word was still hanging in the air around him. Rob felt his ears jerk as if someone was speaking the word directly into his ear at such a distance, that he could feel their breath brush up against it. He frantically looked around either shoulder for the speaker of it, but there was no one there, yet the word came.

"Join"

Act Three

Among the Shadows

Part One

The days groaned with cold as they passed on by. Each passing day seemed to get colder and colder as the weeks went on. The harsh winter that had hit the world appeared as if it was never letting up. Every new day brought a new layer of snow upon the ground.

As the survivors of the Farm got further and further away from the day that the madman had escaped they began to feel secure once more. The first few days had come and gone uneventfully. He watched from the shadows as their leader gathered them all outside the bonfire and told them the news. He said that Rob had escaped and in the resulting struggle he had killed David. He had decided to be honest with them by telling them that he had got away, rather than saying that he himself had killed him. A few of their faces had turned concerned and worried, but the big man with the shotgun slumped over his shoulder and Molotov cocktails hanging from his belt, told them that night crept over moments later, and he assured them that the man called Robert must have been devoured by the creatures of the shadows by now, after all he had no light, no weapons, and no shelter. He was as good as dead; his words.

It was a safe assumption Rob knew. From all he had witnessed since the beginning, anyone who had been left out in the dark was consumed by them. Every single one of the survivors gathered around their fearless leader knew the price of staying out of the light. They had all seen a friend or family member taken from them in this way.

But Rob had managed to survive the night on his own before. Of course he had previously had a light source of some kind, such as the incident with Mike by the stream, or the shelter the night he was left alone in town. But for all intents and purposes John could have very well been right.

The truth of the matter was very different. Rather than kill and mutilate him, the creatures had given him something he had never had before; a purpose. All of his life he had been carelessly floating through it day by day, watching as people he knew changed and became something better while he had remained the same. Now he had something to drive him forward. He had made a deal with the devil, and the devil wanted something in return. In this case he had saved his own skin by giving in to the creatures. They had plagued him with words such as 'join' and 'acceptance' since the beginning, slowly converting him over to their side to do their very bidding. They wanted the survivors and they wanted Rob to hand deliver them on a platter for them.

As far as Rob knew, these people; the survivors who had banded together when the power in the city went down, fought their way through the streets as others were slaughtered all around them, and fled into the woods, they were the last people on earth. The rest of humanity had fallen and this Farm, this small remote place situated in the middle of a decaying forest, was the place where humans had taken their last stand. Rob had stood amongst them once. He had tried to fight and to live. He had tried his hardest to keep going, day by day, with the smallest glimmer of hope that things could get better. Maybe humanity could rise once again from the ashes of this new world. He had once believed that they were worth saving. He had now seen the true face of human nature in the vision the creatures had shown him.

All of those people on the Farm had some kind of darkness hidden away inside of them. He had seen the horrors that these people, the so-called last survivors of their species, had done throughout the course of their lives. He only knew a few specific people's darkness, but he had seen what the rest of them had done. Murder, rape, robbery, and many more sins that they had tried to live with in the old world, and now tried to hide within the new.

Conflicting emotions and thoughts fought one another in an endless battle inside of his mind.

"Not all of them had to be punished" a slight whimpering voice grew somewhere inside of him.

A shred of humanity still lay within the deepest, darkest recess of Rob's subconscious, even after all this time. It reminded him that Peter, and a few others; they deserved to be saved. They had not done anything wrong. He did not know the others by name, but he knew where they would be when the time came. If he could help get them out when he completed the creature's wishes and destroyed or shut down the generator, bringing the Farm into darkness once more, then maybe the creatures would listen to him.

That was Rob's original thought process when he had first returned to the Farm. He had sat in the same bush for what felt like days. He watched the big man give his speech about him, and he saw the faces of Peter and the others when they had heard the news. It was only Peter who had shown the slightest hint of sorrow over Rob's departure, from what he could make out beneath Peter's still bruised and battered face. The rest of them were more worried about the idea of Rob returning and slaughtering them all in their sleep, which to be fair on them, was not too far from what was awaiting them on the horizon.

The more he watched them, the more he could see them for who they were. All the things that had previously gone unnoticed during his time with them were now coming into full view. He saw a married man within the group, whose partner was still alive and sleeping in their room, sneak out to fornicate elsewhere with another survivor. Jennifer; the woman David had kept drugged, eventually hanged herself. It was a clear sign that without David providing her with the drugs that she so dearly needed, the reality of their situation had sunk in and she finally cracked. They found her the next morning and didn't even bother burying her. Instead of laying her to rest in the plot of land east of the Tool Shed, John ordered them to take her into the woods. Rob agreed with them that the ground was far too hard to dig, but his thoughts were on Matt again and the idea that his body was off rotting somewhere in this forest.
Rob thought about following them, but decided it was best if he was not seen. Stepping out from where he hid during the day, would have put the whole plan at risk.

He saw Maria, sneak out of the back of the Barn with food she had clearly stolen from the group, and sell it on to another man for a packet of cigarettes.
Two men fought on one of the days a few hours after noon. Rob heard a ruckus coming from inside the Farmhouse, soon after they burst out of the backdoor and brawled it out in the snow. John and his henchmen eventually broke it up, but not before one of them took a swing at the big

man. It was either intentional or he was aiming for the other guy, but the fist connected with John's face. It did not look as if it hurt the man, but that didn't matter. John lost it once again and beat this man to within an inch of his life. Rob watched as no one dared intervene until John was finished. It was only then that they carried the broken man off and back inside the Farmhouse. The other man had been stuck on guarding the Tool Shed, where the generator was kept, for the next few nights in a row. Rob had heard John tell him that if he was caught asleep, then he was going to string him up and leave him out in the woods for the monsters to get him. For the next few nights, Rob watched as the man used every willpower he could muster to keep himself awake.

The other survivors did nothing as John continued to grow in power and stoked fear in the hearts of everyone. No one dared step out of line, at least when John was looking.

The more Rob watched the group, the more it filled him with a burning rage that somehow kept him warm throughout the winter nights. He could not feel the cold burning at his skin, the same way it had done so before his pact with the creatures. Whatever they had done to him had made him resistant to the cold.

He did not feel hunger, nor did he eat, in fact no feelings of any kind were felt within his stomach. As for sleep, Rob felt tired but in a different way to how he had done before. He felt as if he had gone past the point of being tired and was now running off a second wind. It felt similar to the days he had spent all night studying and drank only coffee to help him get by.

His hands and feet felt phantom, as if they were not his yet he was still in control of them. Many a night, when the survivors of the Farm had gone to bed, Rob had sat there staring at his own hands, trying to get the feeling back, but all he could see was the endless blood on them that would never wash off.

He was a drone; an automaton that served his dark masters. They had given him a new lease on life and Rob was biding his time before he could repay them.

Days must have passed before the group had fallen into a comfortable place once again. The creatures had left them well and truly alone, for now, but Rob knew that this would only be until his work had been done. The survivors of the Farm had expected them to come every night at first, but after a week or so, nothing did. They had no near misses and no one wandered out of the Farm at night. They had no power failures and not even so much as a whisper from the shadows could be heard. Although Rob seemed to remember that it was only he that the creatures whispered to.

He could still hear them however. They wanted him to get to work. They wanted him to get beyond the fence, and the lines of LED lights strung up overhead, a place where they could not step, and they wanted him to destroy the generator, letting in the foul beasts so that they could rain their destruction upon the group.

Even if he did not do a single thing, the act of cutting their lights would be just as bad as killing them himself. They would die by his own hand, he knew. By destroying their light source, he would be leading these people to their deaths.

Most of them he had not known. He had made sure to keep his distance from them. He had witnessed first-hand what it felt like when someone he knew was killed right before him. Matt's murder had left a bigger scar on him that he had first thought. It had left almost as big a stain on his subconscious as all of the murders Rob had committed, in self-defence or otherwise.

In the nights when the survivors had gone to bed, Rob sat there behind the trees or in the foliage, thinking of Matt and the man who had killed him.

Once again differing emotions washed over him during this time. It was the same thoughts that appeared when he questioned about going in there to rescue Peter from what was coming. The questions that burned inside of Robert's brain were along the lines of 'Did they too have darkness inside of them?' and 'Would he still be living amongst them if all of what had transpired over Rob's last few days with the group had not gone down?'

Rob believed that he would. He would still be living with people who lied and deceived, who were being led by a murdering tyrannical maniac, who was willing to kill whomever stepped out of line.

If the opportunity had not arisen for Rob to turn his coat and join the 'enemy', then he too would be with the group, waiting for the time that they were caught off guard and the creatures' came for them.

As for if Peter, Matt, and anyone else he thought was 'good', had a darkness inside of them that they were trying to keep hidden from the world, he did not know. All he knew was Matt was a kind hearted person who was the only one to stand up to John, other than when Peter finally cracked and tried to defend Rob himself, and he had suffered greatly for it.

All the time his mind raced like this. During the day watching the Farm survivors shovel snow and make the Courtyard easy for them to move across. They made additional repairs to the surrounding fence, and they catalogued their provisions. The group had not made any runs into town during the whole time that Rob watched them. In fact not a single one of them left the safety of the Farm once. The harsh winter, that had befallen them, had kept them tight and enclosed within the boundaries that they had created for themselves.

John had told them that they had enough food to make it through until the snow cleared, most likely thanks to the extra mouths that they no longer had to feed now that Robert and David were no longer around. It was also helpful to them that both the apparent food thief had been killed, and the actual food thief was also now dead.

John had also told the others that it was far too dangerous to head out into the forest in this weather. They would hunker down and try to ride it out.

It was a good plan Rob knew. It was the right thing for them to do. The snow was hard to move in. It was deep and it slowed the pace of everyone. It would have taken nearly twice as long to do a supply run to town, if there was even anything left to find there after the survivors had previously picked it clean.

There would be no animals to hunt. Any that still remained in this dead forest were hiding or hibernating, Rob assumed. They could have most likely all succumbed to the horrors that awaited everyone in the shadows of those trees.

It was blisteringly cold beyond the heat of the bonfire in the Courtyard, not to mention that the dark grey clouds would bring nightfall onto them far more quickly than before. All in all it was far better for them to stay in once place, but at the same time, it was also better for the creatures. Even though he did not know that they were out there, when the wind blew and when the sun went down, he could hear their whispers from all around. The words, that were once inaudible except for a few key ones, were now all clear as day. They reminded him of what he needed to do, a few of the people that needed to be punished, as well as encouraging Rob to begin. They were close. They were excited. And they hid in the shadows, the same way they had always done, the same way Rob was doing now, waiting for the right moment to strike. The creatures were hungry. The thirst for the blood of the survivors and eagerly awaited as their snake in the grass sat and bided his time. Rob was that snake. He had betrayed his own species for these things, but at this point in time, after everything he had been through and all he had witnessed and done, he did not care. He knew what he was and he knew what the people in the Farm were. What he didn't know was what came after.

Did the creatures intend to let him and whoever else he helped escape the Farm live? Or was it all just a trick and he would be killed and mutilated the same way that was waiting for the Farm? He did not know. All he could do was continue on with his purpose.

His anger fuelled him. The time was soon. He wanted to wait for the right moment and that moment was fast approaching. The group had got sloppy. Some days, no one had wanted to brave the cold and light the Tiki torches. They stood there like more dead trees as the tops were covered in snow. The only lights in the Courtyard were the string of LED ones connected to the generator in the Tool Shed. It was only that which needed to be cut off.

The cold had caused most people to stay in their respective buildings, the Barn, the Farmhouse, or the Storehouse, with only a few people moving back and forth between them from time to time if they absolutely had to. These all had their own individual light sources, and they would need to be dealt with in their own way. Some of this Rob had planned for, whereas others, he needed the plan to form as and when everything occurred.

The Storehouse did not have any lights of its own inside, at least not any built into the building itself. Instead the survivors had torches, flashlights, lanterns and other such portable lighting devices that they kept in each of the rooms. Most of them were turned off at night, other than just a few. The hallway of the Storehouse, Rob remembered from the time he had confronted David, did not have any lights whatsoever. As soon as that outside door was shut, or a light in one of the rooms, the hallway became an eternal tunnel of darkness.

This was the same for the Barn. Rob did not know what kind of lighting John had arranged to be fitted inside of it. He had only been inside it once or twice in the whole time he had lived at the Farm. From his days watching, he had learnt that John kept something on all night. He could see the warm yellow glow coming from the cracks in the wooden planks nailed over the top window.

As for the bottom, Maria still lived within this section, but now with one of the other goons that had taken up David's previous residence there, and they relied heavily on the outside Courtyard lights for safety. A big mistake. Rob knew that if he was to take them lights out and bring darkness to the Courtyard, the creatures would cut off the top floor of the Barn, effectively trapping John. Rob wondered what he would do with him, considering he would probably stay up there until morning. He would have to figure this out once everything had been done. He didn't think that the leader would try and fight his way out. The man was a survivalist. But with him trapped up there, Rob would be free to move around freely during the chaos.

As for the Farmhouse itself, the survivors used the lights inside of it, connected to the fuse box. Rob was not sure if it somehow operated off its own electrical grid, or if a nearby power station was still up and running, either way the lights in the Farmhouse worked as normal. Matt had been the one to help get this up and running.

Rob would need to get inside and disable it to allow the creatures access. He would need to find Peter and anyone else he wanted to take with him, before cutting it off. Once that happened, the Farmhouse would fall into darkness the monsters of the shadows would descend upon it, tearing the flesh of anyone who dared remain.

There was only one guard stationed outside the Tool Shed at night. It was clear that in a repeated incident where the generator stopped working once again, someone was standing by to repair it the same way Matt had done before.

John had put all of his faith into the generator to keep them safe. It was another sloppy move, which Rob was surprised to see John do. He was grateful for it however. With David's knife still gripped firmly in his own hand, Rob knew that this one person, alone in the middle of the Farm's Courtyard, was the only thing that stood between him and achieving his own goal.

After days of watching them, and the eager hunger of the creatures growing more apparent all around him, Rob knew that tonight was the night that it was going to happen. He had to prepare and get ready for what was awaiting him and the survivors of the Farm community.

As dusk began to take form in the sky, he saw that the clouds had started to depart. It was the first time he had seen the sky in what felt like forever. Between the cracks in the clouds were bright glimmers of orange that were slowly fading to black.

Rob watched quietly from his post in the shrubbery beside the trees, as Maria went inside the Farmhouse, along with a few others, possibly for their evening meal. John headed off into the Barn, and a few moments later Rob saw the little light at the top come on. At that point the man who had been ordered to guard the Tool Shed tonight, a different man from the one who had been stationed there for a few days, this was one of John's men, flicked the switch and the string of lights came on illuminating the Courtyard in a variety of faint colours.

As the sun faded beyond the horizon, night began to fall over the Farm. The time had come.

Part Two

Night fell across the land. The thick grey clouds, that had once covered the entire sky, had now dispersed and only remnants of them remained. They had once been enormous, spanning overhead like a ceiling enclosing itself around the small world that the survivors had carved for themselves. Now they were nothing more than patches of grey spread sporadically across the deep black sky. The moon had finally peered its head from behind them and now illuminated a section of the sky, causing nearby stars to be almost invisible in the satellite's glow. It was the perfect backdrop for the events awaiting to unfold that sat just upon the horizon.

Further down, the string of LED lights shone brightly all around the Farm's Courtyard. Mainly whites and soft yellows, the lights circled and zigzagged all across the ground. The bonfire had not been relit this night. The frost had made the burnable wood in the bonfire far too wet to maintain, and the fire had died around the same time the sun began to set.

This would play to Robert's advantage. With the unlit Tiki torches and the bonfire, the only light sources were those that were connected to the generator in the Tool Shed.

Rob had moved around the woods to the other side of the Farm. He was now facing towards the Tool Shed, with the Storehouse on his right and the Farmhouse on his left. As he moved through the foliage, a leaf brushed against his face. He lifted up his hand and gently wiped away the sensation. His hand was foreign to him. Although he had complete control over it, he could not really feel it. The hand was cold to the touch, so Rob brushed away dark thoughts that had started to creep into his head, and convinced himself that it was just numb from the chill on the wind. The truth of it was that Rob had started to feel less and less in control of himself the longer he had watched the survivors of the Farm. He felt almost like a puppet, dancing on a string to a mysterious force that had assumed control. Now that it was closer to the inevitable horror that must soon follow, the more it felt as if Rob has having some kind of outer body experience.

As he brushed away the leaves, he tried to remember why he was doing this. Not everyone in there deserved to die. Pete had tried to defend him before Rob was exiled. He was sure that not all of the other gawkers deserved what was coming either. While most of them had lived as parasites since this whole mess had gone down over a month ago, leeching off of the hardworking members of the community, others had pulled their weight around the Farm. And yet they all still hung on every word that their 'benevolent' leader uttered. The more he thought about it, the more he could feel the anger building up inside of him. At first it did not feel like his own emotion. It felt almost like it was the puppeteer's feelings, as if the dark force that was driving him had consumed and devoured his own emotions and replaced them with its own, but then Rob began to remember how the survivors of the Farm had stood and watched, doing nothing, when Matt was killed and when Rob himself stood trial before them. It helped make what was coming all that easier.

Rob took a long deep breath as he quietly moved his way closer and closer to the Farm's perimeter fence. The makeshift panels, combined pieces of old doors and rotted wooden planks, which they had gotten from inside the Storehouse when they had first arrived, stood around three and a half to four feet off the ground. It was relatively easy to get over, as Rob had done so many times while taking residence within the Farm. The issue here was the guard posted outside the Tool Shed. John had stopped posting a guard at the bottom of the Barn, given now that the food thief had been taken care of, so the one man leaning against the side of the Tool Shed was all that stood between the Farm residents and their destruction.

The lights that hung between a nearby tree and the side of the Storehouse would give Robert away in a second if he made his approach while the goon was looking. Although the rest of the world around the Farm had fallen into the dark abyssal nothingness, the Courtyard was still very much illuminated.

The few Tiki torches that were lit would play to his advantage. None of them were in the vicinity of Rob's path between the fence and the Tool Shed. All he had to do was get past the LED lights when the guard turned his back.

Just then Rob's conscience flickered. It was just for a brief moment and it was gone as quickly as it came, but the thought left behind a lingering feeling of humanity inside of him. He glanced down at the knife in his other hand; David's knife, the blade he had tried to use to murder Rob, which he was now, in turn, going to use to kill this man. Those thoughts did not last long. He had been the same man that had tried to hold Rob back while Matt was being executed, as well as one who had hit Rob in the face in the past. Although that all felt like ancient history by now, the passage of an unknown number of days or even weeks had made the memories, that had transpired whilst living in the Farm, seem almost like a serial dream from long ago.

Just then the man turned his back to Robert. It was time to go to work. Rob moved out from the bushes and the shadow of the nearby tree and entered into the light. It was the first time that he had been beneath the Courtyard's lighting system in a long time. Rob placed one hand on the top of the fence and in one quick and quiet motion, he hopped over it, gently landing on the snow below. This section of the fence was barely used, and it was clear that no one had been over here in a long time as the snow was still crisp and untouched. It softened the sound of Robert's landing, although now the snow had clearly been disturbed. If he did not act quickly, the goon would soon notice. Thankfully it appeared that he was too busy at the moment expelling urine in the mushed well-trod snow at the back of the Tool Shed.

"Probably too focused on spelling his name correctly" Rob thought to himself as he began making his way over towards him.

He would need to do this quickly. If the man saw him approaching, then all he needed to do was yell and it was all over. Rob believed that he could get to him before he could draw his weapon and fire it, but the yell alone would be loud enough to wake someone. In the dead of night, any sound out here could be heard at a great distance.

The familiar feelings washed over Rob as he made his way closer to the Tool Shed. Inside the Courtyard and the Farm itself felt like an entirely different world to the bleak dark forest only a few metres away. Rob had been watching this place from afar for so long, thinking of what had to happen and how it was going to occur, that it did not even seem real that he was now, once again, on the other side of that fence.

Suddenly the man let out a sigh of relief that gave Rob the impression that he was done. He now had very little time to get to the guard before he turned around and realised something was wrong. Out here, other than the Tool Shed itself, Robert had nowhere to hide. He had to act now.

He clenched David's knife tighter in his hand and moved in. As he approached the side of the Shed, he heard the man's trouser zip before he cleared his throat and spat upon his masterpiece. It was moments later that Rob ended the guard's life.

Rather than the man who had begged for his death in the woods during the first few days, who Rob had killed so mercifully, Mike being shot in the chest, who Rob had killed accidently, or the mad man in the Town, or David, who Rob had killed both in self-defence, the man who John had appointed to watch the generator in the Tool Shed, Rob had killed in cold blood. This had in fact been a murder.

The man had no time to react. He had been taken completely unaware when Robert grabbed him by his hair, pulled him backward enough to bring him lower to the ground and reveal his neck, complete with its throbbing muscles, and slide the knife's blade across his throat.

It had all happened in about a second. A slight yelp was released from the guard when Rob pulled him back, possibly due to the surprise, but that was soon replaced with the sound of gurgling and choking as blood pumped out of the wound and began to flood down his torso. He brought a hand up to his neck, most likely in an attempt to stop the bleeding, but

Rob pushed him down to the ground, disorientating him, causing his arms to flap about wildly for a moment.

As Rob stood over the man whilst he was dying, the two of them locked eyes. Rob could see that his eyes had turned wide in disbelief that the man who had cut his throat and was now standing over him, had previously been one of their own; someone who John had told them all had been killed.

Rob did not wait around for the man to take his last breath, there was still much to do. At any moment, someone could have either heard the commotion, or they could just pop out for some other reason. Time was very short.

He went over to the Tool Shed door and opened it. It was unlocked, thankfully. The guard at the door was all the security the Farm survivors thought that they needed. That had made Robert's job easier. As the door opened the sound of the humming generator filled the area around him. He could see the homemade belt that Matt had put together to keep the thing running after it had shut down that one night long ago. All Rob needed to do was cut that and it was all over. The creatures would swarm into the Courtyard and that would be it, in theory. But the reality was that the generator only controlled the lights outside. The Farmhouse had its own power, and both the Barn and the Storehouse were using their own lights. What Rob needed to do was get them outside, and it was then that he had an idea.

Other than the sound of the generator, the entire place was silent. All of the survivors were either tucked up in their beds or just hiding away inside and out of the cold. It was time to warm them up a bit.

Rob opened the door to the Storehouse and the dark hallway lit up. A large dark shadow of Rob poured onto the floor and stretched out all the way to the far end where David's room had been. The shadow was contorted in the light behind Rob, making his fingers and legs look far longer than they actually were.

He glanced over to the side and saw that the fuel canisters were still piled up. He grabbed one of them. It was about half full judging by the weight, and he carried it outside, carefully closing the door behind him. He did not want to alert the Farm survivors before the time was right.

Rob moved to the side of the Storehouse and unscrewed the lid of the canister. The smell of petrol drifted out. He turned it upside down and began splashing it against the corner of the building. The liquid hit against the wooden structure and soaked into it. When the canister was nearly used up, Rob began pouring it onto the ground, creating a puddle that began pooling down into a stream towards the entrance.

Once it was done, Rob tossed the can onto the ground, allowing any remnants of fuel to spill out, and walked back over towards the Tool Shed. In the path between the Storehouse and the Shed, a solitary Tiki torch stood, its flame flickering in the gentle breeze. Rob grabbed hold of the torch by the wooden stem, hoisted it out of the ground and tossed it into the stream of petrol. Instantly the fuel caught alight and fire began racing up it towards the puddle and the corner of the Storehouse. As it did, Rob moved into the Shed and got himself ready.

Although the creatures recoiled at light, even the flames of a fire, the fire would serve to get enough of the survivors out and into the Courtyard. Ones inside the Barn and the Farmhouse itself would come outside to gawk at the fire, as few would actually bother to help, whilst the people inside the Storehouse would escape outside to avoid the fire. His plan would hopefully draw John out from the Barn.

It wasn't long before Rob's plan came to fruition. A scream rang out from inside the Storehouse. It was a woman's and it was loud enough that Rob knew it would wake up quite a few people. Now all he had to do was wait for the right moment.

A man exited the Storehouse first yelling "Fire! Fire!" over and over. He was closely followed by another three or so people getting outside. A few of them tried to put out the flames, but they had nothing that would help. The sheet that one of them had brought outside with them, had only helped to spread it further. By this point the flames were already creeping up the side of the building.

Rob heard the Farmhouse backdoor open, closely followed by people descending down the few wooden steps crying things along the line of "Oh my god", and "How could this have happened?"

Rob peeked his head out of the Tool Shed and around the corner. Everyone who had been inside the Farmhouse were now out. Peter stood in the entrance, watching. Rob could see the bruises still visible on his face from John's beating. Maria stood in front of him, at the bottom of the steps out the back of the Farmhouse. She too was staring in disbelief at the fire as it began to make its way onto the roof of the Storehouse. Rob's gaze went over to the Barn, and it was then that he saw the man himself. John pushed open the door of the Barn and stepped out into the Courtyard, his shotgun held close to his chest. His beard and his hair were a mess, indicating that the big man did in fact sleep. His eyes went wide at the sight of the flames as they consumed more and more of the old wooden building with each passing second. He took a few steps out of the doorway and watched for a brief moment as the other survivors scrambled to try and help put out the fire, or merely stood staring at it, as Rob had predicted. Shortly after, John tried to say something. Rob saw his mouth move as he desperately tried to put it all together and figure out how the fire had actually started. Rob could see that it was almost instantly when John realised something was wrong. His eyes slowly glanced over towards the Tool Shed and the location of the one man who he had personally put in charge of watching the Courtyard that night. "Where..." he tried to shout, but was drowned out in the chaos. "Where the fuck is Alex?" he managed to blurt out, but no one was listening.

Rob tucked himself back inside the Tool Shed and held David's knife up to the belt of the generator. Maybe it was the fact that John had started to catch on to the fact that something was wrong, or maybe Rob just could not wait any longer, the excitement had started to grow inside of him as his plan of luring them all out into the Courtyard had proved successful, but either way Robert pushed the blade upwards, cutting and dislodging the belt from the cogs it was attached to. It flung off, getting itself caught in various other gears and being torn to ribbons as the generator shook, coughing out black smoke as a small fire began to spark inside of it.

"Lights out"...

Part Three

At first Robert thought that the thing wasn't going to die and that he had trapped himself in the belly of the beast, with all of the survivors swarming around him and John himself marching towards the Tool Shed, his great gun in hand. He knew that if the lights stayed on, then they would see the body of the man Rob had cut the throat of; Alex, Rob believed he heard John say. It was only a matter of time before either the lights went out, or Rob needed to make a break for it and head back to the fence, having failed the dark mission he had received from the shadow creatures lurking in the forest. There was no telling what they would do to him if he allowed the people living on the Farm to survive. The ones with darkness inside of them, their sins would be unpunished and Robert would be left to face up to the fact that he could not be one of them. The Farm survivors had exiled him, and he would have botched the best attempt that the creatures had of getting what they wanted. After this attack, and seeing the body of Alex with his throat cut, John and the others would know that someone was out there. John would know it was Rob instantly. They would change their tactics and keep the Farm locked down tighter than Fort Knox.

It was then that Robert got a sign that everything was going to be okay. He released a sigh of relief as the generator ceased to function. Almost instantly the string of lights surrounding the Courtyard, and crossed over all above them, went dark. The few light sources inside the three buildings, as well as the ever growing flames burning away at the side of the Storehouse, were all that remained.

"Oh shit!" Rob heard someone shout as he moved out from the Tool Shed and saw that the crowd had gathered only around twenty feet away from him.

There was a moment of silence that followed. It was the same one that had come before the creatures attack after the lights went out last time. It was strange for Rob to be on the other end of it. The darkness had consumed the entire Courtyard and it was not long before they were attacked, but Rob felt nothing as he watched the survivors begin to panic and run.

Out of the shadows of the trees, inhuman roars and shrieks erupted. Some of the people stopped dead in their tracks, as if the sounds had a spell that had frozen them, while others tried desperately to make it across the Courtyard to the Farmhouse or the Barn.

Of course this all happened in about as much time as it takes to blink, because almost a second later the creatures showed themselves. They moved out from behind the side of buildings and behind the fence, almost as if they had been hiding there the whole time. Some had even appeared from the section of fence that Rob himself had been at not too long ago, and he was sure that there had not been anyone or anything there then.

As a few monsters squealed with excitement at the fresh prey they were about to kill, the rest began to flock inside. They jumped the fence with the greatest of ease and sped across the Courtyard at a ridiculous speed. The first ones to get kills however were the ones that had already appeared inside the Farm's perimeter. One of John's other goons was the first to go. He had broken away from John and made a run for the Farmhouse, clearly thinking that the Barn must have been too far away. He was caught in the path between the two buildings, where an unlit Tiki torch stood. The man locked eyes with the creature as it hissed and drove its dark claws into his stomach. The man gasped in disbelief and a shot of blood spurted out of his mouth as the beast pulled back its hands, bringing with it the man's intestines and streams of gore that began to pour out.

The woman near the Storehouse, who Rob suspected was the one who had woken up and screamed, bringing everyone out to the Courtyard, had tried to get back inside the Storehouse. She must have thought that she had more of a chance inside with the fire than she did out here in the darkness, which was right, if the fact that one of the other men nearby hadn't pushed her out of the way to get inside first. She fell to the ground as one of the creatures leapt on top of her and began clawing at the back of her skull. Chunks of hair and flesh flew up into a cloud of pink mist while others tried to get past, only to be captured and devoured by more of the shadows as they moved in all around.

Rob glanced over towards the Farmhouse and managed to catch a glimpse of Peter dragging Maria inside, most likely in an attempt to save her. Rob knew that he needed to get inside and tell Peter that it was going to be alright as long as they stayed with him. As for Maria, he was not sure if she truly deserved saving, considering her actions had resulted in a death, but as he thought it, Rob looked around at the chaos that was happening and wondered who he was to be judging someone else. His own actions had resulted in the deaths of so many already, and that was just the beginning.

An explosion occurred inside the Storehouse. The fire had seemed to reach David's narcotics on his workstation, and the entire thing had detonated in a blast that took out the back corner of the building. The fire had now completely covered the roof and he could tell that the inside was now beginning to collapse onto itself.

A man came rushing out moments later. Rob was unsure if he was the same one who had pushed the woman over, as he was now ablaze. Flames had ignited his clothes and hair as he ran frantically out of the doorway, causing two nearby creatures to recoil. One of which had finished tearing into the back of the woman's head and left it a hollow bowl-like shell, her blood and brain matter dripped from the creature's claws as it turned away from the man on fire, and sped off in search of another victim.

A gunshot blast broke out over the top of the sounds of screams and squeals and flesh being torn into. Rob, still standing beside the Tool Shed merely staring at the slaughter that was occurring, turned his attention to the sound. As he did, a voice called out a word in such a horrifying tone, that it made Rob's heart feel as if it restarted for a moment and true human emotions began to flood back inside of him.

"ROB!" John's voice called out from across the Courtyard as he backed away into the Barn, his shotgun firing huge blasts of light towards the creatures trying to get to him. He was doing well at keeping them in front of him and using the shotgun as an enormous flashlight. The light emanating behind him from the inside of the Barn shone outward as he kicked backward, knocking the door open.

Before he disappeared inside, Rob saw the fire in his eyes. He knew that it was not the reflection of the Storehouse ablaze, but instead it was a fire that burned deep inside him. His anger was fuelled by Robert's betrayal. Rob's very appearance here proved whatever theory he had about how the fire started and the power went out.

His attention soon turned back onto the beasts before him as they began to move back, trying to avoid the light from inside. Rob caught one last look at his face as the Barn door closed behind him. He was sure that John would have already thought of some contingency plan, most likely having a prepacked bag prep for such an eventuality, in the case that the Farm did get overrun and he needed to cut his ties and run.

Rob did not know what he would be able to do. It was the middle of the night and the forest was pitch black. He might be able to escape using flares and Molotov cocktails, but they wanted him. The creatures of the shadows would not rest until they had destroyed him. Rob had seen this in their vision when they had surrounded him. The big man was one of the biggest wrongdoers of the lot of them. He knew that they would not let him leave.

They had already began to swarm around the bottom of the Barn. More of them had flooded out of the forest and appeared around darkened corners to join in the feeding frenzy, or hover around the buildings, waiting for the few survivors that had managed to get inside; John in the Barn, and Maria and Peter in the Farmhouse. They were the only ones that he knew.

In what felt like only a few minutes, the slaughter was all over. Most of the screaming had stopped, other than one woman Rob could see being torn apart by four of them over by the bonfire. That too soon became contorted as the creatures tore away her insides, leaving behind only a gargled desperate attempt at calling for help.

It had only taken mere moments for most of the Farm survivors to be overrun by the darkness. They had been caught unprepared and unequipped, except for John, and their lives of living safely within the confinement of the Farm's defences, such as the fence and the lighting system, had made them sloppy. The few Tiki torches, which they had bothered to light, still burned brightly in their small areas and kept the creatures away. If they had lit all of them, then Robert would have had a much harder job in blacking out the Courtyard. There would have been much more time to get caught in the act, which could have resulted in a much different outcome to how this played out.

Rob began to move across the Courtyard. He could hear the sounds of the beasts devouring their victims. Some of them were still tearing them apart. It looked almost like one of the creatures was pulling red confetti and shredded paper out of the man beneath its feet and throwing it into the air. The blood rained down upon him, but still did not manage to penetrate its thick black skin. As soon as the blood got anywhere near it, it disappeared into the dark colourless void.

One creature was squatting on the path between the Tool Shed and the Farmhouse, in Rob's way. It was feasting, as far as he could tell, upon one of the survivor's organs that it was pulling out of a hole in the man's chest. He had left the man's heart for now, which it was clear, was still beating. Rob could see the man breathe slowly as the creature drove its long dark claws into him, and pulled out something deep red, almost purple, and pull it up to its face. Whether or not it was actually eating it was still up for debate. Rob could not tell as he walked past.

The man's eyes flickered and moved towards Rob. They followed him. The man's expression was that of pure agony, as if he could feel every little thing that the creature was doing to him. Blood ran out of his mouth and across a deep cut running down the side of his face. The skin on his cheek hung on by a thread. It had probably been this wound that brought him down to the ground where the creature could finish him off.

Rob's thoughts turned to the first man he had killed. It was a similar situation for him to be in. A man being torn and consumed alive, with his gaze fixated upon Rob. A look in the man's eyes told him that he wanted Robert to end it for him. He wanted him to finish his suffering. As if by some strange telepathic magic, the creature stopped what it was doing, pulled its hand out of the man's chest, and glanced up towards Rob. He stared into Rob's eyes and that same familiar feeling that he had suffered during the visions began to wash over him. He felt light headed and his eyes started to water. In that moment Rob could see what the man had done. He saw what darkness this man had locked away inside of himself and tried to hide within the new world. Rob saw it all. The sight of it disgusted him.

As quickly as it had come, the vision was gone. The creature stared at him for a moment before turning back to the man and continuing his feast. The man's eyes were still glued onto Rob, even when Rob turned and continued walking forward towards the Farmhouse.

When he reached the steps, any whimpers of suffering had stopped. The noise the creatures made as they devoured and toyed with their meat was all that could be heard, that and the roaring fire as it continued to destroy the Storehouse.

Rob turned around and took a look at it. He saw that the string of LED lights coming off the tree near where Rob had entered the Farm from, was now on fire. The flames were slowly burning their way towards it, catching the closest possible dry dead leaf alight. Soon the entire tree would be on fire. The fire would most likely spread to the nearby trees to that one and soon enough a large chunk of the forest would be on fire. When he checked the other side of the Storehouse, he saw that the lights connecting the building with the Barn, were also alight. The fire was slowly moving its way towards the Barn with John inside. Whatever he was planning on doing, either in there or while making a run for it, Rob knew that John would have to act fast. It would help lure him outside, and sooner or later, the beasts would get him and his inner darkness would catch up with him. It was all just a matter of time.

Part Four

Rob turned back to the backdoor of the Farmhouse. A light inside had stopped any of the creatures from getting in. Inside Peter and Maria had taken refuge. The LED lights were connected to this building as well and it would be before the sun came up, that the Farmhouse would have caught alight and began to burn. Although they were safe in there for now, and even if they waited by the fire until morning, all of their supplies would be destroyed and they would only be safe until the next time the sun went down. Then they would be on their own. All they would do was postpone their inevitable deaths for one night longer. Maria, Rob did not care what happened to her. The creatures had come for her, in the same way that they had come for everyone. Rob had not been able to save any of the others. He was not sure if he believed that they all had it inside of them, but it was far too late now to do anything about it. Peter on the other hand, Rob could still save him. He would need to convince him that if he stayed close to Rob, then he would be okay. Rob would be able to tell the creatures no, and without them chasing them in the darkness, they could go wherever and do whatever they wanted. That was the pipe dream anyway. The truth of the matter was, what was stopping them from tearing into Rob when this was all over? All they needed him to do was shut down the generator and let them in, which he had now done. But then again, with that in mind, they would have had no more use for him and slaughtered him with the rest of them. Rob took that as a good sign. All he had to do was get Peter out. After that, then they could figure out what or where to go from there. If Maria got in their way, then Rob might have to do something drastic, but at the same time, if she needed help then he might be able to spare her too.

The door swung open and Rob moved inside. The door closed behind him and he took a few steps through the hallway. The noise of the fire and the feeding frenzy had now disappeared. The Farmhouse was eerily quiet.

Robert almost forgot himself for a moment. He went to speak and call out "Hello?", but he remembered who he was now. They all thought that he was dead. As far as John had told them, Rob was rotting in the woods somewhere. He needed to just find them and explain. But of course what was he going to tell them? How would he explain the fact that he had walked amongst the darkness and survived? Was he going to say that the creatures had allowed him to live if he sabotaged the generator and allowed them to enter, mutilating the other survivors here? How would someone explain something like that and still manage to come out looking good? Although what was their alternative?

Just then Rob heard a bone chilling scream come from the room above. It had been Peter and Matt's room if he had remembered the layout of the Farmhouse. The scream was a woman's. It had to have been Maria. The only other women who had lived on the Farm, Rob had already witnessed their horrific deaths outside in the Courtyard. The scream was cut abruptly short, as if someone had put a hand over her mouth, or something much worse. Had the lights gone out upstairs and now those things had managed to get in up there? If that was the case then there was nothing he could do. Both of them would have been killed and ripped apart by now. That was if they were still together.

Rob moved to the bottom of the stairs and grabbed hold of the bannister. It had seemed like forever since Rob had last ascended them. The last time he had been here was when he had spoken to Maria on the morning before his imprisonment in the Shack. He had not been back to the Farmhouse in a long time.

As he climbed the stairs, he began to think about all the hours he had spent locked up inside of this place. He remembered sleeping on the floor in the living room beside all the other survivors when they first arrived. He used to have to watch out of the window to make sure the rest of them were safe. He, Peter and Matt would take it in shifts, but Peter would almost always fall asleep every shift.

He remembered when they finally expanded and moved out into the rest of the Farm. People had been too scared to even go upstairs, let alone sleep in another building entirely. When they finished making the individual rooms in the Storehouse, and some of the others moved into the bedrooms inside the Farmhouse, Rob remembered how quiet this place became.

It was just as quiet right now. If the creatures had got inside and had killed Peter and Maria, then there should have been at least some noises of them feasting upon them, but right now all Robert could hear was the sound of the steps creaking as he slowly climbed them.

About halfway up the stairs, Rob began to hear a faint buzzing sound. It was distant and he could not pin point exactly where it was coming from.

It grew louder and louder with each step that he climbed. His breathing started to get heavy and he could feel his brain begin to throb inside his head. It was happening again. He was experiencing another apparition. He knew the feeling intimately. His eyes filled up with water. He blinked and tried to wipe it away, but everything went completely dark for a moment.

As his vision came back, he realised that he was no longer climbing a set of stairs, but instead he was now descending an entirely different staircase. Unlike the large wooden on with the deep red carpet in the middle, like the one in the Farmhouse, this set of stairs were tiled, covered in filth, that made a clang sound as he placed his foot onto each step. They had no railing he noticed as his hand hung there beside him, previously holding onto the railing of the Farmhouse stairs.

He was heading downwards towards a dark basement room. He knew right away that he was no longer on the Farm. He could hear the distant noise of the city somewhere above him. He looked backwards to try and see if he could see where the noise was coming from, but nothing but eternal darkness surrounded him. All that there was in this world were the tiled stairs leading down.

Rob continued on. The closer he got to the bottom, the more the room below started to take shape. A flickering light lit up the nearby corner Rob was approaching. After that he would need to move around the silhouetted wall. The floor beneath the stairs and leading into the room could be seen at this distance. Every time the light came on, a strange puddle of liquid appeared, reflecting the light back, for only a few moments before the basement fell back into gloom.

When Rob reached the bottom of the stairs, he pressed his foot into the puddle and it did not react. Not a single ripple occurred. It made Rob feel almost like a ghost. He knew he was not truly here inside this strange place. It was all just in his head, or a past memory, or something he could not quite explain. All that he knew was that the shadows wanted to show him the truth.

With that in mind, Robert told himself that whatever was waiting for him, just around this corner, could not hurt him. It was the same when he saw the truth in Mike as he held down that woman in the alley, or with John who had murdered all those people in the village in the sand. All of that had already happened. There was nothing he could have done to change the events that had occurred. He was nothing but an audience member to some horrifying opera being conducted all around him.

He took a deep breath and moved into the room. The flickering light fixture turned off the moment he stepped through the doorway, almost as if whatever was waiting inside had timed it perfectly to hide it for just a brief moment. Instantly he could tell that no one was here. The room was lifeless. A dank and miserable subterranean cellar that stored nothing but junk. Shelving units lay flat against the walls, with another single door up ahead that could be seen through the darkness. It was almost as if the door was calling to Rob, pulling him closer and closer towards it. He felt his legs impulsively head towards it, through the damp cellar in the dark.

The light had previously taken only a few seconds before coming back on, but this time, it felt as if nothing was going to change in that moment as Rob found himself being drawn towards the door. A strange force was almost dragging him forward, dying to show him what was on the other side of it.

Suddenly the lights flicked back on. Unlike before, the lights never went out again. They shone brightly and illuminated everything inside the basement. As soon as the light went on, the force disconnected it from Rob's subconscious. He found himself standing right in the centre of the room, facing towards the door. Beside it were newspaper clippings taped to the wall. Some of the papers were quite a few years old and had not adapted greatly to the dampness around them. From here Rob could only see the article headers. They spoke of missing woman and corpses that had been found. All around the body of the text were pictures of the girls. The clippings were damaged and most of the pictures unrecognisable, other than the fact that they were women. Some of them, the body of the article itself, were almost unreadable.

It only took a few seconds of scanning over them before Rob saw the word 'Bridgefield' appear. Almost instantly some of the other headlines came into focus; the ones about the severed heads that were not found at the crime scenes. Each of them saying the word 'Butcher' over and over again. Mutilated, decapitated, murderer, a city wide manhunt. The newest newspaper clipping was dated the day before the power outage.

Right then a feeling of dread came over Robert. He found his head turning to his left, towards the junk filled shelves he had passed moments before when the lights were out. He knew what was there, but he had to look anyway. Some uncontrollable urge, almost a curiosity, took over him and he gazed over at the contorted faces of seven or eight woman staring back at him. Their faces stuck forever in their last agonising moments of life as their killer disconnected their heads from her bodies. Dried coagulated blood pooled around their open neck wounds, one missing their lower jaw and her red stained teeth dug into the wooden shelf, her eyes sunken, almost disappearing into the back of her skull.

All of them were in different stages of decomposition. One on the bottom was so rotted that her grey skin was barely holding onto her bones. Her hair had become frizzled and wild. Another, her head was warped by decay and part of her scalp was now almost concave, warping her.

Two were fresher kills. One of which, her blood was still liquid that dripped off the side of the shelf and into the puddle below, running off towards the bottom of the staircase. She still looked the most human of the lot of them. Her skin looked as if it had not yet started to rot, as if a good doctor could still reattach it and she would be right as rain.

Robert only stared at them for a second, but what he saw had burned itself inside of his brain. He had murdered people in the new world, but the people who had died had caused nothing but suffering to others. This type of horrific mutilation, when the world was still whole, before the darkness came... this was something else. This was the type of pure evil that the creatures had been created to wipe out.

Before he had a moment to gather his thoughts, he found himself already at the door, his hand tightly gripped upon the blood soaked handle. Unlike before, he knew what he was going to find on the other side of it. He could already feel the buzzing in his brain begin to fade. He had not noticed it throughout this experience, but it must have always been there. His vision was starting to blur itself once again.

He turned the door handle and with ease he pushed it. It slowly opened, letting out a whine as it revealed what horror awaited him beyond it.

As he was wandering down the tiled staircase and through the darkened basement of the house in Bridgefield, his true form was here on the top floor of the Farmhouse. It had finished ascending the stairs and crossed the landing to the room right next to his. He found himself standing in the doorway of Matt and Peter's bedroom. The light from a nearby desk gave off a warm orange glow inside the room. The door now open to find blood soaking into the floorboards and dribbling down the cracks into the room below. The body of Maria lay on her back, motionless, as Peter made the final cut with his knife, detaching her head. His hands and forearms were soaked in her blood, making it look as if he was wearing a pair of red rubber gloves, while placing the knife beside his feet, he took her head in both hands and slowly lifted it off the ground. Maria's face droops the higher it went, spilling gore from her neck onto the floor.

"I waited so long..." Peter said, staring into her cold dead eyes. "All I wanted was them back. I never wanted to leave them".

Thoughts flashed back through Robert's mind of all the times he and Peter had been on watch together. All the late nights they had sat up talking. Rob wasn't one for mindless chit-chat, but he didn't mind listening. Peter would often talk about the "people he had left behind". Rob always tried to change the subject. He had no idea how to comfort people he really didn't know. He stopped him from ever spilling his guts and talking about the ones he had left behind. Rob thought that he, like every one of them, had all lost someone. Every person on the Farm had either seen someone they loved be taken by the creatures of the darkness, or had left them to save themselves. He would have never imagined in a million years what Peter truly meant.

Rob had come here to try and spare Peter from the monsters that hungered for him outside. He glanced down at Maria's lifeless body and thought that maybe if it came to it, then he would spare her too. Now, as Peter slowly rose from the floor, still clutching Maria's head in both of his hands, Rob realised that he did not know what to do. The evil that he had bared witness to, in the vision and now right before his every eyes was the true stuff of nightmares. It was not those things out there in the shadows. The real evil in this world was the acts that men and woman had committed all around the world. Acts of violence and evil that they had tried to hide away from everyone else, keeping them locked inside themselves in the deepest, darkest places of their souls.

As Peter's eyes locked onto his, Robert could see that now. He could see that they all had to be punished for what they had done. Some of them he had made a connection with and would probably have called them 'friends' in another life. But right now the curtain had been pulled back and the true face of humanity had been revealed. Even Peter, the kind hearted and shy man that Rob had known since the beginning, was in fact the worst one of the lot. His darkness had been hidden so far inside of himself for so long that he could not bear it any longer. In the face of death, he had decided to take it upon himself to get that one last final fix to his addiction. Maria had just been the right person in the wrong place and time.

Rob's mouth was dry. He licked his lips and went to speak, but as he did, he felt as if the words were not coming from him. The dark puppeteer was no longer moving him as he pleased. Rob felt in control of his body and any actions he was about to take were purely down to his own choices, but the words that came out of his mouth were not his own.

"You will suffer for what you have done..."

The words were cold. Rob could see the fear grow in Peter's eyes as he stared blankly across the room at him. It was almost as if there was something else he was looking at between himself and the man standing in the doorway; something terrifying that shocked him to his core. Rob could see his chest rising and falling faster with each breath. His mouth dropped open slightly as his eyes widened even more. He let go of the severed head and it fell to the ground with a thump, before rolling over to the rest of the body.

Rob looked over towards the desk and knocked the lamp onto the floor, smashing the bulb and sending the room into darkness. The orange glow of the lamp had now been replaced by the white of the moon shining in through the window on the far wall.

Peter, still in a state of pure terror, maybe realising now that he was about to die, slowly began to crouch and took a step or two back towards the chest of drawers behind him.

"N... No..." he stuttered. "I... I didn't... I..."

There was no excuse for what he had done. No forgiveness and no mercy. He frantically looked all around Robert as the creatures themselves had swarmed behind and waited eagerly for their kill.

"No... No!" he repeated it over and over again, even when Robert walked over to him, picked up the knife from the floor and he and the creatures finished it.

Part Five

By the time the creatures had finished with Peter, there was nothing left. Maria's body they had left untouched, but Peter's was no more. All that remained of the 'Bridgefield Butcher' was a large deep red mush with sections of tattered clothing sticking out of it. The window, draws, walls, and bed were entirely covered in the splashes of gore while the creatures tore him limb from limb. Robert had been the one to drive the knife into his throat and watch as the man swallowed pints of blood, all the while struggling for air. Rob had pulled the knife out moments later and watched as the darkness moved passed him and began their frenzy. Rob had decided to stay and watch. He saw the moment that the serial killer's heart had given out and he had succumbed to his fate. His face, whenever Rob did see it behind the vale of shadows tearing into him, was the same contorted horrified expression that his own victims had. Rob thought about how it seemed poetic justice, the man who had brought suffering to many, now suffered the same fate, but in reality it was nothing but a butchery.

By the time Rob left the bedroom, the creatures had flooded back into the rest of the house. The few lights that remained did not house any of remaining survivors. They were all dead. There was just one last loose end to tie up, and then it would all be over. He could tell that they knew it too. The beasts of the shadows no longer frantically searched every corner of the Farm, as they had done before. Instead the creatures roamed slowly through the gloomy hallways, almost purposeless, whispering through the corridors as they meandered through. Their words spoke to the darkest regions of Rob's mind. They were waiting for him to set the wheels in motion to finish it all. He knew what he had to do. There was just one last person who had not yet been punished.

When he looked out the window at the top of the stairs, Rob could see the entirely of the Farm's Courtyard. The burning Storehouse was completely engulfed in flames, burning brighter than the bonfire had ever done. The fire burned so bright that the entire forest behind could not be seen. The whole Courtyard was lit up and Robert could see the aftermath of the massacre. Blood and meat lay splattered all across the ice sludge that covered the ground. Some of the warm flesh had melted away the snow to reveal the dead grass and mud beneath, now soaked in blood. Pools of it filled small holes making them look like red basins from this height.

The tree near the Tool Shed was ablaze. The fire had in fact travelled the length of the lights strung between it and the Storehouse, and it now burned in almost a biblical fashion. The sight made Rob turn and see that, on the other side of the Courtyard, the Barn was now aflame. Plumes of smoke pushed their way out of the window at the top. The dark grey cloud dispersed upwards and disappeared into the night's sky. It was all truly a sight to behold.

Suddenly a blast of fire erupted from the bottom of the Barn. Rob could see that the creatures were trying to get inside. The door swung open as another blast shot out, sending chunks of wood from the door flying in all different directions.

Rob turned and descended the stairs as quickly as he could. He knew what was left to do. The big man had managed to keep himself safe throughout the carnage. He was a survival expert. His skills had been what had kept the rest of the group alive all through their harsh experience. Rob knew that if it was not for him, then they would have all succumbed to their fates long ago. He might have even said that it was because of this very man that Robert was allowed to keep his life and survive the darkness of the last few nights, or however long it had been since he had escaped from the Shack and strangled David. If John had not got the survivors to fortify the Farm, putting up a lighting system and other defences against the creatures, then they would have never needed to seek out Rob's help. If they could have somehow got beyond the string of lights surrounding the Farm, then they would have most likely slaughtered Robert the moment they found him out and alone in the woods that cold night.

Outside, the air was humid. A chill still crept throughout it. It whistled through the trees and circled around the Courtyard, before fading off once more. The fire, eating away the Storehouse, lights, trees and various other structures, warmed the entire area up. Rob had not felt the warmth in a long time. He basked in it for a moment, closing his eyes and remembering something that he had thought was nothing but a dream. He remembered the sun and the sand of a past holiday from many years ago. The sea gently brushing against the shore. And a woman. A woman who he had not thought about in a long time. She walked towards him and he could see her face. She was beautiful.

"J..." he went to say, but suddenly the collapsing roof of the Storehouse brought Robert back to the moment. He opened his eyes and the black and red surroundings came into view. He could see that the building was slowly caving in on itself. The wooden support beams inside were being eaten away by the flames and now it too was giving in to its inevitable destiny. The Storehouse had probably been built years ago and had managed to survive for generations, but now it was a hollowed burning husk of its former self.

When Rob looked, more of the shadows had appeared from the forest. There were hundreds of them, thousands even. They surrounded the Farm. If he thought that he could not see the forest before, now he could not see anything but endless black emptiness all around them. They moved in closer and closer, still avoiding the light given off the by the fires burning here and there, but within moments they had almost completely covered the Courtyard. Their hissing and snarling could be heard over the sound of the fire crackling away as it consumed everything in its path.

John was there, standing in the doorway of the Barn, behind him a large piece of burning timber had fallen down from the floor above and was now blocking the way. Rob could see that the cases of food and other supplies were now also alight. It had been them that had cost Matt his life. It had led to Robert's banishment, and eventually the downfall of the Farm. Now the fire had taken hold of them and soon they would be no more.

The big man was clutching his shotgun tight to his chest as he glanced at the endless hordes all around. He desperately searched for a way out, or some kind of obvious solution to his situation. Attacking in the middle of the night had left him completely unprepared. He was not wearing his signature belt across his chest, which he used to carry his homemade Molotov cocktails. Rob could see that he was devastated that he had been caught out like this, but he knew he was not going down without a fight.

He pointed the gun into the crowd and fired. The creatures withdrew from the blast of light that emitted from the end of the barrel, but were otherwise unmoved by John's attack. The projectiles fired from the weapon did not seem to affect them whatsoever. They returned to their positions and even began to slowly move in closer towards him.

"Shit..." Rob heard John say to himself, pulling the trigger and realising that it was now completely empty.

Robert began to move in through the masses, heading towards him. He knew that it was only the flames of the Barn behind him that was keeping the creatures from swarming over him.

The closer and closer he got to the Barn, the more the world all around began to change shape. He started to see the creatures begin to change from their usual forms into something else. Instead of the strange darkness in long and thin, female-esc looking, humanoids, the creatures had all changed into shabbily dressed Arabian men, women and children, all of whom featured bullet wounds still leaking their own blood. They were the same kind that Rob had seen before. They had been present in his visions of John's past. They creatures had morphed themselves into physical manifestations of his own victims. Maybe they were just showing Rob the torment that John had been suffering since everything had changed. Perhaps he was finally seeing the world as the big man now saw it. He was haunted by the dead. They hungered for his soul in a vendetta of unquestionable proportions.

As Rob moved in closer, he could see that John's face was now locked in a state of fear. They had all had to face their crimes and inner darkness before the end had come for them. John cast his eyes over the horde. He could see their true forms as much as Rob could. He knew why they had come. That was until he spotted Robert standing in the crowd amongst them.

"R... Robert?" he said, stunned at the very sight of him. "Why... are you?" He spoke in broken sentences, most likely stuck in total disbelief by what he had just witnessed and what he could now see standing before him. It was clear that he, and no one else for that matter, had ever seen another human being not being gutted and ripped apart by these things, but here Rob was, walking among them, standing side by side, shoulder to shoulder, with the dark creatures who had destroyed everything and mutilated everyone he knew.

Rob stepped forward. "The dead need their revenge" he started off by saying. The words flowing out of him from some unknown recesses deep within. "You must face what you have done... what you have hidden for so long".

John looked across the sea of bullet ridden faces in front of him, before he turned back to Rob, his face twisting in anger. "What of you?!" he questioned. "What about all the people you have killed?" He stepped forward, disregarding the closest monster only a few feet away. "Look around. Look at what you have done! These people are DEAD because of you!"

Rob could feel his own anger bubbling up inside of him. "None of them were good people. You least of all. You have murdered and butchered the innocent". He could see that his words had hit John in a place he thought had long been hidden.

Rob could see that by his expression, he had no idea how Robert could have possibly known. Whatever operations he had been on, back in the day, had all been covered up. No one knew the truth of what had happened that day, other than the operatives and the people in command. Them and the dead. The dead did not forget, and they did not forgive. They knew the horror that had befallen them that day, and they wanted their vengeance. Blood for blood and an eye for an eye. This was what all this was for. The guilty needed to face what they had done and be punished for it. Robert had killed them and had been corrupted into becoming one of them.

Whatever words came out of his mouth, Rob could not remember. All that he did know was that it was not him who was speaking. The dark force had returned and had used him as a conduit to relay whatever message of punishment the darkness wanted to deliver.

The fear in John's eyes when the words came out were something unlike anything Rob had ever witnessed. It was almost as if everything had suddenly made sense and he was having a moment of clarity. The truth had stabbed through him like a sword, cutting through his soul and tearing it into a million pieces.

The shee shock of it caused him to drop to his knees. It was then that another piece of wooden debris collapsed from inside the Barn and completely obstructed the doorway to it, blocking out the light from the flames behind. This gave the creatures the opening to capture their pray, and they did not hesitate for an instant. They moved in for the kill. They were no longer the victims of war, when Rob watched the creatures charge forward, they had returned to the soulless monsters of darkness that he had always seen them to be.

Unlike the other people Rob had witnessed or heard being mutilated by the beasts, John didn't scream. He remembered that Karen had cried out for her husband, all the others that were grabbed when the lights went out, even Peter cried out for forgiveness as he was being disembowelled. John, on the other hand, did not express this kind of pleading when the creatures began slashing at his torso, carving out chunks of his flesh and sending blood clouds of mist into the air. Although his face did show a degree of pain, whenever a new wound opened up, he never screamed or yelled. His eyes stared into Robert's, as they had done in the past, only this time it was not an interrogation of what happened to Mike, or during an explanation of the task he was being given. This time John's eyes told Rob that the man had accepted his fate and knew the reason why this was happening to him.

He gritted his teeth as a large black claw covered his face and pulled him down into the dark abyss below. His body had already submerged beneath it and was now barely visible. From what little Rob could see of it, his body was now just a mass of exposed muscle and bone, caked completely in a thick quantity of blood. His blood would occasionally spit out of any gaps between the beasts as they clawed and tore frantically. Rob stood there, motionless, watching and waiting for the man to finally expire. Just before John completely disappeared into the darkness, he tried to open his mouth and say something, but nothing came out. His vocal cords had most likely been severed by this point. Instead he moved his mouth in a way that Robert managed to understand what he was saying. In his head, he could hear the big man's final words to Robert as the John; the ex-military, gun-fanatic, survival expert, and fearless leader of the survivors at the Farm, completely vanished from sight into a cloud of eternal darkness and pain.

"Thank you…"

For him, his torment was over.

Epilogue

The Farmhouse caught alight by the time that dawn was starting to appear in the sky above. By this point the Storehouse had burned down to a pile of rubble and the Barn was only moments away from completely collapsing. Robert stood there for hours watching it. He stood in the middle of the Courtyard, beside the bonfire, in the midst of the slaughter that had occurred the night before. The creatures had all but disappeared by this point in time. When there was nothing left of John, the creatures soon retreated into the forest, where it had remained dark for another few hours after the sun rose in the sky.

The Farmhouse was now only a pile of burning wood hours later. Rob realised that it must have been just a little before dusk, which meant that he had been standing there and staring at the fire destroy the only sanctuary he had known within this godawful place for hours. Time seemed to have flown by and when he thought about it, Rob couldn't remember doing anything else except standing there and watching the entire place burn throughout the course of the day.

When he decided that enough was enough, that it was time to move on, the sun had begun to make its descent beyond the reaches of the horizon and the forest was beginning to fall into the shadowy undying wilderness that it became during the twilight hours.

Amongst the trees, with streams of snow laid across their dying branches, Rob felt at peace. He took in deep breaths as he moved aimlessly towards the unknown. He was heading in the same direction he and the other survivors had come from when they first entered the forest a lifetime ago. The City was somewhere this way, but their original journey there was in the black of night, so Rob was not a hundred percent sure that he was even going the right way. The slightest little turn and he could end up somewhere completely different.

He wasn't sure why he was heading back there; to the City, but he had no reason to stay in the forest anymore. He had become one of them now. Before he had spent the last few weeks hiding and running, struggling on the brink of destruction in a dying world. With the dark pact he had made with the unknown forces of shadows, he would be free to travel within the City. It was no longer feral ground for him to walk, whether it was day or night, light or dark.

Just as he reached a small clearing, a natural circular formation of trees surrounding a patch of snow covered ground, Robert felt that unnatural breeze again. The darkness hid anything beyond the realms of the clearing, illuminated by the moonlight shining onto the cold white snow. The wind was gentle at first, causing gooseflesh to appear all along his skin, but shortly after it began to pick up. The frost and snow started crumbling off the nearby trees as the wind shook them, making it look like small patches of the forest were caught in the middle of the blizzard. It was sporadic when the wind had started, however by the time that Rob realised something was amiss, it was happening all around him.

As he moved into the centre of the clearing, he could feel the eyes of the creatures watching him. He couldn't see them, but it felt as if there were hundreds out there, and for all he knew there could well have been. For all he knew, he was the last man on the planet and the last one of his species. If the creatures wanted to exterminate the human race, then he might have been all that stood in their way.

His heart began to pound inside his chest. The dark force that he had felt controlling him before was now gone. That had managed to keep his emotions in check. The whole time he stalked the Farm and during his task it destroy the power, he had not felt his heart beat the way it had done before. All familiar feelings were beginning to surface. His heart had beaten this hard when he had been left by the stream as the sun disappeared behind the clouds. His chest had tightened like this when he was stuck in the apartment building in the Town. His eyes had watered similar to the time he had meandered the woods at night by torch light. And his mind had wandered like it was doing now when he was locked up inside the Shack.

His thoughts became filled with images of being torn apart and devoured. He had not thought about this sort of stuff in a long time, and now that he was, he was beginning to feel something else he had not done in quite some time. Fear was now coursing through Robert's veins. It filled his bloodstream with dread that spread and poisoned his entire body. Right then, as the wind blew and the trees shook, whilst eyes watched him from every dark corner of the blackened forest, Rob felt scared.

"What was happening?" he thought, bringing his hands up to look at his palms. Despite the cold air all around, his hands were moist with warm sweat. As he rubbed them together, he could feel the sticky sensation between his hands. "Am... am I..." Rob's mind could not find the right words, or it knew what it wanted to say, but it could not bring itself to say it. He thought about dark force that was no longer in control of his actions. When that was driving, he had felt like something else, maybe even one of the creatures in the darkness, but now that it was gone, he felt alone. He felt like his regular old self again. He felt human.

He was cold as well. The numbing chill had taken over and it now felt as if his body was slowly succumbing to hypothermia. He could feel himself shake at every breeze that rushed past.

It was then that the whispers began once more; the demonic callings of inhuman beasts echoing from some dark plane of existence. It started off faintly, but within seconds it was as loud as standing in the middle of a fully packed football stadium, only by the sheer number of things whispering at once, all completely different words, it made it near enough inaudible. Rob could not make out anything that the creatures were trying to say. Normally he would eventually hear something, a word or a phrase that filled his ears with answers as to what it was they wanted from him. But this was different. At this point the whispers had grown so earsplittingly loud that it was almost deafening. He wanted to bring up his sweaty hands to his ears, but he was so focused on trying to find the source of the noise, that his arms were now frozen in place. His legs, on the other hand, were moving around in a circle within the clearing. He slowly spun around, searching the forest for something, anything.

He wanted to know why it had all changed. The moonlight was not bright enough to have stopped them moving in and killing him. He had seen the creatures slaughter people in light much brighter than this. So he wondered what was happening.

Eventually he thought that enough was enough and went to move towards the treeline. He had no idea which direction he was heading in now. The turning had disorientated him and for all he knew, he could have been heading back towards the Farm. All he knew was that he wanted to get as far away from this clearing as he possibly could get. When he reached the edge, a few feet away from the nearest tree, the whispers suddenly stopped. It as abrupt, almost as if the power had been cut to a television set. The unexpected halting of the noise stopped Rob in his tracks, but the silence only lasted for a fraction of a second before a single word replaced it.

"Robert" a voice said behind him. It was familiar and caused his stomach to sink. His mouth went dry and he turned around to see that, at the other side of the clearing, the woman in blue stood in between a couple of trees. She stood out like a light in the darkness, as a white aura covered her entire skin.

"J..." Rob went to say, but he could not bring himself to finish. His mind knew exactly who she was, it had always done so, but Rob had sealed away the memory inside. It was then, in that moment, staring across the snow and into her eyes that seemed to unlock it.

She turned and moved slowly back into the trees.

"Wait!" Rob cried, his eyes filling up with tears, reaching out a hand towards her, as if he could just grab her in the palm of his hand. "Joanna... wait".

She disappeared further into the forest, but the white aura around her could still be seen. Without even thinking about the danger he could be in, Rob ran across the ground and made it to the other side within moments. He stopped beside the tree she had been standing next to and peered into the woods. It looked different to the rest of the forest. This part of it was so dense that it felt more like a jungle than just your average forest.

Rob didn't care. He stepped forward and moved inside, climbing over fallen trees and broken branches, before looking back and seeing that the moonlight and the clearing had completely vanished from view. He did not know how to get back even if he wanted to. His only choice was to keep pressing forward, closer to her.

The jungle was so much darker than anything else Rob had witness that he had to check to make sure he was not going blind. He put out a hand in front to, not only guide him, but to make sure he could see it in the pitch black. His hand was completely situated in darkness, but he could still see the sleeve of his coat. His arm trembled at the unknown which lay ahead.

It was like this for quite a while, scrambling through the cold dark silent nothingness, until the white glow could be faintly seen. It grew from around the side of some of the trees ahead. The trees themselves were so tightly packed together, that it seemed unnatural and almost wall-like in appearance. As he got closer to it, he could see that the white light now shone brighter. It was not bright enough to light up the floor, that was still a black void beneath his feet, but he could see the dry bark of the side of the trees as Rob rested his hand against it and peered around the corner.

The source of the white light was not exactly clear. Rob couldn't make out if it was coming from somewhere off in the distance or was just suspended in mid-air, but as he turned the corner, he could see what it was the light wanted him to see. Strung to the wall, held together in the vines of the trees, twined with dark black shadows holding everything in place like rope, was the body of man. He was dark skinned and wore blue blood stained overalls. His face was contorted and twisted in the horror of his last agonising moments. He was dead, but at the same time he looked as if he was still suffering. Visions of Mike's past began to flood into Robert's head like a dam had broken. He saw, not only the same rape he had witnessed before, but now he saw all different ones.

Rob turned away from him and stepped aimlessly in a different direction. Another body came into view. This one was of a man, his head was severed and tied to the tree above it. Blood ran down from his neck and covered the branches holding him in place. This one was the Bridgefield Butcher; Peter. The memories came quick and fast then. He saw women crying out in terror as Peter murdered them, before removing their heads from their bodies and parading them around in his dark damp basement. Sickness started brewing up inside of Rob. He felt as if he was going to throw up all over him. He moved and saw that the white light was now somewhere else entirely. It was at the end of a long dark corridor of trees. Either side were the bodies of men and women, all of them tied together to different trees. They formed hellish statues leading down towards the light.

As Rob began to move down, he took a moment to turn and look at each of them. Every time that he did, he would be greeted by a flash of memories of the darkness that they had tried to keep locked up inside of themselves. He saw Karen, who was the only body strapped with another. Her husband was tied to the same tree as her. Rob saw what they had done to their son. The story he had read in the newspaper article weeks ago came to life before his very eyes. He could only stand a few moments of it before he turned away in disgust. "You had it coming" he said aloud as he did.

Next he saw the man Rob had shot when they had first got into the forest. It was strange seeing him again. Rob did not know his name, but he remembered his face when he saw him. His eyes still spoke of the pain he had been suffering before Rob had pulled the trigger. The bullet wound was still present in his face. Shortly afterwards Rob's mind was invaded by a memory of armed robbery. He saw scared shop keepers handing over their money as the barrel of a gun was pressed against their cheeks. A lone man trying to stop the robber, only to be met by a bullet ripping through his abdomen, bleeding to death in the middle of a store as his blood pooled out onto the ground.

After that they all seemed to fly by quickly. Maria was there. Rob saw the effects that her blackmail had on the family of the man who had hanged himself. He saw David's drug dealing, overdosing young men who lay dying on a dirty mattress in the middle of an abandoned tenement building. Jennifer, as she stole an old woman's gold necklace to pay for her addiction. Even Matt was there, strapped to the side of the tree, half of his face still missing from when John had blasted it off with his shotgun. Rob saw that he had hacked into bank accounts and stolen thousands. Families were left without their savings and small businesses had to let people go because they simply could not afford to pay them. This vision had made him realise that there was no one worth saving at the Farm. The one kind hearted person who Rob knew, was really a cybercriminal, using his knowledge of computer systems for villainous means. All of them had got exactly what they had coming.

The homeless man Rob had murdered was next. He saw what he had done in his past life and any sickness he had started to feel was soon gone. He had done terrible things. Thankfully the vision had spared Rob the true horrors of what the man had done, but it had given him just enough information to make him realise that he had done a good thing by killing him.

At the end of the dark tree corridor of death, Rob saw the big man himself. John was strapped to the last tree beside the natural archway. Rob didn't need to see his past crimes. He already knew what terrible things this man had done. The look of acceptance still lingered on John's face as Rob turned his head away and carried on.

Passing through the archway, the white light had now moved further away. When Robert looked, he saw that there was one more body strapped to a tree beside it. Its head hung down towards the ground and its arms were bound above it.
He moved over to it, looking around to see if any more of them were present, but other than the endless black staring back at him, there was no more. There was not even another white light to help him figure out where to go next. He was looking for Joanna, he needed to find her. Once he did, maybe all of this madness would end. Maybe it would soon be all over.

He approached the final body and placed his hand on the person's head. It was a male body that Rob did not seem to recognise. Confused, he started to push back on the top of the head, bringing the face into view. It took him a few moments to figure out exactly who it was he was staring it, but then the realisation hit him harder than John's shotgun had done. It was Rob. It was his own face that he was staring into. He let go of the hair and stepped back.

"Wha…" he blurted out. "No!" he thought. "How could this be?" He was not dead. He had not suffered the same fate that all of the other Farm survivors had. He had not been torn apart by the darkness inside of him.

And right then, the memory came to him. Rob's heart filled up like a balloon. Inside of his chest, he could fill it growing and growing, pushing against his ribcage as if it was trying to get out. His vision spoke of Joanna, young and beautiful. When Robert saw her face again, that was when his heart could take no more and it felt as if the balloon had burst. He loved her more than anything else in the whole world. She was everything to him. With her in his life, he did not need anything. He wanted to spend the rest of his life with her. He wanted to father children and grow old. He wanted her to be by his bedside as he took his last breath as an old man.

It seemed that she wanted something else entirely. The woman that Robert had loved and the life they had made was nothing more than a lie. She did not feel the same way that Rob did for her. He had come on too strong and it had scared her. She thought that she could love him, if she spent more time with him, but the longer they had stayed together had only lead to her wanting other things. Her eyes had begun to wander and she had started to develop feelings for other people. She had not said anything to him and let the lies wash over her, telling him that she loved him too, telling him that they would be together forever and beyond, but the truth was she yearned for another.

The day came when she finally decided that she had had enough; the day she told him that she did not love him, admitting that she did not think that she had ever done so, was the day she had worn her blue dress. It was a subtle outfit for the warm climate outside.

Rob had fought against her decision, telling her of the good times that they had had together. He recited the things that she had told him; loving words and plans for the future. He offered to change, telling her that he would do anything not to lose her, almost to the point of getting down on his knees and begging, but she would not listen. For her, her mind was already made up. She had already planned out the rest of her life, and it did not involve Robert anymore. He was no longer going to hold her back from her own personal happiness.

Rob had been lost in total disbelief. He had no idea that she had felt this way for so long. She had never mentioned it once. He thought about how if she had said something, anything then he could have tried to fix it before it became impossibly unrepairable. His heart had been shattered into a million pieces. His whole world had come crashing down around him in a matter of moments. All of his plans for the future were no more and everything he had been working his whole life towards was going.

He pleaded with her not to go, but she was already heading towards the door. It was then, in that fatal moment, when his everything was about to fade away and never come back, knowing full well that he had lost the only person he had truly loved, that something snapped. He felt his head go light and his eyes glaze over. With tears still streaming down his face, he moved towards her. He grabbed her by the arm and she pulled it away, saying something that Rob could not quite remember, but he knew that it had filled him with such uncontrollable rage that he grabbed her arm once more, pulling her towards him. She tried to fight him off but it was no use, by this point she had already lost her footing and fallen to the ground, Rob falling on top of her, his hands moving quickly to her throat. He was not thinking. He did not know what he was going to do with himself without her. If he could not have her in his life then he didn't want anyone.

He never noticed that his hands clutched tighter and tighter around her neck. Her face began to turn a shade of purple as she struggled for air. Her hands tried clawing at him, but they only managed to scratch against his jacket, some of her nails breaking.

It was all over in a few minutes. He felt the last of her blood pump to his hand, still holding onto her throat, before slowly dispersing away. Her life too had slowly faded away from him.

It was then that the lights went out. Rob got to his feet, over the body of the woman he had loved, and looked around in the pitch black. It seemed that the entire street had fallen into darkness as well. In fact the lights from the City were all out. It wasn't too long before the screaming started. The roars, the hisses and the shrieks could be heard. The death and the chaos followed shortly after.

Robert blinked for a moment, but it felt as if he had his eyes closed for hours. When he opened them again, the strange jungle of darkness, containing the mutilated bodies of his fellow survivors had gone, as too did his own corpse before him. The vision and the nightmare was over. Now he was back in the shadowy forest he had known all along, only this time he stood right on the treeline of it. Ahead of him lay a large grassy plane leading upward to the top of a hill. He could see the night sky above him, yet the stars were not at all visible as they had been before, when he was much deeper in the forest.

Was this it? Was he truly at the edge of the forest?

Rob, without even thinking, almost as if he was being slowly lead, began to make his way up this hill. The snow had completely turned to slush. The mud beneath it squelched and squished as he struggled to climb higher. It seemed that the further he got, the more his feet felt as if they were going to sink completely in the muck below.

After a few more hard steps, Rob managed to persevere. The ground began to harden the closer he got to the top. The melted ice became less and less apparent, almost as if the snowfall had never made it this far. By the time he had almost reached the top of the hill, Rob could see that the sky was changing from a deep soulless black, to an almost navy blue. A glow from something beyond the other side of the hill was emitting a source of light.

His mind was still racing from the return of his hidden memories, almost in a daze, the pull Rob was feeling towards the top of the hill was far too great for him to resist. He knew that if he fought against it, it would be futile. He was in no position to resist. His thoughts were still on Joanna, flickering and haunting the dark recesses inside of him, yet the light ahead had sparked his curiosity. Was it the same light he had witnessed in the dark jungle moments earlier? If it was another chance to see her then Rob was happy to let the force continue to guide him towards it. The way it had taken over the sky above proved that this was far greater than anything else he had witnessed before.

When he got to the top of the hill the urge appeared to leave him all at once. His body jittered for a second as if the release of whatever it was that had over him, had now gone. His legs felt weak beneath the weight of his torso. He managed to stop himself from toppling over, but only just. He dropped to one knee. As his hands touched the grass below himself, he realised that it felt slightly warm. The ground was not wet or even cold. It felt so foreign to him that his brain took a good few moments to even register what it was he was touching.

His eyes turned forward and his gaze drew him to the source of the light. Up ahead of him, maybe two or three miles in the distance, Rob could see that, over the vast fields and roads, was a magnitude of different buildings all clustered together. It was the city that Rob and Joanna had once lived in. It was most likely the city that all of the Farm survivors had lived in only a few weeks ago. His memory of it being a dark and frightening place had vanished. Thoughts of people being torn apart in the city streets as he and the others ran for their lives, seemed to fade away, as if they had been nothing more than fragmented memories from a dream.

The noise of the city could be heard even from this distance. Cars driving and beeping, the general hustle and bustle of a never sleeping metropolis. Even the roads leading into it were filled with cars and buses, traffic jams and bright headlights shining out towards the shadows.

Rob took a look back towards the forest. The snow on the tops of the trees was no longer visible. If it had been snowing there, then there was no longer any evidence of it. Rob knew that the Farm had only been a couple of miles behind. At the very least he should have been able to see the plume of black smoke rising into the air from the smouldering ruins of the Farmhouse. When he left he remembered that it was still burning intensely enough that smoke was pluming up into the sky.

Rob wondered how long he had been walking for. Perhaps by this time it had stopped and was now a barren wasteland of the horror that had taken place. The bright lights of the City, off in the distance, shone over the entire scene. He was so close.

Movement caught his attention and Rob's gaze turned to the side. His heart, still shattered by his past, tried its best to re-inflate itself. A tight hold squeezed around it as Joanna appeared a few metres away from him. She looked the same as she had always done. Her beautiful face stared at him, it almost felt as if it was looking through him and into his very soul. The feeling was agony. He knew what he had done to her; the pain he had caused her and the life he had taken away. But there was still something inside of him that wanted to smile at her. Maybe it was just the idea that she had returned to him, for however short a time it might have been, was enough to make him feel some form of happiness.

Was it a noise that caused Robert to turn around in the opposite direction, or was it more of a feeling? The sensation that eyes were piecing through him became ever more apparent. He glanced behind and saw that she was there again. Another Joanna, still wearing her blue dress, only now standing at the other side of him. He looked back to the first one and she was still there, now a few feet closer to him, only this time another entity with the appearance of Joanna was standing beside her. More began to appear from all around. Some spawned out of the darkness of the forest, while others merely appeared whilst Rob had his back to them. He spun around frantically as the horde grew closer and closer to him. Each one of them stared coldly at him with each step that they took. They were emotionless, now only a few feet away. Rob could feel his heart pounding in his chest, almost to the point where he thought it was going to explode. His muscles tightened. He could feel the cold icy air close in around him, as each of them appeared to grow darker. Their skin and clothing became almost impossible to see, and after a moment, it was. Within seconds each one of them had metamorphosed and now all the dark creatures of pain and suffering; the shadows that had stalked them in the gloom and the clawed beasts that punished the guilty for their sins, the inner darkness that Rob and the other Farm survivors had tried to hide away inside of themselves.

They had finally come for him now. Just as John and Peter and David and all the rest of them had been punished for what they had done, Robert must also face the same wrath. He had borne witness to his own crimes, and with every criminal there must be repercussion.

After all, that was why they had all been brought to this place.

"This is the judgment, that the Light has come into the world, and men loved the darkness rather than the Light, for their deeds were evil. For everyone who does evil hates the Light, and does not come to the Light for fear that his deeds will be exposed"

John 3:19-20

THE END

Danny Hughes

From Harlow in the UK, Danny has always had a fondness of writing and designing even from a young age. He is a qualified computer game designer, although never having actually worked in the field, only on projects at home for his portfolio.

He is a self-published free-lance writer who enjoys writing all types for all ages.
He mainly enjoys writing Sci-fi, fantasy, war, zombies, and noir crime stories, drawing inspiration from absolutely anything. Mainly enjoying designing and creating the entire world that the story is set within to help bulk out the story line.

Danny begun writing more seriously and trying to get his first book published after wanting to base a fantasy series on his daughter; Freya Iris Hughes.

Freya Fables

Written & Created by Danny Hughes

Freya Fables: Book One
The Prince in the Shadows

ISBN-13: 978-1499302844

Freya Fables: Book Two
The Golden Legion

ISBN-13: 978-1499399202

The Valour of Sir Henry
A Freya Fable

ISBN-13: 978-1499609721

Freya Fables: Book Three
The Age of Darknes

ISBN-13: 978-1502879561

Special Thanks

Carleyann Claridge, Geraldine Hughes, Gary Hughes, Rob Brown, Sandra Claridge, Jude & Eva Hart,

And of course
Freya Iris Hughes

I love you

x

Printed in Great Britain
by Amazon